AFTER COUNTRY

AFTER COUNTRY

Kenneth Camacho

for all fellow travelers

"For the Benefit and Enjoyment of the People."

> *Inscription on the Roosevelt Arch of
> Yellowstone National Park, a supervolcano
> now 200,000 years overdue for eruption,
> 24 April 1903*

*"And we fight. We fight like hell. And if you don't fight like hell,
you're not going to have a country anymore."*

> *President Donald J. Trump, speech at the
> Ellipse in Washington, D.C.,
> 6 January 2021*

"My Dad is the most useless person on Earth."

> *Caleb Henry, unpublished entry
> from a personal diary,
> 31 May 2030*

PART ONE

Decay

River of Grass

Henry Henry never found the crocodile he was looking for. Unbeknownst to him, it was already dead: expired in 2024, on the eve of the last presidential election in what had amounted once to the United States of America. There was no material connection between the events, of course; but if anyone had been around when it happened, they might have noted a symbolic one. In the end, the crocodile—nicknamed "Sally" by park rangers and, at 18 feet long, a reptile of near-mythical proportions—dug its aging dinosaur claws into the earth and flat out refused to keep living. It starved to death in one of the most food-abundant biomes on the planet.

Imagine that.

Henry had first read about Sally years ago in an oddities-themed guidebook for a road trip through Florida he'd found once in his wife's study. There was even a photograph of the monster, enormous and hovering just below the brown surface of the pond, a kayaker nearby for scale. The kayaker's life jacket was red, which Henry had thought more than a little ominous. He'd wondered if its wearer knew Sally was so close— that there was a killing machine no more than a few feet away. Was the kayaker oblivious, and the photographer too focused on the shot to tell them? Or were they in on the plan from the start? A fact Henry does know: posing for a photograph was once the second-leading cause of death in national parks. The first, by a mile, was suicide.

Still, for the last day and a half, and while doing his best to sneak across the half-flooded roadways of the most rural stretches of what he guessed was still the Patriot Republic of Florida, Henry's mind kept wandering back to Sally. It went without saying that finding the pond in which an enormous crocodile lives was precisely the kind of thing that had become exponentially harder these days. There was no more cell service, no more rangers, and to ask a stranger for help was to take your life in your hands. So, Henry decided to begin with the park visitor map on page 44 of his fraying and dogeared Rand McNally road atlas, along with two questionable assumptions: the first was that the pond was named "pond." If not, why his memory of that word? And the second was that it would be near some road-shoulder parking lot or pull out. If not, how the kayak? And a question hiding just beneath that one: how else was he going to get there?

And so it was that in the mid-morning of an uncomfortably warm day in late January 2034, Henry turned the key in the ignition of a stolen truck and began working his way south along the only remaining road in what used to be Everglades National Park. He stopped first at Sisal Pond, then Ficus, and then Sweet Bay, and at each he held what he found up to his memory of an image he had seen maybe twice in his life. Was it big enough? Roundish enough? Did he remember pines in the background, or low tangles of mangroves? Just as importantly: was there a giant crocodile?

He did not feel very confident in his answers. More typically, he stood on the edge of this body of water or that one and second guessed himself until he got too hot to want to stand there any longer. The temperatures were bearable, but the humidity was suffocating. The rich-to-rotten smell of the swamp clung to him, and his mouth tasted like it was full of dirt. He had once heard this sort of thing—the spending of time doing a fruitless task—described as "sweat equity;" as in, "if you want to get results, you've got to be willing to put in some sweat equity." He stepped up into the open door frame of the truck and looked back at Pond #4, Paurotis. He could no longer believe people used to say things like that.

It seemed inescapably foolish to think he could walk up to the same place a picture was taken no less than fifteen years later and find the very same creature once he got there. But there were many inescapably foolish things about Henry Henry, and in any case, crocodiles do live for a very long time. Still, when the truck reached the nearly-lost parking area at Nine Mile Pond, he was startled by his own certainty: this was the right spot. It was the right patch of Bermuda grass on the near shore, and the right boat launch. The water was deep enough and dark enough to hide the leviathan between its lily-padded surface and the limestone bedrock below. And the icing on the cake: as he opened the door of the truck and stepped down, Henry saw a pair of Canada geese standing at the near shore by a foreboding cluster of reeds like bait. He felt like he was just outside the frame of a nature documentary, and any second now, there would be an explosion of white spray and both geese would disappear at once into a thing barely recognizable as a mouth. He couldn't take his eyes off them. He couldn't even walk more than a step or two away from the truck, for fear of missing the show. But as he waited, the one closer to him dug its beak into the folds of its wing, and the goose by the water sat down and promptly fell asleep.

In the end, Henry missed his crocodile by nine years, three months, and around two hundred feet. Sally's final resting place was just around the bend of a tributary among the stalagmite knees of a small cypress grove, and if he had found her then, he could have shaken her empty, leather claw. But instead, after giving up on the geese, Henry followed the remains of a trail in the opposite direction and towards the other side of the pond until it disappeared into the murk and mud of the mangroves. When he turned around and made his way back to the Bermuda grass and cattails, he tiptoed out to the water's actual edge and looked into the brackishness, still half-expecting every rock under the surface to open its eyes and stare back at him. But none did.

It was never much of a plan. Henry turned one last time to take in the expanse of things: green unrelenting and still. The sense that the swamp was holding its breath. The smell of root and earth and salt. The shadows just beginning to emerge again in the afternoon sun. Life was everywhere, and also nowhere, and as he looked, some kind of something felt close to him—if just out of his reach. The scene was not quite beautiful.

Take a picture with your mind, his wife had once said to their son, Caleb, after riding all the way to the top of the Willis Tower in Chicago and leaving the camera in the car. This was during the time when they were both experimenting with dumb phones, in the years before phones stopped working at all. *You can draw it when we get back to the hotel,* she had said.

So Henry took a picture with his mind.

In the truck again, Henry cranked the engine, pulled down the gear shift, and turned the wheel towards the main road to Flamingo. He knew it would be potholed to all hell; all the roads were. But he would make it to the visitor center by late afternoon, and with any luck, he would have a night to himself at the soaked and seeping edge of the world. The Everglades is a river, the mildewed park brochure told him, sixty miles wide and flowing less than a foot every hour. A river of grass.

Henry could relate.

Ingo, the sign said. There wasn't much left of it. Some unnamed and unannounced hurricane had swept across the southern peninsula years ago and wrought unthinkable havoc there. The palm trees still standing looked like they had been throttled within an inch of their lives, and what had once been an idiosyncratic oval of grass in front of the visitor center was now overgrown and littered with the trunks of the trees which had not been so lucky. Everywhere there was rot: high tides now pushed detritus and dead fish well up over the seawall and into the roadway and parking lot. Now, with the water receded, Henry's tires squished through banks of tangled seaweed until they came to a stop on what he hoped was high enough ground.

He looked through the windshield at the ruins of the complex. The roof sagged over the main portion of the visitor center. Across an old walkway, the lesser wing of the structure had been swept away entirely, leaving only a concrete and rebar-studded foundation. A smaller third building, in that fickle way of disasters, seemed almost untouched by the flooding. However, a later lightning strike must have set it ablaze, and the charred skeleton of its two-by-fours had become a cage for an enormous pile of windblown palm fronds.

Enough sand had washed in that morning for Henry to see a dozen animal track lines criss-crossing the space between his truck and the front doors. Apart from their makers, wherever they were, he was alone. He reached down in the space beside his seat and extracted a bright yellow crowbar. Then he stepped out into the mid-afternoon sun.

The earthy smell of the ponds was gone, but it had been replaced by the reek of aggressive decay. Insects hummed. As he picked his way towards the building, he made unintentional eye contact with a great blue heron hunting frogs in the morass. The bird stared, and Henry looked away embarrassed.

A rusted and padlocked chain was knotted between the handles of the door to the vestibule. There were no scratches in the keyhole or gashes from bolt cutters, which Henry took to mean that Flamingo was well and truly abandoned. He felt genuine surprise: even before Florida had become a Patriot Republic, its governors had a habit of refusing federal funding. It had been eight years since non-natives and itinerants were barred from state citizenship, and Everglades–along with Big Cypress, Biscayne, and Loxahatchee–all shuttered shortly after that. Without money and without workers, there was no way to keep them open. But empty places (and especially empty places with parked vehicles and a probable weapon or two) rarely stayed empty for long. So all Henry could figure was that this place was far enough out of the way, and had been taken by storms too quickly, to stick in anybody's memory. In any case, it was a stroke of luck: with his first smile of the day, Henry raised the crowbar and gave the door a good whack.

Glass shattered inwards, and the shadow of the heron blinked over the scene as it took flight. Henry took a careful step over the threshold and looked about. It was a large center with high ceilings and enormous windows offering up views south and east over Florida Bay all the way to the tiny train cars of the Keys stretching out along the horizon. He could hear the surf, and he realized there must be another opening somewhere in the space. It was unbearably humid, and there was a sheen of condensation coating every surface. Molding curlicues of wallpaper slowly peeled their ways down the walls.

The rangers had done their best to clean up on their way out all those years ago: maps had been put away, pamphlet trays were empty, and merch kiosks were tucked back behind the lowered and locked shutter gate closing off the gift shop. But it looked more like the place had been shut down for the night than abandoned forever, so Henry liked his chances. He blinked a few times to try and clear the sweat from his eyes and walked around the far side of the ranger desk, scanning the bins and boxes beneath the counter. There were stacks of coloring books, a charging rack for walkies, an old lost-and-found hamper piled with sweatshirts and water bottles. And then, in the corner, a brown cardboard box ripped partially open at one end. The smile from before returned, and Henry took a step closer. Then, and altogether mindlessly, he reached his hand into the box. In that very same moment, he heard the sudden, clear, and quite loud sound of maracas in his left ear: rattlesnake. He closed his hand around the contents of the box and then jerked backwards, hitting his wrist hard on the bottom edge of the counter. The box had come with him, stuck now around his closed fist, and he began to shake his arm wildly.

"*Shit!*" he somehow both yelled and whispered. "*Shit!*" The box would not come off his hand, and the maracas were all he could hear. He kept shaking, and after a half dozen swings, his brain finally caught up to his body and he reshaped his hand inside the box, pinching his treasure between his fingers. On the next swing, the box flew off into a corner, and Henry checked himself: there were no bite marks on his fingers, but something had poked a single hole in his palm and there was a small trickle of blood there. "*Damn it,*" he said to himself.

He could still hear the snake, wherever it was, and he grabbed the crow bar he had set down on the counter and looked around again. He turned his head, first one way and then the other, listening for the source. After a moment, he zeroed in: the sound was coming from the old hamper on the bottom shelf. He gave it a jab with the crowbar, and a juvenile timber rattler, no more than a foot long, slithered away under the counter. Henry let out a shaky breath and realized that, until a moment ago, he had not spoken in a week.

The rest of his search was surprisingly fruitful. There was a box of snack-sized potato chip bags in a storeroom, along with a stash of granola bars and a big can of cashews. The employee kitchenette yielded plastic baggies of salt, pepper, and sugar packets, cleaning wipes, a new knife, and a few spoons in a drawer. The real haul, however, came from the gift shop, which he was able to open after finding the key to the shutter in a lockbox beside the radio bay. Henry filled a trash bag with branded t-shirts, socks, sweatshirts, and a hoodie with the words *I Survived the Everglades* written across the shoulders above a screen printed picture of an alligator wearing sunglasses.

By the time he was finished with this, the sun was setting. He thought about the mattress in the back of his truck, and then he thought again. On the east side of the lobby, a staircase led to offices on the second floor. The hole in the center's roof had exposed a number of them to the weather, but what was once the park director's office was still intact. Inside there was a fake mahogany desk and an enormous leather sofa. It looked unimaginably comfortable. After an unceremonious dinner of Doritos and beef jerky, Henry took off his boots, stretched out on the couch, and slept like a stone.

In the morning, Henry Henry stepped back over the shattered door frame and emerged into a world of infinite glass. The tide was in, and the entire parking lot was now covered by perfectly still water. The palm trees left standing were reflected in it like strange, vertical barbells. A gull flew across the grounds, and its twin, mirrored beneath it, matched each beat of its wings. Henry's breath caught in his chest. Slowly, he began to walk, and with each step, ripples spread out across the surface moving silently and out and perhaps forever.

He'd chosen the right spot for the truck: although doubled under the cloudless sky, the tires were standing in no more than an inch of water. He unlocked the door, tossed the garbage bags of clothes and food into the empty space where a passenger seat should be, and then stepped inside. On the floorboard of the driver's side, Henry kept a small, gray lockbox. He picked it up, set it in his lap, and lifted the lid. Then, he reached into the pocket on the front of his new, ridiculous hoodie and extracted his treasure: a gold plastic badge, in the style of a ranger's, with the words

Everglades National Park engraved on the front. The pin from the back had cut Henry's palm when he had grabbed it from the box the day before, and there was still the smallest bit of dried red on the latch where he had pushed it closed. He held it for a moment. Then, he set it down in the box next to the others: *Biscayne. Congaree. Chesapeake Bay. Shenandoah. New River Gorge. Acadia. Catskills. Cuyahoga Valley.* In the lockbox there was a black Sharpie, and Henry reached in carefully to pick it up. He closed the lid and turned the box over. On the bottom, there was a sequential list of numbers, one through sixty-six. The first eight had been circled, and he now drew a black circle around number nine. He returned the Sharpie to the box and then tucked it back underneath his seat.

No, it wouldn't be quite right to say that Henry had a plan. In his fifty years of life, it was possible no one had ever said that about him. After all, plans were slippery things, evolving and changing and adapting. But a quest was something different, Henry thought. A quest freezes the world where it is. A quest endures. If plans have obstacles, quests have dragons: cunning reptiles who live forever, guarding their hordes. You could sneak past a giant on a quest. You could creep around the crumbling edges of things. It didn't matter if you ever went home, so long as you made it to somewhere else.

It was a long way to whatever it was Arkansas called itself these days; too far to guess how long it would take to get there. But no matter: however slowly, Henry Henry kept moving.

Fort Lonesome

For the last ten days—which is to say, since escaping South Carolina—Henry had been driving something called the Roving Ranger. In truth, it was an ice cream truck wrapped with Imagestock photos of swamp creatures and emblazoned in a half dozen places with the old NPS arrowhead. In the last few years before the parks in the secessionist states went completely broke, several of them latched onto such vehicles as a way of cutting visitor center costs: why pay for a building that sits still when you can trade it in for one that goes anywhere—and comes with a deep freezer? Henry had checked it for ice cream after he first found the keys, but all he'd found were a few empty boxes and a black widow spider.

The way he'd ended up with the Roving Ranger was actually more-or-less of a miracle. After drifting for a day and night in a rusted canoe through what seemed an endless swamp in the South Carolina midlands, he had spotted the splintered end of a boardwalk leading up from the Congaree River and back towards the interior of his Park #7. He'd followed the dilapidated and badly twisted ribbon of wood for more than a mile, his sense of balance devastated first by floating all night in the canoe and then by walking on this flood-warped funhouse path deeper and deeper into the largest old growth bottomland hardwood forest in North America. A thing he hadn't expected: there were pigs everywhere.

In his raid of that visitor center, which had also seemed utterly untouched, he'd found a set of keys on an actual rabbit's foot keyfob next to a pink sticky note with *RR* written on it. However, when he'd stepped into the parking lot, his heart sank: there was nothing there. Then, after a second and closer look, he realized that the carpet of kudzu which had swallowed almost the entire blacktop rose up in one corner in a conspicuous mound before stretching over a gap and swarming across a stand of nearby trees. That mound had a shape. And that shape was an ice cream truck.

Once Henry had cut away the vines, he discovered the full extent of his luck (thank you, rabbit's foot): not only did the truck still run, but its diesel engine had been rigged by some do-gooder or other to operate on vegetable oil. When Henry finally got the rear doors to open, he found that there were, in fact, three drums of the stuff already sitting in a row near the back. The key worked. The engine roared to life. He adjusted the one seat in the cab and checked the rearview mirror.

Over time, Henry turned the Ranger into something not unlike a very sad apartment. In the floor, he stacked two stained mattresses he requisitioned from an abandoned motel. In the space between this bed and the far sideboard, he jammed a large white fishing cooler, a plastic crate piled high with loose maps and brochures, and two totes he helpfully labeled *Food* and *Not Food*. And in the very back, he left the oil drums in just the places where he'd found them. Their seals were tight, but it didn't take long for Henry to realize that there was still no stopping the smell: the whole truck reeked of popcorn, and after a week of living in the Ranger, Henry began to suspect his own skin had become flammable.

*　　*　　*

Back in the Everglades, Henry navigated the sputtering Ranger over the ruined park road and thought about the day ahead. There were back ways north that would skirt around whatever fires he had seen burning before towards Naples. But even so, he knew this was dangerous country. The swamplands stretched forever, and the precious few corridors through them were prone to unofficial checkpoints manned by overeager locals looking for anyone without a good reason to be there. Henry's Ohio driver's license was long lost, but it wouldn't have done him much good with these renegades anyway: he knew the Republics didn't recognize yankee motorists.

All Henry had going for him was that he certainly didn't look like much of a threat. He was a soft fifty–tall and paunchy, with shaggy gray hair and an egg-shaped face dominated by a patchy beard and glasses taped together at one corner. In another life, he had been a mid-level executive for a meal kit delivery company specializing in synthetic proteins, and it showed. In this life, he had the survival instincts of an especially googly-eyed opossum.

Still, by late-afternoon, he had covered more than two hundred uneventful miles and was a few itchy mosquito bites away from feeling relaxed. Florida in January could still be pleasant, he thought, and a day that had started with pure cobalt skies was now streaked with the sort of clouds which might produce a good sunset. Henry didn't have a dime that would spend in the Patriot Republic, so he knew a white-stripe diner was out of the question. But there were enough odds and ends in the back of the Ranger to make a meal, and he started to keep a lookout for an empty enough place to sit.

It took a little while, but a few miles north of Duette, Henry found what seemed to be a perfect spot. The sign said *Fort Lonesome: Population 6*, but someone had spray painted over the *6* and drawn a *0*. This wasn't a promise, of course. But it was a good start.

The town, such as it was, consisted of a derelict gas pump, a half-collapsed barn, and a way station for the double-circuit power lines tracking east to west across the intersection. The lines seemed operational, but the crossroad was closed in both directions by old and faded sawhorses reading *Road Out Ahead*. He noticed even more smoke to the west off towards St. Petersburg, but he couldn't guess what was making it. Of significantly more interest to him was a little lane between the station and the barn that was just the right size for the Ranger to nestle in peace.

As he cut the engine, he gave the rabbit's foot a squeeze and then climbed into the back to make himself a peanut butter sandwich. He wondered if bananas grew in Florida now—or if they ever had. When he was finished, he stepped down from the rear doors and left them open as he walked to the far side of the pump island to watch the sun disappear over the fenced and humming transformers. The sky was just beginning to take on an orange hue, and the high cirrus clouds were already turning pink at their edges.

He was down to the last bite of his sandwich when he heard the bell over the gas station door ring. Henry froze. He didn't even chew. He strained his whole body listening, and after a long pause, he heard slow steps beginning to crunch over gravel and broken glass in his general direction. His back was still turned, and he realized he was holding his breath.

"Hey there?" he heard a shaky voice ask from somewhere behind him. "Mister?"

It sounded like a question, and Henry hoped it was directed at somebody else.

"Hey, you at the pump?" Henry turned around slowly, his sandwich still in his hand. As he did, he saw someone less than a dozen feet away from him. It was a young man, maybe twenty. His clothes were filthy and hung from his frame. His hair was long, and he was wide-eyed. He held a camping backpack in one hand and his other out towards Henry with the palm open, as if he was trying to calm a wild animal. "Easy, buddy," he said, "Easy. Easy. You're okay." The man set the pack down, and when he did, it lost its shape altogether: there was nothing inside of it. "I'm safe, see?" his eyes were still trained on Henry. "I'm safe."

Henry very specifically did not feel safe.

"M'name's Alex, alright? I'm Alex. I don't want nothin' from ya. I was just in here lookin' around when I saw you pull up, and I didn't want you to freak out if ya found me." He offered a weak laugh to try and calm Henry down.

Henry looked around for his car, his bike, his anything. But except for the two of them, the station was empty. "How'd you get here?" he heard himself ask, and his voice still sounded strange in his own ears.

"I walked that way yonder," Alex said, gesturing towards the fires in the west past the barricades. "Road goes to Tampa."

"Why did you do that?" Henry asked.

"Well," he said—and then took his chance: "Truth is, I think I've been lookin' for you." As soon as the words escaped his mouth, he realized they were wrong, and he tried to backpedal: "Not *you*, buddy. I mean I've been lookin' for *some*body. Somebody from somewhere else. Somebody *like* you, alright?"

Aside from blinking and breathing, Henry was still. Alex changed his approach. "Hey, I didn't mean'ta scare you. Hell, you scared me! But I'm glad you did, okay? I'm glad you're here. I—well, I didn't think I'd ever see nobody out here. But now…" His voice trailed off, and as it did, he gestured towards all of Henry. As if to say, *here you are.*

Henry didn't care for it.

Still, Alex took a step closer. "Hey, it's okay. Truly it is. Why don't you tell me your name, and we'll be off on the same foot."

"I don't want to," Henry said.

"Well, okay," Alex said. "That's okay. I getcha: you don't wanna have a name. No problem. But whoever you are…you ain't from around here, are ya? You ain't supposed to be in Florida?"

That question confused Henry. "I think I'm supposed to be here," he said.

"I mean you're *travelin'*. Your truck back there: it's got Carolina plates on it."

Alex had said he'd been in the store. Henry wondered how he knew about the Ranger. "Why aren't you still in Tampa?" he asked.

Alex laughed. "Hell, Tampa ain't where anybody oughta be! Don't go visit." As he said this, he thought of something and his face changed. "When you came down, you drive through Georgia?"

Henry nodded.

"Well, you're not gonna be able to get out that way. At least, not no time soon." He gestured towards the alley where the Ranger was parked. "You listen to news in that thing?"

Henry said nothing. Until this moment, he had not considered whether or not the Roving Ranger even had a radio.

"Well, Georgia's closed up again. No travel on the interstates; not on any big roads. Whenever that happens, ports like Tampa get busy, and that means extra hands, and 'hands' means Trupas. That's bad news for most folks. It's bad news for me." Alex didn't fill the space those words left, and Henry tried to guess what sort of folk he was. The way station hummed. The sky was a rich orange. Deep purple stained every cloud.

"What are Trupas?" Henry asked. He hadn't heard the word used before.

"Trupas? That's just True Patriots," Alex said. "Militia-types. Same old rednecks as always, but a bit more high-n-mighty than most, and a helluva lot meaner. When they come around, people're supposed to stay in their houses 'less they gotta reason to be somewhere. If they catch me out here"–Alex kept his eyes locked on Henry's as he said this–"they won't have a good reason to take me back, right? My point's this: I left Tampa, and I'm lookin' ta get a bit further away soon as I can."

If the situation was clear to Henry, his face didn't show it. Alex kept talking: "Look, I don't know who you are, but I ain't gonna hurt you, okay? If I was, I'da done it already. I don't want your stuff… "

At that, Henry's eyes widened perceptibly.

"… you just look like somebody movin' through, and I'm wonderin' if you might let me move through for a while with ya."

For the first time, Alex let his gaze move fully away from Henry, and when he did, everything about him seemed to soften. He looked towards the Roving Ranger. "I wouldn't be no trouble," he said. "I could probably help, even." His breath trembled as he let it out, and Henry realized he was just as rattled, just as frightened, as he was. Something was rising up in Henry, and he suddenly felt desperate to keep it down. He wondered if he was about to throw up. And then he knew what to say:

"I don't have a seat."

"What?" Alex asked.

"I don't have a seat," Henry said again. He pointed, helpfully, at the truck. "It only came with one."

Alex didn't say anything.

"There's just the driver." And as soon as Henry said this, he felt the words settle over him like a blanket. They felt magical: *there's just the driver*.

"I don't really need a seat," Alex said. He could feel the situation shifting, but he didn't fully know to what end yet. He looked again at the Ranger, and then back at this strange man in front of him. "Even if there's just room in the back…"

Henry realized he was still holding the last bite of his sandwich, and he had squeezed it into roughly the size and shape of a quarter. He let it fall to the ground and toed it, like he was putting out a cigarette. "There's not really any room in there. It's just me. And I'm trying to be careful…" The words all made sense to him, but they also weren't quite right. He looked up to see how they were going over, and when he did, he finally saw Alex. He had been wrong before; he was a kid, surely no more than sixteen. His hair was long but clean. He was so thin. Henry saw him, and he hated himself for what he already knew he would not do.

"I don't know," Alex said. "I can't go back there, mister. I can't go back…" His voice had cracked, and he could feel everything sinking. He wasn't about to cry now, but he looked like he would cry later. "I don't know what to do," he said again. "I don't know what to do."

"There's just the driver," Henry said, and he hoped the spell of these words would at least keep its hold over him. The kid said nothing, and instead, he sat down on the bit of curb in front of the station doors and stared out at the last colors in the sky. The sun was below the horizon now, and all that remained was the deep red-becoming-purple of civil sunset. Alex reached out for his empty backpack, pulled it in between his feet, and put his head in his hands.

The hardest part was over, and Henry started to walk slowly back towards his truck. He swung around the gas pumps in an excessively large orbit, and at the apogee, as he prepared to drift off again into his own space, he looked back and spoke to Alex one last time. "My name is Henry," he said, and he meant it as at least some token of goodwill. He nodded his head towards the boy kindly, and then he started to walk again.

Alex was already sniffling, and when he looked up, he wiped away a tear. "Yeah?" he said.

"Yeah."

"Well. Get fucked, Henry."

The kid put his head back down, and Henry walked on.

So long, Fort Lonesome.

Stars Fell On

It wasn't that Henry couldn't care. It was that he was afraid to. He wasn't alone: in this After country in which he lived, the air everywhere had become thick with fear. Henry took fear in with each breath until his lungs became heavy with it. He felt fear coating his skin like sweat. He moved because he knew fear would suffocate him if he stayed still. But every place he went, he found fear was already there, too—waiting for him as soon as he arrived. Fear had become a kind of primal humidity in his world, making everyone irritable and defensive. Making everyone myopic. So, Henry didn't give Alex a ride because he had learned to believe that it was better not to get involved. He didn't give Alex a ride because giving that would have led to questions, and questions from other people would have led to questions for himself. His answers would have become a story, and a story always turns where you're going into an arrow pointing away from where you've been. And that was the most frightening thing of all. So, Henry drove with the windows rolled down, because it's not the heat that gets you.

It took him two more days to sputter across the rest of the erstwhile farmlands of the Sunshine State. The roads were eerily empty, and everywhere Henry looked what were once fields of cotton or tomatoes had been uprooted, furrowed, or otherwise left to seed by people who either couldn't get anything to grow, or couldn't sell anything that did. Roaming forest fires had created nightmare tunnels of black and twisted branches out of old citrus groves, and Henry could see patches of soot stains on the sun-bleached asphalt which marked the places the fires had lept back and forth, from orchard to orchard, whenever the wind changed direction.

The kid–Alex–had seemed serious about not heading back through Georgia, and that made sense to him. It had been more than a year since the territory had voted to become a U.S. protectorate, and that made it a new island in a sea of confederated Republics. Even Henry knew this was a big deal: there weren't many of these enclaves, and the bargain they made was handout money in exchange for being hated by everyone around them. The official trouble would be on the old interstates and along the railways–places where constabularies could rally enough of the angry and bitter to keep up a blockade. But even in the empty spaces, Henry knew folks were still capable of laying out tire strips and setting up lawn chairs with a cooler and a shotgun if they didn't have anything else to do. The good news, for him at least, was that Alabama and Florida were still friendly. So, Henry opened his old atlas across the steering wheel and set his sights on a crossing north of Malone and south of a place called Grangeburg along highway 71.

Henry had learned in the Carolinas to always cross borders at night, and never to cross them with your headlights on. This time, however, it couldn't have mattered less: there wasn't a soul on the road, and the spot seemed to be utterly forgotten. Neither former state had even bothered to update their signage, and the darkened Ranger crunched over the cracking pavement while Henry held his breath. It was just after ten when he rolled past the words *Welcome to Sweet Home*, lit up by silver moonlight.

A few miles later, the road curved to the north and took him past not one, but two, Dollar Generals in a stretch of less than a half mile. The town, like all the others, was quiet. But the second of those Dollar Generals had lights on inside and a car parked out front, and Henry slowed. As he drove past the Methodist church at the end of Main Street, he could feel the world beginning to stir.

Henry checked the map. He knew Dothan was next, and he also knew it was large enough to be ringed by a highway bypass. Henry wanted nothing to do with that road, in large part because Henry wanted nothing to do with anything. So he marked three cross streets heading west, each capable of getting him to the safety of county roads across the delta. But as he approached the first, he realized it was closed off not only by orange and white striped sawhorses, but by a full set of concrete jersey walls. The black words *Road Closed* drank in his low beams while the rest of the sign, covered in reflective white, bounced the light back at him. He squinted and looked around. There were no people. But there was no way through, either.

The second road was also blocked when he turned in to check, and he saw the third closure without even having to brake. His stomach sank hard and heavy, and he could feel his heart beating in his chest. There was a squeal in the A/C compressor that Henry had been ignoring for a week, but it now sounded to him very much like a tea kettle about to boil. He slowed down and realized that the roads to the east were all closed, too, which meant this wasn't a fire, a flood, or tornado damage. It was a trap.

And then there it was: another mile ahead, spotlights had been set up on both sides of the bypass interchange along with several white pop-up tents through which vehicles could be funneled. A handful of police officers were standing about, and his heart beat faster still. Henry was still looking for any potential escape path. He even imagined gunning the Roving Ranger at a dirt ramp beside the checkpoint and trying to jump the gate. But just as that fantasy took flight, a flashlight was already waving him forward, and as soon as the beam hit him through the windshield, Henry's opossum instincts took over. He froze, and then slowed the Ranger to an impossibly low idle. The engine threatened to stall—five miles per hour, then four, then two–and as it crawled towards the checkpoint, Henry's foot hovered over the brake, tapping it whenever the needle of the speedometer dared to register movement. The flashlight from before sped up its waving, growing increasingly impatient. But things had moved beyond Henry's control: this would just take as long as it took.

The Ranger stopped on its own accord against a rubber cone, and the instant it did, the officer behind the flashlight walked to the driver's side and tapped on the glass. Henry rolled down the window.

"No big hurry, huh?" he said.

Henry looked at him without blinking.

"Republic license'n registration." The officer paused for a moment and then added, helpfully: "Carolina's valid here, too." He had had plenty of time to look at the Ranger's plates.

But Henry still didn't move. "I don't have one," he said.

This gave the officer pause. "You ain't got a Carolina license for this vehicle, or you ain't got a license?"

"I don't have a Carolina license."

The officer clicked off the flashlight. He wanted Henry to see that he was trying to be patient. "You got a license from any Republic 'r state?"

"No," Henry said. Then, to avoid causing offense, he added: "Sir."

"And why'd that be?" the officer asked.

At moments like these, Henry oscillated wildly between two unhelpful approaches: the first was silence and the second was oversharing. He went with the second.

"I lost it in a swamp."

The officer's brow furrowed. Somehow, he was still more amused than angry: the whole checkpoint was the mayor's idea, he knew, to show he was a hardass about immigrants after he almost lost the last election. On most nights, they were lucky to get a half dozen cars, and those were almost always bleary-eyed locals on their way back from skirting the town's blue laws in the woods. So whatever else the "Roving Ranger" was, it was at least a story. Still, this was thin ice.

"Ease my curiosity," the officer said. "What jurisdiction was'at license from *before* you lost it in a swamp?" he asked.

"It was an Ohio license." Henry couldn't hear it, but the officer's ice was cracking.

"You lost your *Ohio* license… in a swamp?"

"Yessir."

"In a truck outta South Carolina?"

"That's correct."

The officer looked again at the Ranger. It was spattered with mud and dust; the quarter panels were rusted through, and the faded face of a bobcat stared back at him from a decal on the hood. "Let me ask you: s'this vehicle yours?"

Henry gulped. "Well, in an important sense, yes."

And with that, the ice broke.

"Okay bud, you're gonna need to get on out now." The officer stepped back and rested his palm on the handle of his service weapon: the man before him did not seem remotely dangerous, but he certainly seemed *something*.

The door opened and Henry, wearing flip flops, cargo pants, and a hoodie from the Everglades, felt surprisingly naked in the humid night air. His glasses immediately fogged. The officer's hand relaxed, and he suddenly remembered an essential question–a question he could not believe he had forgotten to ask: "What's your name?"

The officer couldn't see them, but Henry's eyes closed. He was concentrating as hard as he could. "It's Henry, sir. Can I ask what this is all about?" This seemed like the kind of thing people in this situation might say.

"Henry what?"

*   *   *

It turned out that Alabama jails had not been noticeably impacted by the decline and fall of the United States of America. The officer from the checkpoint—McKinney was his name—had taken Henry to the police station first. It was a sprawling cinder block building with a low, flat roof. He had had questions:

"So, you're saying your name is Henry Henry?"

"That *is* my name," Henry Henry said.

"And you're from Ohio?"

"In the United States, yes." Officer McKinney ignored this little dig and pressed on.

"And you've been on a road trip since November two-five?"

"Since last Thanksgiving, yes."

"What happened on Thanksgiving? Bad turkey?" McKinney asked.

"I don't eat turkey," Henry said. But he understood what McKinney was asking, and he offered a partial truth: "I left on Thanksgiving because I don't have any family any more, and it seemed like a good day to leave."

"Is that so? What happened to your family?"

Henry paused. "My wife died last spring."

Officer McKinney was quiet. He jotted something down in his notepad.

"When you left Ohio, where'd you go?"

"I drove to upstate New York first, to the Catskills. And then I went up to Maine."

"Tough time'a year to go up that way, ain't it?" McKinney himself had never been north of Tennessee.

"I guess so," Henry said. He thought for a moment about that drive, and he remembered there actually hadn't even been snow on the ground yet. Winters came later and later these days.

"And what'd you do up there?" For Officer McKinney, this was the central mystery. He already knew that Henry had left a job, a mortgage, and a handful of unpaid parking tickets in Ohio. He knew about the dead *ex*-wife. He also knew that Henry's old boss was the only person who ever called in a wellness check for him after he left without notice.

But what Henry knew was this: the man talking with him was a dragon, and now that he was awake, Henry needed to slip by him carefully.

"I had never been to the coast, and I wanted to see things. My wife always wanted to travel, and we never really did. We always pushed it off." Henry did not like using her like this—as a deflection. What he said wasn't untrue, but it wasn't the real truth. So he said another thing, and he meant it two ways at once: "I wanted to go because of her."

Officer McKinney wrote something down in his notepad. There was also a tape recorder on the table between them, and Henry didn't know which one was the prop. "Where and when'd you leave the Federal States?" McKinney asked.

"It was New Years. I crossed into Beckley because I wanted to see the Gorge. I stayed in the Republics after that, and that took me all the way down to here."

The Ranger had been heading north not south, but Officer McKinney chose not to chase that rabbit quite yet. Instead, he said, "I didn't know they was lettin' tourists come through in West Virginia. I thought those borders're shipping only."

Henry didn't say anything to that. Honestly, he didn't like talking this much at all. His throat was sore, and the water Officer McKinney had brought him tasted like pennies.

McKinney continued: "Okay Henry, there're two things I really need'ta know. First, I need'ta know how you ended up with that ve-hicle. It's registered to the old park service, and nobody works for them no more, so I don't know where in the world you got it. The second thing I need to know is what in the hell you're doin' in Alabama."

Henry realized he was very much ready for the interview to be over. "I found the truck," he said, "when I was in the swamp."

"That myst'ry swamp? One where you lost your license?"

They were different swamps technically, but Henry let that go. "Yes."

"And you just went and took it?"

"Well, yes. Like you said, nobody was using it. The parks are all closed. At least, down here."

Down here. McKinney wasn't Alabama's biggest patriot, but he was still beginning to get annoyed. "By that you mean the parks're closed in the Republics?"

"Yes. The Federal parks down here are all closed, I mean. You couldn't afford to keep them open, I guess. At least, that's what I read."

Federal. Afford. Read. Officer McKinney put down his notepad and leaned back in his chair. *This fucker right here,* he thought to himself. "Well, Henry, it's been awhile since I've been a part of things up your way, but I seem to remember it's frowned upon to claim gover'ment property as your own."

Henry rolled his eyes. "That's sort of what *you* did though, isn't it?"

Good God, did Henry have a punchable face. McKinney grit his teeth.

Suddenly, Henry remembered the officer's second question: "I'd also like very much to *not* be in Alabama, sir, if possible."

Henry waited in the jail for three days stretching over a weekend. No one told him about any official charges, but also, that sort of thing didn't really matter. On the bright side, they fed him bologna and cheese sandwiches everyday, and those were an upgrade from the peanut butter and beef jerky he'd been eating for the last week. The bed was also more comfortable than he expected. Toilet paper was a luxury, too.

On the second day—a Saturday—a drunk got tossed into his cell with him, but he didn't say much. Henry did his best to blend in with the walls and avoid eye contact. Still, he learned the man's name was Cletus, unbelievably, and he cursed a lot. He was released as soon as he sobered up, and when the guard came, he tossed Henry a newspaper called *The Alabama Son*. Henry did not read it.

Time passed slowly. Although it was warm out, the heat in the jail was on and Henry's cell was uncomfortably damp. The paper slippers he'd been given to wear stuck to the floor whenever he stood up from his bunk. There was a small window near the ceiling over the sink, and he could see clouds in it sometimes. Even through the glass, he could hear occasional birds. Time passed slowly, but it passed.

On the third day, Officer McKinney appeared with a plastic bag containing all of Henry's worldly belongings. He was holding a clipboard, and while he spoke, his eyes stayed fixed on it. "Henry, I'm lettin' you go. You're a weird sonofabitch, but there's nobody who cares about that truck. The license is a problem, but I'll be goddamned if we're going to pay'ta feed and house some dumb fuckin' yankee drifter. You take these keys and get the hell out of Alabama."

"Okay," Henry said. He was already standing, but Officer McKinney was blocking the doorway, eyes still on his clipboard. Henry took a tentative step forward. "Um?"

"Je-sus Christ," McKinney said and tossed the bag into the cell. He left the door open and walked away.

In the bag was the rabbit foot keyfob, and in the parking lot was the Roving Ranger, looking not much worse for the wear. His things had been shuffled about a bit, the glove box rummaged through, his bins dumped out onto the mattress in the back. But still: it was sweet home. He cranked the engine, adjusted the mirror which had been knocked askew, and pulled up to the rolling security fence leading to the exit. It buzzed, and as he waited for it to open, he looked over at the officer in the guard shack and gave him a little wave. The officer shot him the bird. Henry rolled on through.

West of Dothan, he followed signs to Enterprise and then slipped back off the main roads and into the safer emptiness of the backcountry: the state highway to Brantley, 106 to Georgiana, then a county road under an interstate overpass and on through Old Texas, Pine Apple, Oak Hill. If Florida had been desolate, Alabama was simply abandoned: scorching summers had baked the countryside an even and empty brown, and the only signs of life were those same symmetrical stands of pines that were leftovers from attempts in the 2020s to replace the dying cotton crops with cheap lumber. Everywhere, houses were boarded up or burned down. Nothing had succeeded.

It was near evening when Henry first caught sight of the Alabama River to the north, and as the road turned to cross it, he found an old and overgrown picnic area along the roadside. He pulled the Ranger into what was once a parking space and turned the key. He'd been thinking, as he drove, about sneaking around empty places. About how he had come to this. About what it was he was doing, and the little metal box under the driver's seat. He'd been on the road for three months now, and it was still just as foolish a quest as it had seemed on the day that he left. In the past three weeks alone, he'd been lost, he'd been robbed, and now, he'd been arrested. If he had hoped, once upon a time, to be able to tiptoe through this old country, he'd learned his feet were much too clumsy for such work. Henry was a fool, but he wasn't that much of a fool.

The stars were coming out, and his mind wandered, as it often did, to the woman who had been his wife. To Shannon. It was true what he had said: that she had always wanted to travel. She sold houses back in Akron, and she used to joke that it was the perfect place to live if you never wanted to see a tourist ever again. Her nightstand had been stacked with quirky guidebooks to unusual places—*50 Best Roadside Attractions in the West, The Most Haunted Places in America, 100 Sights to See Before You Die*. But in twenty years together, they had made it to no more than a half dozen of them. It was a boring story: work, taking care of dying parents, raising a kid. Nobody's fault, really. Henry wondered now if the books did more for their imagination, for their ability to believe other places were even *out there*, than anything else. Sitting here now, looking out at the wide expanse of the Alabama River, Henry was pretty sure travel wasn't worth it. The whole place was a wasteland, ready to crumble at the slightest touch.

Do you think people will ever live up there? Shannon had asked him once. They were looking through a telescope—one of his hobbies—at the moon.

Maybe they already do, he said hoping she would laugh. But she didn't. They were both quiet for a while.

You know, it's been fifty years now since anyone walked around up there, she said. *Fifty whole years. When I was a kid, I thought for sure we would live to see colonies on Mars. I thought my grandkids might live in them one day. Now, I'd settle for them to get out of Ohio.*

Their son was two. They didn't know it, but their worst day was still years ahead of them.

Ha ha, Henry laughed sarcastically. *There's still time. You never know. Maybe somebody will figure it out. It's NASA: that's what they always do.* He said this as if it explained everything. *You just wait: Henry Junior will be an astronaut yet.*

I swear to God, stop calling him that. Henry had been committed to this bit since they came home from the hospital. *If you don't stop calling him that, I'm going to leave you, I'm not kidding. You'll never see him again.*

Henry laughed, genuinely this time. *You're the one who wants to send him to space.*

Shannon elbowed Henry in the ribs and bent to look again through the eyepiece. *Getting out of Ohio is not the same as going to space.* She paused for a long second, her head still down, and Henry couldn't read her expression. *I'm just saying that it used to seem like we were all going somewhere. And it doesn't really anymore.*

Where were we going? Henry had asked, and gotten no reply.

It was dark now in Alabama. The flittering shapes of bats were swooping and diving for bugs over the river. It was actually cold for the first time in a long time, and Henry thought about the thousand miles between where he sat and Akron.

He might as well have been on the moon.

Henry slept in the next day and then, on an absolute whim, went skinny-dipping in the slow, brown dirge of the Alabama. Time after time, he dove down to the very bottom, dug his fingers and then his toes into the soft silt of the riverbed, and sprang to the surface in an ecstatic rush. For no reasons which made sense to him, he laughed like a maniac each time. After nearly an hour of this, he beached himself on the shore, still fully nude, and let himself dry. It was barely 60 degrees out, and he was shivering despite the sunshine. Still, he felt bolder somehow. He felt better.

Later, back in the Roving Ranger, he drove much too fast for the backroads. The landscape was still apocalyptic, and he was eager to be rid of it. Alabama: it's all brown roads, scraggly trees, and empty shacks. As far as Henry was concerned, Officer McKinney could keep it.

He'd picked a place just west of Aliceville to cross, and it was early in the afternoon when he passed the shotgun-blasted town sign. Things were as rotten as everywhere else, and Henry pushed the Ranger towards its ceiling of fifty miles per hour. His hope was that this road would keep him well south of Tupelo on the other side, and if his luck held, he could stay in the backcountry for at least a day before needing to cut north. The last few mile markers were counting down, and he remembered what the kid in Fort Lonesome had said about the radio. For the first time he turned it on, and like magic, it latched immediately onto a station: Rock 106.3, "Tuscaloosa's Home of the *Bad Attitude*." The song was mid-riff and Henry recognized it, even if he couldn't name the band. Ozzy Osbourne? AC/DC? Papa Roach? He turned up the volume until the speakers fuzzed and then rolled down the windows. He wished he could wear sunglasses. He felt fucking amazing.

And then, as he rounded the last bend and stared down the last four hundred yards to the border, he saw it: unbelievably, incredibly, there was something in the middle of the road. At three hundred yards, he could make out a chair and an umbrella. At two hundred, he saw a man stand up and lift his hands to begin waving the Ranger down. At one hundred, he could tell the man's hands were empty: no gun. *No gun!* Something like delirium came over him, and Henry floored it.

The man, who must have been in his seventies and was dressed like a Civil War veteran, waddled out of the way in plenty of time. But his folding chair wasn't so lucky: Henry obliterated it with the left corner of his bumper and the old man watched as it flew twenty feet in the air and got stuck in the top of a tree.

Keep Alabama the Beautiful.

Fifth Country

Over the next day and a half, two things happened. First, Henry's brief bout of confidence evaporated like rain on hot asphalt and he became convinced somebody was after him. The man from the roadblock, bumpkin though he may be, would certainly have had a way to call Henry in. The cops from one patriot republic or another would be on the hunt, perhaps Officer McKinney among them, and how many ice cream trucks with turtles and raccoon stickers on them could be on the roads in Mississippi? He couldn't believe he had been so stupid.

And the second thing: Henry discovered there was a lot less of this state left than he expected. The parts that had once been a delta were now a swampy wetland, and the routine of storm surges from summer hurricanes pushed the water closer and closer to the treetops, even fifty miles inland from what used to be the coast. The tributaries snaking across the flatlands towards the Mississippi were experiencing hundred year floods almost every spring, and whole roads had been washed out and left unrepaired. Henry had to detour, and then detour from the detours, until he was good and lost in a ravaged nowhere. Plastic and other garbage was tangled in every low bush or branch, from whichever disaster he knew not. For all the "Don't Tread On Me" flags still flying over the scattered homesteads, Mississippi seemed to have been well trod.

Still, Henry's dread of whatever Law there was around here pushed him to drive through the night. He slept through the next day after hiding the Ranger off an old forest road, and once the sun set, he kept going with only his running lights on for hours along winding dirt tracks through shadowed woodlands. The sky was clear and there were moments when he could see that it was beautiful, despite his fear. To hear better, and to dissipate the odor of vegetable oil, he kept the windows rolled down as he drove. Although it was warm for February, the air was still sharp and smelled of pine needles. The moon hung low in the sky, and it surprised him each time it appeared to dart out from behind one tree and run to the next.

Years ago, when he and Shannon and Caleb would take trips, he would play games with the miles-to-empty gauge in their little car. He knew the readings were finicky—that there were always secret miles waiting for you past the zero, if you just had the courage to get to them—and he would stretch each tank of gas to its very limit. You won the game when you finally got to the pump: if you could put seventeen gallons in a sixteen gallon tank, you had uncovered the secret, and in some small way, the car became more yours. But on a handful of occasions, the car would win, and Henry would have to coast to a stop, seeking shade if he could find it. When that happened, Shannon's anger would burn towards him with a heat he could feel and a brightness he knew not to look at. Caleb would sometimes begin to cry.

What Henry never told either of them was that these, too, were moments he longed for. He would hang his head, complain about the gauge, and maybe mumble an apology. But when that was done, he would do what he could to make them comfortable and then set out on what he thought of as a hero's journey. If the next gas station was close enough, he would walk to it; if it was more than a mile or two, he would hitchhike. He particularly liked hitchhiking: the sense of danger, of stepping out of his world and briefly into the world of someone else, used to be intoxicating to him. It was sometimes hard for him to imagine this side of himself now. Then again, he *was* driving across the country in a stolen ice cream truck.

But the gas: no matter the means by which he arrived, Henry's routine once he reached his destinations was consistent and clear. He would go into the store, buy one of those red plastic cans, and a pack of the cheapest cigarettes the store sold. Sometimes these were Winstons; sometimes they were Marlboros on sale; most often, they were Newports. Whatever the brand, he would wait until his gas can was full and then unwrap the pack hastily, take out just one, and throw the rest in a trash can. Then he would make his way to the edge of whatever lot he was in, sit down on the tarmac, and watch the strangers at the pumps as he smoked it. He knew Shannon hated the smell of smoke, but he also knew the gasoline would cover it, and both odors would dissipate before he got back to the car. Henry lived for these little moments of strangeness and rebellion. For his time in limbo, at the far edge of his own life.

As soon as the cigarette was gone, though, Henry would feel the pull of Shannon, of Caleb, of people waiting *for him*. The time he had been gone would rush at him in a flood, and then guilt would break like a thunderclap over his head. He would scramble up, dust himself off, and sometimes even run on his way back to the car. He would strain for the first moment it came into view. He would fight down panic as he looked to see if Shannon's silhouette was still there in the windshield. The gas can, which when he first set out he imagined as the carcass of a freshly-slain deer to be brought back over triumphant and proud shoulders, would become a blemished and pitiful offering. He would fill the tank in silence, then take his place again behind the wheel.

*   *   *

But of course now there was no Shannon. They had divorced in 2031, and she had died from another flu last spring. And there was no Caleb. So there was no more sun at the center of things, either to run from or to bring him hurrying back. He was free in Mississippi, he understood. Launched out into silent space.

Henry made his way out of the woods sometime after midnight, and lo and behold, there was a sign: *All Points North*. The sign was new—not a relic of the old highway administrations—and it was painted a brownish orange. The road towards which it gestured had recently been paved and seemed strangely well maintained. All in all, it was the sort of thing Henry typically went to great lengths to avoid. But after all the detours, the truth was that Henry had no idea where he was, and he thought the road might at least lead him to some crossroad or town he could recognize from his atlas before dawn. So, he made the turn, and as he did, there was another orange sign waiting for him: *Fifth's Highway*.

Henry didn't know what that meant, but it seemed to mean something. As he drove, he began to see plywood signs along the roadway with "God Bless the Fifth" in big, hand-painted block letters and even the roof of a barn reading "Regiment 5 Keeps Mississippi Alive." There were more and more old Confederate battle flags sprouting from poles in the soybean fields, as well as a new flag he had not seen before with what looked to him like a white lotus blossom surrounding a single black star. At a surprisingly frequent rate, there were also small white crosses along the shoulder. Henry's first thought was that they were for car crashes, but there was a strange consistency to them: a uniform shape, size, and tiny inscription. After passing more than a dozen, he realized they all had that same black star dead in their center.

* * *

As the sky began to lighten, the road stayed mercifully empty, and Henry began to get his bearings. The highway had finally found a way to cross the Yockanookany River, and although most of the original signs had been torn down or covered over, he spotted a few faded Park Service arrowheads which told him he was on the old Natchez Trace Parkway. That road, he knew, led to Tupelo, which was too big of a town and too close to Alabama for Henry, border-runner and fugitive from justice that he was. So, he broke north again as the sun rose, passing out of the piney midlands and into flat and mist-covered fields.

Now that he was no longer focused on the absence or presence of headlights behind him, Henry was finally able to notice another troubling thing: the Ranger was making a distinct sputtering sound. Henry had grown used to many of its rumbles and groans over the last thousand miles, and he typically chalked them up to the quirks of running an old and long-disused biodiesel engine. He'd found the truck in a swamp, after all; he knew their time together would be fraught. But this sound was different than any he had heard before. It was more like a phlegmy and knocking cough, and he also noticed that the dashboard lights dimmed with each of its rattling wheezes. "This isn't good," he said out loud and to no one; he had been experimenting with keeping his voice familiar.

Even though it was morning, Henry was hesitant to stop. There were no guarantees the Ranger could get going again, and so he decided to drive it as far as he could. Along this older highway, he lurched through a half dozen one-light towns. The truck, covered in animals and backfiring every hundred feet, couldn't help but draw attention. What was odd, however, were the differences in each town's reactions: in Slate Spring, in Calhoun City, in Pittsboro, residents heard him coming and came out to more or less stare him down. More than a few had rifles in their hands, caressing them tenderly as the Roving Ranger knocked and rattled along their respective Main Streets. But in other towns—small ones, with names like Banner and Paris–Henry could feel he was being watched from behind drawn curtains and through cracked doors, but there wasn't a soul in sight. Still, Henry knew they were there. Surprising numbers of dead possums and armadillos lined the streets. Packs of mangy dogs disappeared together into roadside culverts. The sound of insects swelled, even with his windows rolled up, growing louder until it was a roar.

The Ranger performed heroically, but Henry couldn't get it above twenty miles per hour as he passed the sign for the Oxford city limit. It was larger than any of the other towns he had seen that morning, and it seemed to Henry like a 1920s mosquito stuck in mid-apocalyptic amber: century-old oak trees gave shade to boulevards lined with perfect little postbellum houses, each with a wrap-around porch and painted in the same faded pastel hues you find in a carton of dyed Easter eggs. There were squirrels in the trees and cats dozing on wide and sun-dappled sidewalks.

Henry realized the road he was on had entered into a perfect grid of cross streets, and just a couple blocks from what he could already see would be a perfect courthouse square, the gazebo inevitable, he by God's good grace spotted a white stripe on the awning above a nearby storefront. The Ranger knocked and sputtered and was in the actual process of stalling when he turned into the next alley and rolled to a stop in the vacant space behind a rundown diner. He turned the key, pocketed the rabbit's foot, and popped the hood to inspect the damage.

Henry knew nothing about cars. The various shapes of plastic and metal were a uniform blackish-brown; he understood a certain amount of smoke was to be expected in such an environment. He wiggled a hose that seemed wiggle-able. He brushed off some dried leaves that had nestled into the creases of what might or might not be an intake manifold. Birds sang to each other overhead.

He looked around and considered his options. The first, as always, was to run away. Henry could grab his lockbox, stuff the pocket of his hoodie with a day's worth of snacks, and keep moving. In time he would probably find an untended bicycle. But he could sense that the place in which he found himself was a long way from any other sort of place, and he thought about the unfriendly faces he had passed on his way here. Did he want to run into someone on foot? And yet, his second option was no less dangerous: he could ask one of these people for help. He thought of Officer McKinney. He thought of the man who shot him a bird at the gate. He thought, needlessly, of Cletus. And he didn't like those chances any better.

He was going to have to bet on that white stripe, and he prayed they didn't have a radio: *...on the lookout for a white, middle-aged male...driving a stolen truck...unarmed, but a danger to pedestrians and patio furniture...* He gulped and set out from the parking lot towards the diner he had passed when he turned in. As he walked around the corner of the building, the sign under the awning came into view, and he squinted, making a puzzled face as he read it: *Bunch's Lunches.*

Bunch's Lunches?

An actual bell rang when he opened the front door, and he immediately heard, of all things, jazz. He stepped into a dusty, dark, and surprisingly smoke-filled room. The near wall had formerly been a large window looking out on the sidewalk, but the inside had been covered in old newspapers which tinted the space an odd brown as the sunlight streamed through them. A half dozen booths sat against the window, but only two were free of boxes, bags, or other odds and ends. He was pretty sure an actual engine block was sitting on the table of the booth in the corner, which he took to be a positive sign.

Across from the booths was a long counter which was like every counter in every diner, and as Henry's eyes adjusted, he found the source of the smoke: a waitress had just emerged through the still-swinging doors to the kitchen and she had a lit cigarette dangling from the corner of her mouth. Another was tucked behind her ear. She had skin like an old leather purse.

"Well, good morning, stranger" she said. "What can I do ya for?"

"I saw the stripe. And I think I need a little help." Henry didn't have a hat, but it still seemed like he was holding one in his hands. The air felt heavy and thick to him, and he fought back a cough.

"Well, sweetie," the woman said, "that stripe means we're safe, not that we're a charity." She seemed ageless: somewhere between 35 and 100, a bold amount of lipstick, and red Lucille Ball hair piled on the top of her head. As Henry put all of this together, she took her time with him, too: she looked him up and down, from his still mostly-new hoodie to his shorts and flip flops. She thought he looked like a cartoon of a person. "Exactly what kind of help mightcha be lookin' for?" she asked.

"My truck broke down," said Henry. "And I'm not sure I can get it started." The issue of money (and his failure to have any of it) seemed relevant to the conversation, so he offered what currency he could: "If I can, I'll get right out of your way. I'm just hoping to pass through."

She wrinkled her nose at that. "Well, ya don't just 'pass through' Oxford, hon. Folks only come here when whatever place they're headin' ain't a place they can rightly get. So, in your case, where might that be?"

Following her sentences was like making his way through a maze, but she didn't seem wary, and Henry thought she looked like someone who had heard every possible answer from every sort of traveler. He went, uncharacteristically, with a partial truth.

"Near Little Rock."

The wrinkled nose made a snort. "Well, that right there's your first mistake," she said, shaking her head. "Little Rock? Nothin' but trouble, and you ain't the first in here who's wanted a look. But every cart needs a horse first: what'd you say was the problem with the truck?"

The proprietress agreed to call a friend who might be able to help, and although she promised he would be right over, it was noon when a panel van with Christmas Auto stenciled on the side met Henry behind the diner. The man who emerged from it—middle-aged, heavy, gray scruff on his face—took one look at the biodiesel engine and then spit a loogie on it. He shook his head skeptically, made a grumbling noise, and then set to tinkering. "It's gonna be a bit," he said, not looking up. "More like a while." Henry backed away slowly.

Inside again, he didn't know what else to do besides sit at the counter. He made a little church out of his hands. If the music hadn't been on, he might have actually whistled. And after ten minutes, the proprietress got tired of waiting him out and came out again from the kitchen to see what she could see. She told Henry her name was Cece. In reply, Henry confessed to her that he was penniless. But Cece was unphased. Instead, she listened to his rambling—promises of wire transfers, future mailed checks from somewhere north—and then raised a finger towards his mouth to shush him. It was such a familiar gesture, but Henry could not remember if he had ever seen a person actually make it before. He felt immediately like an infant. But once he was quiet, she told him to at least wait until the verdict was in, and they might be able to work things out.

"Sweet tea?" she asked him, and he thought for a moment she was using the term of endearment again. But her hand was already reaching for a glass, so Henry just nodded. She filled the glass with ice, reached for a pitcher on the back counter, and poured. "Joe's anything but quick," she said. "So you're gonna have ta sit. What'd you say your name was again, Little Rock?"

"Hank," Henry had said, and when he did, he felt an old boldness. *Why shouldn't it be?* But he sensed immediately she didn't like it. The corner of her mouth quirked up, and she said, "Hmm. I'll give it a try. But Little Rock's gotta ring to it."

As the afternoon wore on, it became clear there was virtually no business in this diner. Henry spent most of his time staring into empty space, trying to avoid Cece's questions, and feeling increasingly sick to his stomach. Time was stretching out in a pool around him, and he felt like he was back at one of those gas stations buying a red can, and then being forced to smoke the whole pack of cigarettes. Eventually, Cece came over again and leaned against the counter.

"Well, Little Rock, I might as well ask ya, even if I already know you're gonna lie: what really brings you out this way?" She slapped her hands on the counter and dust puffed into the air.

"It was the only road I could find," Henry said.

Cece nodded at that. "But then there's the thing," she said. "Bein' the *only* road don't always mean only's the *best*." Working his way through that sentence left Henry exhausted, but he didn't yet know the half of it: by the end of the afternoon, Cece had shared her life story and then some: she was born and raised in Oxford, but the politics disagreed with her, so she moved to Missouri. When the country was crumbling, her mother crumbled, too, and she moved back to see things through to the end. By the time that came, Mississippi had already seceded from the rest of the United States, and the new ways of things made it impossible for her to leave. So she was stuck, and after pittering about for a few months, she took the diner over from a neighbor who was too afraid of one virus or another to risk running it herself. In the end, Cece liked the work. But after a year of having her ass slapped by militiamen and church deacons, she added the white stripe out front just to keep their kind away. For that sin, she dealt with mean looks from neighbors and vandalism from time to time. But her skin was thick enough for all that.

She liked the leftover academics and graduate students who stayed in Oxford after the university fire: the secret anarchists and closet liberals, holed up in their houses and selling whatsits by mail or sending "dispatches from the Front" back to New York news outlets for a few hundred bucks. When they poked their heads up around her counter, she sold them company more than anything else. In the end, it was enough to keep her fed and to pay the power bill, and that's all she really needed: the flu outbreak in '29 had killed her landlord, and nobody in town had taken any notice. A hurricane had barreled through that same year. Then, so did the Fifth.

Henry was unused to listening to anyone talk about anything for so long, especially in such an exhausting way. But when he heard Cece mention "the Fifth," his ears perked up. He had found himself dragged forcefully and unwillingly into her story, and now he was having what could best be described as an out of body experience: he could see himself sitting there at the dusty diner counter, and he knew this other, fleshy version of him was on the verge of taking the bait she was dangling. He saw his own mouth beginning to twitch, and his brain starting to turn over a question: "what *is* the Fifth?" It was like watching water beginning to boil, the bubbles threatening to break the surface. But he willed himself to silence, to distance, and he came back into his body. He forced himself to break eye contact; to smile, and to nod. And Cece didn't seem to notice how close he had come to caring. Instead, she went right on, talking about this traveler and that one; where they'd been heading, and how long each had stayed.

Henry knew—he had known for a long time—that *not knowing* was his secret. It was the key to quick stops and long drives. It was what allowed him to keep moving, drifting further and further out from something he was afraid to be pulled back towards. But Cece seemed eager for the opposite. She was a collector. Her diner was a reservoir in which moving things came to rest.

Mercifully, a customer came in. He was well-dressed and had dark skin. He was holding a notebook in his hands. Henry realized he was the first Black person he'd seen in he didn't know how long, and Cece looked at him with recognition. She stood up, and as she did, she turned back to face Henry one more time. "I'll tell you what, Little Rock: if you'll work for a few days, I wouldn't mind it if you kept eatin' and stayed parked out back. You'll be more or less safe there, and if Joe figures things out, we'll work that in and get you on your way."

Her attention shifted. "Billy, Billy," she said to this new man. "We ain't filled up that damn notebook of yours yet? What in the world do you wanna hear now?"

Joe did not figure things out. The Ranger stayed stuck, and Henry stayed stuck with it. In the kitchen after they spoke, Henry made Joe dinner and then came around the counter to bus the dishes. At some point, Cece had handed him an apron and stepped out for a few hours. But Henry didn't mind. He liked the quiet. And he had always liked to cook.

When she came back, Cece reassured him. She would make another call to a man she knew who worked on lawnmowers who had helped a traveler out with a busted axle a year or so ago. There was a kid who knew tractors in town, too; she said Henry wasn't without hope quite yet. As Henry listened, he looked down at the cup of sweet tea he hadn't realized was yet again in his hands, and his thoughts drifted to other options: could people still stowaway on railcars? Were there still traveling circuses? The hum of the ventilator hood over the grill was endless white noise, and the tea had the flavor and consistency of molasses. It made his teeth hurt. He could hear cicadas, brought out from the ground months too soon by a too-warm winter, buzzing in the trees along the boulevards. A dog, with no collar and no owner, walked by the propped-open door of the restaurant.

That night, in the back of the Roving Ranger and finally asleep, Henry dreamed of deep woods and soft earth. In his dream, he saw enormous roots forcing their way down between heavy stones, their motion sped up and frightening as they wrapped themselves around boulders and turned them into anchors and weights. In his dream, no storm could shake them, even though many storms tried. In his dream, no wind could blow them free.

Yoknapatawpha

The lawnmower man was just as perplexed, and the tractor kid never showed. Every day was the same: Henry woke up, went into the diner, took in a glimmer of new hope from Cece along with his coffee—a man who used to work on an assembly line at the Toyota plant, a ham radio operator who was good with electronics—and then got to work. A few days passed this way; then a week. Outside the diner, the town of Oxford never changed. The sun shone mercilessly, roosters crowed, and the same faces drifted in and out of Bunch's Lunches. He was at the end of a tether, but whoever had been on the other side had dropped the line and left him in limbo, the rope still tied around his waist. He didn't want to know what had happened to them. He had acquired a taste for sweet tea.

Cece was kind and curious, and Henry worked hard to keep her at bay. Each morning she would pry for more information, and he would answer back with only a word or two. He told her his age. He told her where he used to work. He told her he had learned to make a mean omelet from a roommate after college. He did not ask her any questions. He did dishes, wiped down the counter, took out the trash. He shooed away raccoons and left saucers of milk out for stray cats.

And then one day at dawn, there was a knock on the vending window of the Ranger. Henry woke up like someone who finds themselves suddenly underwater, lunging upwards and gasping for air. He heard the knock again, and he was unsure of what exactly to do. Why wasn't it at the back door? He stood up and faced the window. Tentatively, he turned the latch and the whole panel rose up and outwards on little hydraulic pistons. The smell of french fries filled the parking lot.

Before him was a man he had come to recognize. His name was Billy. He was Black and thin; maybe thirty. He'd been in the diner a handful of times, and Henry had made him a tuna melt. He was wearing what he always seemed to be wearing: a buttoned-down shirt tucked into plain brown slacks, looking for all the world like someone on their way to work. Henry couldn't fathom where that could be: an architect? A florist? A teacher? Were there still schools here? The man was smiling, but he seemed like he was working not to seem nervous.

"What I'd do for a Klondike Bar," he said, making eyes at the Rover and ready to share a laugh. But the joke never landed.

"What?" Henry said.

"I said, 'I'd do anything for a Klondike Bar.'" He drummed his fingers on the serving board on the outside of the window. "Because you're sleeping in an ice cream truck."

"Oh," said Henry.

"Well?"

"What?"

"Do you have any?"

Henry wondered if he was still asleep. "No," he said. "It's not really an ice cream truck." Billy had fought hard to break the ice, but Henry could be a cold son of a bitch.

"Yeah, I guess not." He kept standing there, searching for a new approach. "Your name's Henry, right?"

Henry sighed. "Yes." *It could never be Hank.*

"Right. Well, I'm Billy," he said, touching his whole hand to his chest. "I've seen you around in the diner. You stuck out here?" Henry knew that everyone knew that was the case. So, Billy went on: "If so, I thought I might try to work on it. I don't know a lot about ice cream trucks," he said, "but I know a thing or two about cars."

When Billy had practiced the line, he had assumed they would have already shared a laugh about the ice cream. This whole encounter was important to him: he'd been watching Henry for a few days, and he'd asked Cece about him. The night before, he had been lying in the backseat of his own car trying to figure out if Henry could be the train he'd been looking for. Now, he was trying to find the tracks again. "I could give it a look," he said. "That's what I'm saying. If you're interested."

Henry was still groggy, and he felt more than a little confused. But he sensed that old hope glow in him for just an instant at the sound of Billy's voice. He'd given a chance to a drunk VCR repairman yesterday; what could this really hurt? There was at least the chance of movement. He looked again at the man's clothes.

"You probably heard I don't have any money," he said.

"That's fine," said Billy. "I'm not looking for any. Consider it a favor." He hoped it would turn out to be more than that, but Billy kept this card close. "It's just a good turn," he added. "I'm willing to offer a hand if you're willing to take it."

Henry spooked at that, like always. "I have to work in the diner today," he said, not hearing the strangeness of his words. "I told the others I'm not really much help…"

Billy laughed, and it sounded like a stream bubbling. "I don't need it. I've got some time this morning. Hell, I've got time every morning. If I can figure things out, I'll come in there to find you, and we can talk. Is it a deal?"

Henry didn't like that word. But then again: *what the hell?* "Okay," he said. "Okay."

"Sweet tea?" Cece asked him again as he walked inside. She already had a glass poured and waiting for him on the counter. It was seven in the morning.

"I'll have some coffee, if there's any up yet," Henry said.

Cece looked disappointed, but she went back through the swinging door into the kitchen. There was something warm rising up again inside of Henry, something like what he had felt forever ago in the river in Alabama. It wasn't the first time: ever since Joe Christmas left a snot rocket on his radiator housing, he'd felt himself rising up with the arrival of each new tinkerer. If nothing else, the news gave him something to look forward to on those days. But by midmorning, as he drank his third cup of coffee, Henry was surprised to discover the feeling hadn't gone away.

"Do you have another cigarette?" he heard himself ask Cece. It was the first time he'd thought of it; he kicked himself for not asking before. She did, and they smoked together, indoors, in the twenty-first century. Henry ashed into an honest-to-God ashtray, and it was glorious. He felt like he was materializing, for the first time in a long time, right there at the lunch counter. Then he surprised them both by asking his first question since the day he rang the little bell over the door: "What's the Fifth?" he asked Cece.

"What's that, Little Rock?" she said back, making her mouth into an "O" and blowing a smoke ring as she waited for him to repeat himself. She was visibly excited.

"I asked: what's 'the Fifth' mean? When I drove up here, I was on Fifth's Highway. There were signs on barns about it. And then you mentioned it. What is it?"

Cece paused for just a moment, making sure he was serious; that he was really there. Satisfied, she began: "'The Fifth' is what we call the folks who're a part of the Fifth Regiment. They were militia-types in the old days: doomsday preppers and 4-Fers; the kin who have guns and eagles on all their clothes. Where the name comes from is an old Confederate regiment, back from the first War, I heard. Can't remember the general's name; Dickey, maybe? But there's a monument down in Vicksburg. Where'd you say you were from again, Little Rock?"

Henry hadn't said yet, but he took another chance: "Ohio." He'd never heard of Vicksburg.

"Hmm. Well, y'all stayed Federal, of course. But I'm guessin' you still had some of the same folks out in the sticks there too, at least at first: gun nuts, Qs, off-grid homeschoolers. I'd imagine you eventually rounded 'em all up."

Henry nodded, thinking of men with goatees who tucked their t-shirts into jeans.

"Well, when Mississippi stepped out, the Fifth became our Green Berets: big talkers, always sayin' what they were itchin' to do. Before long, they swallowed up all the other backwoods folk and you'd see 'em all around the place. Pretty soon, kids jumped in with 'em, then soldiers back from wherever, then old men scared they'd die without ever havin' a real fight in their lives. Just about everybody fifteen to fifty: all the little-dicks.

"Anyway, within a year or so, they was bigger around here than the state guard ever got ta be, and they set to puttin' up checkpoints everywhere. Policin' whole towns, if folks'd let 'em. Botherin' anybody without some place ta be. And all this on direct order of the governor, who realized he'd have to either be on their side or against 'em, so he deputized the whole gang."

Henry thought of the flags and the crosses. "Were they the ones who used that flag with the lotus star on it?"

"The hell's a lotus?" Cece asked. It took her a moment to puzzle it out, but then she understood: "No, sweetie; that there's a magnolia blossom. It was the old state flower. But sure enough, that's them."

Henry stubbed out his cigarette and sat back as Cece continued. "But the *big* thing that got 'em famous was when Cassie come through in '29. I imagine you read about that, even back in Ohio." Henry looked at her and just barely shook his head. "Well, it was a goddamn tragedy, Cassie. A Cat 5 hurricane headin' straight for New Orleans. Just like Katrina did. Louisiana was still Federal at the time, and the Army came down to try to get people out on buses headin' north. They picked a road for the evacuation right through here, since the interstates had fallen apart and the only good road left was the ol' Natchez Trace. Army even asked the governor if they could use it. But he said no, and told 'em it was all 'encroachment,' that there probably wasn't even a storm to begin with, and the whole thing was just a carpetbaggin' land grab. He told everybody if they let the Army take the roads, Mississippi'd never get 'em back. So those buses would have to go some other way.

"Course, by the time the decision'd been made, it was too late for any of that. Your president up there told the Army to take the roads the old fashioned way, and that's what they did, at least as far as Jackson. But the Fifth stepped in and stopped 'em right there, holdin' the line all the way south to the border. Once they had it, they wouldn't let it go, and nobody could get up or down. By the time the storm eventually did come, they'd fought the Federals all the way back down the Trace and pinned 'em in Tupelo. Then, they opened the roads to true Missippians only: folks from Biloxi and Pascagoula could come up it, but nobody outta New Orleans. There were dead boys and dead old men from the Fifth all up and down the highway, and folks would stop on their own during the evacuation to put 'em in the ground themselves. They left markers everywhere. Put strings in trees and made up piles of rocks with writin' over 'em on cardboard. Then the next spring, Mississippi sent trucks down the road to dig 'em all up and bring 'em home for funerals, and they put up those crosses in whatever places they'd found 'em at. The Federal ones got left on the ground wherever they was. I'd guess their bones're out there still."

"Oh," Henry said.

"In the end, they all got their fight," Cece said, and raised her eyebrows. She spit, took the extra cigarette from over her ear, and put it between her lips. "That's all they really wanted. And folks up here love 'em for it," she said, then cupped her hands around the end and lit it.

"What about the buses?" Henry asked.

"The buses didn't leave New Orleans," she puffed. "They're still there, too, I reckon, if you want to see 'em." Smoke hovered a foot over her head stretching out in a thin, sharp cloud. "Folks who were supposed to be on 'em are gone, though. Ten thousand people washed all the way out into the Gulf of Mexico. A man came in here once who said they still find shoes on the beach down in Galveston, from time to time."

Henry was quiet.

"Didn't keep up with the news much back when things were fallin' apart?"

Henry was caught off guard by this question—by the story turning back on him. He thought about that year, about 2029, and he felt that old panic rising up. He felt that need to run back to people waiting for him. He remembered locked doors. He remembered a note, stuck to the screen of his old cell phone one morning when he woke up: *Talk to him!* it said in Shannon's hand.

"I didn't," he said. "I guess we were falling apart, too."

"Well," Cece said, "Unless there were ten thousand of you, I'd say you might have had your head in your ass."

* * *

53

It was near dusk when the bell over the door rang and Billy walked back in. Cece had gone home for a few hours and left Henry in charge of the place. How was he left in charge of a place? He needed desperately, *desperately*, to leave. Henry noticed that Billy's clothes were as clean as they had been when the day began, and his heart fell in his chest. But then he noticed Billy's hands, stained from grease and busted open on one knuckle. He found a dish towel and handed it over as Billy took a seat at the counter.

"What did you figure out?" Henry asked him.

"Well, it was a few things," Billy said, "but it was the air filter that got them started. The man who turned that thing over to oil did a lot of things right—even a few things I didn't know you could do, really. But I don't think he counted on anybody driving quite as much as you." A question he'd been waiting to ask for a week had to make its way out: "How'd you get it, anyway?"

Henry didn't see much point in a lie. "I found it in a swamp."

"No shit? And just like that?"

"No shit. Just like that."

Billy finished with the towel and set it on the counter. Then he reached in his pocket, pulled out the rabbit's foot, and set it down, too. "I think your luck's holding," he said. Then he smiled. "I got it going."

Henry actually gasped. "What?"

"I got it up and running. It'll go for you in the morning. I had to shuffle a few things around, but it'll do. It'll get you to Little Rock, anyway."

Henry didn't know what to say. Was *thank you* appropriate? "Thank you," he said.

"You're welcome," Billy said. "I was glad I could help. I know you're looking to get out of here, and you've got a good thing going with that truck. A *real* good thing: oil's a nice trick down here. Gas can be tough to get."

Henry nodded. He was still in something like shock. "Thank you," he said again, like a reflex. He felt like another spell had been broken, and his mind was already racing ahead, thinking about itineraries and provisions. Could he work the morning shift for some bread rolls and a bag of coffee? Would anyone miss a handful of ketchup and mustard packets?

With his hands now empty, Billy placed his palms on the edge of the counter and drummed his fingers. "You're welcome, Hank," he said, again. He was realizing conversations with Henry weren't easy to rehearse, and so he figured it was best to be out with it: "I want to ask a favor."

Henry never had a chance to really hear him: his mind was already miles away. "I lost my wallet," he said, "but I'm good for anything I owe you. I can send you money when I'm up north again." *Up north again!* he thought. "If you could give me your address—"

"No, no—it's not like that."

Henry seemed to be visibly expanding on his chair. "Well, whatever it is..."

Billy interrupted: "Hank?" he said. "Hank, give me a minute."

Henry stopped. He actually seemed to lurch forward in his seat, his momentum physically arrested.

"I want to ask you something," Billy said. "I want to ask if I can ride with you tomorrow. Just as far as Little Rock. I know you didn't agree first, and we don't have a deal. But I'm stuck here, too."

Henry looked at him blankly. So Billy kept going:

"I've been here a month. But I'm from Illinois. I ran out of gas, and I was parked right out there where you're parked now. For a day or two, it wasn't a big deal: I picked up shifts here, just like you. Got to know Cece. But neither of us could get anybody in town to sell to me. I screwed up by going to the stations first; then, when *she* went around, they all knew who she was asking for." He looked Henry in the eyes. "It's not that they weren't selling gas," he said. "It's that they weren't selling it to *me*. Do you understand?"

Henry was beginning to. He remembered the towns where the folks watched him with guns. He remembered the other towns, too, where eyes peeked out from behind curtains.

"On the fourth morning I was here, I came out of the diner and found my windows busted and a bag of sugar in my gas tank. I'm not sure what that proves, really—it's hard to get chased out of town if you can't leave. But it was part of the joke, I guess."

"Cece couldn't find any?" Henry repeated. He seemed like he was always at least two sentences behind. It was a defense mechanism he'd learned. It lowered expectations.

"No," Billy said. "She couldn't. Here's my point: I don't want to stay here if I don't have to. And I'm hoping that, tomorrow, I won't have to." Everything he had said was true, and so was the last card he had brought to play: "If it helps you make up your mind, you should know that even though my car was shot, the air filter was just fine. And now it's on your truck, ready to go. And that's fine: it wasn't doing anything for me, and I hope it gets you wherever you want. But I'm also hoping it gets me at least a little farther up the road, too."

Things were getting all confused for Henry. This was what he wanted, but not the way he wanted it. He felt exposed, and he regretted the cigarette. He wanted, more than anything, to disappear.

"I've got some money, if it helps. And I've heard Little Rock is a friendlier town. If I can get there, I'm sure I can get back on my own track. So, I want us to make a deal: you take me with you, and in exchange, I'll get you back on the road in the first place. Does that work for you?"

There's only the driver, Henry thought; that had worked before. But instead of saying these words, what his mouth said was: "There's only one seat."

Billy smiled for the first time since he told Henry the Ranger was resurrected.

"I've already thought of that," he said.

By mid-morning the next day, Billy had bolted a half-sized bench from a booth near the door of the diner into the passenger seat space of the Roving Ranger. It was plush, stained, and covered in a cracked and tacky red vinyl. It was also entirely at home, and even beautiful, in the cab.

Cece was sad to see them go. She had gotten to know Billy well in the weeks before Henry arrived, and she made a point of telling Henry she liked *him,* with her eyes set on the younger man. But she still sent them on their way with a generous helping of food, ice, and a fill-up of leftover cooking oil from Bunch's Lunches. The cicadas thrummed. An alley tom wound around her legs as she waved goodbye. Henry squeezed the rabbit's foot and turned the key. When he did, the Ranger roared back to life.

He and Billy backed out of the parking lot behind the diner and made their way slowly towards the town square. Henry hadn't spoken and didn't really intend to. But Billy broke the silence: "I know I'm second seat here. But do you mind if we make a quick stop?"

Henry shrugged like they had all the time in the world, and the Ranger followed a series of rusted signs to the abandoned campus of the University of Mississippi. Every building was burned and most had fallen down entirely. The lawns, which Billy told Henry used to be famous for their groves of old-growth trees, were now little more than charred ruins. The parking lots were cracked and bubbled tar pits.

The truck crawled over the rubble in the direction Billy pointed and towards a forgotten corner at the southwest end of the campus. They stopped at the edge of a small wood which had at least partially escaped the fire, and Henry could see a weed-choked opening in the trees there that could have once been a walking trail. He put the Ranger in park, pocketed the old rabbit's foot, and stepped out.

Billy led him down the path, high-stepping through the underbrush, until it opened onto a little clearing. Although the forest here had not burned completely, the small, plantation-style house in front of them had: it was a blackened shell of its former self, the inside filled with sunlight streaming down through the charred and roofless rafters. Billy and Henry stared at it, perfectly framed at the end of a short lane lined with the destroyed trunks of a half dozen oak trees standing uselessly at attention. A metal sign nearby, dark with soot, was still legible:

ROWAN OAK

Built c. 1848. From 1930 to
1962 home of novelist William
Faulkner, who named it for the
rowan tree, symbol of security
and peace. Now maintained as
a literary landmark by the
University of Mississippi.

"I know him, I think," Henry said. "He used to be famous."

"He was," Billy said back. "Did you ever read one of his books?"

"Did he write *Gone With the Wind?*"

"The book?"

"Yeah."

"No," Billy said. "He most certainly did not."

They walked up the drive and then up the narrow steps to the empty doorway. There was nothing to see: no furniture, no writing desk, no long-forgotten and miraculously preserved typewriter. There were just buckled floorboards and the scaly-black charcoal of burned timber.

"So…" Henry said. But Billy was now somewhere else. He had walked to the far side of the room and put his hand on what was left of a mantelpiece above an empty fireplace.

Something came to him. "You're just not a 'Hank,'" he said. "I know you're older than me, but I've been thinking about it. You've just got 'Henry' written all over you. 'Hank' doesn't stick."

"It never has," Henry admitted. "I've been trying all my life."

Billy smiled at that. "Well, what's your last name, then? Maybe we can make something out of that." Billy couldn't see it, but Henry's shoulders slumped. Even in February, the air was heavy and thick.

"Henry," he said.

Billy laughed out loud, and Henry heard that stream in his voice again. It sounded right in the space. "Really?" he said. "That's just awful. Truly." There was something soft and sympathetic about the way he said it, even as he kept on laughing. "Henry Henry? I can't believe it. Your mom and dad should be ashamed. They didn't give you much to work with, did they? 'Hank Henry' isn't any better. I can't believe they stuck you like that."

Stuck you like that. Henry hadn't ever thought about his name as being anyone else's doing. But his dad's name had been Alexander, and he'd had an older brother, too: Michael. Why was *he* Henry Henry? He felt much too old to be wondering about any of this; it was a child's question, and his father was dead in the ground.

"Maybe we could go with Mr. Henry, if it doesn't sound too formal," Billy said.

Henry didn't like it. "I don't know," he said. "How old are you?"

Billy smiled again. "The same age he was when he bought this place: I'm 32."

"You know that much about him?" Henry asked.

"No, not too much, really." Billy put his hands in his pockets. "I just read a few things. Had lots of time for that the last few weeks, and he's a big deal around here. Famous White man, writing about angry White people. Folks can relate."

Henry didn't have anything to add to that. He had never read one of his books. "What did he write about?" Henry asked.

"Being stuck mostly," Billy said. "Not being able to let go of a place. Digging in and dying there instead."

Henry thought about this. He looked down and noticed that Billy's pants were smudged with charcoal dust from the fireplace. "Your pants," he said. He had noticed how clean Billy kept his clothes, even while working on the Ranger.

Billy looked down and clicked his tongue. "Thank you, Henry." The "mister" had already been abandoned, and it was just as well. Billy produced a handkerchief from a pocket and wiped off his hands. Once they were clean, he set about trying to brush off the dust.

When they got back to the truck, Billy put the dirty handkerchief in a side pocket on the small duffel bag he had brought with him. Then, he unzipped the top and produced another, cleaner one, folded it in quarters, and put it in his pocket. He seemed to Henry to be a man out of time.

"What about you?" Henry asked. "What's your last name, William?" He had suddenly become lousy with questions. The Ranger had not yet moved, but he could feel himself accelerating, achieving escape velocity once again. Nothing would catch up with him. Did it matter if he was alone? He still believed it did, but it was only for a few days more, and he was so close. The sun shone down, ever present, and created a glare across the windshield that made him squint.

Billy laughed again. "You wouldn't believe me if I told you, Henry Henry," he said.

Henry smiled in spite of himself. His own name was ridiculous. It had always been that way. "Try me," he said.

"It's Faulkner, actually," said Billy. He tipped an imaginary hat in a gesture of formal greeting. "William Gentavius Faulkner. But I've been 'Billy' all my life."

Lay Me Down

Parks, huh?" Billy had finally gotten that much out of him. They'd been on the road for most of the day trying to find a place to cross the Mighty Mississippi. The first bridge they'd tried–an old truss east of Helena–had been washed away years ago. Trees sprouted from the cracks in the asphalt as they approached its edge, zigzagging through the young wilderness. When they arrived at the empty span, there was nothing to see but brown water a quarter mile wide rolling indifferently past them. "Well," Billy had said. Since then, they had been following backroads south looking for any way over, and Billy had spent the time trying to learn anything about Henry beyond his name.

"Mmhmm," Henry said in reply.

"You see, I'm not going to let you off the hook with that," Billy said. "*Why* parks?"

"What do you mean?"

"I mean everything is falling apart around here, you're wandering through all of it, and I want to know why. No offense, Henry, but you don't seem like all that outdoors-y of a guy. You're not making paintings or writing poems. What are you doing out here?"

Henry was quiet, but Billy could see he was thinking.

"I don't know," Henry said. "I started, and then I just kept going."

Constant pressure, Billy thought to himself; *just constant pressure*. It was only a few days, but he didn't want to spend them with a stranger. "Okay, where'd you start?"

"I went north first. I went to Maine and Bar Harbor."

"And how are things up there?"

"They're mostly the same as Before."

"Before, huh? So still street lights and apple pie?"

"Mostly. Maybe. I didn't see any pies," Henry said. "They like lobsters."

People always talked about the world Billy and Henry were living in as the After. But nobody really knew when the After started: was it when the elections stopped? When the phones turned off? When the Republics began? When people realized they couldn't talk with their grandparents anymore? It *had happened*, everyone knew, but only because it had first *been happening* and no one had stopped it. They had thought noticing would be enough.

"The roads were free. And the parks were open. That was the big thing," Henry said.

"Who was running them?" Billy asked.

"I don't know. There were still rangers…" Henry thought on that. "At least, in Maine there were. And in New York. But that was it. After that, they were mostly closed."

There was that white noise sound of tires over asphalt, and Billy started to actually wonder about something, beyond simply making conversation. "What'd you do at the closed parks?"

Henry kept his eyes on the road. "I would sneak into them, maybe." He had done this a half dozen times, but he'd never named it out loud for what it was. "Sometimes I would have to go around a gate or walk for a while. I would find a way to get in."

"Where'd you go when you got in?"

"Just around. Overlooks, maybe."

Henry was giving something, and Billy sensed it like a crack in the pavement.

"Did you hike?"

"Some. Never very far."

"Did you go anywhere else?"

"I'd go to the old visitor centers, sometimes."

That was something. "Just to see?"

But at this point, Henry's bridge was out. Billy could go no farther. "Yeah," Henry said. "Just to see."

The tires rumbled on. And then, suddenly, Billy jumped up in his seat.

"Pull over!" he shouted. "Pull over, pull over!"

They were passing through another one of the quiet towns: places where a dozen or so houses bookended a dusty and boarded-up Main Street, seemingly no different than any other. But as Henry brought the Ranger to as quick a stop as it was capable of, Billy was already half-leaning out of his open window: "Back up, real quick! Back up!"

Henry reversed until they were even with what seemed to be an entirely unremarkable bungalow: two or three bedrooms, run down, a car on blocks filling most of the tiny yard, a ramshackle hutch near the street with *CAMPFIRE WOOD $5* scrawled on a piece of cardboard nailed to the frame. Before he could even park, Billy was out of the truck and on his way up to the door.

"What are you doing?" Henry called after him. He was instantly terrified. "*What are you doing?!*" he said again, whisper-yelling now, as if this would prevent a man in an ice cream truck from drawing attention. Billy was already knocking. "*What are you doing?!*" Henry asked the empty diner seat. "*What is happening?!*"

As he watched, crouched down so that only his eyes peeked over the edge of the passenger window, the front door opened and Billy stepped inside. Henry's heart was beating so hard he could actually hear it.

Then, after a few minutes in which Henry aged most of a decade, Billy walked nonchalantly out of the house, waved once behind him to some figure in the dark, and then stepped back into the truck.

"There's a bridge near Greenville that's still open," he said. "It's just a little further south."

Henry's mouth was hanging open. He had to think about closing it before he spoke. "How do you know that? Who told you that?"

Billy smiled. "There's actually people in these houses. You know that, right?"

Henry didn't have an answer. "You can't do that!"

Billy laughed. "Not everybody's trying to kill us, you know. Some people are; don't get me wrong. But not everybody."

Henry looked at him.

Billy rolled his eyes and sighed. "There was firewood," he said.

Henry kept looking at him.

"Hey man, have you seen anybody camping anywhere? In the last decade?"

Still looking.

"Wood for sale means the house is safe. It's a code. The person there isn't going to bother you. Usually, it means they would actually love for somebody to stop in and ask a question. Turns into the best part of their day."

Henry thought on that. Then he shifted the Ranger into drive.

"What if they're serious? What if the wood's really for sale?"

"Then you end up buying some wood," Billy said.

"Okay," said Henry, still puzzling it over. "But what if someone really just wants it?"

"Well," Billy said, "then you make five dollars."

They made it to Greenville by the middle of the afternoon. Finding it to be a surprisingly lively and sizable town, they swung wide to the east and then circled back, coming up a rutted levee road until the bridge was visible against the white but cloudless sky. A car passed along it. Henry pulled the Ranger to a stop.

"What are you thinking?" Billy asked him.

"I only cross at night. It's safer that way."

"Even here? It seems like it might still be lit up after dark."

"Maybe. But I don't see anything up there that looks official. And there's more of the city on the other side of the river, so it might be an open crossing. We can probably get over. There's another levee road on the other side; we can duck onto it as soon as we cross and before we hit any stops."

"That's pretty smart, Henry. Damn. I wasn't sure you had it in you."

Henry heard the compliment and chose to keep it. "I got to Oxford, too. And I got into the parks."

Billy smiled and let him brag. They sat for a long moment.

"What do we do until then?" he asked.

Henry looked in the rearview mirror. "It looks like this road goes south a little ways. We can see if there's somewhere down there to wait."

As they crunched slowly over potholes and gravel, Henry realized he was sinking into Billy's company. He asked too many questions, maybe, but he was nice. He respected movement. Before long, they realized the road had led them onto an island formed by a gooseneck in the river that was utterly uninhabited and overgrown. They parked in the middle of what had once been a small crop field but was now a grassy space between stands of trees. It was a comically perfect place.

They made a meal together in the back of the Ranger, and then they got out and sat on a pile of old stones at the edge of the clearing. More early cicadas were whirring in the trees, and they could each smell the river, earthy and mild. There was what felt to Henry like a peaceable silence. As the sun began to set, a surprising chill floated in off the river and the first stars appeared in the air through the gloaming. Billy sat with his back turned, and Henry let himself drift away…

When his son, Caleb, had been nine years old, he and his wife took him to what would be his only park: Cuyahoga Valley, an enigmatic green space halfway between Akron and Cleveland. It was only a half hour drive from where they lived, but before Shannon found it on a map, they had had no idea it was even there. Henry couldn't remember what had stirred them to that first visit: a good word from a co-worker, maybe; the sinking dread of failing to do enough, between work and themselves, to give Caleb a memorable childhood. Whatever the reason, they woke early on a fall morning, paid the fee, and drove in.

The primary feature of the park was a towpath along a 19th century canal route with woods lining its eastern shore and a railroad line to the west. They parked in an open lot and, unsure of what else they were intended to do, began walking. The trail meandered alongside the waterway, stands of cattails and reeds hiding the near bank. Squirrels skittered over the path. A doe and her yearling grazed on the far side of the train tracks. Within a half hour, they found themselves walking over the shadows of I-70, which crossed the park on an impossibly high overpass.

In short, nothing happened: they walked for a while, tired, and then walked back. It was still nine in the morning. Back in the parking lot, a visitor center which had been closed when they arrived had since propped open its door. They went in, if only to find out if they were doing this right. Inside, a ranger dressed in brown and wearing a flat-brimmed hat gravitated immediately to Caleb. She squatted down to talk with him at eye level:

Did you and your mom and dad walk the towpath? She asked. Caleb nodded, and Henry looked at Shannon over his head: had either of them called it that? The ranger was asking him what he had seen. He told her about the deer and the overpass; he told her he had seen a blackbird.

Do you know what that path used to be used for? Caleb shook his head. *Well, people who needed to get heavy things from where we are right now either all the way up to Cleveland, or all the way down to Akron, would put those things on boats in the canal. But the boats didn't have motors to move them. So, the people would tie a rope from the boats to horses, who stood on the path you and your family were walking on earlier, and then the horses would pull them where they needed to go.*

Caleb's eyes stared at her as he turned all of this over. Then he asked her what the horses would eat. She was patient with him, and after a few minutes, she looked at Henry and Shannon as she asked him how long his family was going to be visiting. He told her without hesitation they were going to be there all day. Shannon gave her a nod, and she led Caleb over to the main desk and found a booklet for him under the counter. *Why don't you and your family work on this while you visit, and if you finish it, you can come back here before you leave and I'll have something for you.*

For the rest of the day, Caleb led them from sight to sight, working all the while in his booklet. They hiked under cliffs in the woods and followed a short boardwalk to a waterfall. They read signs by an old country store and went on a scavenger hunt for tree leaves. Henry remembered that he and Shannon had argued in the afternoon; something dumb about plans for Halloween. But before they left for the day, their feet sore and Henry significantly sunburned, Caleb ran back into the visitor center to turn in his project. He emerged a few minutes later and climbed into the backseat of the car, a plastic ranger badge pinned crookedly on his shirt. Henry could still remember the ranger's name. It had been Lopez…

The sound of a truck somewhere far away pulled Henry back into the clearing. He looked around for Billy, but he was gone. Lightning bugs dotted the woods. Walking back to the Ranger, Henry saw light around the edges of the vending window, and he knew Billy was in the back. He walked around to the driver's side, opened the door, and got in.

It was quiet, and he enjoyed the stillness. After a moment, the light in the back turned off. He closed his eyes. Billy's voice came from the dark behind him. "You didn't ask me how I knew about the wood," he said. "I could tell you wanted to know."

Henry didn't say anything.

"I don't think you asked me anything all day, now that I think about it."

"I'm not really very good at that," Henry said. Billy's voice wasn't mad; he sounded like he might be off somewhere else, too.

"But you want to know," he said.

"Maybe," Henry said. But that wasn't the truth. "Yes."

"Well, if you had asked, I would have said that I knew about the wood because I'm out here writing a book. That's what I came down here for, from Illinois. I'm writing a book about getting around in all this. In the After."

Henry was curious. "Like a travel guide?" he asked.

"Yeah, actually. Like a travel guide. For people who want to go see family, or still want to visit somewhere. It's not safe for everybody to do that. But there are still ways to make it work, if you know where to look for them."

Henry thought about that. "I know about the white-stripes," he said.

"Most people know about those. They were in the news a lot, for a while. But there's other signs, too." Henry could hear Billy beginning to head down a path. "Things like the wood, for example. Or an empty coffee can on somebody's porch. Green balloons tied to a mailbox. People know other people are scared, and they try to help."

"People are right to be scared," Henry said. He thought about the wastelands he'd snuck through across the angry and bitter South. "There's nowhere to go, really."

"Says the man visiting national parks."

"That's different," Henry said, but he wasn't sure why he said it. "Nobody should do what I'm doing." It was a slip. Maybe it was also an admission. Billy started to speak, but he stopped himself, and the moment stretched.

"Maybe not," he said. "But I think they can choose. And if they want to do it, they should be safe. As safe as they can be."

Henry thought about the hobo signs. "Why are the balloons green?" he asked.

Billy laughed: that bubbling stream. "I don't really know. It's not really a birthday color, I guess. The people I've asked about it aren't sure. One man said it was like the old green books from the '50s. Those listed out what hotels were safe for Black people, what gas stations would sell gas. Did you ever hear about them?"

"I don't think so," Henry said.

"Yeah, that checks out," Billy said, and Henry felt stung. He realized Billy couldn't see him. They were quiet again.

Then, surprising himself, he spoke. "I got arrested in Alabama," he said. "For having the truck. And for not having a driver's license."

"No shit?" Billy asked.

"Yeah. I was in jail for three days. It was nice, actually."

"Why'd they let you go?"

"I know it sounds weird," Henry said, "but I don't think they could see me. Or maybe they didn't want to."

"Like you were a ghost?"

"Maybe. They did see me once. I said something dumb to the officer, and it made him mad. I knew that. But the rest of the time, it's like I wasn't what they were looking for. I was just there."

Billy thought on that. "What were they looking for?"

"I don't know. Trouble, I guess. Somebody who wanted something from them."

"Somebody like me, maybe?" The words were a question, but Billy's voice wasn't asking.

"I don't think it was like that," Henry said. He sounded like he was defending someone, and he didn't know why he was doing that, either.

"They let you go, though. And gave you your car back," Billy said.

"Yeah, they let me go," said Henry, "but they didn't like me."

"Yeah, well. There's always been more than one way to be Black in America," Billy said, "but there's only ever been one way to be White."

The Ranger was quiet a third time, and the night sky was a void overhead, offering no answers and asking for nothing at all.

"You're not a ghost, Henry," Billy said. "People in Oxford talked; they took you for another drifter. Cece said she figured you had shot somebody and you were on the run, but you weren't doing a very good job of it. People can see you. They're just not afraid of you."

"I don't want them to be afraid of me." He looked for stars, but he couldn't find them through the windshield. "I just want to be left alone, I think. I want to keep moving."

"Maybe. But maybe you just don't want to be still."

"I'm being still right now."

"And just look at all the talking it's getting you to do."

Henry laughed a little. "I'm not very good at talking, either."

"You don't try it much."

That was true. And then Henry tried something new: he tried to wonder about Billy, and something came to him. "What's Illinois like now?"

"You mean in the middle of the Apocalypse?"

"Yeah."

"It's different. The cities are the same in some ways, but there are more people than there were, and it's hard to live in them. My family tried to move out once, down towards Springfield. But the people there made it hard. There are a lot who are angry, just like down here. They're mad the state went Federal. And they don't want to give it up."

"You mean White people."

"Yeah, I do. They're afraid, mostly. Everybody's afraid."

"Are you?"

"Some days. But I don't think everything's over yet. I think this will pass, too. People forget things have always been bad for *somebody*. You don't get used to it, but you stop being surprised. Maybe this makes it easier to see."

"What did your family do?"

"They moved back to Chicago. And I came down here."

"Hmm," Henry said.

"Hmm," said Billy. Henry wished for anything at all to happen: a shooting star, the hoot of an owl; a UFO descending right on top of them.

My wife, Shannon," he said, "she was Black."

"Well, goddamn, Henry! You mean like *me*? What in the hell am I lecturing *you* for?"

Henry let a sound escape from his mouth that surprised him: it was a low groan, shaking up from somewhere deep inside him in a tremor. "That's not what I meant," he said. "It's–it's–" He couldn't find the words. Why could he never find them? "Nevermind," he said. "I'm sorry. That was dumb to say."

"It *was* dumb to say."

"I don't say the right things," he said, and somehow, this made Henry laugh. The sound rose up from the same place deep inside, and he felt stupid. He felt clean. "I never say the right things," he said, and he kept laughing. "Not ever." He didn't know how he knew it, but he could tell Billy was smiling, too.

"That might be on me," Billy said. "It's my fault for getting you going. I didn't know you were an idiot."

Henry felt like he was on a wave that wouldn't crest. "I hope you learned," he said.

"I did." Billy was chuckling now, too. "I did."

Sometime after midnight, the Roving Ranger made its way over the bridge and into the West. They kept the lights off, and the truck moved from circle of light to circle of light under the streetlamps. They shone like tractor beams. All was quiet in the moonless dark.

As Henry and Billy turned onto the levee road, the town around them fell away, and Henry's mind wandered again to what had been his family once. He thought about needlessly late days at work and dinners in separate rooms. He thought about early morning runs and secret cigarettes. He heard his wife's voice over the phone: *What did you do? What did you fucking do?*

Nothing, he had said back to her. *Nothing. Nothing. Nothing.*

He turned on the headlights, and as he did, Billy stood up and put a hand on Henry's seat, moving towards the back again. "Let me know if you need a rest," he said.

"I will," said Henry.

They drove north, and Henry thought again about that day they had all spent along another shore…

What do you have there? Shannon had said to their son as he climbed into the backseat.

It's a badge, Caleb told her. She smiled.

Does that make you a 'ranger' now? Henry had asked.

So stupid, he thought to himself now; *stupid, stupid.*

No, he could hear his son's voice say quietly. Henry remembered watching him in the rear view mirror as he looked down at the piece of plastic, frowning at it now as he bent his neck. *It's just a dumb thing they give to kids.* The next night, after tucking him into bed, Henry noticed the badge again. It was pinned to the bottom hem of his son's blue window curtain…

Alongside him now, all these years later in the dark, the Great River churned on. As it did, the waters drove deeper into the earth and ate the banks with a steady and unending hunger. It did not thunder or roar. It simply slid past: enormous, ageless, and indifferent. Henry felt a vague sense of vertigo as he moved against its current. For a short while, this River had been a vein running out from the very heart of a country. Boats moved up and down it like cars on a highway. Now, though, it was again what it had always been. It was the way mountains are sent to the sea.

Hot Springs

rkansas was a different story. As Henry and Billy drove through the night, a glow persisted in the sky to the north from the direction of Little Rock. Billy had trouble keeping his eyes from it, although worry did him no good. It was true that he had heard good things about the former capital from people he'd met between Illinois and Mississippi. But the reason his mind was set there was because his heart had been set there first: his grandfather lived in Little Rock, along with a cousin he hadn't seen since his family's short-lived move from Chicago. The car waiting for him had been his grandmother's, and the money a loan from a friend. When Henry had shown up in Oxford with his sights set on Arkansas, Billy had been angling for a ride from the start.

But now, he wondered what he had gotten himself into. Even in the dark, they could see things were different: crop fields were burned and towns weren't just quiet, they had been abandoned. Twice, the Ranger had to detour because roads actually disappeared into cratered holes in the ground, the second of which had a charred and ruined station wagon sitting in its center like the ovule of a flower. What had happened here?

Henry drove them through the night in a shared and anxious silence. No working cars were on the road. There was nothing beyond the sound of the engine and the rhythmic thumps of the tires over the breaks in the pavement. It occurred to Billy, somewhere in this wasteland, to turn on the radio. Static and voices filled the Ranger: *—flict continues in the areas around Two Rivers, where peacekeep——orces maintain a de facto—iege of Arkan—— iberate the cap——————ill not rest————election res———————— stimated——————lions of doll…*

The signal could not hold against the intrusion of country music from a neighboring station, and Billy turned the radio back off. He looked at Henry, but Henry's eyes stayed on the road. They had been making their way west for an hour, but before hitting Camden, they cut north. Whatever was waiting, at least now it was in front of them.

The old county road led them to the edge of another small cluster of farmhouses. This one was Leola, and as they crawled on through the dark, they came across a low building declaring itself to be The One True House of Holy Hope. In front, there was a low marquee, illuminated unexpectedly:

GOD STAND5 WITH THE PE0PLES ARKAN5AS.

They both saw it. There was nothing else to see.
"Against who?" Billy said out loud to himself.
Henry surprised him by speaking. "The Devil's Missouri, maybe?"
"The Devil's Missouri?"
"It's the 'Show Me' state."
"*Was*," Billy corrected. He was looking again towards Little Rock. "Who knows what it is now?"

Leola disappeared behind them in what was becoming a thickening pre-dawn haze. The landscape was changing again; it seemed to have recently been on fire. The smell of smoke pushed its way into the Roving

Ranger, and as the sun rose over the horizon, the air caught its light and swallowed everything up in grit and gray.

"We should stop," Billy said, his voice just a whisper, hiding.

"Here?"

"Soon."

"Okay."

Still driving slowly, they skirted the eastern edge of an overgrown patch of wilderness that was once a state park. Billy asked if Henry wanted to stop, if he wanted to see anything, but he didn't. Then, they moved on to what their atlas said was the town of Prattsville. In truth, it was a lone gas station guarding an intersection amidst flat and scoured nothingness. Like something out of time.

At first, the building appeared as ruined as the small farms they had passed on their way to it. But when the Ranger slowed for the junction, Billy saw a lit window in the apartment over the store: a yellow light, beaming out into the smog. He pointed. Henry braked, looked over at Billy, and then turned in.

The pumps of the old station were long gone, and the concrete pad was overgrown with weeds. There was an unmistakable band of white paint running vertically down the plate glass cashier's window, behind which someone had hung a faded and upside down American flag: a signal of distress. Some vandal had taken issue with this and scratched a message into the glass: *FED CUCKS = DEAD FUCKS*. The sky darkened overhead.

The Ranger came to a stop at the farthest edge of the tarmac and Henry let it idle.

"Do you want to go inside?"

His doubt was unmissable, but Billy thought about the radio. "I want to know what happened."

They left the engine running. Still, the squeaking hinges of the doors were deafening above it. As they walked towards the station, the first drops of rain began to fall and dotted the oil-stained concrete. It was cold on Billy's skin, but neither he nor Henry quickened their steps. As they reached the modest shelter of the store's faded and torn awning, Billy looked over his shoulder at the Ranger, now impossibly far away.

Under the cover, there was a plate glass door, but before they could reach for it, they heard the sound of a key turning in the lock. Billy's heart stopped in his chest. He looked over and saw that, as usual, Henry was frozen in place. Then, the door cracked open and a sinewy hand emerged from the darkness, propping the door for them to enter. The hand became an arm, its skin wrinkled, weathered, and the color and texture of an old paper bag. Then, the arm became an old man, his hair short and white, his face and neck covered in gray stubble. He looked at them with cloudy, green eyes which moved first up, then down, then up again. Those eyes met Billy's, and he gave him the faintest nod.

"Y'all're lost," he said, then took a step back to make a way for them to get in out of the rain. "And you're gettin' wet. But bacon's in the pan, and I'd be a damn fool to try'n eat it all by myself."

An old electronic door sensor dinged for Henry and Billy as they entered the store. As their eyes adjusted to the gloom, they realized the man was somehow already gone, his voice now carrying back to them from the far side of the long and empty shelves. "May be that the good Lord's sent y'all to me for some purpose. I don't believe that. But may be you're holdin' off this heart attack for 'nother day, and that I'll take..." The sound of his footsteps on the tile stopped, and he had realized his guests were still in the doorway. He raised his ancient hand above the racks at the far end of the room and waved them over. "Y'all come back this way. There's stairs." Then, the footsteps started again, followed by the creak of weight on wooden boards.

Billy stepped forward and instinctively held out his arm to keep Henry behind him. It wasn't for his protection. He made his way towards the secret staircase and, perhaps understanding, Henry followed. There was an ice machine in the corner, and in the space just beyond it, a doorway lit from a light shining down from an upstairs apartment. The sounds of the old man's footsteps were already on the floor above them, and he called out again: "I ain't sure where y'all boys're headed, but I hope it ain't Ar-*Kansas*." He said it wrong, and with venom in his voice.

They reached the room above the store and caught sight of him again now standing in a kitchenette in the corner. They could hear the sound of bacon sizzling. A single yellow light bulb dangled from the ceiling above the man's head. A small window over the sink looked out over the station below with the Ranger in the corner of the frame, parked apologetically in the furthest possible spot.

"What happened in Arkansas?" Billy asked, saying it the way he had grown up hearing it said.

"What's happen*ing*, you mean. Every damn thing." It seemed the man had been saving up for just this conversation, and his words were like pennies stored in a jar. For a day like this. For who knows how long? He let them out: "In January, them goddamn country boys finally decided they'd had enough of the Damn-o-crats and went to get Little Rock back from 'em, by God. That's how they said it. Stormed the town with pitchforks 'n torches. Then they got themselves all shot to hell by the National Guard."

"Stormed?" Billy heard Henry say. The old man didn't hear him.

"I thought Arkansas was Republic." Billy said.

"Republic? Hell no: not here, no way. State's been divided 'gainst itself since '30. The politicians voted Union and took Federal money. But nobody anywhere else was with 'em, and after talkin' about it for two years, seems some whiteys finally got themselves riled up enough to do somethin'. Went up there and set off pipe bombs in a park and started shootin' at police. Didn't go well for nobody. Now you can't walk outside without seein' Army drones in the sky, circlin' around like it's damn Puerto-Rico." He shook his head. "I always knew white people were gonna kill me," and then he looked squarely at Billy: "but I figured it'd be some hillbilly redneck and not some Yankee playin' a video game."

He started to plate the eggs with one hand and turned off the burner with the other. "This is the stupidest time to be alive," he said, "and I'm goddamn serious about that. It's embarrassing."

They ate breakfast together holding plates in their hands and standing in the kitchen. Billy kept asking questions, researching. The old man's name was Reese—whether first or last he did not say—and when Billy asked, he told them getting into the capital was a fool's errand: the roads were closed and guarded, and anybody heading that way was sure to be turned around—or arrested. "*Especially*," Reese said, "people in a ice cream truck." Billy wanted to know if anybody from the city had gotten out before things were locked down, but the old man didn't know. He said if they had, they could only have gone north: everything east of the river had declared itself the One True Arkansas, and the people there had sworn to fight the Feds to the last man. Or so the radio said. The rain outside was coming down now in earnest.

The eggs weren't half bad. The bacon was better. Billy realized he'd been eating pepperoni sandwiches for two full days, and he wondered how long it would be before he had another chance to eat anything different; Henry was a man of quiet habits. He was a man quiet in most every way. Billy and Reese talked more as they ate: how long he'd run the store, who all he'd seen pass by, what he'd heard from this traveler or that one. He had questions about Mississippi, but he snorted at Billy's answers. "It's just true-dyed shit this time," he said.

In the end, he sent them on their way shaking his head. "If you got any sense, you'll get the hell outta Arkansas," he told them. "And if you don't, you're in the right damn place." He seemed satisfied with that bit of wisdom and nodded to himself. When they went downstairs again, he locked the door behind them and was gone before they could thank him for the eggs.

It was raining hard enough that by the time they made it back across the tarmac to the Ranger, they were both soaked through. The engine was still running. They shivered from the wet and the cold. *No Little Rock*, Billy was thinking. He could sense Henry didn't want to be the first one to speak. There was nothing new about that.

Out with it, he thought. "What do you want to do?"

Henry turned on the heat and Billy was grateful. There was caution in his voice: "There's a park," he said.

"One of your parks?"

"Yeah." Henry paused. "It's not very far from here."

Billy thought about it. "I've got nowhere else to go," he said.

Henry reached for the atlas. "It's not far."

As they got closer to the town of Hot Springs, faded and sometimes ruined billboards started to appear at intervals. Local pizza places. Messages from God. Small market phone companies, bringing landlines back from the dead. *Your Sign Here*. Someone had tried to light one of them on fire, with limited success: it advertised a free prenatal clinic and "zone of refuge" somewhere ahead over the stars and stripes of an American flag. Someone—perhaps the attempted arsonist—had spray-painted the words *BABY KILLERS* in black over the address.

The barricades started before they reached the sign for the city limit, but they had been forgotten and neglected some time ago. The cross beams of sawhorses had been stolen for the lumber, and the occasional old road crew signs were either knocked down or moved aside to make room for vehicles to get through. The rain was coming down steadily, and the Ranger crawled in a serpentine path over pits and potholes in the asphalt.

Things continued this way until the low mountains at the north end of town emerged from the fog at the far side of what seemed to be a modestly-sized city. They were the first notable changes in the terrain Billy and Henry had seen in their three days together. Neither of them spoke a word. On the eastern rise, there was an odd tower too substantial to be a cellular array or radio transmitter but not immediately identifiable as anything else. It was topped with a blinking red light to warn planes away. Billy wondered how long it had been since that was a real concern.

Their luck with the road ran out just past a lightning-struck and long-ruined Wal-Mart. Two tractor trailers had been dragged sideways across the street for reasons Billy could not guess and did not want to fathom, and the way forward was blocked. Henry pulled the Ranger into the small parking lot in front of a shuttered ice cream hut whose sign declared it to be the _ORIGINAL KING KONE_ in block-red capitals. There was a drawing of a gorilla wearing a bib and holding a spoon, climbing the "K." Henry turned off the engine.

"I think we'll need to walk from here," he said.

Billy grabbed the atlas and puzzled over the roads through downtown to the small green square labeled Hot Springs National Park. "What kind of park is this?"

"I think it's bathhouses, mostly," Henry said. He had put on his coat and was visibly bracing himself for the cold wet. "Or it used to be. Like old health spas."

"That still doesn't sound like much of a park."

Henry didn't seem to know what to say to that. His attention was elsewhere. "It was old," he offered.

"What is there to see?"

"I guess we'll find out."

Billy was thinking about the rain now, too. He was also thinking about the barricades and the fires he'd seen in the sky coming from Little Rock. "What are we looking for, exactly?"

Henry didn't answer. He opened the door and paused before stepping out. "You could stay," he offered.

Billy considered it. "It seems like a bad idea to split up," he said.

"Yeah."

He shook himself all over and reached for the door handle. "I'm coming. Let's go."

Perhaps because of the rain, the streets were quiet. It was early afternoon. They stuck to the shelters of store fronts and scurried under the darkened lights of intersections. Just past Grand Avenue, they could make out the blackened and collapsed shell of a police station, and for a moment, Billy saw Henry's posture change. He had been someplace far away, Billy realized, but now he was here again. He waited to see if Henry would speak, but he didn't. Billy pushed his hands deeper into the pockets of his raincoat and lowered his head as they walked on. Something rumbled in the distance, and they both knew it could have been thunder.

Two blocks later, they turned onto Main, and suddenly there were human beings: three of them, maybe a hundred yards away, standing in ponchos beside a lifted pick-up truck. Two were holding rifles, but they had not seen either Billy or Henry. Their attention was to the north, towards the hills. The rain kept beating down. Henry looked at him, and they both moved to the lee side of the nearest shop front. They huddled.

"That doesn't look great, Henry," Billy said.

"I know."

"What are they doing?"

"They're looking the other way."

"*Towards* where we're going."

"Yeah."

"We could go around."

"We could go home," Billy said quickly. He was surprised to hear his own voice say it. He didn't want to be here.

"I think we can go around," Henry said. "We could stay over here for a few blocks and then cut back over." Billy realized he was serious. He wasn't frightened yet, but fear was getting closer. Henry continued the negotiation: "There's no reason for them to be watching a park. It must be something else. Maybe the Army or something." They were both thinking about what Reese had told them. But that was Little Rock, wasn't it?

Billy's mind raced. "Maybe, but they don't want to see us."

"It's just a few blocks. Then we can check again."

Billy peeked around the corner again. The man without a rifle was holding a bullhorn. It was down at his hip, and he was talking to a fourth man they had missed before who was sitting in another vehicle. It was an old mailcar with the USPS logo crossed out by a spray-painted, red *X*. The men with the rifles were talking to each other, their heads down against the rain. Together, they were certainly blocking the road, but they weren't exactly guarding it.

Henry looked at Billy, waiting on an answer. He could have asked, "for what?" He could have asked why this seemed so important. But instead, what he said was, "Those better be the last ones we see." They retreated from the corner, crossed back a block, and kept walking.

They made their way up one alley, and then another. They passed a vacant and badly dilapidated convention center, its windows broken and a section of the roof ripped free by some storm or another. On the far side, they caught sight again of the twin hills, the blinking red light. A sign told them they were on Reserve Street, and in the shadow of what looked like an abandoned factory building, they could see new barricades and another sideways tractor trailer. There were no men in ponchos, but they could both sense they weren't far away.

"I think this is it," Henry said, pointing ahead of them. "It's just around the corner here."

"There are gonna be people on that corner."

"No, not all the way on the main street. Just before that. There's a back path."

"A back path to where?"

"To the main building. To the old bathhouse, I guess. I don't know exactly."

"You think those guys we saw aren't looking this way? We can't be more than a few hundred yards up from them."

"Maybe, but the path comes first. The road they're watching goes straight up between the mountains, and there's just the park up that way. Whatever they're watching for, it's gotta be back towards town. They won't see us."

"But what if they do? I don't want to get shot at, Henry."

"Why would they shoot at us? We're not doing anything wrong."

"Like you weren't doing anything wrong in Alabama?"

Henry was barely there with him. He was going; he was dead set on it. "You can wait here." He came back to himself again and looked Billy in his eyes. "Wait here for me, and I'll go. I won't be long. I just need to see something."

Billy looked up at the factory building. *What for?* he could have asked. But instead, he said, "I said it's a bad idea to split up."

"Then are you coming?"

"Yeah. Yeah, I'm coming."

* * *

They made their way to the back path, turning away just before the barricade. It wasn't another alley: it was wider, with planters at intervals in the center of the sidewalk and benches lining the sides. But half a block up, the entire path was obstructed by an enormous white tent. It was some kind of intake center: there was no getting around it. Not ten feet in front of them, a sign topped a metal stanchion that was driven down in a gravel-filled bucket:

YOU ARE ENTERING U.S. GOVERNMENT PROPERTY

"We should go back," Billy whispered.

"But this is it," Henry whispered. "The park office is in there."

"In the tent?" The scene reminded Billy of the pandemic years: of testing sites and drive through vaccinations and endless quarantines, one after another after another. There was nowhere else to go, but before he could make up his mind, Henry was already moving ahead of him. He followed behind, and when Henry reached the door at the tent's entrance, he reached for the handle and it pulled open. Henry paused for him, and they entered the darkened interior together.

In the light from the opening, Billy saw a chair to the left of the door, a clipboard and radio sitting neatly in the seat. Not ruined by weather; not covered by dust. He tapped Henry on the elbow and gestured when Henry looked at him. He mouthed: *"who is here?"*

There was no answer. They moved slowly up the darkening corridor. Billy saw more stanchions and signs: *Federal Identification & Registry, General Welfare Services, Pregnancy Care.* They passed them in silence. There was no other word for what they were now doing: they were sneaking.

The tent was maybe two hundred feet long. Now that their eyes were adjusting, they could see another door, this one without a window, on the far end. There were alcoves to their left side, perhaps heading back into the bathhouse buildings they were currently behind. Billy felt the presence of some invisible line in front of them—maybe twenty more feet ahead; maybe only ten—when a trap would spring and there would be no escape. But he took one step, and then another.

And then, just as he feared it would, it happened: there was the unmistakable sound of a breaker being flipped and the tent suddenly filled with light. A voice—much too close—said, *"Got it!"* and then, almost instantly, a woman emerged into the hallway from one of the bathhouse doors. She was wearing hospital scrubs, and as she saw them, she let out the shortest burst of a shriek.

She was frozen. Outside somewhere, a generator roared back to life, and the lights flickered in the tent as the power caught up to itself. Billy's hands went up, as if she were a bank robber. No, as if *he* was a bank robber, and she had caught him in the act. Henry had turned into a statue in front of him, and he thought he could actually see the hairs standing up on the back of Henry's neck.

"We're sorry," Billy heard Henry say.

"What?" the woman in hospital scrubs said back. Billy realized her hands were up, too. Bank robbers all around.

"Is it closed?" Henry asked.

"What?" The woman seemed to be close to hyperventilating, and she didn't know what to do with that question. "What?" she asked again.

"What?" Henry said back.

Billy jumped in. "The park," he said. "Is the park closed?"

The woman kept blinking rapidly. "What?"

No one moved, and the three of them might have stayed there forever just so, but then another woman came barreling through the doorway, oblivious to the scene that had stalled out in front of her, and almost ran the woman in scrubs over:

"Ave, what?" Her eyes were fixed on the clipboard she was carrying, "we're going to need to reset–" and then she saw the men, too. Her eyes went wide.

"What are you doing here?" she asked them.

They didn't speak. She repeated her question.

Billy broke free first. "Is this Hot Springs?" he asked her.

"What?"

"Is this Hot Springs National Park?"

The second woman took that in. "It is," she said. Her friend, Ave, was beginning to come back to herself, and she finally lowered her hands. She took a cautious step to the side to move out of the clipboard woman's way. They exchanged a look. "Why are you here?" the clipboard woman asked, but something had changed in her voice and it sounded like the question at the top of a flow chart.

This caught Billy off guard. His answer seemed suddenly meaningful, but he didn't know how. "I'm… not sure," he said.

Everyone stared. That wasn't right. He gestured to Henry. "He wanted to come."

Henry Henry said nothing.

The clipboard woman tried again, looking at Henry this time. "Are you here for the clinic?" she asked.

Billy didn't understand. "No. No, he's here for the park." He reached over and put his hand on Henry's forearm, holding him as if he were a grandfather addled and drooling. "He wants to see the park."

The women looked at each other again.

"There's nothing here to see," the first woman said. "This is a clinic now." As she spoke, her words tied themselves to a script she had repeated so many times she could not, even in the strangeness of this moment, keep it from pouring out of her mouth: "This is a federally-operated healthcare clinic operating on U.S. government property. It is free for use by citizens of the United States, and if you are in need of asylum—"

Billy interrupted her: "No, no, it's not like that. He just wants to visit. He's traveling…"

The woman's auto-pilot switched off, and for the first time, she really saw them. They were soaked to the bone and held nothing in their hands. Billy was young; the other man was middle aged. They weren't lovers. They weren't kin. They weren't emissaries, or terrorists. "Well," she said, "the park is closed. It's not really here anymore. But you can step inside…" She gestured towards the doorway behind her, the one the clipboard woman had come through. The clipboard woman chimed in. "There's nothing up in the park except the old tower. No one goes anymore. The trails are closed to the public."

"But there are trails," Henry said. His voice surprised them all.

She looked at him. "This is a clinic now," she repeated. "But it's open if you'd like to step inside. We don't have many men come through, but it's safe…"

Something about that word lapped up high against a dam somewhere inside of Billy. He felt a building pressure. "It doesn't look safe outside," he said.

The clipboard woman understood. "You mean the trucks," she said.

"We saw them coming in here. The men had guns."

"They're always there."

That was no comfort to Billy. The waves kept lapping, the water level kept rising.

"They come most days to try and scare people away. To intimidate defectors, I suppose. We aren't set up to take people in here, but we can help them with the paperwork if they're looking for asylum. But you're already in here—"

"And scare you?"

"Look, I wouldn't know about that. They're here every day. Do you want to stay? You could dry your things…"

Henry spoke again: "What's in the tower?"

"You're welcome to stay if you're afraid."

"Is there anything in the tower?" She looked him over. His old coat. His unwashed clothes. His worn out shoes.

"There's nothing in the tower. The elevator is broken. No one uses it anymore. We just use the gift shop to store things."

"What things?"

"Leftovers from the Park Service. Old equipment." Billy watched her, and she was no fool: "What are you looking for?"

"Could we get there?"

"It's all locked up. Why?"

Henry didn't say anything to that.

"Come in first," she said. "Tom can take you up later. He's an officer, and he can keep you safe if you really want to look… " Billy saw she was calculating. She needed more data about them, more time to work it through. He looked at Henry, and he opened his mouth to speak–to plead to go back, he knew–but as he did, a sudden, deafening cracking sound filled the wholeness of the space. It was a rifle, and all four of them knew it. The clipboard woman crouched reflexively and looked back towards the doorway to the bathhouse. The other woman had already disappeared inside. "I'm sorry," she said. "Get down. Stay here."

"What was that?" Billy asked her. It was a helpless question, and she didn't answer it. In fact, she was already gone, the door in the side of the corridor now swinging on its hinges. "What was that?" he asked again, interrogating thin air.

Henry had flinched at the shot and now stood frozen with his shoulders hunched. But another report broke the spell, and suddenly the two of them were moving, crouched and racing, towards the far end of the tunnel. There were voices talking quickly but without panic beyond the walls, and now a three-round burst rang out from somewhere inside the bathhouse. It was an automatic rifle. At the far end of the tent was another door, and they rushed through it, expecting gunfire to explode the bricks around them.

But no more sounds came. They had cover here–more buildings stood between them and the men in the trucks; they were out of lines of sight– and they paused to gather themselves. They were both already winded, panicked, hearts racing. A megaphone squawked and someone began talking. Billy could not make out what was being said.

"I don't think this is working out," Billy said between breaths. His pulse was pounding in his ears.

"What are they shooting at?" Henry asked, panting.

"How could I know? But they're shooting!"

"Someone inside shot back."

"What?" Billy wanted to leave.

"It was probably Tom."

Billy's mind was racing. Henry was standing now, his hands on top of his head as he tried to catch his breath. "The tower," he said. "I want… to see… the tower."

"The *tower*?" The talking continued over the megaphone. "You're shitting me. *No!* We need to go."

"There's probably a way up here…there's trees…"

"No, go *home*, Henry. Damn!"

Henry was collecting his own thoughts, trying to hold things together. "But the people are all that way," he said.

He was right, goddamn it.

"*Fuck me!*" Billy said, still breathing hard. He was turning things over. There was nowhere else to go: the men were to the west and south and the hill was to the east. "*Jesus Christ.* Do you think there's a way down the backside? If we take this path up through the trees, can we get down that way and go around?"

Henry was catching his breath now, too. "It's not very steep. We could make one," he said.

There weren't any better options. "I don't want to get shot, Henry. We'll go up this way," he pointed at the path leading up the side of the hill in front of them, "and then we'll come down on the far side. We'll do it quick while everybody's talking, before any guns come out again." The megaphone voices continued.

"Okay," Henry said.

"But no *chances*!"

"Okay."

"And *quick*! No fucking around up there."

"Okay."

Billy paused one more time, gathering himself. "And what are you *looking* for, man?"

"Okay," Henry said.

Billy shook his head. They set out.

The path stayed low as it exited from behind the buildings. They moved into a tunnel of trees, and as they walked, the chatter behind them—both parties were using megaphones now—faded to a background murmur, to static. After a few hundred feet, a set of sharp switchbacks appeared on the hill to their right and they began their ascent, still in the apparent safety of the forest.

"I guess that was just a day at the office back there?" Billy said. He knew by now that Henry wouldn't answer. "I guess that's just what you gotta do to keep your daughters from running off to join the circus?" He didn't know what he was talking about. Adrenaline still surged through him, and he wanted to be down off this hill. He wanted to be home, home, home. Which was where, exactly? "What's that even gonna do? Shoot at some volunteer nurses and drive your own damn doctors away? What sense does that make?" Footsteps, footsteps. "They can keep goddamn Arkansas. Nobody else wants it. But you can't keep *people*," he said. "You can't keep people." They were walking too fast, and he couldn't keep his breath, even when he caught it. "What are we *doing* here?"

Henry's breathing was a rhythmic and raspy sawing beside him. "It's not far," he said, putting one foot in front of the other. "It's not far."

The path switchbacked up the western side of the hill and then joined a gravel roadway which swept around to the south of the modest summit. They were well-sheltered by the trees here, and they finally slowed their pace. Billy was beginning to edge away from the panic he had felt before, and something like grief was threatening to fill the empty spaces opening up within him. He kept talking; he pushed it further away. "There's a tower here?" he asked.

"Yes," Henry said.

"What's it for?"

"I don't know. For sightseeing, I guess."

"Sightseeing what?"

"I don't know. Arkansas. The river, maybe."

"This is the only hill anywhere. What's there to see?"

"Nothing, maybe."

"Nothing," Billy said. "Nothing."

"Look over there," Henry said in reply. "There's a clearing. You can see for yourself."

Just ahead of them, on the right side of the road, was a small, white gazebo perched on a low ledge looking south over the town of Hot Springs. The trees had been cleared away from the viewpoint, and there was a stone bench inside it. Leaves from the previous fall had piled up within the structure and there was the strong smell of rot. They didn't enter, but they stood to the side and looked down. They could see the row of bathhouses, along with the makeshift barricade still lined with these new men with rifles and bullhorns. The indistinct sounds of mechanical voices drifted up to them, and as they watched, a figure pointed a rifle in the air and a puff of smoke burst from its end. The sound of the shot took nearly a second to reach them, but it was still sharp, reverberating across the hill. A cheer followed up after it.

"Look," Billy said, pointing down the hill. "Even that mailman's getting in on it." They could see the vandalized post office vehicle parked now in front of the main bathhouse in the no man's land between the barricades and the front door of the clinic. "Neither snow nor rain nor sleet nor shine…"

"There's no sleet," Henry said.

"What?"

"In the post office motto. 'Neither snow nor rain nor heat nor gloom of night stays these couriers from the swift completion of their appointed rounds.' That's how it goes." Billy looked at him. "Everybody thinks it says 'sleet,' but it's 'heat.'"

"'Stays these couriers,'" Billy said, still looking down the hill. "Jesus Christ. What about guns?"

"It doesn't say anything about that."

"Of course it doesn't."

The tower was at the far end of a parking lot. It was perhaps two hundred feet tall and topped by an enclosed octagonal viewing platform. The blinking antenna poked up from its center, along with two shorter posts of now-defunct cell phone transmitters. Billy had been wrong about that. An external stairwell was fixed to the side of the main elevator shaft, and at the base, there was a small ticketing counter and gift shop. The tower looked only like what it was: a machine for turning what was freely-available into a commodity.

Around the gift shop, the windows were covered by weathered plywood boards with the letters *NPS* scrawled across them in green spray paint. The double doors at the front were chained at the handles and padlocked. At some point in the past, an angry or inebriated driver had jumped the curb and rammed an old, two-door hatchback Honda into the side of the structure and left it there. More dead leaves had piled up nearly to the buckled and rusting line of the hood. They had been caught between the wall of the tower and the crumpled bumper of the vehicle. Everywhere was the smell of decay. Burrows were dug into the mound where foxes might be sleeping. Windows were broken out. Wires dangled. Tires were flat on the ground. The sky was gray above it all. The wind, here above the trees now, was biting and cold.

Henry didn't speak. Instead, he found a chunk of loose concrete from the curb that had been broken by the undercarriage of the hatchback before it struck the tower. He weighed it in his hand. Then, he carried it to the tower door, gripped it tightly, and brought it down as hard as he could on the lock. The sound boomed in the small alcove. Billy flinched. Henry paused to re-evaluate his plan, but there were no better ideas. He brought it down again.

Boom!

Billy turned away from him. There was nothing left to say. They were here; soon, they would go.

The tower complex sat on a small rise from which the little gazebo was still visible, and Billy walked to the edge of the hill and looked down: first at the covered white structure; then beyond it to the row of bathhouses, the strange blockade, the town still and sleeping out there in the distance. No, it wasn't sleeping: it was dead. No, it wasn't dead: it was desolate.

Battered to a point past weariness. Broken in its soul, he supposed. Like everywhere else: a ruin.

Boom!

It was another blow at the lock. He heard the sound of the chain moving against itself as Henry lifted it, probably checking for any signs of progress. Probably looking for something that Billy now knew was not the park. Looking for Billy knew not what. The wind gusted, and dry leaves skittered across the empty, concrete spaces.

Boom!

There was no sound of the chain falling freely to the ground. There was no cheer from Henry. Below, there was no movement. But here, the leaves to his side were swirling into a little vortex now, lifting up into the air before the current lost its grip on them and they each spun out a different way, settling again to the ground. Billy loved this quirk of atmosphere and pressure. In his life, he had looked for it often: on playgrounds, in front of office buildings, under the elm tree in his own front yard.

boom.

Another blow at the lock? No, that sound was different. This was an echo; perhaps bouncing the sound of Henry's efforts back off some stone wall or storefront somewhere below–

Boom!

But then there was Henry again, and no softer sound followed. It wasn't an echo. So, what? Then Billy realized: it was the sound of another gunshot, drifting up to him from the strange stand-off at the clinic. *Was that what it was?* And then: *boom. boom.* This confirmed it: the sounds of two more shots, with an interval between them just long enough to shift a person's aim. Billy shuddered at the thought. Or was it at the wind? He listened close and thought he might hear the mechanical squelch of the bullhorns again, of new shouts and demands. But things fell silent.

Boom!

Henry. The lock was stubborn: the tower held tight to itself and kept its secrets. That was a fanciful thought, Billy knew, for a cheap tourist attraction likely filled with nothing more than blank shift reports, cheap postcards, and boxes of branded t-shirts. He heard the sound of the chain rattling as Henry re-checked it. He braced for another collision.

Boom!

Billy, stirred up by their journey through the tent and up the hill, now drifted back down into himself. If not Little Rock, he wondered, then where? Should he go back to Illinois? Who was still there? His father? Billy realized he had no idea where Henry was off to next. He had no idea how he might move on again, either with him or without him. Three days ago, the air filter had been a coup. It had been a ticket to movement. But now he was less sure about where it had led him. He knew there were other networks for travel in the dying world. There were also still outposts, like the clinic below, for asylum seekers. He wondered if their services applied to travelers who had entered the Republics voluntarily; he wondered if that was what he had done, or if it was what he was still doing.

Boom!

Another blow from Henry, and then Billy heard the smaller reports after it: the "down there" sounds of a shot being fired, and then another answering back. He wondered if Henry could hear them from where he was. The front doors of the gift shop were under a portico of sorts, which put him in a small kind of cave, so sound might not get in. He wondered if, hearing them, Henry would know what they were. He wondered if he would care one way or the other.

That thought caught in Billy, and just as he was about to re-examine it, there was a sudden flash of light somewhere below. It filled the sky for an instant and was gone. At the same moment, behind him, he heard the crash of the chain rattling to the ground and then heard Henry's voice: *"Hey, I got it!"*

And *BOOM!*

The ground shook under their feet and the windows of the tower rattled and came loose from their frames. Sheets of glass from the observatory platform fell in whole panels onto the sidewalk, where they exploded into foot-long shards that went spinning through the air and planted themselves inches deep into tree trunks. The air was swirling with dead leaves, a blizzard now of trash and glass. In the distance, a hundred car alarms went off at once.

Billy realized he had fallen to the ground and picked himself up. He ran down the embankment to the white gazebo and looked to the town below:

The street-facing side of the bathhouse in which they had been no more than a half hour ago was entirely gone. The rest of it was already in flames. The trucks at the barricade were gone, too. No: one was now overturned, balanced on the collapsed roof of its cab, and the other was twisted into rubble unrecognizable. He could see men, at least two of them, lying on the street. Between the wreckage of the trucks and the collapsed bathhouse, there was now a deep crater—a crater where the mailcar had been—smoking and steaming in the fast-cooling air. There was the sound of the car alarms. There was another sound, a human sound, beginning to rise, too.

He realized he was expecting Henry to materialize beside him, but when he did not, Billy remembered the falling glass and turned to make his way back up the hill. The tower was still standing, but Henry was nowhere to be found: not in the parking lot, not on the ground outside the tower, not in the portico, its doors now wide open. The doors?

Billy stepped inside. The darkness was jarring; the damp smell of mildew overpowered his other senses. He felt like a bag had been pulled over his head.

"Henry?" he called. No answer. "Henry?"

As his eyes began to adjust, he could make out the basics of the room: ticket counter, empty racks in a gift shop, cardboard boxes stacked to the cobwebbed ceiling. Some had already been rummaged through, their contents strewn across the floor and the half-emptied containers tossed to the side. It was still too dark for Billy to make out exactly what had been in them, but his feet yielded clues: the crunch of cheap plastic; the softer give of piled fabrics. His toe kicked something small and metallic, sending it clattering across the tiles of the floor.

"Henry?"

The space was small. It was clear Henry wasn't here. And then: the sound of metal straining under weight somewhere above him. A rhythm to it. The staircase. He looked around and saw a door beside the defunct elevator.

"Henry?" he called as he opened it. He was outside again, at the bottom of what resembled a fire escape. The noises–the steps–were harder to hear out here over the sounds of car alarms down the hill, but he could make them out. He started up. More steps; his breath heaving in his chest.

At the top, he found himself in the old observatory. It was exposed to the elements now that the windows had all fallen to the sidewalk below, and wind gusted through it. He saw Henry immediately: he was standing at a railing facing south.

"Henry?"

"I'm here," he said, finally looking in Billy's direction. His face was noticeably pale, even in the shadow and gloom and cold of this space. He was turning something over in his hands, rotating it too quickly, but Billy couldn't see what it was. Something small; some whatsit of mindless fascination. "They blew it up," he said.

"It was the mailcar," Billy said in reply.

"The mailcar," Henry said, looking back out the window. "Neither rain nor snow nor heat nor gloom of night…" His voice seemed to be drifting away.

"We should help," Billy said. "We should go down there and help."

"'…will keep us from our appointed rounds.'" But Billy already knew that was the ending.

He repeated himself: "I think we can help. People down there might need help. Those nurses…"

"You can go," Henry said. His voice was still just more than a whisper. The sounds from below were unrelenting, drowning him out.

"*We* can go," Billy said. "No splitting up…" He noticed now that there was blood on Henry's hands, even as they kept spinning, spinning. "What's that?" he asked.

"Nothing important," Henry said, pocketing the trinket suddenly in his coat.

"The blood, Henry," Billy said. "You're bleeding."

Henry's eyes widened. "Am I?" He looked himself over, and there it was: a shard of plate glass, the size and shape of a kitchen knife, sticking out from his left thigh. "What's that?" he asked, but before Billy could stop him, he pulled it out of himself—an inch, two, three—and held it before him, pinched between his forefinger and thumb. Studying it like it was some strange and enormous insect. "A piece of one of these windows, I would think." He gestured to empty space. An oval of blood was rapidly expanding on his cargo pants. "What do you make of it?"

Billy expected him to collapse in his arms, but he did not. He went to him, put Henry's arm over his shoulder and slowly, together, they made their way down the sixteen flights of stairs and back into the visitor center. Henry's leg was bleeding significantly, but it did not seem to Billy like anything vital had been damaged. Still, Henry was woozy, weakening, and Billy could feel his grip loosening on his friend's shoulder. A wound deep in the muscle. In the gloom of the gift shop, he picked up one of the old sweatshirts Henry had tossed out of the storage boxes before and made a quick compress, wrapping it around Henry's thigh and knotting it by the sleeves behind his knee. It would hold; Henry could walk, more or less. He led him through the door.

Later, Billy would think often of that afternoon. Moving so slowly down the far-eastern side of the hill. Limping down deserted streets and alleys, pausing every few hundred yards to rest and tighten the sleeves of the makeshift tourniquet. Worrying vaguely about more men in trucks; worrying more specifically about the frozen woman in the tunnel, and then the woman with the clipboard. Praying the rain would hold off for another hour, or for another two.

It was well past dark when they found the Ranger again. Billy settled Henry on the bed in the back, and he was snoring before Billy could even adjust the driver's seat and put the key in the ignition. He paused. He didn't know where he was going, but he chose roads north, winding his way on asphalt and gravel and dirt until well past midnight. He drove until he was sure they were somewhere well over what was once the Missouri state line. He never saw another car.

Later, he thought often of that afternoon. He wondered what might have gone differently if he had run down that hill instead of turning around for the tower. If he hadn't heard the sounds of Henry's feet on the steps of the stairwell. If he hadn't called his name. If he had snuck up and slipped the rabbit's foot from Henry's pocket and left him there, bleeding and spinning something in his hands, lost in the top of his tower.

Tonight, though, he thought of getting miles away. The radio was no comfort—just static, and news he didn't want to hear. He drove and drove. Years ago, his dad told him there was nothing to do anymore. He'd been a mechanic, but cars outpaced him; his mother had been a minister, but she had died in an automobile accident. Billy wanted to be a writer, but his world was tired of reading. *What's there to say that ain't mean?* his father asked him once. *Who's gonna say anything different?* Dinner in the garbage and dishes in the sink, he sat each night not in the worn chair in the living room but under the single light hovering above the kitchen table. He'd play cards against no one at all, drinking until he was sleepy, but never a drop more. Spinning the draw with his fingers until he could see where he wanted to play it.

Billy watched him from the other room with his phone in his hand, until there were no more phones, and after that with a book or crossword puzzle. *Nowhere to go, nowhere to go,* his father would say. Billy would fill in the last word and then turn the page.

Henry's One-Stop

enry dreamed again about his son. Caleb a month old, sleeping on his chest. Caleb barely able to stand, bracing himself on the back of Leo, the family dog. Leo: another goldendoodle in The Age of Goldendoodles. Caleb: clutching Leo's fur so tightly Henry couldn't believe it didn't hurt him, or that he didn't seem to care if it did. What a wonder, that dog.

Once, Shannon received a 5-gallon bucket of gourmet ice cream in the mail from a client after selling their condominium. It arrived in a styrofoam box lined with two blocks of dry ice. Caleb was four. Henry had taken out the blocks and put them in the sink, then called Caleb into the kitchen. As soon as he walked into the doorway, Henry turned on the faucet and a white fog erupted like the ash plume of a volcano, overflowing the sides of the sink and rolling out onto the floor. Caleb shrieked and clapped his hands, bouncing up and down on his toes: *Again, Daddy! Again! Again!*

Caleb turned six during the first pandemic, in 2020. He hadn't been able to go to school, and Henry had been frustrated: he'd been counting on Caleb's absence during the days so Shannon could go back to work full time. But instead, she kept showing houses on the side and stayed home with him four days a week, managing listings on a laptop at the dining room table while Caleb went to school in the kitchen. She would hire a sitter whenever she needed to go out; usually a neighbor girl whose classes were also online. Her name was Bella, in The Age of Bellas. She would sit beside Caleb at the table and read her phone with her computer on mute. The voice of Caleb's teacher going over letters and primary colors beside her. Shannon putting on lipstick in the mirror beside the door before covering her face with a mask as she left to meet a client. Henry imagining all these things from the safer distance of his mostly-empty office.

Alarm early. Shower hot. Toothbrush in need of replacement.

Traffic light. Office quiet. An order on Amazon that would be delivered by noon.

Days not just empty, but nothing at all.

Shannon's guidebooks started arriving during this time. Ways to imagine being somewhere instead of nowhere. Ways to be outside when inside was out-of-the-question. Henry would find them in conspicuous places: his nightstand, on the side of the sink in their bathroom, on the table where he kept his car keys. He would take the hint and ask her about them:

Where do you want to go?

Anywhere.

Pick a place, and I'll try to get off.

Somewhere.

It might be tough to find the days…

Shannon's mother died in a nursing home. The last time Caleb saw her, it had been through the window of her first-floor apartment. He had waved and she had placed her palm against the glass. 2021.

Henry's dad died in a hospital bed. Caleb was home with Bella when it happened. Henry and Shannon were in the room but somehow missed it: an ad on the television had caught their attention, and they were looking away when the beeping stopped. 2022.

Caleb was well-behaved at the funerals. He cried, but never loudly so. He was dressed in a black suit tailored for children; for events such as these, Henry supposed. Curly brown hair cut short and parted in a way it never was at home. Small and shiny dress shoes. He would have been seven, then eight. Just starting school in a real classroom.

In second grade, he had trouble. Most kids did. He sat still but couldn't pay attention. He was described by a counselor as "morose." Shannon took him to therapy, and Henry asked her how it went. He was attentive. He was appropriately concerned. When he was awake, this is how he remembered himself. But when he dreamed, he knew differently.

Caleb: sitting at the small desk in his room, drawing in the journal his counselor had given him. Simple figures and shapes, scribbled dark. Arrows, fist-drawn letters. Henry watching from the doorway. *Don't speak. Don't speak. Walk on by.*

Caleb: older now, on the other side of a shut door. *Don't speak. Don't speak. Walk on by.*

Caleb: older still, playing video games at a friend's house. The door not quite shut. The journal is under the pillow now. Henry knows it is there. *Walk on by. Walk on by.*

What did you do? The door is cracked and he hears Shannon's voice.

Again, Daddy! Again! Again! The volcano erupts and fog spills out onto the floor.

What the fuck did you do? The door is shut.

Nothing. He says it into a telephone. The door is open.

Again! Again! It is the second number he's called.

Nothing. Nothing. There are sirens outside. The door is shut.

I did nothing. But that was not the truth.

I did nothing! But it was.

*   *   *

He woke and there was blood on his hands. He saw it on his sleeves, on the mattress he was laying on. He was in the Ranger. It was moving.

He looked down and saw his leg. A sweatshirt had been tied around his thigh, and although it was stained a dark reddish-brown, it was not wet. The bleeding had stopped, and he tried to remember what had happened. He remembered the sharp pain like electric shocks that came with each step on a stairwell. He remembered being carried (or was he dragged?) for what seemed like both an eternity and no time at all. He remembered clenching and unclenching his fist around a knot he had made of some part of Billy's shirt; focusing all his attention on that one action: squeeze, release, squeeze, release. Like a heartbeat in his hand.

It took him a moment to decide to try and sit up. He still had not spoken. And then a bump in the road caused his whole body to lift up in the air and crash back down on the mattress in an absolute explosion of pain. His eyes were so wide he thought they might pop from the sockets. After surviving that, he thought: *what the hell?*

He propped himself up and realized things were not unbearable. He felt something inside his leg pull and burn, but it held. He felt the dried films of blood stretched across his leg, his stomach, his arms crack and separate, tearing tiny hairs out at the root, ripping a dozen Band Aids off at once. He winced and made a sound somewhere between a whimper and a groan.

Whatever it was, it caught Billy's attention. His voice called back from the driver's seat: "You're alive."

"Where's my jacket?" Henry realized he wasn't wearing it. Billy must have stripped him down after he passed out, and he looked quickly around himself. He saw the bins and barrels and loose piles of clothes and scattered trash. He saw smears of his own blood everywhere. He saw a partial red handprint–Billy's, he thought–on the panel of the rear door.

When his eyes got there, he had trouble focusing on anything else. It made him want to vomit. *How long?* he wondered.

"It's back there." The voice from the front said to him. Billy didn't offer any additional guidance, and his voice sounded tense, angry.

"I don't see it," Henry said. There was no reply to that. And then, there it was: wadded in a ball under the overhung lip of the service window. He reached to pick it up, and when he did, he felt the cut muscles in his thigh rage against him. This didn't stop him, and now with the jacket in hand, he began feeling for the pockets. He found the right opening and fished out his treasure, holding it in his red-stained palm: a gold plastic badge with *Junior Park Ranger* pressed into its crown and the words *Hot Springs* stamped in black across the banner. He couldn't believe it had stayed clean.

He needed his lockbox.

"Can we stop?" he asked, his body still turned away from the front of the truck. Still, he felt Billy's eyes on him in the rearview mirror. The moment went too long. Then:

"Yeah," Billy said. "We can stop."

Billy parked the Ranger in a gravel lot outside a long-abandoned bait and tackle shop. The sign, although Henry couldn't see it, said *Henry's One-Stop*. Whether that was a first or last name, no one could tell. Henry scooted his way to the rear doors and swung them open. There were trees everywhere: oaks, sweetgum, and a few pines, still dark green in the February light. Henry could see the highway they had been driving, too: it was a two-lane blacktop, still mostly whole, although the lines had faded to invisibility.

He was looking for a road sign when he heard Billy's door open, and then the crunch of his footsteps as he made his way to the rear of the truck. Henry gently lowered his legs over the bumper and sat until Billy came into view. Henry realized he must have stopped and changed clothes at some point in the night because he was completely clean now, a fresh shirt tucked neatly into slacks that, although a bit wrinkly, were still crisp at the pleats.

"You look great," Henry said.

Billy looked down. "Yeah, well. You made a mess."

Henry nodded at that. Then he looked down, too. "Did you keep those clothes?"

"Where was I going to wash them?"

"So, 'no' then." Henry's eyes fixed on the knotted sweatshirt around his leg. "Am I gonna make it, doc?"

"You have so far."

Henry pondered that. "You carried me all the way back," he said. He'd been struggling to imagine it; they had walked so far. He thought about the convention center and the burned police station and the awnings over the shops up the street from the Walmart. While he was rewinding their journey, Billy kept quiet. "I must have been heavy," Henry said.

Billy shuffled his feet. He had yet to make eye contact. His hands were pushed deep in his pockets. He seemed to be letting his sight drift over every piece and part of the storefront on the far side of the Ranger now. Henry couldn't read from where he was sitting, but he could see Billy taking in some detail, then another: Fishing Lines, Lead Weights, Live Blood Worms. "You weren't light," he finally said, and it was Henry's turn to be quiet. He realized, as he looked around him, that *everything* was that way: there was no breeze, no cars passing by. Even the birds must have stopped to listen to their conversation unravel.

"Where are we?" he asked, breaking the silence.

"A bait shop. Somewhere in Missouri. I don't know where."

Henry was squeezing the badge in his hand, and he understood something important. "You're mad at me," he said.

"I think I am," Billy said back. His eyes had finished with the store and moved on, but not to Henry. He took in the trees, a squirrel in the corner of the parking lot, some cloud in the sky.

"You saved me, though." Henry said.

Billy took one hand out of his pocket and rubbed his eyes with his fingers, then cupped his mouth in his palm. He looked Henry in the eyes. "I didn't leave you behind," he said. "That's not the same thing."

For the first time in a long time, Henry felt afraid: not of Billy, but of something else. He was getting closer to something he didn't want to find, and his stomach was clinching inside him like a fist. It dawned on him—and it truly was like the sun peaking over the horizon—that he didn't want to be alone anymore. He squinted his eyes against the discovery. "Are you leaving?" he asked.

Billy laughed and that old bubbling-creek sound was long gone from his voice. "And go where?" he said. Then something bizarre happened: Billy's entire body tensed as if he had been struck by lightning. The charge of it moved up him from the soles of his feet, causing his legs to shake, then his hips, and then he started to wave his arms around looking for all the world like an inflatable man outside a used car dealership. Henry could hear the sound of his starched clothes flapping and chafing against themselves, and finally, whatever energy he was conducting reached the top button of his collar and burst out: "*AND GO WHERE?!*" he shouted into the Missouri sky. His voice echoed off the bait shop, and Henry didn't know what to say, because he was in awe.

Billy looked him square in the eyes again and locked in: he would say his peace. "I. Am not. Someone. Who leaves," he said. "No, I didn't leave you. I didn't *leave* you. But you took me there, and people got hurt, and for what? You didn't tell me. You took me, but you didn't tell me…" And then: "But you would have left *me*."

As soon as Billy said it, Henry knew it was true. Billy kept talking: "I didn't do it because I *couldn't* do it. So I dragged you all the way down, and I got you back here, and I got both of us to wherever *this* is. But…but…" And suddenly all that energy was used up, and something changed in his face. He didn't know how to finish his sentence. He didn't know fully why he was so angry. He knew Little Rock was on fire. He knew he had heard people, newly blown apart, crying out for help. And now, all he could see was Henry back in that goddamn tower, turned away from him, spinning something in his hands. "There's nowhere for me to go," he said finally, and that was the bottom line. "Nowhere. But you have to tell me, Henry. You have to tell me what you're doing. I deserve to know."

Henry thought, *I'm not doing anything.* Over the past three months, he had said this to himself so many times he had lost the ability to disbelieve it: *I'm not doing anything.* But instead, what he said was: "I can't."

Billy glared down at him. "No," he said. "No, that's not going to work. You have to tell me."

"It won't matter–"

"It will matter *to me*. It almost killed me, so it will matter *to me*."

"I can't–"

"Henry, you have to tell me, or else you can sit in that ice cream truck until you get better or die in this parking lot, and I will break down the door of that *goddamn* bait shop and live there until the next person, *in a fucking car, comes along*!"

"I don't know," Henry said, and he was looking down at his legs now, at the bloody sweatshirt now, "I don't know, I don't know…"

"Know better, Henry. Know better. You can do it." He pointed to Henry's closed fist. "What's that in your hand?"

Henry felt like his whole being was about to burst apart, and once it did, he would never be able to find all the pieces again. There would be no one left to even look for them. He was already crying, and he wanted to disappear into the earth; he wanted to rot away into nothing.

"Please, Henry," Billy said. "Don't choose this."

What choice? Sitting there in his own dried blood, Henry felt his dissolution beginning, his seams separating. He let his fingers fall open, and Billy saw.

"It's my son," Henry said weakly, and he was still so afraid. "It's my son…"

He could feel Billy looking at him, but his own eyes were squeezed shut. He didn't know what else to say, so he said all he knew: "I don't know why I'm doing it. I'm not trying to do anything. Nobody needs to know I'm even here. I don't want to hurt anybody… I don't know why. I don't know…"

"What happened to him?"

"I can't–"

"Tell me, Henry," and his voice was suddenly so gentle, the air around them so still. *You can't say it,* Henry screamed at himself, *you can't!* But he knew he would, because he had no substance left.

"He shot himself," Henry said. "I was downstairs, and I went up…" But he couldn't go any further that way because the door was shut. He saw Caleb, sleeping on his chest. He saw Caleb, walking the towpath. "He wanted them when he was younger. And I know it's too late now. Nothing's even open anymore… but who would care? Who misses them? It doesn't matter. It doesn't *matter* to anyone. It doesn't matter. It doesn't matter." It was all he had, and for a moment, he wondered if Billy was still there. He hoped he wasn't. He hoped he was. He was crying, and he had no power to stop it. Splitting, breaking, coming apart.

And then he heard Billy's voice.

"What happens when you're done?"

What's at the end of the tether? He didn't know, and he said so.

But it wasn't enough. Neither of them spoke for a long time. Then, Henry heard the sound of Billy's shoe move once on the asphalt. The rasp of it was enough, and in a voice he thought might not be heard, he whispered: "Please don't leave, Billy."

The sound stopped. And then Billy answered him: "The keys are in the truck." The dress shoes moved across the gravel and Henry strained as hard as he could to hear them, even as they walked further and further away.

There was no stripe on the bait shop as Billy approached it, but there was a bronze plaque by the door. It read:

<u>HARTVILLE, MISSOURI</u>
POPULATION CENTER OF
THE UNITED STATES OF AMERICA

The plaque was a gift from the National Geological Survey, and it had been presented to the town council in 2020. Billy wondered if the council met at Henry's One-Stop. He wondered if those first lockdowns had sabotaged some grand ribbon-cutting once upon a time; if the plaque had arrived in a padded envelope instead of making its way to Hartville in the briefcase of some middling supervisor from the erstwhile USGS. *What a goddamn thing to celebrate,* he thought to himself; *'you're standing in the empty hole of a people donut.'*

He tried the door and it swung open. He stepped inside. *That selfish fucker,* he thought; *that stupid bastard.* Billy had never been a fisherman; he'd never even been on a boat. But there among the rods and tackle he knew he was still hopping mad. He realized it was Henry's face that pushed him over the edge: that blank look Billy knew was both a reflex and shield to him; the way he pretended that he couldn't understand rather than that he chose not to try.

He pushed the return on the cash register and found a few useless coins, a jumble of paper clips, and a stamp for signing checks. There was a phonebook on a shelf under the counter next to a worn and folded highway map. Next to that was a box of old ammunition; he shook it, but it was as empty as all the others. He set it down next to a dog's old chew toy with the squeaker pulled out, and then he walked back out from around the counter.

The truth was that Billy was almost as afraid as Henry was, and he knew it. He was getting dangerously close to becoming what Henry only pretended to be, which was a ghost. His whole life he'd felt invisible. He had an older brother: Robbie, the Athlete, named after their father. He had a younger sister: Busola, the Artist, named after their maternal grandmother. He was the Academic, named after the author of the first book his grandmother could remember reading in school: it had been *As I Lay Dying*, and she'd loved the part where the boy thinks his mother is a fish.

But that label never fit Billy. He was a so-so student who had done well enough to get by, but never well enough to stand out. He'd gone to college at the Illinois-Chicago campus, but his last two years were remote. He'd dabbled in creative writing, if only to the tune of two B-minuses in the courses he tried. After the First Insurrection, in 2021, he'd latched onto journalism. But by the time he graduated, computers were doing most of the writing. The damned thing was, he'd never actually even received his degree: his commencement ceremony was virtual, and the physical copy got lost in the mail. After college, he waited tables and caught Covid. Then, he tried substitute teaching and caught Covid again. When his mother died, he thought his dad might finally be someone who needed him. But he'd been wrong about that, too.

Now, after six weeks on the road for his own Great Adventure, he'd interviewed a dozen waitresses and gas station attendants, lost his car, and ended up in the company of a barely functional–if not suicidal–White man. Worse than that: a White man in crisis. With a Black wife. With a dead kid. In another life, Billy thought, maybe he would have been good for an interview. But probably not. He thought of his own father playing solitaire: *Busted*, he'd say to the empty kitchen, and then reshuffle the cards.

A newspaper article on the wall caught his eye. It was a space-filler of a piece: "Local Fisherman Reels In State-Record Sunfish." There were maybe 300 words, accompanied by a photo of a grinning and shirtless man holding up his catch. Billy guessed he was a regular at the old One-Stop–or maybe even someone who worked here. The clipping had been mounted and framed, and a thick layer of dust had collected on the glass. He rubbed his thumb over the author's name so he could read it, and he wondered what Glen W. Robertson was up to now.

Billy realized the Ranger hadn't started up, and he looked back through the door to see it right where he had left it. *The lazy, indecisive sonofabitch.* It came as a surprise to him that he felt relief.

In the corner of the parking lot of Henry's One-Stop, a red fox made her way out of the nearby wood and paused to clean her paws. The rain from the day before had muddied her usual path from a small forest creek to the east where frogs were plentiful to the meadow on the other side of the highway where she lived in a series of burrows, and soft earth had pushed up between her toes and made her going heavy. She was pregnant with a litter of kits, but their arrival was still some time off. Yet, in the mornings after feeding, she often busied herself preparing a place for them in the warm and folded-over straw.

As she groomed herself, a sound like the croak of a fat toad punctured the quiet of the place. She paused, mid-lick, to find it. Her ears twitched on the top of her head. It came again, and this time she knew. There was a truck in the far corner of the lot, rich with strange smells, and as the sound repeated a third time, she could see it jostling on its springs. She watched.

In time, a man emerged. He was propping himself up with something, and so, so slowly, he began making his way from the truck towards the building where she knew mice to play. He croaked and sighed with every breath. And then he saw her.

Mud still between her toes, she trotted across the road way and underneath the low bushes into the spaces beyond.

Henry Henry had found a trekking pole that had once been the property of Congaree National Park in a locker beneath the vending window of the Ranger. He hadn't needed a key for it; the rabbit's foot was still lying in the driver's seat. His little golden badge was still in his pocket. With pain in every step, he limped towards the bait shop.

The door was unlocked; Billy hadn't needed to break in after all. It groaned on its rusted hinges as Henry pushed it open. The inside was dim and dusty, but it was still mostly intact. There were boxes and cartons on the shelves, a rack of fishing rods on a far wall. The cooler of nightcrawlers and crickets had been raided. The bins of beef jerky sticks were cleaned out. But still, it had been subjected only to light anarchy. Perhaps the owner had been well-liked.

As Henry's eyes adjusted, he spotted Billy standing in the marine supplies aisle. "Hey," he said.

Billy looked at him. "Hey," he said back.

"I don't want to leave."

"Do you want a medal?"

"I meant I don't want to leave without you."

"I know what you meant." He turned and made to rummage in a tote of plastic funnels of various colors and sizes.

"You drove away from Little Rock," Henry said. "Why'd you do that?"

Billy picked something up, looked it over, and set it back down. "The man said there was nobody there."

"But you had people?"

"I hoped I did."

Henry shuffled over and propped himself against the counter. His leg hurt like hell. "Where else do you have people?" he asked.

"Nowhere," Billy said, and they both knew it was the truth.

"I can take you where you want to go."

"You can't really take anybody anywhere right now."

Henry looked down. *Jesus Christ,* he thought to himself. "It's just my left, though."

"Yeah," Billy said. He had moved to the next bin. This one held assorted hoses.

"Look, if you want to stay together, I want to stay together. Not just because of yesterday. Because you know things. You're better with people than me. Reese. Those ladies–" and when Henry said it, he saw Billy tense. He decided he should go another way: "I thought I was supposed to do this on my own."

"You still can," Billy said. He'd made his way to the end of the row.

"But I don't have to."

Billy faced him. "I'm not here to babysit you, Henry. I'm not waiting for an apology. I'm not your sidekick. We're not stuck with each other. If you want company, we have to do that the right way–" And he paused. "I can look for things with you. I don't think there's anything wrong with that. But it can't be just you."

Just you. Henry hadn't thought of it that way before. *When is a door not a door?* What other way was there to be? Dust motes swirled in the air. The smell of stale earth from the emptied cooler caught in his nose. Mice nibbled at a baseboard behind the cashiers' counter. He turned it all over, and he made a choice.

"Okay," Henry said, and he wanted to know how to mean it. And then he thought of something like a miracle: he'd found it more than a month ago, in the clerk's office of an abandoned motel he'd raided for blankets and courtesy shampoos. When it happened, he hadn't been able to believe his luck. He'd thought to save it for… well, for he didn't know what. But he'd kept it beside his lockbox under the driver's seat this whole time. It was an unopened bottle of Heaven Hill bourbon, still in the brown paper bag from the liquor store.

"Can I ask you something?" he said.

"Yeah, you can."

"Do you want to get drunk?" He was starting to wonder how much longer he could stand up. He felt like this was among his very best ideas.

Billy looked at him, and he didn't laugh. But the old creek burbled in him, anyway.

"I think I do," he said. "I think I really do."

The day passed. They drank. Henry showed Billy the front pages of his atlas, where he'd mapped a route before leaving Ohio that road closures and natural disasters and militiamen had turned entirely to shit. But the sketch of his quest was still there, moving up the Mississippi, then across the Great Plains, into the mountains by springtime, and then to the coast. He would come down through California over the summer, and then turn east again, through the deserts and canyons until he got to the baked emptiness of Texas. The route stopped at the Mexican border, and Billy asked him, "where will you go then?" Henry's eyes looked at his home but his mouth said "Alaska," and he laughed and Billy laughed, too. Billy told him that was the stupidest plan he'd ever heard; why would you cross the mountains in the spring? Why would you drive across the desert in the middle of the summer? Who in their right mind would try to get *into* Texas? But Henry didn't have any answers, and they weren't real questions, anyway. He'd never make it to Texas. He had barely made it to Missouri.

As the sun was going down, they opened the back door to watch it, and Henry remembered the badge in his pocket. He shushed Billy, who had started in on a story about an uncle who had been abducted by aliens, and said, "Look, look." Then he crawled from the back of the truck through the doorway into the cab and retrieved his lockbox. He set it on his lap like the treasure that it was to him, and when he opened it, Billy honored the secret as if he were a pirate peering into a chest of gold doubloons. Henry took the Hot Springs badge and set it inside next to the others. Then he took out the marker and handed it to Billy. "Can you do it?" he asked, "I'm too…I'm too…"

"Drunk," Billy finished for him, and Henry laughed in a way that might have been crying, but for the smile on his face. He tapped the box and then turned it over to show Billy the numbers and circles.

"I don't think I can hold it straight," he said. Billy obliged and drew a clean circle around the ten.

"Tell me what you saw," he said, putting the box down between them.

"Where?" Henry replied.

"Anywhere. Any place."

"I saw a mess," Henry said, shrugging and letting his eyes close. In the dark, pictures came back to him of dark mountains swallowed in clouds, blue waters stretching forever, tunnels of mangroves leading on and on into he knew not what. The smell of decay. Crossroads, with smoke in the distance.

"I saw *country*," he said, and he was well and truly drunk. He opened his eyes. "Messy, rotten country."

"What do you want to see?" Billy asked.

Henry knew not to close them again. "Who knows?" he said.

"Something beautiful?"

"Sure, let's go with that."

They both laughed. As they did, the stars came out overhead, though of course they hadn't gone anywhere. Bats fed in the dark. Trees waited in the stillness of the night. And not so far away, a fox, her chores done for the day, nuzzled her face over her growing belly, covered herself with her tail, and slept.

Gateway

enry and Billy woke slowly the next morning to a clear sky and late winter cold. They could see their breath in the Ranger, and Henry made them a breakfast of corned beef hash and stale toast from the last of their Oxford supplies, while Billy washed his face and dressed. It was their fifth day together.

As they ate, coffee gurgled in the percolator atop the single burner of their campstove. In the small space, the smell of the roasting grounds did battle with the everpresent odor of vegetable oil, and it won, thank God. Billy swallowed a bite, wiped his mouth, and asked the day's question: "Where to?"

"Depends on where we are," Henry asked back through a mouthful of hash.

"Newspaper inside says Hartville, Missouri." Billy was already reaching through the opening to the cab for the atlas. He found it and flipped to the right page. There was already a circle around St. Louis.

"Then we're off to see the Arch," Henry said. "That's almost in Illinois. Do you know anything about it?"

"I know it's not there anymore," Billy said. Three years ago, in 2031, a small plane crashed into the observation deck and turned the Arch into a set of broken snake's fangs. A dozen people had died. It had been an accident, according to what was left of the FAA, and the pilot's family spoke to the media about his usual stability and plans for the future. There had been fog that evening, and a warning light on the Arch was malfunctioning. Still, the word spread that he was a terrorist, or perhaps a lizard person, or perhaps that it was a false flag and he didn't exist at all. Meanwhile, cranes moved piles of carbon steel and glass, and engineers tried to work out what to do with the leaning towers that were left.

Henry took another bite. "The museum underneath might still be there, though," he said. "They would keep the badges. If we can get into it. How's St. Louis?"

"It's a Federal town. I haven't heard much about it. I'd guess it's pretty okay: power, phones, still a few McDonalds."

"Want to see it a bit? Might be something for your book."

The coffee was ready, or at least it was ready enough. Neither of them said it, but they both felt like shit warmed over.

"It's worth a stop."

They followed a state highway east through what used to be the Mark Twain National Forest, but there had been no management for years and it had been left to wild. It was still beautiful. The road wound up through rising hills dense with old growth trees, and with spring leaves still a month away, they could see through the latticed branches for miles and miles. The landscape tumbled down away from them like the frozen rapids of an enormous river, rising and falling in ridge after ridge. Twice, wild turkeys scurried across the cracked asphalt in their path, and everywhere sunlight glinted off the wet surfaces where ice from the night before was just beginning to thaw.

There were tiny hamlets along the drive. Most seemed long abandoned, but some still showed signs of life: a ribbon of woodsmoke from a chimney; a dog barking at them from a front porch. Once, Henry saw a green bandana tied to the flag of a mailbox and he turned to ask Billy if he wanted to stop. But his companion was sound asleep with his head against the cool window glass. They changed roads in Leadington, and then again in Crystal City. The Mississippi River came back into view for the first time in three days, and they traveled north along its west bank until, in the early afternoon, the skyline of St. Louis came into view.

As Billy predicted, they had no trouble getting into town. There was a commercial checkpoint in the middle of a bridge next to a closed riverboat casino, but as Henry approached, he saw that it was unmanned and the gate had been left up. The truth was that he didn't know quite where to go. He pulled over and checked the inset map of the city: Gateway Arch National Park was a tiny rectangle of green along the river in the heart of downtown. It was just past the interstate bridge back to Illinois, but the old waterfront road to get there had been washed out and left unrepaired. He figured their best bet was to work through the gridded streets of downtown and then possibly walk over. After he woke Billy, Billy agreed. But he had another idea, too:

"How about one damn good meal?"

"It's been awhile. Better than McDonalds?"

"A lot better."

Like all midwestern cities, St. Louis spread out instead of rising up. Rather than head straight to the park, they approached to the west of downtown and came up on Kings Highway. As they neared an overpass, they could see an intact geodesic dome in a park to their right, and the glass caught the noonday sun and shot it back out at them and in every direction: it was a genuine marvel. A few blocks further on, they picked up Old Route 66 and headed east towards the skyscrapers there. However, the road was not empty: although it was nothing like the traffic of Before, cars dotted the lanes in both directions and Henry looked over at Billy. "It's been awhile," he said.

His friend knew what he meant. St. Louis was a step back in time, if not to the glory days, then at least to something like the pandemic years, when people would poke their heads out of their holes like mice and scurry anxiously from place to place. Around them, men moved with heads down and quickness in their steps. And yet, they were there: what was happening in the Republics was not happening in St. Louis. At least, it was not happening yet.

Because the city was Federal, dollars were accepted and white stripes weren't necessary. However, as they neared the downtown, store after store carried the mark in solidarity. It could have brought comfort, but instead, it left Henry and Billy both with an eerie feeling. Henry thought of Ohio, where his ignorance had come easier. And Billy thought of Springfield, where things pushed down tended to brew into a different sort of poison.

The most famous highway in America turned north before the trainyard and the river, and in the shadow of an old major league stadium where neighborhood club teams now played, Henry spied a sign in the shape of a pig with *Lewe's* painted on it in cursive script. There was a neon in the window blinking *OPEN*. There was a stripe on the awning. So, the Ranger pulled in.

The building was empty aside from a young Black man and an even younger White woman chatting by the register. Neither of them could have been more than 20. As Henry and Billy stepped inside, the man called out, "Welcome to Lewe's" and the woman made her way to the prep line. "What can we do for you?" he asked. They ordered two house specials and took a seat at the counter. It had been God only knew how long since they had bathed, and Henry, at least, looked as road-hard as he was. He was still limping dramatically, and although he'd put on new pants to hide the blood, it spotted through. In short, they were a mess. But the young man said nothing of it. Instead, he asked them the usual counter-clerk questions: "Where are you in from? Where are you going? What do you think of St. Louis?"

They told him they were on their way West; that they were there just for the day; that they had come to see the Arch. He told them what they already knew: there wasn't much left of it to see. Henry asked about the museum, and the man was confused at first, but then he told them about a place called Drury's which might be helpful. Henry tried to clarify: "I mean the old museum, the one underneath. The park service used to run it. Have you ever heard of it?"

"I don't know it," the kid said. "But it would be blocked off, anyway. Everything under there is."

Their food arrived and Billy had been right: it was a damn good meal. Billy paid their bill, and as they turned to go, the woman called out from behind the grill: "You really should try Drury's. It's by the old courthouse. It's easy to find, and if Auggie is there, he'll be able to help you. He keeps track of all that stuff."

They thanked her for her time, too, and then Billy asked one more question: "What's it like here?"

She thought about it for a long moment. "An aquarium," she finally said. "Or a zoo, maybe. It's nice enough. So long as you don't want to go anywhere else."

After lunch, they bartered with the couple at Lewe's for some leftover peanut oil and then worked their way east along the city mall. Billy stopped in at what seemed like an antique store of all things, and Henry rebandaged his aching leg. It was late afternoon when they got where they were going. "Drury's" turned out to be the lobby of an abandoned hotel off of Market Street at the very edge of the old park boundary. Just beyond it to the east, a ten foot (and apparently permanent) barricade blocked any view of the monument grounds or the river beyond; all they could see were the shattered ends of the two remaining spires poking over the top of the wall and bent towards each other, as if they were speaking. There was no door or gate in the blockade as far as Henry could see, and a new kind of resignation began to settle into the pit of his stomach. At least, he hoped that's what the lead-weight feeling in there was.

As for the lobby, it was open and maintained, if also a bit dusty. The lights were off inside, but the enormous glass windows let in more than enough sun to see by. As they entered, Billy was the first to call out. A moment later, an older man—squat, disheveled, and with a Santa Claus beard—appeared from behind one of the dozens of large, glass cases spread around the otherwise empty space. Henry looked in the case nearest to him and saw an old typewriter underneath a picture of a man he recognized to be Mark Twain. Drury's *was* the museum.

"You found me!" the man said.

"Are you Auggie?" Billy asked.

"August in the flesh!" he said. "Welcome in. What can I do for ya?"

Henry was already beginning to wander the floor. "What is this place?" he asked.

"It's an 'unlicensed recreational space intended for educational purposes,'" August said back, checking their faces for something. Not finding it, he continued: "Turns out you're not supposed to use the 'M-word' with every clientele."

"Why's that?" Billy asked.

"Well, history's become a matter of opinion these days, hasn't it? My business is trying not to let on that I have one."

"Is it a business?" Billy asked.

"Not in the strictest sense. No money to be made, anyway. But there's business and there's business," said August, and he seemed satisfied by the answer. Then he clapped his hands and tried to start again: "What'd you say brings you fellas in?"

"The old park," Billy said this time, and then he looked over at Henry, who was staring at a display of sundries salvaged from a Conestoga wagon.

Henry spoke up. "I set out to visit them. Last year. As many as I could, anyway."

"Well, I'm afraid this is as close as you're gonna get, my friend. Not that there was all that much to see there aboveground before, anyway."

Henry took that in. "You mean the old museum," he said.

"There's that 'M-word.' Yeah, that's the one: it was under the arch. But they caved it in after the crash with dyn-o-mite. Lost…oh my, they lost just about everything down there."

"Where did all this stuff come from?" Billy asked. He was wandering now, too. He walked past a scale model of an old riverboat, fixed in blue resin on a table with miniature trees.

"Well, some of it came from park service *storage*, once they closed up shop; I had a friend there who let a few things slip out. And the rest is my private collection." He moved towards the center of the space and held out his hands. "Was there somethin' in part-ic-ular you had hoped to see?"

"Badges," Henry said, and then he realized that was unhelpful. "From the Junior Ranger programs. I know it's silly—"

"No, not silly. Did you collect them?"

"I do," Henry said. "I do now."

"Common hobby, once upon a time!" August put his hands back in his pockets. "I wish I could help you," he said, and his voice carried a kindness with no obvious home. "But that stuff is all buried now."

"Even if we could get past the wall?" Billy asked.

"Even if. It's a shame, what happened over there. That big old croquet wicket was always a distraction, I thought. What made St. Louis St. Louis was the River, one, and the trailways, two. At least, those were the happier sides of things." He looked at Billy as he said this, and then he quickly looked away. His eyes locked onto something invisible in the distance somewhere beyond the boundaries of the room. "Still, it was a shame to see it get knocked down the way it did. But it was a bigger shame to lose everything else. And the courthouse, too."

"What's wrong with the courthouse?" Henry asked.

"It was the park's, and they left it to rot when they pulled up stakes. You can't hardly stand near it, the mold's so bad now."

Billy had learned how Henry's mind worked, and he tried to head him off at the pass. "No chance there's any badges in there, though?"

"Can't say there is." He was hedging, and they could tell. But he couldn't keep it up: "I'm tellin' you because I checked. Not for the badges exactly, but I went in just after they shut it up, and I've been in a time or two since."

Billy looked around the room. "And found a few more exhibits?"

August smiled, just a bit sheepishly. "Maybe just a few."

"Why do you have this place?" Henry asked. It occurred to him that he loved it; that he could limp around and see everything and read every word. As museums went, it was nothing spectacular. But to him, it felt courageous.

"Truth is, I don't remember," August said. "Once upon a time, I just didn't want to lose things. But the harder work is keeping 'em."

They looked around a bit longer and talked more with August. Soon, Henry's leg began to hurt in ways that were new and deep, and they said their goodbyes. They walked slowly back to the Ranger and before Henry settled onto the bed in the back, he looked again at the stems of the old Arch above the curls of barbed wire there. It had been a gateway once—or at least it claimed to be. A symbol of the opening to the Old West. From where they stood, it was already night in the places beyond it, back towards Illinois, and Ohio in the dark beyond that. A sunset not much different than any other was settling in behind them, and in the morning, they would go that way, too.

Suddenly, Billy chuckled to himself. "Hey, what's the difference between an aquarium and a museum?" he asked.

Henry's eyes were still fixed on the eastern sky. "Time," he guessed–and was proud of himself for his answer. He thought of fossils buried in silt.

"That's probably right, actually," Billy said. He opened the driver's side door. "I was going to say water."

Henry thought about it for a moment. "That's pretty good, too."

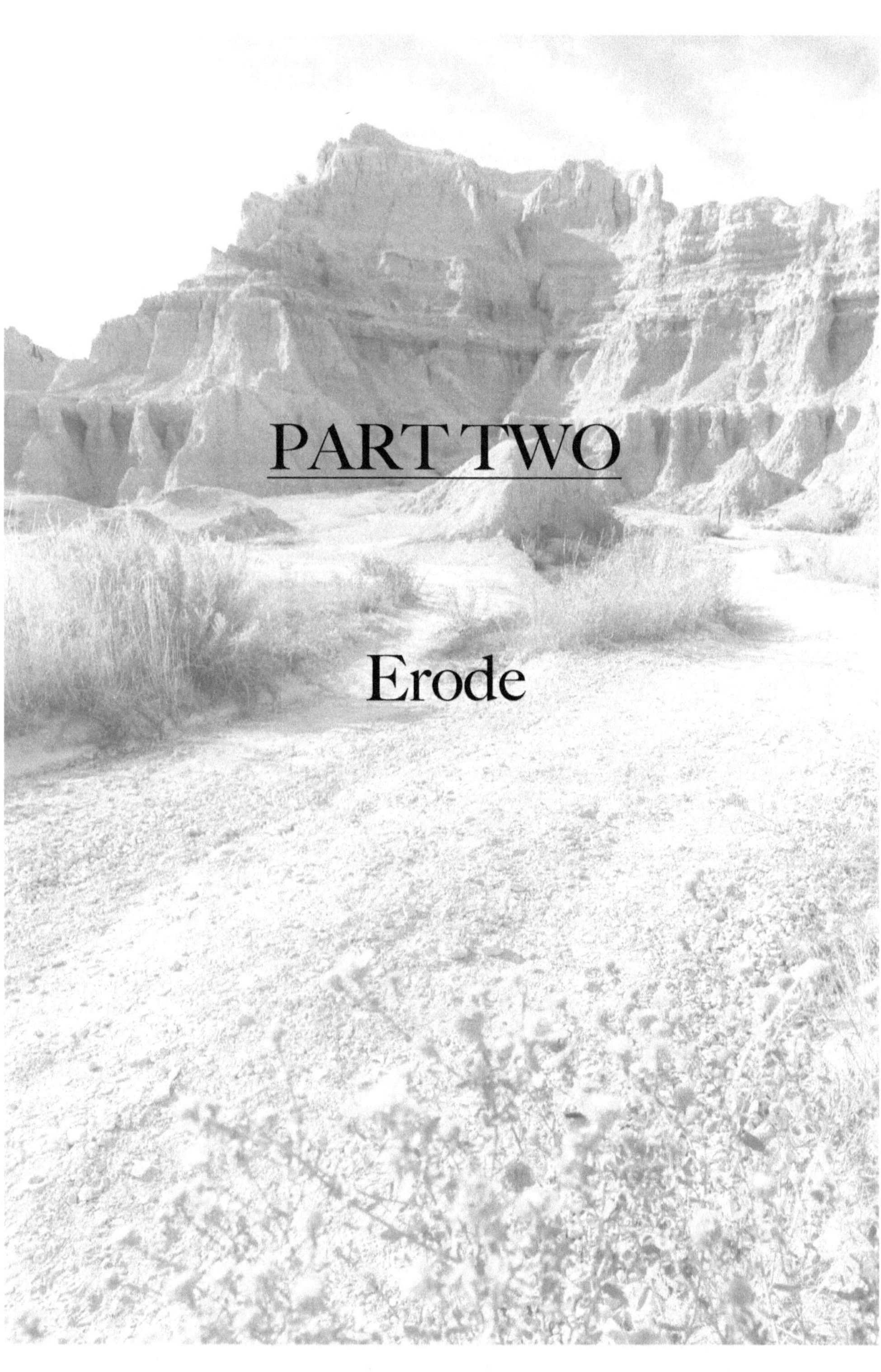

PART TWO

Erode

Great River Road

Henry Henry and Billy Faulkner did not go west the next day. Instead, they took the road north from St. Louis and wound their way along the bank of the Mississippi. The route was marked everywhere by little square signs with an old pilot's wheel on them and the words *Great River Road* written above a picture of a paddle steamer. It seemed seldom used these days, and the dense foliage at both shoulders was not infrequently interrupted by views of wide brown water to their right and modest palisades rising on their left. They passed through small townships with at least a little life left in them, and as the morning stretched on, they both forgot, if only for a few hours, that their world had fallen apart.

But just south of Hannibal, Missouri, the road was entirely washed out and a detour brought them back to the broken present. As they backtracked to find a path which might connect them to the federal highway, a gray-haired and disheveled looking man holding a rifle stepped out from the end of a driveway on the far side of a bend and flagged them down. He was wearing a flannel shirt tucked into work pants with an oversized buckle on the belt. There was also a pistol. Henry was sitting in the passenger seat, and his eyes went wide with sudden fear. "Keep driving!" he said. But Billy slowed calmly to a stop and rolled down his window.

The man kept his rifle pointed at the ground as he walked around the front of the Ranger to talk with them. When he got to Billy, he said, "You're just passin' through." It wasn't a question.

"Yessir," Billy said back to him. His tone was quiet but friendly. "We're just trying to make it to Hannibal. But the road's washed out."

"Hell, I know that," the man said back. "But we're not gonna have trouble here, understand? So get on up there, do what you're doin', and keep on goin'. Long as I don't see you again, we won't have any problems." Henry could see the man clearly now: he was wearing a hat that had become its own sort of uniform over the last decade that said *Take America Back* in frayed white stitching on its dirty red fabric. Once upon a time, his type had been called "Tabbies." It was a moniker that minimized all sorts of insurrectionary foolishness. After the majority of southern states seceded, Tabbies became more common in the flyover places where politicians were more prone to try and take a peaceable course in the hopes that the Great Divide might leave them out of it. People like the man currently eyeballing the two of them felt that was downright cowardly, and the end result was a lot of self-deputizing, grocery hoarding, and homeschooling. Of course, Henry couldn't hear the word and not think of cats.

Billy took a beat, staring straight ahead. "You won't see us again," he said, and then reached down for the window crank, assuming the conversation was over.

But the man flinched when Billy lowered his shoulder, and he started to raise his rifle. "Easy boy," he said, emphasizing the last word.

Billy stopped and then looked the man square in the eyes. He did what he could to keep the venom out of them. "You won't see us again," he repeated. "You don't need to worry."

"Who's worried?" The rifle stayed half-raised. The air between them seemed to thicken somehow, and Henry realized he could see the man's breath steaming in the late-winter air, the clouds appearing before his face and then drifting away. Billy put his hands back at ten and two and looked out the windshield. He stayed quiet. They all took another breath, and then another. The vapor from their nostrils like puffs of cigarette smoke.

Finally, the man seemed satisfied. "I'd better not," he said. "You got another half mile to go, then you're gonna turn past the water tower. You can just about see it already over there above them trees." He stepped back from Billy's door and lowered the rifle again. "You wanna eat in Hannibal, you stay riverside. Then you move right on. Boys."

Billy reached for the crank a second time and did not look at the man again. The window closed, and they started moving. The anger building up in Billy had nowhere to go, and Henry could feel it trapped in the truck there with them. When the Ranger slowed to a stop at the intersection beneath the water tower, Henry picked up the atlas from the dash and checked again to make sure of where they were. Hannibal was just another three or four miles away. He touched the spot with his forefinger, and then the Ranger started moving again.

"Fuck him," Henry said, staring ahead through the windshield. The Ranger picked up speed, and dead trees slid past. "He can go straight to hell."

In Hannibal, on riverside, they found a small and modestly-stocked market on the ground floor of an old depot building. They were in a stretch of storefronts which had once been a tourist trap but were now mostly boarded up and vacant. A wide berm of tall grass protected the town from floods, but it blocked any kind of view of the river at all. The only place that seemed to have been kept up was a two-story lodging house called *Pudd'n'heads* where a row of sparrows were perched on the gutter above the door.

In the market, they stocked up for the days ahead as best they could: more peanut butter, more beef jerky, and a gamble on an expired box of old Cup O'Noodles. They also picked up, of all things, a twelve pack of Coca-Cola. After shopping, they bought lunch at the counter for a song, and then they kept their word to the Tabby and moved on.

The air was crisp and the sky was clear. The noonday shadows of naked tree branches on the road made it feel like they were driving over cracked glass. But somewhere, they had lost track of the pilot wheel signs and they were now cruising towards the gridded straightaways of the real Midwest. By mid-afternoon, the forests had given way to infinite fields where soy, alfalfa, and corn would sprout in the months to come, but now they were tilled and spotted with patches of late-winter snow. The cobalt blue above them was like an ocean, and they sailed across it upside down.

Together, they chose roads that bypassed that strange nose on the state of Iowa but still skirted east of Cedar Rapids. Things were spread out and quiet, but there were enough graffitied billboards and strange flags atop the occasional barns to make them nervous. Neither of them knew local politics well enough to know how things fared here; they'd crossed the border from Missouri without incident, but they'd also done so on what was little more than a dirt road. The fallow land around them made things feel plausibly abandoned. But who could know for sure?

Their solution was to drive, check the radio at least once every hour, and make conversation. Billy told Henry about his siblings, about this odd job and that one in his last decade of wilderness. Henry told Billy about ice fishing trips in Canada with his brothers and father when he was a boy and dreaming, back then, of going to space. He'd fixated on Mars, he said, until one day his high school science teacher told him it would be a one-way trip: there was no fuel there for a ride back home. He'd been terrified, and all his life he'd had a recurring nightmare about a lost colony of geriatric Martian explorers, withering away inside their spacesuits until to dust they returned. In the dream, he could look down and see the skulls inside their helmets. Then he would realize that if he could see them, he must be there, too. With that, he would wake in a cold sweat.

They found the Great River Road again just south of the town of Guttenberg. A detour skirted again to the west on an old mining road and then rejoined the river path under the boarded up windows and doors of a place called the Eagle View Motel and Resort. It was on a relatively expansive, if also now overgrown, head of land. A sign advertised a Lakeview Ballroom somewhere among the terraces of the place, and they both saw it and imagined farmhands of yesteryear dressed in their Sunday bests courting land-owning debutantes while a band played. It all seemed like so many lifetimes ago. And it was.

But the Ranger was at home along the river, winding again atop a modest bluff as the wide brown water of the Mississippi slid past them. They drove through McGregor, and then past the rusted truss bridge that connected Marquette and Prairie du Chien. It was late in the afternoon, and the sun would only give them another hour and change. So, when they saw a sign for an old park service site–Effigy Mounds National Monument–they turned in.

The place seemed long-forgotten, but it was just off the road. They were stopped by a rusted chain holding an old iron gate in place. Billy parked the truck and Henry dug around in the back for a tool that would have eased their adventures in Arkansas considerably: a bright red bolt cutter. They snapped the lock, opened the gate, and drove the Ranger through. Then, they made a show of resetting things by looping the broken chain around the hitch post in case anyone drove by in the night.

On the other side of the gate, there was nowhere really to drive: it was just a modest parking lot, shielded from the highway by a stand of trees, with a visitor center at the far end. They backed into a handicapped space by the door and looked at each other. It was getting cold.

"I'm guessing it's not really a Park," Billy said.

"It's a Monument," Henry said back.

"Are there more of those?"

"A lot more."

The watch Billy wore and kept said 4:30 p.m. "Want to see what there is to see?"

They broke a window with Henry's other tool—his trusty yellow crowbar—and when the glass shattered, Billy felt bad about it. But they made their way inside the old and dim space to look around anyway. Things were much different than the cluttered and moldy storeroom at the base of the tower in Hot Springs: the air was dry and musty, and a thick layer of dust covered every tucked and tidied surface. Things had been put away as if the park might reopen any day, and Henry said this was closer to par for the course. Because nothing like a real Civil War, Part 2 had ever erupted, everyone must have assumed that when the parks closed it would only be a temporary state of affairs. Rangers had still been paid for most of the following year, until funds ran out entirely. And yet, even after states separated (some through formal declaration; others through good, old atrophy), there was hope that local governments might step in to keep the places up. That's what happened at the more famous sites: Fort Sumter in South Carolina, Muir Woods in California, the Alamo in the Great Republic of Texas. But most of the others were left to time and the slow working of the same nature they had once protected. Parking lots filled with weeds; walking paths became game trails. The roofs of buildings collapsed under the weight of winter snow, or were blown off by increasingly common tornadoes. The collapse had come much more quickly than anyone—aside from the old park rangers—had predicted. And America's Great Idea went back to being only that.

Henry limped around the space, looking at pictures and maps on the walls. Billy picked up a folded park brochure from a stack still on the counter and held it up to the fading light coming in through the windows. He started to read aloud:

"The construction of effigy mounds was a regional phenomenon of the Effigy Moundbuilder Culture."

"That's a helpful name," Henry said.

Billy ignored him and read on: " Mounds of earth in the shapes of birds, bear, deer, bison, lynx, turtle, panther or water spirit are the most common… they were built for burial purposes, but sites lacked the trade goods of the preceding Middle Woodland Culture. The sites were also used for ceremonial purposes that are still a mystery." He finished reading and unfolded the map. "Seems like that's where the trails lead to."

"To the burial mounds?"

"That's what it says here."

"In Iowa?"

Billy folded it back up and put it in his pocket. "It wasn't always Iowa."

Henry thought about that. He wondered what a mound shaped like a bear might look like. He wondered how many people might be underneath it. It was getting late, but his belly was full and there was still an hour or so of daylight left. "How far away are they?" he asked.

They walked the overgrown paths up and along a ridgeline to what the park map said was the Little Bear Mound Group. If they hadn't spotted an old sign half-hidden in the unkept underbrush, they would have walked right past it. Even if it had been the middle of the day, they would have struggled to know what they were looking at. The sign faced what seemed like a knobby meadow with young trees beginning to rise up from the knee-high grass. At first glance, it didn't look like a bear, little or otherwise.

But the longer they stood, the more Henry started to detect some purpose to the humps that were visible in the clearing.

"Look there," he said, pointing to one that extended like a finger from the larger berm beyond it. It was no more than a foot or a foot-and-a-half high, but it had a strange symmetry. "What do you think that is?"

"It could be a leg," Billy said, recalibrating his expectations from the park map to fit them within the landscape. "See here?" He pushed away a climbing vine and pointed to the drawing on the placard: there were four distinct protrusions extending down from the south side of the main mound. Henry and Billy matched them to the shapes in front of them.

"What do you know?" Henry said. "There it is."

"Yeah. There it is."

They stood for a moment, looking. Then the cold caught up with them, and their breath steamed in the dusklight.

"There are people there," Billy said, and it was an uneasy thought.

"Still, you think?"

"Where would they go?"

"I wonder how big they used to be," Henry said. "They must wear down over time."

Billy didn't have anything to say to that. He was thinking about burials.

"There are more of these?" Henry asked.

"It says they're all through these hills. Dozens of them. Circles and animals and lines."

"More animals?"

"That's what it says."

"Wow," Henry said.

"Yeah," said Billy. "Wow."

*   *   *

When they got back, they raided the visitor center for what they could. The haul wasn't much: a few park jackets, flashlights, a pair of new boots that were a size too big for either of them, and a thick wool blanket to replace the one Henry had bled on three nights before. To both of their surprise, his leg seemed to be healing well: no fever, no infection, and a manageable amount of pain as long as he kept it tightly wrapped. On that front, they found a full emergency medical kit in the visitor center, too. It was still mounted on a wall in the back office, and after retrieving it, Henry sat on a chair in the main lobby, opened an only slightly expired tube of antibiotic ointment, and re-dressed his wound.

As he worked, Billy opened drawers and cabinets at the ranger counter. He found a stapler and a stamp pad and a box of pre-sharpened pencils. Henry liked listening to him rustling around. In fact, today Henry liked most everything—roadblocks and rednecks excluded, of course. And then the rummaging sounds stopped and Henry realized Billy had squatted all the way down somewhere below the counter. Henry heard his voice:

"You're not going to believe this," he said, only the top of his head visible above the wooden lip.

"What did you find?"

"They've got badges." And then Billy's hand poked up and Henry could see a piece of golden plastic. "Does this kind count?" he asked.

Henry was pulling up his pant leg gingerly, taking care not to bump his fresh bandages. He thought about Billy's question for no more than a second or two.

"It counts," he said. "I think it counts."

By the time they settled back into the Ranger for the night, it was well below freezing. The slightest flurries were dotting the windshield, barely visible as gray specks against the darkness of the sky. They tried the Cup

O'Noodles over the camp stove and ate deli meat they'd purchased from the market wrapped in butcher paper. It was good, and they didn't speak again until Henry was settling in under his new blanket and Billy was back in his own place, stretched out across the diner seat he'd bolted into the front. Their voices carried through the open hatchway between them.

They made small talk about the day behind and the day ahead: a little further up the river, then west into the Great Plains. Billy told Henry about the Indigenous Lands Act, which had been passed through a partial Federal Congress four years earlier. Henry only knew what he'd read in the news then: reservation lands across the country had been formally ceded back to tribal nations as autonomous states, freed finally from the faltering governance of a quickly splitting America. As always, Billy knew, the root was far from altruism. The vast majority of returned territory existed in places no longer interested in being part of one country, and by declaring them independent, the president effectively halved the sizes of many of the Republics before they really began. This, everyone knew, would create new trouble. The Dakotas–into which they were headed–had effectively become a new Sioux nation, Billy had read. But he didn't know much about it. And he didn't know if they would be welcome.

"We're not really welcome here," Henry said.

"We'll see," Billy said to that.

The night grew longer and a thin line of snowflakes formed along the wiper blades and began rising slowly up the windshield.

"I wanted to ask you something, Hank." Billy had been trying out the nickname all day, even though they both knew it wouldn't stick.

"Okay," Henry said.

"What happened to your wife?"

There was a pause from the back. "She died," Henry eventually said. "She got the flu last year. She was living in Indiana with her family then.

We talked when she was sick, a few days before the end. But I didn't see her."

"I'm sorry," Billy said, and then waited. "I meant before, though. What happened to the two of you?"

Henry looked up at the roof of the truck. He tried to find patterns there, and to trace them with his eyes. He thought of Shannon's face the last time he'd seen her; it had been a video call from his computer. Things for her had just begun to turn, but neither of them believed then that it was the end. *I'm sorry,* he'd meant to say to her. *I'm sorry, and I'm afraid. You didn't deserve this, and I didn't know how to stop it.* All of that would have been mostly true. It would also have been honest. But instead, they had just talked about what might happen if he sold their house, about her sister's search for a job, and then her aunt's awful cooking. Shannon had laughed at a joke he made about her meatballs with a rasp Henry had tried hard not to notice. "I don't know," Henry said. "I let her down."

"And she divorced you?"

"No. It didn't happen like that."

"How did it happen?"

How did it happen? He had never practiced these sentences before, and he didn't know if he could form them for his friend now. He looked for words, but all he found were moments that wouldn't make any sense if he described them: a night when he couldn't come home; a night when she wasn't there when he did.

"After Caleb…" Henry said, "before then even, it was so quiet. She felt like what happened was my fault. We couldn't talk about it. We couldn't talk about anything, really. We didn't argue or fight. We were just there." He could remember how she looked at him, and how he had wished for her pity, or her blame, or even her contempt. But there was always just unreachable grief in her face, and every time he saw it, he tried so hard to make his own face something other than a mask. He had realized even then that he wanted her to be able to find him. But, somehow, he had already known she was done searching.

"We just wore down," Henry said. And then he closed his eyes, giving up on the patterns above.

"Did you love her?" Billy asked him. It seemed like a stupid question. But it seemed like the only question.

"I did. I wasn't always like I am now. I don't know; maybe I was. But she was good," he said. "She was good, and she was someone who always knew what to do. When things happened, when she *didn't* know anymore…" And then another moment came to him in the dark. "When I met her, it was raining. I had an umbrella, and we were students at school. I had an umbrella, and it was raining, and she didn't have one. I didn't know her then, except that we had classes together. But she just came in under my umbrella, right there on the sidewalk. She grabbed the handle from me, and then she held it out…" Henry raised his own hand just like so, even though he knew Billy couldn't see him. "She grabbed it like *this*, and then she put it up so we both could stay dry. And the crazy thing was that she knew my name: she said, 'do you mind, Henry?' And I said I didn't mind, because she was beautiful to me, and because I didn't. And we walked to class together, right through the rain. When we got there, she said, 'I'll see you, Henry,' and I said, 'I'll see you, Shannon,' and I knew she was impressed I knew her name. But she also smiled, like she wasn't surprised, either. And when she was walking away, she didn't even turn around, but she said over her shoulder, 'You should ask me out.' I was so dumb. I don't know why she said that. I don't know why…" His eyes were welling up. "She was always the one who knew," he said. *She was,* he thought; *she was.*

"How long were you together?"

"We were together for twenty years."

Billy watched the snow falling gently on the glass, flake after flake after flake. There was an inch now, and he wondered how high it would be when they woke. "How old was your son?" And as he asked it, he heard Henry sniff somewhere behind him.

"He was sixteen."

"Do you know why?"

"Yes."

Billy hesitated to ask the next question. It was so quiet tonight, and so peaceful. He had decided back at the bait shop that he could go wherever this journey took him. But still, he needed to know. "Why?" he asked, and he waited for Henry to answer.

"Because of me."

Snow fell on, and no one spoke.

Voyageurs

This is why.

When Caleb was sixteen, and for once out at a friend's house, Henry read the journal his son kept hidden in his bedroom. But this wasn't his unforgivable offense: Caleb had kept journals faithfully since he was in second grade, and in those early years, when Shannon and Henry had been most worried about him, they would skim through them with some regularity in search of clues and portents. But new boundaries had been set in middle school—for the purpose of cultivating independence; for the sake of avoiding their own embarrassment in reading about Caleb's first crushes—and the snooping came to an end.

The endings hadn't stopped with the journal. Consumed by the busyness of what everyone treated as post-pandemic life, Shannon and Henry paid less and less attention to what their son got into in those years. He spent most of his time in his room—first on a school computer, and then on his phone—and so long as everyone came down for dinner together, each was left to their own. Shannon would worry about him sometimes; Henry would point out his passing grades and general compliance. Their lives would go on: school, work, grocery shopping, sports practices, Shannon showing houses, all of them visiting their surviving grandparents.

But then, when Caleb was in tenth grade, Henry stopped one afternoon in the hallway and opened the door to his son's bedroom. For a long time afterwards, he tried to invent an explanation for why he did this on that particular day. But there was none. He went in, closed the door behind him, and Henry snooped. And then, on the bookmarked page in Caleb's journal, he heard his son's voice explaining how he was going to carry a loaded gun into his pre-calculus class and shoot his teacher, Mr. Kimbrough, in his awful fucking face.

Henry flipped backwards through the pages before the bookmark looking for *why*, but there was no answer to that, either. How could there be? What would have explained it? So he took the journal to his own bedroom and hid it on top of a box in his closet that, he understood later, was the same box in which he kept a loaded handgun his own father had given him when he was eighteen.

That night, he showed Shannon what he had found and they talked and talked about what on earth they could do. They would not call the police because Caleb had not committed a crime, and there was no clear plan or timeline in the journal; it was a matter-of-fact statement written in scratchy pencil by a child. They would not tell the school because it would lead to panic and reprisals for Caleb, all for something he might not have been serious about really trying to do. They would not accuse Caleb, or lock him in his room, or have him committed at a hospital because, for the love of God, he was their *son*. But they had to do *something*.

They realized it was a Friday night, and although it was macabre to think of it this way, they felt they had time. So, Henry said he would talk to him: he would apologize for reading the journal, he would tell him what he found, and he would ask him about whatever it was that was going on. He would be a father. He'd seen how to do it on television a hundred times. Shannon said this to him: *You have to do this, Henry. It's really serious, and you have to.*

I know it is. I will. I will, Henry said to his wife, to his partner and his anchor. It was a promise.

The next day was Saturday, and Caleb had a basketball game. Things felt, in every way, like they were normal. But Shannon and Henry were on edge, looking for more signs and omens; looking for… well, they didn't know what. But there was nothing to find. And Henry let the day pass.

The next morning, on Sunday, Shannon went out early to see a client, and she would be gone most of the day. She left a sticky note on Henry's phone on the nightstand: *Talk to him!* it read. Henry was not offended by this; in fact, he was grateful. He always needed reminders, and this was important to them both. All morning, he rehearsed what he would say and how he would say it: he practiced the tone of his voice, the look on his face. But by the time he went downstairs, Caleb had already made plans to meet a friend for lunch, and he was out the door so quickly they did not speak. After he was gone, panic started to rise in Henry because the day was slipping away, and because he had made a promise. He stayed home and did little other than imagine the conversation, and each time he went over it, it went worse and worse. It was the suddenness, he knew, that would shut Caleb down: the mix of embarrassment and fear that would come the instant the fact that *Henry had seen* was revealed to him. Henry knew this would happen because he knew his son: if he felt accused, he would lock himself away, grow defensive, put up walls. Henry wished there was a way to help him brace for the conversation, so he could see his dad as someone who wanted to help instead of seeing him as an accuser. But how?

And so here's what Henry did that could not be forgiven. He took the journal from on top of the box in his closet and laid it out on his son's bed. He opened it to the page about Mr. Kimbrough. And he left it there for Caleb to find.

No matter how hard he tried in the days and months to come, he could not make anyone understand what he thought would happen. In his mind, Caleb would find it, he would realize Shannon and Henry had seen, and instead of feeling angry, instead of feeling defensive, he would feel grateful. Henry would wait an hour, and then go up to his son's room. Caleb would be sitting there on the edge of his bed, the journal in his hands. His eyes would be red, but the tears would have stopped. Henry would sit down next to him and hold him in his arms, as he had done years and years before. He would have told him he understood what he was feeling. He would have listened to Caleb explain how hard things had been for him, that he didn't really mean it, that it was a stupid thing to have written, or even to have thought. And his father would have said it was okay to feel scary things, but that he could always share them with him, and with his mother. That he wasn't as alone as he felt he was. That they loved him, and that he was safe. They would rip the pages out of the journal and Henry would say, *this isn't who you are*, and Caleb would say, *I know*, and Henry would ask, *what do you want to do with them?* and Caleb would say, *let's burn them*, and they would go downstairs together and put them in the fireplace and turn the fireplace on and watch them disappear, watch them turn to nothing, and Henry would never stop hugging his son and his son would be okay and the future would be a safe place for him and the world would be whole forever and forever.

But that is not what happened. Caleb came home, he went to his room, and he shut the door. Henry waited in the kitchen downstairs. He looked at the clock on the microwave: it was 2:17 in the afternoon. He did not know it then, but later, he worked out the math from the police report. He had exactly 48 minutes.

He thought about checking emails but decided against it. He would be present in this moment. He checked the clock again and it was 2:32. He folded his hands on the table. There were 33 minutes left.

He expected Shannon to be home for dinner by 5, and he remembered thinking that, if everything went how he planned for it to go, they could go out to eat. They could go somewhere Caleb loved—which meant they would get Thai food. Henry didn't like it, but that didn't matter. It was 2:48 now, and he thought about going up the stairs, but he did not. 17 minutes.

At 3:03, he decided he was ready. He rehearsed everything one last time: his voice, his words, whether he would sit on Caleb's left or Caleb's right. He stood up from the chair.

But it was already too late. And as he put his first foot on the stair, the world ended.

Billy and Henry woke to unexpected darkness: the storm had picked up during the night and buried the Roving Ranger in more than a foot of snow. Billy pushed his way out of the passenger door and high-stepped backwards through a drift to look at things. The truck was a white mound jostling slightly as Henry started to move around inside of it. Billy went to the back door and swung it open.

"Merry Christmas," he said. It was March 5.

"Well, Jesus Christ," Henry said, looking past his friend to the transformed landscape behind him. Everything was blanketed. Tree branches drooped under the weight. "Did you see a shovel inside?"

"There has to be one," Billy said. His feet were freezing in the dress shoes he always wore. "I think I'll try out those boots, too."

There was, of course, a shovel, and they spent the next hour digging out. Things weren't as dire as they seemed at first, and although the temperature was barely above freezing, the late-morning sun was already turning the snow in the parking lot to mush. They were on their way again just before noon.

* * *

They decided against any and all conventional wisdom (as well as the route Henry had outlined in his road atlas) to go north. There was a national park at the top of Minnesota called Voyageurs, and that became their target. It took two days for them to get there. The roads were sludgy but passable, and there was no one out in the snow. Everywhere, they saw ribbons of smoke rising from chimneys, but the good people of Minnesota seemed well and hunkered down until the spring thaw. There were no billboards, no roadblocks, no Tabbies keeping watch in their driveways; just endless fields of white under empty blue skies.

They traveled through Sauk Centre and Motley and Chamberlain and Bemidji. They moved east through Tenstrike and Blackduck and Northome, and Billy joked that even the words were so cold they huddled together. They wound their way through alley streets in Littlefork and, late on the second afternoon, forged fresh tire tracks through old snow in front of the Kabetogama Visitor Center. There was no gate. The front door wasn't even locked.

Inside, things were as they often were: dusty and put away. There was nothing to loot, but the cardboard box of junior ranger badges was sitting in the expected place under the counter. Henry collected his treasure and they walked out behind the center to look out over the park itself.

According to the brochure, Voyageurs was mostly water. It protected a series of lakes, islands, and portage paths once used by Native peoples, and then later by French settlers, to connect the fur trade of the northwest to the villages and markets of the east. But right now, it was frozen over in winter ice and stretched out from the bluffs Henry and Billy were standing on in a perfect sheet of snow, broken up only by little pine-topped islands scattered at picturesque intervals. As the sky turned orange to the west, they marveled at all of it. They were quiet together. They breathed slow. It was a good day.

Later, real cold began to set in, and they decided to break into a small cabin at the edge of the park property that had once been part of a summer resort. It looked long-abandoned, but there was still dry wood in a storebox next to the fireplace. They lit it and warmed themselves as the dark came on. There was a half-empty bottle of gin in a pantry, along with some tins of meat and beans. After two days of peanut butter sandwiches, it was all a feast. They laughed into the night and then slept soundly on the floor.

The next day, they retraced their steps to the southwest and continued on towards Fergus Falls and the open spaces beyond. They stayed on still-quiet farm roads, traveling slowly but steadily. They crossed the Bois de Sioux River at Mud Lake and entered into South Dakota. On their atlas, they saw the old I-90 running parallel to the newer interstate and west towards the Black Hills. It seemed like the safest way to go. They could pick it up in the town of Mitchell, for which there was no inset map in the atlas, nor any superlative save one: it was home to "The World's Only Corn Palace."

The World's Only Corn Palace

itchell, South Dakota was a wasteland. Henry and Billy entered the town from the north on state highway 37, and every building they passed was boarded up or burned down. The remains of strip malls sat far back from the road, their enormous parking lots dotted with ruined cars and abandoned shopping carts. The infinitely flat horizon was broken up only by the totems of old fast food restaurants, their plastic signs long since shattered and chains identifiable now only by the shapes of their frames: here the empty "M" of an old McDonalds; there the archway of what could have been a Taco Bell. Further into town, there were frayed and misshapen wreaths still fastened to the street lamps, possibly from the previous Christmas, but more than likely from the one before.

"What happened here?" Henry asked Billy, who was craning his neck from behind the steering wheel to look around them as the Ranger crept along.

"I don't know," he said, because it was the only answer he had.

It didn't take long for them to spot the Corn Palace. It was the only building more than a story tall, and its strange, onion-shaped domes were visible from blocks away. There were at least two dozen flag poles along the roof, most of them still flying wind-shredded rags of indecipherable origin or allegiance. As they moved closer, they found they couldn't take their eyes off the place: every side and surface was decorated in rotting corn husks and cobs of various colors, patterned into murals of prairie life: a farmer behind a plow, a woman churning butter, a brown corn-bison atop a field of gray corn-grass under a gold corn-sky. Around each panel, even more dried and bird-pecked ears and leaves were arrayed in stripes and shapes of decorative patterns. It was a marvel. It was also insane.

So transfixed were Billy and Henry that they stopped the Ranger in the middle of the street to gawk, and it was a long moment before they turned to look at the other side of the street, where another building, nearly as bizarre, lay in the Palace's early morning shadow. It was a castle, built of real stone, with a sign over the lowered portcullis reading *Valtiroty Bible Land Park*. What *was* this place?

"I want to see inside," Henry said.

"Which one?"

"Both."

Billy looked to his left, then back to his right. "Let's start with 'The World's *Only* Corn Palace.'" He was reading from the darkened neon sign over the entrance. "I prefer my crazy secular."

"Yeah," Henry said. "Amen."

Billy checked his mirrors, but nothing had changed: there wasn't so much as a stray dog on the streets. He put the Ranger in park and they left it in the middle of Main.

The front doors of the Corn Palace had an old and rusted chain through the handles, but it was only looped over itself. Billy shook it, and the links clattered to the ground. The doors swung open, and the two of them moved inside. The truth was that they weren't prepared for what they found. Who could be? The doors opened onto a concourse with a ticket office and reception desk. An interior set of glass panels and doors were all shattered, but strange and narrow paths had been cleared through the littered shards of debris. There were tracks of dirt, and even small footprints, visible in them. Beyond this, wide staircases led up to a darkened space above. Henry looked nervously at the ground as they wound their way through.

The staircases led to, of all things, a wide balcony of stadium seats ten rows deep. Although the light from the front doors was dim, they realized they were in what had once been some sort of sports arena. The metal struts of raised basketball goals along the ceiling shone faintly in the near-black space, and as their eyes adjusted, they could make out an enormous scoreboard and speaker array suspended from the ceiling. Underneath it, on the old court floor, they could see the toppled and destroyed racks of what must have once been gift shop displays. It looked at first glance like a bomb had gone off: there were boxes and clothes scattered everywhere. But they also saw broken glass gleaming in a half dozen neatly-broomed piles.

They stared down at the ruins, and suddenly, the silence was broken by a scurrying sound off to their left. Then the clatter of something perhaps falling from a shelf somewhere along the farthest wall. The hair went up on their necks.

"Rats?" Henry asked in a whisper. His eyes were like ping pong balls in his skull.

"Or stray dogs, maybe."

"I didn't see any dogs."

"Maybe rats, then."

Henry thought for a moment, and he tried to smother his fear. "There might be food down there, then."

"I was thinking that, too." Billy paused. "Do you want to go?"

"I think so."

They descended slowly and carefully on the stadium steps and then through a gap in the railing to the arena floor. They could see more and more, even though the bleachers were now between them and the front door. Billy looked up and saw dirt-covered skylights in the ceiling above letting in faint light. He looked around the edges of the arena, and saw there were more corn murals here, too. But even in the gloom, he could see that they were patchy and changed somehow; he looked closer and realized they'd been picked over. Something had eaten them right off the walls.

"Billy," Henry said, pulling at his sleeve. "Look."

Henry pointed between a row of standing racks, and there, at center court, was a small table. It must have been from a cafe in some lost nook of the gift shop. It was round with a lacquered top and supported at waist-height by a single spoke and weighted base. On top of the table were three lit candles, and beside the candles was a paper bag with an actual McDonalds logo on the side.

"Jesus," Billy said. There was no mistaking its intention.

"Is it a trap?" Henry asked.

"It's bait."

"For what?"

Billy looked around in the darkness.

What could they do but move closer? The pair inched towards the table, which was twenty feet away at first, and then ten. The candles were each burned down nearly to the base, but whether because they'd been lit for a while, or because they'd been lit before, was unknowable. Henry and Billy squinted their eyes in every direction and swept their heads back and forth, but they saw nothing. They listened for any sound of movement and heard only silence. The bag on the table–just a few feet away now–bulged at the bottom: there was definitely something inside it. Neither of them spoke.

And then they were there. Henry and Billy looked at each other, their faces orange in the glow from the candles, and Billy gave the faintest nod. With that, Henry reached towards the table. He picked up the bag, handling it like a bomb, and pulled it close to him. He slowly unrolled the hand-wrapped end and looked inside. As he did, Billy realized he couldn't smell anything.

"It's candy," Henry said, reaching in. "It's full of candy." He pulled out a handful of Dum-Dum suckers. "What… ?"

And then chaos. Somewhere much too close, a voice shouted *"NOW!"* and something dropped down from the ceiling. Billy sensed the movement and flinched backwards to avoid it. As he did, he looked up and saw ropes. They glanced off his shoulder but caught Henry in an odd tangle. Billy took another two steps back and stumbled into an overturned shelf. He realized he was falling to the ground, but he righted himself and kept backing away, kept trying to get distance, so he might find somewhere to hide. He realized the voice from before was still screaming: *"Now! Now! Now! Now!"*

Something hard hit him in the head. It hit him again, and then again. Pain exploded over his ear, but he realized he was not passing out, he was not unconscious. He flailed his arms around him and caught hold of something long and solid as it was in mid-swing; he clenched his hand around it, and yanked with all his strength. Whatever was on the other end resisted at first, but it gave way, and Billy had it now. He clenched his fist and looked around, still searching for the far side of the court floor. His new boots squeaked on the hardwood. What did he have? He could see no one. And then finally, his back slammed into a wall. He tried to find Henry in the middle of the Corn Palace.

Now he could see everything: his companion was standing absolutely still beside the table that had held the McDonalds bag, illuminated there in the candlelight with the sticks of suckers still poking from between his fingers. Something was draped over him, and Billy realized he'd been caught underneath what must have been the net from an old soccer goal: its holes were enormous—much too big to hold anyone—and Henry's head actually poked up through it as if he were wearing the net as a costume. For a moment, Billy was furious: *why wasn't he running?* And then he saw the small and blurry shapes surrounding him, poking him again and again with Billy knew not what. *Monkeys?* he thought reflexively. His mind was still trying to make any sense of the dark limbs, wild hair, the stooped and gangly figures. And then he understood: *Not monkeys,* he almost said aloud; *children.*

Suddenly, one of the figures leaped up on top of an overturned store display. Something large and frayed ringed its neck like a lion's mane, and it held a wooden pole high in the air that was gnarled at one end like a wizard's staff. *"The other one!"* it shouted; *"Get the other one!"* It was the same voice as before.

The other shapes kept jumping and chittering for a moment, but as they registered the command, they began to disperse and spread out through the darkness in the room. Billy saw none close, but he also had no cover: he was simply standing at the edge of a basketball court where anyone could see him. And then, Henry did.

"Billy?" he said, looking right in his direction. The child on the gift rack turned and looked, too. "Billy, run! Billy, get out of here!"

"You dumb fuck!" Billy yelled back. He finally glanced down at what was in his hand. It was a youth-sized aluminum baseball bat, and he moved his grip down to the handle.

He heard the imps before he saw them: four—no, five—children, shirtless and covered in splotches of he didn't know what, wielding sharpened sticks and clubs. One even held a full-sized pitchfork—although he struggled with the weight.

Get him! It shouted.

You get him!

Eat him!

He's got Skull's bat!

So what?

Get him!

We're gonna eat you!!

Somebody grab it!

Get him!

Billy put his second hand on the handle and held the bat out in front of him. The kids had formed a semi-circle, backing him again into the wall. "Let him go!" he shouted. "Let him go!"

They're together!

We know that, idiot!

There are four of us!

He looks delicious!

He won't hit kids—

"The fuck I won't!" Billy yelled back at them. They were inching closer. He waved the bat in a wide arc. He risked a glance up at the leader, who was still standing above Henry and watching things unfold. He could see now he was a boy, too; maybe a young teenager.

Fuckin' poke him, W!

I'm trying!

You're not!

Yumyumyumyumyum

You hit him!

W, fuckin' do it!

The kid with the pitchfork jabbed hard at Billy, and if he had connected, Billy would have been pinned to a wall of rotting corn cobs.

But it was too heavy, and he missed to the side. Billy used his leg to kick the handle away, and as the kid lurched forward, he swung hard and connected the bat with his jaw. The sound echoed in the space and the kid crumpled to the floor. Everyone froze. The sound of what might have been teeth skittered across the court. The kid he'd hit curled into a ball, holding his mouth and beginning now to wail.

At this new sound, the more cautious of the children ran away. The one who had yet to speak stepped back and just stood, watching the others. And then, the one who kept talking about eating him jumped at Billy and grabbed hold of his neck. *"I'll kill you!"* he screamed; *"I'll gobble you up!"*

The bat fell to the ground and Billy spun, the kid grabbing him and clinging to him like an animal. He smashed himself into the wall, trying to knock the boy loose, but the child held on and bit hard into Billy's shoulder. His teeth broke skin even through Billy's shirt, and Billy felt the warmth of his own blood.

"What the fuck?" Billy said. "What the fuck?!" He rammed into the wall again, and then again. Finally, the boy was knocked loose and Billy kicked at him once, then twice. The child moved away, crouching on all fours. "Stay back!" Billy yelled at him, "Stay back, you crazy little shit!"

The boy had blood in his mouth, but whether it was Billy's or his own, he didn't know. *"I'm going to eat you! I'm going to eat you!"* he said, *"You're mine!"* But he didn't stand back up.

Something jabbed into Billy's back. He turned and saw a stick in the hands of the smallest of the children. There was malice in his eyes, but Billy could feel it hadn't done any real damage; it hadn't even gone through his shirt. But he grabbed the stick right out of the boy's hands and raised it over his head. "AAAAHHH!" he yelled at him. He turned in a circle, trying to locate each one of his tiny attackers. Both his hands were in the air. "AAAAAHHHHHH!!" he yelled again.

The biggest of them had picked up the boy with the broken mouth and was now walking him back to the middle of the room where two of the remaining three were already standing. The smallest boy skittered away. The only straggler was the young cannibal, who glared at Billy from where he still crouched on the floor.

"You can't leave, you bastard!" the leader of the pack said from across the room. "Give up! We have your friend!"

"I know that!" Billy said. He spotted the baseball bat where he had dropped it before and traded his stick for it. "Tell them to back off!"

"*Say you give up!*"

"Back off!"

"We're going to get you!"

"Then do it!"

"We will! You're ours!"

There were two more children now, even smaller than the others, who had emerged on each of Billy's flanks. But they were unarmed, and when Billy raised the bat at them, they scampered back. Billy swung hard at a rotating rack of audiobooks and sent the cases spinning across the floor. "I said call them off!"

"I will!" the leader said, but it didn't matter: his minions were shaken, and the fight was already over. The boy sensed it, and he looked up towards the ceiling. "Blood Angel!" he shouted.

Billy heard a breaker switch and the room was suddenly filled with light. He squinted against it. There were twice as many kids as he had thought at first—at least twenty, and maybe twenty five. They were much younger than he expected, too; some no more than five or six, and none older than their mid-teens. They were filthy and covered in what Billy thought at first were rags, but then realized they were actually costumes: the kinds of tunics street urchins would wear in an old movie. Most of the children carried some kind of weapon or another—broken mop handles, hockey sticks, and even a few leather pouch slings. They were already gathering around the leader in the center, circling their king and his captive.

"Let him go!" Billy shouted again. "Let him go or I'll whoop every last one of you!"

You won't do shit!

Jump on him!

Get him with a rock, Bullseye!

Eat his friend!

Make him watch!

Kill him!

The leader pounded his staff down on the rack. "*Enough!*" he shouted. The crowd quieted down. "What do you think you're going to do?" He was talking to Billy now.

"I want him!" He pointed the bat at Henry.

"Tough titty! He's ours now."

"You're not going to eat him!"

This produced a round of giggles from the hidden places behind the racks.

"You'll see," the leader said. "Unless you get out of here. Go on and get. He stays with us."

"The hell he does!"

"*You shut up!* He stays, and we're going to eat him!"

Tell him, Omega!

Get them both!

Kill him now!

"Nobody's eating anybody!" Billy yelled into the room.

"You wish," the boy who must be Omega said.

Billy's mind was racing. Everything was absurd, and he couldn't believe his next words even as he said them: "We can make a deal!" More giggling came from children he could not see.

No deals!

Don't, Omega!

They're both ours!

The staff pounded again. "What kind of deal?"

"We can talk about it! Get everybody where I can see them, and then we'll talk!"

The leader mulled this over. Billy realized the boy's mane was made of dried cornhusks woven together in a kind of necklace. His face was painted, as were the faces of the other children. Over his tunic, he wore a belt of dangling bones. Even from this distance, Billy thought they were too small to be human. He thought, *they must be.*

Omega spoke: "Okay, interloper. Let's hear it." Then he raised his staff again in the air: "Take the prisoner to the Temple!" he shouted.

To the Temple!

To the Temple!

Kill them there!

"What's the Temple?!"

"Take the prisoner to the Temple!" the lead boy repeated. There was movement everywhere, and the children at center court began leading Henry, still tangled helplessly in his net, towards the far side of the arena. To Billy's sides, children streamed out from their hiding places, and even in the catwalks above, he heard footsteps.

And then the floor of the Corn Palace was empty. He heard the bang of double doors on the far side of the room, followed by silence. His breathing was heavy. He looked at his shoulder and saw a rose of blood from the cannibal's bite forming on his shirt. He adjusted his grip on the bat handle. And then he followed them.

* * *

The emergency exit the children used led into a wide fluorescent hallway with locker rooms on one side and a water fountain on the other. Dozens of metal buckets were piled and scattered beneath it, and as Billy approached them, he saw names scrawled in Sharpie across the fronts: Blood Angel, Scar, W, DeathKing, Skull, Princess Emily, Wulf, Small Paul. Most were decorated with drawings of bones and knives. One depicted a cat underneath a black rainbow. At the far end of the hall, and somehow surpassing all the strangeness he had seen so far, there was a plaster Tyrannosaurus Rex with a saddle and a human figure on its back. It was eight feet tall. There was a bit between its blunt, sculpted teeth and real leather reins looped through the mannequin hands of its rider. The rider wore a cowboy hat, and nothing else.

He's coming!

The voices came from another set of double doors next to the Tyrannosaurus.

Sssshhhhhhh!!

SSSSHHHHHH!!

He moved towards it. He knew this was the Temple, and he put his hands on the push bar and went in.

It must have been a press room, once upon a time. The space was at least a dozen feet wide and twice that in depth. On the far end was a riser with spotlights aimed at a place where a podium or table would have been. But instead of those things, there was now a golden box under the lights with two angelic figures facing each other behind it. Billy knew it was the Ark of the Covenant.

The boy the children called Omega was seated in front of the Ark on the lip of the stage. His staff was in his hand, and he grinned wickedly at Billy as he entered the room. Henry, still trapped, was standing beside him, being guarded by a boy who had what looked like an actual spear. The other kids lined the walls, sitting on boxes and crates and benches that had been dragged across the floor. They were whispering back and forth to each other in the darkness.

"You came," the leader said. "And so: you wish to seek a deal."

"That's what I said."

The child stood, his thin upper body now in the bank of the lights. "Your kind are forbidden in the Temple," he said, and for the first time, Billy realized that underneath the dirt and grime, all of the children were White.

"You'd better mean adults," he said.

"There are no more adults."

"There are two."

"You aren't adults. You are Interlopers." the boy said, pointing his staff. "Not people of the Palace. Outsiders who don't belong."

"'Interlopers' is a big word for middle school."

"There is no more school!" he shouted, and a few children cheered. Omega was obviously satisfied by this, and he kept up the drama: "No school! No grown-ups! There is only us!" The children were riling. "And we… are… *the Corn Kids!*" At the sound of their name, the room erupted in whoops and hollers. Children waved their weapons in the air and chanted: *Corn! Kids! Corn! Kids! Corn! Kids!*

"Are you fucking serious?" Billy asked.

"Are *you* serious, Interloper?" the boy asked, the room immediately falling silent. "Mock us, and you won't leave here alive."

Billy tried to let the ridiculousness of everything roll off him. He had taken enough bait today. "And what are you, then? The chief?" he asked.

"They call me Omega, because I'm the First Kid," he said proudly. "And this"–he waved the stick around him–"is our Kingdom. We live here. And we protect the Child."

"Omega means last," Billy said. "You're the last kid."

"*Omega means what we say it means!*" the boy yelled, and there were more cheers.

You're dead, Interloper!

Somebody get him!

We eat your kind!

It was the cannibal kid again, and Billy let the Greek go. "What's he keep talking about?" he asked, pointing at the one with Billy's blood on his mouth.

"He's talking about what happens to adults who interfere with our affairs."

We eat them!

We do!

No one escapes!

Yumyumyumyumyum!

"You don't eat people," Billy said. "That's bullshit."

Yes we do!

You don't know!

Shut up, outsider!

"We do," Omega said, "when they deserve it."

"You've never eaten anybody."

We have!

"You don't know what we eat!" cried their chief.

"You eat corn," Billy said back. "It's in your name."

"I said…*you don't know!*"

You're talking too much, Omega!

Shut him up!

Omega planted his staff once again on the riser and composed himself. Whatever else he was, he was a natural actor on the apocalyptic stage. "What we do isn't your business, Interloper," he said. "Right now you want your friend back, and we have him. So you will need to trade if you wish to live."

Billy's hands hurt from gripping the bat. He lowered it, but he did not put it down. "Okay. Okay. What is it you want?"

Omega was ready for this question. "Interloper, we demand… your ice cream truck."

Yeah! We want it!

And your flesh!

Give it to us!

"There's no ice cream," Billy said.

I told you!

Shut up, Paul!

"We don't care," Omega said. "We demand it anyways."

"You can't drive it."

"We can."

"You can't. And it's not an ice cream truck. Where would you go in it?"

"That's not your business."

"No deal," Billy said. "I'm not giving you the truck. If you want us to go, how could we leave? Try again."

There was more murmuring from the children, and Billy could sense their collective disappointment. They had been watching the Ranger from the start. Omega's eyes darted left, then right, as he scrambled to keep control. "Fine," he eventually said, "You can keep your truck. But you must promise never to come back here—"

"Done."

"—and you still must trade."

Billy was growing frustrated. "What, then? Do you want a mattress?"

"We don't sleep."

"Then what?"

Omega grinned again. "We want your weapons," he said. "We want your gun."

And then it was Henry who spoke. His voice was almost a whisper. "We don't have any guns," he said.

Omega stared only at Billy. He pointed his staff. "That's a lie. He does. Skull saw it when you came here: he keeps it on his ankle." This brought the children to a real commotion; the gun was news to most of them. It was also news to Henry. The Corn Kids whispered to each other, and Billy caught a skinny hand reaching out towards his foot. He kicked at it, shooing the boy away.

"I can't give you that," he said, and Henry's eyes locked onto his. There was hurt and confusion in them.

"Give it to us," Omega said. "Give it to us, and we'll give you back your friend. That will be the deal."

"Try again," Billy said.

"That's the deal," Omega repeated.

Billy thought. "You're full of shit," he said. "You can't stop me; I can leave right now."

"No, you can't."

We'll eat him!

Ssshhh!!

Billy ignored them. He spoke only to Omega. "There are no bullets in it."

"But you have some in that truck, I bet."

"I don't."

"Billy," Henry said. "Billy, you can't give them a gun—"

"It's okay, Hank."

"Billy—"

Omega poked Henry with his staff. "You shut up! You: give us the gun."

Billy realized he heard crying somewhere in the room. He risked a glance and saw the kid he had hit with the bat earlier in a corner. His mouth was covered in blood, and an older girl was soothing him. "What about medicine? Bandages?" he said. "We have those. That kid looks really hurt."

"We want the gun. He will be fine."

"I don't know. I hit him pretty hard."

"He'll be fine."

Billy was searching for any other option. He didn't want to do this. "What about a doctor? We could take him with us and take him to a doctor."

"I told you. There are no adults."

"*Why?*"

"Because they left."

"*What?*"

"They left us here. Some were sick. Some left. It doesn't matter, because *we don't need them*. Give us the gun."

"Billy—"

"What are you going to do with it?"

"What do you care?"

Billy pointed at Henry. "I care because I don't want you shooting the next person who tries to grab a hamburger!"

Omega considered this. Then he repeated himself, slowly: "What… do you… care? Maybe there won't be a next person. Give us the gun. And we'll give you your friend."

Billy didn't know what else to do. He couldn't leave Henry here. He couldn't fight thirty kids. So he reached down and lifted up his pants leg. There was a small ankle holster there above the top of his new, oversized boots. In it was a snub-nosed .38 revolver. He took it out and checked the cylinders to make absolutely sure they were empty. "Okay," he said. He walked forward towards the stage. He set the gun down on the lip. "Now let him go."

Omega looked at his prize and the corners of his mouth curled up again in that strange grin. "Okay," he said.

Two other boys—closer to Omega's age and both a head taller than the others—emerged from the pack and started untangling Henry from the soccer net. Omega came forward, and Billy could see that his hair was shaggy and unkempt. He could see the beginnings of a mustache on his upper lip. Omega couldn't have been more than thirteen or fourteen years old. Billy also saw that his staff was made of hard plastic, and there was a sticker at the middle with the word *Valtiroty* printed on it: it was a prop from the Bible park. He looked around the room and realized the Ark, the angels, the costumes, and even the Tyrannosaurus were all props, all looted from the building next door. But even so, the insanity here was real enough. And he had just given a child a gun.

Omega was looking at the revolver now, not quite pointing it in his own face. "There are no bullets in it," he said.

"That's what I told you," Billy said. "I don't have any bullets."

"Lotta good it was doing you then."

"Lotta good it did *you.*"

Omega ignored the remark—or didn't understand what Billy meant by it—and tucked the gun into his belt of bones. The bones were identifiable now to Billy: chickens, pigs. They were real, too. "It doesn't matter anyways," Omega said. "We'll find some. You wait."

Henry was free, and he limped down from the dais. His leg hurt. He was rubbing a wound on his shoulder where there was some blood on his shirt. "Billy," he said, "Billy, you can't give that to them."

"It won't work," Billy said. "They won't be able to use it."

"We will," Omega said.

"They will," Henry agreed. "They'll find bullets. Billy, there's a baby in there—" He pointed to the golden box behind him. "There's a baby…"

"What?"

"It's not a baby," said Omega. "It's *the Child.*"

"*Jesus* is in there, Billy."

"What?"

It's baby Jesus!

We eat him!

"Be quiet, YumYum." Their leader looked at Billy, and his blue eyes were the color of the sky before a storm. "We *keep* him," he said. "His mother watches him for us. He's the only one who gets a mother."

Billy turned to Henry. "There's a baby there?"

Although he was still confused, Henry realized what Billy was thinking— what he was afraid of. "It's not a real baby…" he said, "But Billy… Billy, who would do this?"

"We took him back," Omega said. Billy thought of the Bible park. "*That's* our school now. We know who God is." Omega stared now at Henry. "'Who would do' what?" he asked him. "We do everything we want. We build. We keep. We fight. We eat. Who would do *what?*"

Henry found courage somewhere deep in himself, and his courage was his pity. "I don't think you're okay, Omega," he said. "I don't think any of this is okay."

"We don't care what you think." Omega pressed the barrel of the empty gun to Henry's chest. "It's time to go, Interlopers."

Billy reached for Henry's arm and held him by the wrist. He felt his pulse; he felt his trembling. "Come on, Hank."

"Billy…"

"It's okay."

"It's *not* okay!" Henry said.

"I know it isn't," Billy said. He looked again around the room. He looked at these feral children, and their strange Bible things, and their leader in his lion's mane necklace. "We're going," he said. Then, with his free hand, he tightened his grip on the baseball bat one more time and lifted it up. "Nobody moves. We're going."

As they backed towards the door, Omega pointed his new pistol at the ceiling and yelled so loud it was deafening: "*Corn Kids! Corn Kids! Corn Kids!*" The others took up the chant, and as Billy reached behind him for the door handle, Omega took one last parting shot: "*You are banished from this Kingdom!*" he cried, and all the others cheered. Except, of course, the boy whose mouth was broken, and who was still whimpering wetly as his friend stroked her hand through his dirty hair.

Billy's confusion, his shame, and his fear suddenly gave way to a burst of fiery anger. As he stood in the doorway, he pointed the bat back at Omega and yelled at him: "*That's a dumb name! That sounds dumb! You're all dumb!*" He had no control left. "*You should all go home! You...you dummies!*" Omega looked at him with hate in his eyes. Then, he held his free hand out and raised his middle finger. The other kids followed, all of them shooting Billy and Henry the bird. Some of them blew raspberries.

"*Banished!*" Omega shouted, and the cannibal cackled madly at them: *Hahahahahahaha!*

Then set to licking his bloody lips.

The children didn't follow, but the two grown ups could hear them talking and shouting from the hallway. They turned away from the Tyrannosaurus and started to leave.

"Are you okay?" Billy asked Henry.

"I'm not hurt. Are *you* okay?"

"I'm fine. Keep moving. Keep moving."

They made their way back into the arena, then through the haphazard rows of shelves, and up the bleacher steps to the concourse. It was strange to see the daylight again, beaming in through the broken windows. Billy realized they couldn't have been gone for more than a half hour, and the Roving Ranger was in the middle of Main Street where they'd left it. While they were inside, one of the Corn Kids must have slipped out to investigate and had scratched the word *Inderlooprs!!* on the paneled side with a rock.

"What the fuck?" Billy said when he saw it.

"That's the second time you saved me," said Henry. He was coming back to himself.

"Don't mention it." Billy was in a hurry to get moving, but he waited to make sure Henry could get around to the passenger side, open the door, and climb in. Once that was done, he took his own seat behind the wheel.

"I didn't know you had a gun," Henry said.

"It was never loaded."

"Still."

Billy finally exhaled. "Yeah."

"What are they going to do with it?"

Billy didn't want to think about it. "I don't know," he said. But the truth was that he did. They both did.

Henry still hadn't buckled his seatbelt. "Do you think that's true? About their parents?"

"That they ate them?"

"No. That they left them."

"It's possible. A lot of people got sick. It's not a big town here. Maybe people forgot."

Henry thought about that. Billy expected him to ask about how that could happen: about how parents could leave their children. But Henry was quiet. He pulled at his shoulder strap and fastened it, and as he did, Billy saw the blood again.

"What happened there?" He pointed.

"Oh," Henry said. "One of them stabbed me with a fork."

"With a *fork*?"

"Yeah."

"Like you were food?"

"Yeah."

"Goddamn."

"Yeah."

Billy let out another long breath and turned the key. The Ranger came to life.

"You're right about the name," Henry said. "Why don't they call themselves the 'Children of the Corn'?"

Billy had been thinking the same thing. He'd come to an answer: "It's fifty years old, Henry. I doubt they ever heard of it."

Tracking

The snow came again as they drove west. It stayed first on the roofs of scattered houses and then made white furrows on the shoulders of the highways. The wide fields around them began to fill, and Billy turned on the wipers as larger flakes blurred the windshield. It was afternoon, but the skies had turned deep gray and a real storm was coming on.

They crossed the wide Missouri on a long, low bridge and, just like that, the trees disappeared. They were in the real late-winter prairie. The Ranger's headlights had just caught the snow-patched exit sign for the town of Resilience when the low tire pressure warning came on. Within a mile, they were listing to the right and Henry heard the *thump thump thump* of a flat. They coasted to the side of the empty road.

"I can do it," Billy said, his breath already appearing in front of his face.

"I can get out."

Billy was rummaging for a warmer hat. Henry zipped his coat up to his neck. "Let's go, then."

The snow swirled around them, blowing in every direction at once. The wind cut through their clothes and stung their cheeks. They found the problem quickly enough: there was a fork in the passenger rear tread, rolled flat into the tire by the highway. *Corn Kids.*

"Is there a spare?" Billy asked, his voice loud.

"I think so!" Henry opened the rear doors, pushed back the mattress, and looked for a compartment. He found one with a wheel, iron, and jack inside. They got to work. The lugnuts were rusted tight, and they took turns standing on the tool handle to try and break them loose. First one gave, then the second. They each grunted with the effort.

It was Billy's turn when Henry stepped back around the windbreak of the Ranger and heard, somewhere on the wind, the sound of another distant engine. He took another two steps into the road and tried to see what he could see. The snow was thick, but there was no mist or fog; he scanned the horizon. Low white hills rose one after the other in all directions. He looked east behind them along the highway, and then west ahead. There was nothing—but he could still hear the sounds, revving up, and then dying away again. There was more than one.

"I think somebody's out there," he called to Billy, who had gotten the last nut loose.

"What?"

"I think somebody's out there! I can hear engines."

Billy looked up at him. "Where?"

"I can't tell."

"These are loose. Start with the jack and we'll do this as fast as we can."

They worked together on the tire, but it was slow-going. The sounds of the engines came and went, shifting with the direction of the wind. Billy could hear them now, too. They didn't seem to move closer, but they did seem to move around. Once they had the tire up, they realized it was stuck to the axle, and Billy kicked at it, trying to break it loose. Henry stood up again, and this time he spotted them: there was a pause in the snowfall just long enough for him to see three silhouettes atop a hill, maybe a mile away. They were men on motorcycles.

"Billy, look," he said, and Billy did.

"That's not good."

"I don't think so either."

"What are they doing in a snowstorm?"

"I hope we don't find out."

The figures didn't move. Henry watched them while Billy worked on the lee side of the truck. The rumble of their engines rolled over the prairie, throbbing above the wind.

"Work faster," Henry said. "Work as fast as you can."

"I'm trying."

Henry was afraid to blink for fear of losing sight of the silhouettes. But he couldn't help himself, and the snow kept sticking to his glasses. He took them down and wiped them clean as fast as he could. When he raised them back, he was frantic as he searched, but they were still there, still watching. He would have sworn, though, that they'd moved closer.

"Got it!" Billy yelled from behind him. "Roll the spare over here."

Henry did as he was told, but as he turned his back on the figures, he heard their engines rev. They got the old tire off and Henry wheeled it around to the back as best he could. He grunted, his leg throbbing as he lifted it into the back of the Ranger. He could hear Billy lining up the bolts of the spare, knocking it into place. Frozen fingers worked quickly, and their breath steamed in the cold air, puffs coming faster and faster now. But when Henry stepped back from the rear doors and looked at the hill again, the figures were gone. They had disappeared, he knew, into the gully between where he'd first seen them and the low rise on the south side of the interstate, only a few hundred yards away from where he stood.

"Billy…"

"I'm working!"

"Billy, they're coming…"

"Lower the jack!"

Henry ran back around and squatted beside his friend. He turned the handle as fast as he could. The Ranger crept towards the pavement. "What are we going to do?" he asked.

"It won't come to that."

"Your gun…"

"I know." Billy was gripping the tire iron in his hand as Henry worked. He'd hit a kid; he knew he could hit whatever this was.

The engines were clear now over the sound of the wind. They had spread out and seemed to be everywhere at once. Neither Henry nor Billy could see from where they were kneeled down beside the truck, and as the tire touched pavement, Billy started tightening the bolts: one, two, three… "That's good enough," he said; "grab the jack, let's go!"

Henry ran for the passenger door. He got it open, tossed the jack to the floor, and was buckling his seatbelt as Billy jumped in behind the wheel. "Lock the doors," he said. And then something occurred to him: "does the back door lock?"

"I think so."

Billy pressed the button and listened for the latches. The bikers were on them now. He turned the key in the ignition, but nothing happened. "*Shit!*" he said.

"It's the cold. Leave it turned for a second." Billy did, keeping his fingers on the key.

The snow was falling harder, and they could see the strangers passing one after the other across their headlights. They were circling the Ranger like horses on a carousel. The riders were dirty and bundled in heavy coats and black leather. Snow was sticking in their beards and they were laughing as they passed. Suddenly, there was a loud thump on the side of the truck. What was it? A rock? A club? A human skull? Today, Henry and Billy would have believed anything.

Billy turned the key again and the Ranger roared to life. Gauges and dials sprang to their places, and Billy pulled the gear shift into drive and floored it. The tires spun on the icy asphalt, and the biker currently passing in front of them swerved awkwardly to the side and kicked the front fender with a heavy boot as the truck pulled away. Billy looked in the rearview mirror and saw him fishtail, the other two riders pulling up beside him. Then they revved their bikes again and set off in pursuit.

They caught up to the Ranger easily and flanked it on both sides. It was a strain to get the truck up to fifty miles per hour, and Billy swerved to one side, then the other, hoping to knock them away. But the tires slid in the snow and forced him to straighten back out.

"We can't outrun them," Henry said.

"We're not stopping, either."

In this way, the strange caravan moved west. The Ranger was barely controllable, and the bikes accelerated past them easily, racing ahead and then slowing to laugh and yell at them through the windows. There were more thumps. Henry looked for some sign of what they were saying, of what they wanted, but there was none. He felt sticky with sweat, despite the freezing cold. Enormous snowflakes zoomed past them in the headlights as if they were going at warp speed rather than the crawl they were. The empty road ahead of them stretched ahead forever. But there was nowhere to go.

"What are they doing?" Henry asked.

"I don't know."

"What is this?"

"*I don't know.*"

And then they heard the unmistakable sound of rifle shots–one, two, three. They were close, and both Henry and Billy expected glass somewhere to shatter. But none did, and the bikers peeled off. Henry watched as the one who had been hollering at him through his window so close he could have touched him moved away, dipping smoothly off the shoulder and then cutting a clean line through the fresh snow to the north. He disappeared over a ridge and into the haze of the storm.

"Was that them?"

"I don't know." It was becoming a mantra.

"Then who?"

Billy was looking frantically, first in the side mirrors, and then in the rearview. But the truth was that he felt the blue lights before he saw them. And then Henry sensed them, too. "Oh no," he said.

"Maybe," Billy said back. There was nowhere to run, nowhere to hide. He was in an ice cream truck on an interstate in a snowstorm during the apocalypse… which is to say, he was caught. He slowed the Ranger and held his breath. The patrol car pulled alongside him, both vehicles still idling slowly ahead. The patrol car's passenger window was down and the officer inside was leaning across the vehicle, rifle still in his hand, gesturing to talk. Billy rolled down the glass, and the man inside yelled across: *"Follow me!"* He pointed down the highway with his free hand, steering the car with his knees. *"Stay close!"*

Billy nodded and cranked his window back up. He looked over at Henry. Henry could see what he was thinking, what he was worrying about. But something new and strange occurred to him: he could be calm for his friend, even if he was panicked himself.

"It might not be so bad," he said.

"Yeah, right."

He thought as hard as he could. "The last time the sandwiches were pretty good."

"I'm not counting on any sandwiches."

Henry wasn't, either. "At least it's a story," he said. The patrol car pulled into the lane in front of them and they tried to stay in the ruts it made through the snow. The blue lights stayed on. "It's gotta be better than the one we were about to be in."

Billy let out a long breath. "I hope so."

The patrol car pulled off on the next exit and then turned north onto what Billy and Henry would not have even known was a road. They stayed behind and crept through the gloom. The snow was letting up, but the sky remained steel gray. Billy felt he was in no-time: not morning, not noon, not dusk. They drove straight forever, their three tires and a spare stuck in the grooves being made before them. Mile after mile. Their tracks filling with snow as soon as they were past, leaving no sign left that they had been there at all.

What seemed like an hour later, a long, low rectangle caught Billy's eye near the horizon. He watched it grow nearer until he recognized it as a single-wide trailer. There was a pickup parked beside it, blanketed in snow. Hanging from the front porch, he saw a new flag: a white sun on a bright red field. It was the only color anywhere. It was like a winter cardinal. It looked like it had been dipped in blood. More buildings passed, all long and low to the ground; all covered in new snow. A barn here and a shed there. Sometimes, smoke rose from chimneys. Sometimes, lights were on inside.

And then they were in a town, no more than a dozen blocks in size. The patrol car made one turn, and then another, and then it pulled off the road into a parking space in front of a wide, brick building. As Billy slowed the Ranger, the man's hand appeared again from the driver's side window, pointing at the space beside him. Billy pulled in, shifted to park, and turned the key. He and Henry sat there, waiting for whatever would come next.

Then the man from the patrol car was standing directly in their headlights. His belt, badge, and rifle gleamed in the beams, and Billy reached for the knob to turn them off. The man pointed at the building behind him and yelled through their windshield, *"Let's go inside!"*

What choice did they have? They got out and followed him again.

The man was talking the instant they went through the door, but he was not talking to them. "Hetty, the damn SMC is back on 90 again. I said it, didn't I? Just last week, I said it. Tell Chief and we'll send a car down tomorrow."

They were in what was unmistakably a police station. Every wall was faux wood paneling and there were old fluorescent lights in the ceiling overhead. Corkboards were everywhere, each one filled with pictures and maps and posters for community events.

"I'll tell him. Won't do much good, though." The voice seemed aggressively disinterested, and Billy looked to find it. Henry's glasses were fogged completely, but he turned his head, too: behind a desk was a soft-looking woman in her forties or fifties, her black hair lined with gray and gathered in a wide braid over her left shoulder. She seemed wholly at one with the chair in which she sat. She wore horn-rimmed glasses, and her brown eyes met Billy's, then looked back to the man who had led them in. "Who are these ones, then? Not bikers."

"Don't know that yet." The man had laid his rifle on a table in the middle of the room and was shaking out his coat. He stomped his feet on the carpet. "SMCs were giving them a roper before I chased them off, and we didn't have much time to talk about it. Brought 'em back here to sort that out."

"Oh, big hero you, then?" the woman said.

"Yeah, big hero me. You tellin' the chief or not? Is he in?"

"He's not. He's out at Wayne's. He'll be back soon, though."

"What's Wayne want?"

"He didn't tell me nothing about what it was Wayne wanted. What else is new? He'll be back soon, though."

The man who found them turned to face them square. He was in his late-twenties, thin, dark eyes with long hair also pulled back in a braid. He, like Hetty, was Native. And he moved like an overwound watch, his eyes darting and feet shuffling as if he was late for something before it started. The tag over the pocket of his uniform shirt said Trimble.

"Well," he said, "who are you then?"

Henry was the first to speak. "Nobody, sir," he said.

"Oh, that's no good." It was Hetty. She was resting her chin on her hands and watching them. "'Nobody,' he says."

"We're just traveling through."

"That's even worse!"

Trimble cut his eyes at her. "I can do this, Hetty."

"Okay, then." She made a show of sitting back in her chair and turning to squint at her computer screen. The blue rectangle reflected in her glasses. "Go right ahead."

"Traveling from where to where?" Trimble asked.

"From Mitchell this morning," Henry said, "and trying to get to the parks out west."

"There are no parks out west. So that's a no go."

"Well, to where they *were*," Henry said.

Hetty let out a snort at that and Trimble pursed his lips. "Okay, we'll get there, I guess. But first, what happened out on I-90?"

Henry seemed to have two strikes already, so Billy thought he could give things a try. "We broke down just past the river. We had a flat. Those bikers came up while we were changing it, and we were trying to get away from them," he said. "Then you saved the day."

The attempt at flattery didn't seem to earn him much. Trimble deflected: "The Savages are troublemakers, but they wanted to scare you more than they wanted to hurt you. We're workin' on them." He was fidgeting with a notepad he dug out from a back pocket now. He flipped it open and found a pen. "But here's the thing," he said, his eyes looking down. "This isn't somewhere you can be. I can understand with the weather, that might not have been clear, and we're workin' on that, too. But your people don't cross the Missouri."

"Why not?" Henry heard himself ask.

It was strike three, and Hetty let him know it. "This one's gonna be trouble, Russ," she said. "Watch out for him. Travelin' through. Mr. Nobody, he says."

"Hetty."

"Alright, alright—you can do this."

"Thank you, Hetty." Trimble looked back to Henry: "It's not your country is why. This is Lakota Nation. It's not open to you unless you have cause to be here, and the old parks aren't cause, they're trouble." He looked at the woman behind the desk who was again pretending to be wholly occupied with something else. "And nobody around here needs you to be trouble. Now, it's getting late and Chief's not here. The weather's bad, and we don't need no wrecked ice cream trucks to deal with in the morning, either. So you can stay in the station tonight." The notepad had been tucked away again; it was unclear why he'd ever gotten it out. Wheels were spinning behind his eyes, and he realized there was more to say. "You know where you are?"

"No sir," Henry said. Manners seemed as good a place to begin the road to recovery as any.

Trimble had already moved back to the table where he'd laid down the rifle and slid a map to their end of it. He pointed to a spot neither Henry nor Billy could have differentiated from any other in the middle of a shape they didn't recognize. The only thing that made sense to them was the winding blue of what must be the Missouri. "You're right here. This is Lower Brule township." He pointed at a second spot, just on the other side of the blue line. "In the morning, we can look at your tire and then get you over here to Fort Thompson. You won't have any problems out that way, and you can move on back east from there. You're not from around here, and you didn't mean to cross in; I can vouch for that. But tomorrow, you're out. Okay, then?"

He'd said his peace, and he'd been kind. But Billy looked at Henry, who was still trying to make sense of the map. He'd found I-90, and his eyes were wandering along it west. Billy knew they would need to talk. "That makes sense to us," he said to Trimble. "We understand. Thank you, officer; we won't be any more trouble."

"Peacekeeper," the man said, a new edge in his voice. "Officer's not our word, it's yours. You can call me Peacekeeper Trimble."

"My mistake," Billy said. "I didn't mean any offense…"

"No offense. Just right names." He pushed the map back to the middle of the table and then didn't seem to know quite what to do with his hands next. He put his thumbs through his belt loops.

The woman behind the desk came to his rescue. "Names, Russ," she said. "I can't write 'Mr. Nobody' in this thing or I won't know the end of it." She looked at Henry and went wide-eyed. "Chief will *scalp* me."

"Okay, Hetty," Trimble said. "No problem. And no need for that." He made a finger gun now and pointed it at each of them. "Shoot," he said.

"Billy," said Billy, and then he corrected himself: "William Faulkner."

Hetty typed it in, repeating the words slowly to herself as she went: "*Will-iam Faulk-ner.*" She hit enter, and then clicked somewhere else on the screen in front of her. "And what about Mr. Nobody?" she asked, looking at Henry Henry now over the rim of those glasses.

Henry gulped.

* * *

It was rabbit stew rather than sandwiches, and it tasted incredible. They each ate two bowls full and the warmth of it settled inside them. Peacekeeper Trimble had given them two cots in a jail cell in the back of the station, and he'd paced the floor while they'd eaten, taking the bowls the second they were finished. When he left, he made sure the gate to the cell was open and the lights were off. Still, they could see the yellow glow of the office through the doorway, and more dim gray filtered down from the slit of a window near the ceiling. Neither Henry nor Billy had the slightest idea what time it was, but they knew they were dead tired. They laid back on their cots.

"Lakota Nation," Henry said as his head hit the thin pillow. They'd each been given old quilts, worn and faded but warm, and he pulled his up under his chin. He stared, as always, at the ceiling.

"Lower Brule," Billy said back. "Wherever that is. I'd guess it's one of the old reservation tribes." He didn't know much of anything about Native lands or politics out this way, but the truth was that he was incredibly curious. He hadn't thought about his book in a long time—not since Hot Springs—but tonight it was back on his mind, even as he began to drift away. He wondered how closed was "closed." And he sensed Henry was wondering the same thing.

Henry confirmed the suspicion. "He said there *are* no parks anymore," he said. "What do you think that means?"

"Maybe it means they don't keep them up. Maybe it means they just don't let anyone in. I suppose you could ask him in the morning." But even as sleepy as he was, Billy knew that was a bad idea. "Or I can ask him about it," he said. "I'd like to look around, if they'll let us."

"Yeah, look around." It was an echo and not a sentence. Henry was fading quickly, too. "I don't want to go back east," he said.

"We might not have a choice."

Henry closed his eyes. "Yeah. I'd like to see them, though."

Billy closed his, too. "You always want to see them."

"But *really* see them, I mean."

"We can ask," Billy said. "I don't know about sneaking this time."

There was that word again. Henry knew it was accurate, that this is what he was doing. Once upon a time, it had even felt right: he'd wanted to be a ghost. But that seemed silly now, with his belly full of rabbit stew and the healing wound in his thigh throbbing with each and every beat of his heart.

"Yeah, no sneaking," he said, and then let out a long and heavy yawn.

"Good night, Hank," Billy said, nearing sleep himself.

"Good night."

The Badlands

O h, it's Henry Two-Times, awake at last."

It was Hetty. She was back at her desk when Billy and Henry walked into the lobby, and it was unclear if she had ever left it. The morning sun filled the space, and her head was perched on her hands again as if she'd been waiting for them.

"You got a big day in front of you today," she said. "A big, big day. You get to see the fine Lakota Nation, and then you get to take the story back home with you. I'm jealous of that. Maybe you can go tell it to those strays out east in Mitchell. They'd love to hear it, I bet. Might give them some new ideas."

Billy was surprised. "Do you mean the Corn Kids?" He couldn't believe he was thinking with those words.

"Oh, the 'Children of the Corn,' yeah. I know of 'em. Buncha White kids with no parents, playing *indians*. We hear stories. Buncha *crazies*, I think." She pointed at Henry. "But maybe Henry Two-Times can set 'em all straight. Tell 'em their dads all ran off to join some biker gangs and get scared whenever real 'red men' show up. Buncha *cowards*, their dads. You can tell 'em I said that."

"Those bikers are from Mitchell?" Henry asked.

"What do I know White people?" Hetty said. "Mitchell, Sturgis, Bumfuck—they're *somebody's* dads. If not those corn ones, prob'ly no better.

You're all crazies, I'm thinking. You, too, Two-Times." She laughed and laughed. "Look at you, asking me! Nobody tells me nothing."

Billy prayed for Trimble to appear, and then he did: he barged through the front doors and shook more snow off his jacket. He looked up and his eyes darted from Hetty to Henry to Billy.

"You're up, then."

"We're up."

"Well, time's wastin'. Let's go see about that truck." He looked at Hetty. "Still no chief?"

"He's down at Wayne's again."

"Damn Wayne. You tell him about I-90?"

"I did. He said he'd worry about it."

"He'll worry *me* about it. Radio him and tell him we're at the shop and to meet us there when he gets a chance."

"Can do," Hetty said. Then her eyes lit up. "These two seen the Children of the Corn," she said. "Get some stories out of 'em for me while you're down there."

Trimble pursed his lips again. "You don't need any more stories about that. Sad is all that is."

"I don't have any tears left for those White kids. I used 'em already. I hope they eat each other up."

Trimble went back to the door and held it open. He motioned for Henry and Billy to come with him. "You don't hope that, Hetty."

"See if I don't. Their whole country is eatin' itself up. 'Bout time, I say. You see if I cry about it."

"Okay, then."

"Yeah, okay." She waved her hand at the lot of them. "You have fun babysitting, Russ. I'll try not to interrupt."

"Okay, Hetty."

They went back out into the snow, and the door closed behind them.

* * *

"You two stopped at the Palace?" Trimble was riding shotgun in the Ranger while Billy drove. Henry was sitting on the mattress in the back.

"We did, yeah. They attacked us."

"Fell for the burger trap, then?"

Billy looked at Henry in the rearview mirror. "We knew it was a trap."

"Hard to say no, though?"

"Guess so. What's their story?"

"We don't know much, really. Just rumors from folks who run out that way sometimes. They've been there close to a year or so; since the last sickness passed through. Sad story."

"Yeah, it's a sad story." Billy thought about the kid he'd hurt; about the older girl, mothering him.

"There's no telling with States folk these days. All kinds of craziness. That's why we been keeping to ourselves. Working to stay that way, too. Don't need no extra trouble; we have enough of our own."

"Like those bikers?" Henry said from the back.

"No, they're not much trouble. More a nuisance, really. Call themselves the Savage Motorcycle Club. The SMC. Don't much care for the name, as it's supposed to be some sorta insult, we're thinking. But it does suit 'em. Leftovers from the old Sturgis rallies in the Before times. Folks who were angry about the Independence. But they haunt the empty places nowadays and don't come near our towns. Don't come near us most times. No law out here here but ours, and we're outta patience with 'em." He pointed at a turn up ahead for Billy and then he pivoted around to look at Henry, face to face. "That's why I'd counsel against going to the parks, though. First off, nobody goes into the Black Hills—no exceptions. As for the other one, down Pine Ridge way, I can call over there and see if they're against you nosin' around or not… but you'll run into those men again, and you'll be on your own this time. You're better off getting over the river here and stayin' away." He looked ahead and gestured again to the road. "Turn right and it's the big tin building over there. Pull up out front and I'll go in. Big will take a look." Then he was with Henry again: "You don't seem like a dangerous pair, and I got nothing against you. But 160 years is a long time to wait for visitors to leave, and it don't make anybody eager for more company." He unbuckled his seatbelt. "Now let's get goin'."

He was halfway out the door before he finished the sentence. Henry had never seen a faster man than Peacekeeper Trimble.

'Big' was the town mechanic, Eddie Big Sky. He was, as his nickname implied, enormous: at least six foot four, broad-shouldered, and large-bellied. He talked to Russ and Russ alone. "Heard all about them two," he said. "Hetty kept me up half the night with the story. Mr. Nobody, she says. You want me to look at what?"

"They had a flat and are running on a spare, Big. Just lookin' for a quick patch and some air."

"I got patches and I got air," Big said. "Won't be no problem if you let me get at it." He started to move towards the Ranger when a mechanical trill sounded once, and then again. Henry looked at Billy. They both knew exactly what it was, but they couldn't believe their ears: a cell phone was ringing. Big paused, reached into the front pocket of his overalls, and extracted a smooth black rectangle. It was tiny in his hand. "Oh, it's Hetty," he said. "Gotta take those. You guys just get the bum tire on out and bring it around here to the shop. I'll get to it when I get to it." He swiped with a thumb to answer the call and then walked off towards the far side of the garage.

"You have phones?" Henry asked Trimble incredulously.

"We got 'em where we can. They work here in town."

Henry and Billy lived in a different America. The cell carriers pulled out when the secessions started, first as an act of partisanship and then as a way of claiming neutrality. The truth was there just wasn't clear money in it, with the dollar collapsing and whatever the currency *de jour* was in the Republics changing constantly. Henry had forgotten what a phone even felt like in his hand. "How?" he asked.

"The Canadians made us a deal," Trimble said. For the first time, they saw him smile. He tried to stifle it, but the effort just transfigured his grin into a steady, bubbling chuckle. "Oh, boy," he said. "The foot's on the other boot now, huh?"

Big would be awhile, and in the meantime, Henry and Billy split up: Henry was left to wander Lower Brule and wait on news, while Billy followed Peacekeeper Trimble back to the station. Billy was alive with questions, especially after the phone, and when the tire was done, Henry could find his way back with the Ranger and pick Billy up. Meanwhile, Trimble would negotiate their exit from the Nation.

So, Henry Henry wandered. The town was spread out across the rippled grasslands of the west bank of the Missouri and just south of an oxbow bend held off at the neck by a narrow spine of low hills. The snow from the day before was still a foot deep, but the spring thaw was coming for the river and a thin channel of dark blue water ran between a patchwork of cracked winter floes. The sky overhead was pale blue and the sun sparked on the crusted ice and hurt Henry's eyes when he looked at it. But he looked anyway.

He tried to put words together in his mind for what was so different about what he was seeing. He'd been near pan-flat farmlands all his life, seen fields stretch to the horizon, stood under the crystal dome of true Big Sky. But Ohio was featureless in its broad expanses; it seemed to run out to the ends of the earth because it had no imagination for anything else. This place was humbled by the wind and the sky. Worn low by them, but not giving in. Even now, knots of stubborn earth bucked against the blanket of snow, patches of brown and gray poking through the white.

Henry felt it was beautiful is all, and he swelled up in his scavenged winter coat against the cold. He wanted to see the Badlands, whatever they were, and however they might be bad. And he wondered how, or even if, he would be able to.

For his part, Billy was finding out the answer to this very question. He was back at the station, back with Peacekeeper Trimble, and also back with Hetty, who chided him for the audacity of his presence. He'd asked about the tribe and asked about the Nation. He'd asked about phones and food and industry. He'd learned the people of the seven former reservations—Lower Brule, Crow Creek across the river in Fort Thompson, Rosebud, Yankton, Pine Ridge, Cheyenne River, and Standing Rock—had taken up the mantle of the old Očeti Šakówiŋ, the Seven Council Fires, and formed a new confederacy in the territory west of the Missouri and east of the Bighorn Mountains. Theirs were the tipis arranged in a circle which Billy had mistaken for the sun on the Nation's flag; the red was warrior blood poured into the earth. In the last four years, the united Lakota had reclaimed the Black Hills and driven non-Natives back out to the hodgepodge of Republics and "sovereign States" surrounding them. They had also built up commerce with their neighbors to the north in Winnipeg and Saskatchewan, who were flourishing themselves with expatriates from the last decade of southern dissolutions. The American Invasion had come and gone, Trimble told Billy. "And fuck them forever," Hetty added to that.

At noon, the chief finally returned. He was older and wore an old white cowboy hat over long gray hair that he left loose on his shoulders. His skin was dark and deeply rutted. His eyes were soft, but he seemed to hold his mouth in a perpetual grimace. His nametag read White Plume. "It's bad news from Huron, Russ," he said, taking off his hat and hanging it on a stand by the door. "They're not gonna take these two in."

"They say why not?" Hetty asked from her usual place behind the desk.

"No visas and not an asylum case. Crow Creek says they're our problem." He looked at Billy. "Which means you'll have to sneak out the same way you snuck in. Not on 90, though. And not east."

Billy was catching up. "Peacekeeper Trimble said we could talk to Pine Ridge about going west. Is that still possible?"

The chief realized he had skipped a step and paused. He extended his hand to Billy. "Chief White Plume," he said. "Brule tribe. You're William Faulkner?"

"Billy, yes. From Chicago."

"Billy, then. Not William. Okay." He looked at Russ, who was fidgeting with a clipboard, unsure of what he was supposed to add. The chief moved on without him. "What's in Pine Ridge?"

"The old park there," Billy said. "The Badlands. My friend wanted to see it. We didn't know we couldn't be here. We didn't mean trouble—"

"What trouble? No trouble. Did Russ tell you that?"

"He did," Hetty interrupted. "He was scaring 'em half to death about it."

Russ was beginning to look panicked. His eyes darted from the chief, to Hetty, and then back to the chief again. "That's not so, chief," he said. "The SMC…"

"I don't give two damns about the damn SMCs. And Pine Ridge don't give three damns about that nowhere place. Take 'em down there, Russ, and drop 'em off at Interior. I'll tell Bear about it and he'll have a good laugh."

"Yes, Chief," Russ said.

White Plume looked at Billy. "If you run into those bikers down there—and you will—you tell 'em to go to hell and they'll scatter off fast enough. They don't want anymore trouble with Pine Ridge than they want with us. You and your friend can see what you want and then go out the Nation south there. There wasn't a damn person in Nebraska before your country fell apart and there are even less now. Won't be no trouble."

Billy was stunned by what seemed to be their good luck, but he was smart enough to expect a catch. And, of course, one came. Chief White Plume pointed at his chest. "You say 'parks.' We know what you mean. So, I'm gonna be real clear with you, Billy: stay south of the Hills. That's *Paha Sapa* to us and 'closed' to you. You drift up there, somebody will shoot you. That's a fact, now. There's nothing for you to see that way. We blew those White Fathers' faces right off that mountain and it's all ours again now, same as it's meant to be. So don't go. Is that clear to you, Billy?"

"It's clear," Billy said.

The chief's shoulders relaxed and he turned to the desk. "Hetty, what'd you bring today?"

"Rabbit," Hetty said.

"Always rabbit."

"It's good, chief." Russ said. He had found his voice again.

"I know it's good," White Plume said. "It's just always rabbit."

After lunch, Henry picked up the Ranger from Big and drove back on his sore-but-healing leg to the station. Billy gave him the news and Peacekeeper Trimble loaded his patrol car up for the drive to the Badlands. They would follow him out there, and he would talk to his counterparts in Pine Ridge, get them settled, and drive back the next morning.

They turned over the engine in the Roving Ranger and set out at a slow crawl back through town. The snow was melting quickly in the spring sunshine, and it was no trouble staying in Peacekeeper Trimble's tracks. The long road south was a different wonder in the clarity of the afternoon: stubbled grasslands stretched forever in all directions, interrupted only by the Ts of power line poles running to the horizon like a drawing exercise in perspective. Dripping icicles clung to the wires.

They rejoined I-90 at Reliance, which was barely a pit stop: a dozen or so houses bracketed on one side by a Family Dollar and on the other by a Cenex gas station. The highway was clear both of cars and, Henry and Billy were surprised to see, of snow: the Nation had plows, too. Still, Peacekeeper Trimble kept a slower pace, and it was a three hour drive to the park exit.

Lakota was a wonder, even under a cloudless sky. The Ranger cruised along the undulations of the landscape like a boat on a white sea, their only navigational aid the sun, which was just a week or so from the equinox and seemed to descend towards the horizon directly in front of them.

After a long quiet, Billy spoke. "What do you think we'll see out there?" he asked.

"I don't know," Henry replied. "Shannon used to have guidebooks. She would leave them around for me sometimes, probably hoping I'd take the hint. But I never really did."

"What did they say about it?"

"I don't remember. I think they looked like mountains in the pictures. But smaller."

"Hard to imagine mountains here."

"Not mountains, really. But shapes like that. It's hard to describe."

"We'll find out, I guess." Billy looked out at the prairie passing by. "Why didn't you ever go with her?"

"I…" Henry had been wondering the very same thing. "…I would have said I was just always busy. But I wasn't. The truth was I didn't go because I didn't know I could."

"Hmm," Billy said.

Henry looked over at his friend, and maybe for the first time he really saw him. He saw the crispness of the collar of the white button-up shirt he always seemed to wear and always seemed to keep clean. He saw the rich cedarwood color of his skin. He saw the faintest signs of crows' feet forming at the corner of his deep brown eyes, early markers of age that had not quite arrived yet. He realized he'd never seen Billy shave, but he'd also never seen more than a day's stubble on his face. He looked at his friend, and he thought, *all of him is kind somehow; all of him is curious.*

"Billy, why are you still with me?" he asked.

Billy smiled, his eyes focused now on the rear bumper of Peacekeeper Trimble's patrol car. "Hell if I know, Hank," he said. "It's a story, I guess. You're a story."

Henry considered this, but it wasn't satisfying. "You could be anywhere," he said. "You could write any story."

Billy raised his eyebrows and made a frown. "That's not true. I know because I tried it. The world we're from—which isn't this one, I'm figuring out—is just waiting on the next thing to happen to it. That's how my dad is; how my brother and my sister are. That's how things have been my whole life. But I don't want to be that way. You can be a frustrating son of a bitch sometimes, but at least you're doing something."

Henry looked out the window. Just now, he couldn't look anywhere else. "I don't mean to," he said. "That's what's funny about it. All this craziness just seems to find me."

"It wouldn't have found you if you'd stayed in Ohio."

"Maybe." He thought again of Shannon. "I just wasn't any good there. I wasn't good for anybody." On the last day he had spoken to her, even after all they'd been through, she'd said, *I still love you, Henry. I just couldn't live with you.* He'd told her he still loved her, too. That he always would. And in his odd, hopeless way, he had.

Billy looked over at him and saw the man he always saw: a reluctant astronaut, searching for somewhere to land.

"Lighten up," he said. "It's the Badlands."

Billy was right. Peacekeeper Trimble turned on his blinker, worried and fidgety as ever, and the Ranger followed him down the exit and then back left across the highway. A sign on the far side said Badlands National Park: 2 Miles, and they set off, the sun now a hand's width from the horizon and beaming in Henry's window from the west.

The snow here was melting quickly and had become a spotted patchwork on the ground. Fence posts ran along the side of the road, marking the time as they passed. They approached the abandoned entrance station and slowed as the Ranger passed under the raised and paint-chipped gate. On the other side, the path rose slightly and wound around gentle hills.

And then Henry realized they were approaching the edge of a plateau: the white prairie at the horizon was significantly lower by maybe a few hundred feet of elevation, and if he looked closely, he could see the ragged edge where the earth had sheared up and away from it. Another sign said *Viewpoint Area,* and as the Ranger banked to the right, it was suddenly clear that this break wasn't clean, that there was no cliff, but instead the raised plain on which they traveled had eroded down from them in a maze of steep gray gullies and washes stretching miles out. It was like looking at an entire mountain range, not quite in miniature, but on a scale that made them feel like giants, or like birds. The light from the sun contrasted with the slivers of snow still holding on in the shadowed places and in the millions of dry channels curling in fractal patterns through the soft rock. It was all like nothing Henry had ever seen. It was wondrous.

The road began to descend, and now they were surrounded by strange hoodoos and fairy spires of stone on all sides. Alcoves and cul-de-sacs. Early spring grass grew in patches out of the sandy fills between them, and the green of it was electric against the pale earth and snow. As they went down, they realized lines of color ran through the formations, black and purple and green and red, with a thick yellow band between them. It was a rainbow in hardened mud, and at the sight of it, neither Henry nor Billy could speak.

Signs for trails appeared to their left, urging travelers into turn offs and parking lots. They saw a boardwalk running out from one, disappearing between sharp crags to who knows where. *Notch, Window, Door.* And then they were switchbacking through a pass, winding their way to the still-infinite prairie below, where from the height of a hundred feet they could see a small village. They recognized the long shape of a visitor center with a semi-circle of houses beyond it, and then the intersecting loops of a campground just visible on the far side of a large mound with an amphitheater at its summit. The sun threw the jagged shadows of the Badlands in a long serrated line across the panorama like the teeth of some great dinosaur, and the Ranger wound its way to the bottom and slowed on the flat.

"That was something," Billy said, still looking around him.

"Yeah. It is."

Peacekeeper Trimble pulled his patrol car into the parking lot of the Ben Reifel Visitor Center and cut his engine. The Ranger pulled in beside him and all three men got out. The temperature was still cold, but the air felt warm in the sunshine. The brickwork of the building glowed a deep orange. The flagpole out front still displayed the last tatters of an American flag, the red stripes now faded to pink.

"This is it," Trimble said. "All the dirt and wind you could want."

Henry looked around. "Thanks for leading us here," Billy said.

"Sure, no problem for me. Sorta a day off, really." He clapped his hands together. "So, Chief says you'll have no trouble if you wanna keep parked here for a bit and do what it is you wanna do. But I'd say it's a good idea to pull around back there to the old ranger village, if only to keep outta sight from the road. Not too many drivers come through here, but you'll be all alone if any do. He talked to Chief Bear down in Pine Ridge, and they're gonna let you be, so long as you stay just here. Might send a runner to check in, if you're gonna stay a few days."

"That sounds good to us," said Henry.

"Yeah, well. I'm thinkin' I'll camp down here with you tonight to get you settled proper, then head back east in the morning. Shouldn't get too cold there in your van, but I'd guess the keys to those cabins are in the center, and no one will much mind if you use 'em should you need to." He moved his hands to his coat pockets and bounced on the balls of his feet. "I'll get us some wood and meet you in the village come sundown."

As ever, he was two steps gone before his last sentence was done. They watched as he got in his car, backed it out, and then headed to the far side of the hill with the amphitheater to scavenge the campground.

"Wanna get your badge?" Billy asked Henry.

"Yeah, we should."

"No time like the present."

"Yeah." Henry had yet to move. He was still wide-eyed, staring back at the strange hills through which they had passed.

"It's a hell of a place," Billy said. "Think we'll stay for a bit?"

"Yeah. For a day or so, maybe. I'd like to see it." Henry came back to himself and looked at Billy. "Is that alright with you?"

"I'd like to look around, too."

"Good."

* * *

The visitor center had been looted before. They both guessed it was the Savages, which was partly true, as that gang had certainly rummaged the ruins more than once. But the real pillaging had been done by refugees from Rapid City making their way south years ago: bank managers and car salesmen and burger flippers and housewives broke the glass in the double doors and took everything that wasn't bolted down. Money was raided from the gift shop registers, clothes from the racks, boxes of ammunition from the old ranger office. Someone had half a mind to steal a stuffed coyote, but they'd realized their folly before they got to the parking lot, and it was now lying on its side in the entryway, its four stiff legs padding through empty air. Maps and pamphlets and trash were everywhere. Exposure had stained and warped the drooping tiles in the ceiling. Prairie dog scat littered the floor.

Still, what Henry was seeking had been left where it always was: the Badlands National Park Junior Ranger badges were in a box sitting on a shelf behind the counter. He picked one out, and then, on an impulse, he took a second. "What do you think?" he said to Billy, holding it up for him to see. "Do you want one?"

Billy smiled. "Absolutely," he said. Henry stood up and handed it over.

Then, Billy did something unexpected: he pressed down the latch and pinned it to the breast pocket of his shirt. "What do you think?"

Henry had never once thought to do this. He looked at the badge in his own hand and then put it in his coat pocket. "It looks good," he said.

"Now I'm a Junior Ranger," Billy said. "Is there an oath?"

Henry honestly didn't know. He looked back under the counter beside the box of badges and picked up one of the workbooks from a stack he had seen and ignored just a moment earlier. He turned it over. "There is," he said, surprised.

"Let's have it."

"You're serious?"

"Absolutely." He held up two fingers in a Cub Scout salute.

Henry read: "As a Junior Ranger."

"As a Junior Ranger."

"I promise to explore, learn about, and protect."

"I promise to explore, learn about, and protect."

"Special places like Badlands National Park."

"Special places like Badlands National Park." Billy lowered his hand. "Is that it?"

"That's it." Henry realized he was smiling now, too. "We should keep the book. It's got homework assignments in it. And a map. It might be helpful if we're going to wander around tomorrow. Really, you should have had to do those first."

Billy laughed. "I'll take it on credit. But yeah, bring it." He looked around the lobby. "Not much else in here to find."

"Doesn't look like it."

"What about those cabin keys?"

"I'll look around."

"Hold on. I'll come around and look with you."

Once Trimble finished building the fire, he seemed to finally relax. They'd found a few lawn chairs in one of the cabins and gathered them around an old pit in the ranger village. There was more rabbit, but this time it was complemented by a loaf of bread Trimble had brought with him in his cruiser. The three of them passed it around, each tearing off a hunk and dipping it into the stew. The wood popped and crackled. Smoke rose up into a sky crowded with stars. The Milky Way stretched across them, reaching from horizon to horizon.

They made small talk for a while. Billy and Henry told him about the Corn Palace: how Henry had been trapped and Billy had bartered for him; about the strange props from the Bible museum across the street, and the feral kid who had endlessly licked his lips. Peacekeeper Trimble shook his head about the gun and said, "Hetty would send them bullets herself, then say what they could do with 'em." Billy laughed awkwardly. He kept the news about the boy whose mouth he'd broken to himself. Henry was quiet, off somewhere alone again.

Trimble asked Billy about his badge, and Billy said it was Henry's quest. It was an attempt to bring him back to the conversation, and Henry understood it and laughed a bit sheepishly. He admitted the quest part was true: he was trying to gather them all up.

"How many have you got?"

"Thirteen."

"Lucky thirteen, then."

"I guess so."

"How many are there?"

"That you can still get to? 40 or so. There are a lot in Alaska, and others on islands."

"You gonna get 40?"

"Probably not. I don't know how many."

Trimble thought for a moment. "What one did you have in mind next? Old Mount Rushmore?" He laughed at the thought, his voice sounding out one big *Ha!* "Woulda been hard to recognize now, I gotta tell you. I went up there once, just maybe a year or so ago. We had some poachers at the edge of Paha Sapa; not white folks, I hate to say, but some no-good Natives out from Oglala. They were teenagers with no respect for themselves. But I saw the mountain where those heads once were, and it was as flat and white as a piece of paper." He shook his head.

"Is that better?" Billy asked. There was no cynicism in the question.

"Better?" He considered it. "I don't know. It's not worse. It lets the mountain be a mountain again, and that's no small thing."

Billy nodded, his mouth now full of stew.

And then Henry spoke. "It wasn't a Park," he said.

"What's that?"

"Mount Rushmore wasn't a National Park. It was a National Monument. The Parks are different. At least, they are most times."

"Huh," said Trimble. "I thought it was. Had a big damn complex there underneath it. Buildings and sidewalks and flags." He gestured to the spaces around them with his spoon. "It was a lot bigger than this, anyway. What was the Park you wanted, then?"

"Wind Cave," Henry said. "It was in Paha Sapa, too."

Peacekeeper Trimble took another bite and spoke with his mouth full. "*Wind Cave*," he said. He swallowed the bite and then chuckled to himself. "I gotcha then. Hetty was right sayin' you were gonna get yourself in trouble. I know that place. Maka Oniye is our name for it; it means 'breathing earth.' It's definitely a 'no' for you."

"Why is that?" Henry asked. Then he thought about Hetty, imagined her glaring at him, and he reframed his question: "I mean, what is that place to you?"

Trimble wiped his mouth with his hand and set down his bowl. Then, he brushed his fingers off on his pant legs. "That's a big story."

"Can I hear it?"

"I can do my best to tell it, if you want. But I'm not a storyteller."

Henry put down his bowl, too. "I do. Want to hear it, I mean."

"Okay, then. It starts with the Creator spirit: 'God' to you, maybe; Takuskanskan to my people. He had tried many times to fill the earth with good things, but the things he made were stubborn and kept breaking themselves. They kept breaking the world, too. But he was a Creator, so he couldn't help himself from creating. So, he began again. This time, though, he took the people he made and put them in a cave deep in the earth to protect them. It was at the edge of his spirit land, and he told them to wait there for him while he prepared the world. Then, he went back to work. While he was away, the people made more of themselves, like people do, until there was a whole tribe of them."

He grinned, and his teeth shone in the fire. Then he continued. "All these people waited so long in the cave, they started to wonder if the Creator spirit had meant what he told them about the land above being made ready. They were restless, is how I've always heard it said; but what that restlessness ends up looking like changes with the teller.

"Anyways, in every story, one day a visitor comes to them in the cave. It's a shewolf, bigger than any wolf any person has ever seen, and she has a pack on her back with leather and seeds and strips of dried meat inside. Even crazier, the shewolf speaks the people's tongue so they can understand her, and she tells the people that she's come down from the surface of the world. The Creator spirit has finished all his making, she says, but he's gotten so caught up with it he's forgotten to come back to the cave to tell them—that's how good the world is to him. But the shewolf says she can help and lead them up out of the cave; she knows the way, and if they come with her, she will show them where they can find everything she's brought with her in her pack. She says that's what she brought it for: so they could see. She lets the people taste the meat she's got, and everyone who does falls madly in love with her. Then they all line right up to go.

"But there's another man in the cave, named Tokahe, who doesn't trust the shewolf. He gives a speech to the people, and he reminds everyone that they were told to wait for the Creator spirit, and they need to keep their word. When he's finished, many of the people agree with him, and they say no to the meat and decide to stay. But many other people—meaning the ones who ate the meat already—tell Tokahe it's no real chief who keeps his people away from plenty. And they set off with the shewolf, up from the edge of the spirit world and on the long journey out of the cave.

"Now, this is another spot where storytellers have fun with it. Sometimes, there are traps and monsters on the journey. Other times, the path is full of crazy and beautiful things, like waterfalls and big villages made of mushrooms. But the point is that the people follow the shewolf out, and they don't stop for anything. After days and days of walking, she takes them where she promised to: they see the opening of the cave, and they stop and wonder at the big blue of the sky.

"Once they're all out, they discover that everything is just like the shewolf said it would be. The surface is green and growing, because it's spring. They follow the shewolf around and eat everything they can find, and everybody is happy. But the shewolf has tricked them, because she knows the world *isn't* finished all the way: it's still flat in most places, and even though there's plenty of food at first, when the seasons change and winter comes, the people are starving and cold. They cry out for the Creator spirit, but he is still away working on the earth, and he cannot hear them. Some of the people start to die, and the tricky shewolf is nowhere to be found.

"But one of the men on the earth is a tracker. In the stories we never know his name, but he looks everywhere for the shewolf's footprints and eventually he finds them heading off in the snow. He gathers up a hunting party, and they all set off to follow her, to see if she can fix whatever it is that's happening to them. They walk a long ways across the prairies, through days and nights and snowstorms, until the tracks lead them to a lodge under a lone pine tree. It's dark when they get there, and there's a fire inside that throws shadows on the walls. When they look, they can see there's figures in there dancing. Real slow, they creep closer. And then the tracker pulls back the flap: inside is the shewolf, and she's laughing with a small little woman who's hunched over and's got a shawl on her head. When the woman looks up, they all see that her face is very beautiful. She tells them her name is Anog-Ite, and she's known the Creator spirit for many, many years. She says she's seen other people he's made walk around on the earth before, living and dying, time after time after time. And when she tells them this, she just shakes her head and laughs at them.

"When she's done laughing, she calls the shewolf close. She points at the shewolf's face, and she tells the men to look closer at it. They do, and they can see her skin isn't on quite right. Her teeth are too large in her mouth, and her fur is stiff and dry and hangs wrong on her throat. The beautiful woman laughs again when they see all that's wrong, and she tells them the shewolf's true name: she is Iktomi, the spider, who is the trickster of the world. At that, the shewolf grabs the beautiful woman's shawl in her mouth and tears it away, and there, on the back side of her head, is a second face that is terrible and twisted. It is so awful it puts chills down every person's spine. And then, with that face, Anog-Ite laughs even harder at them, and Iktomi bares her fangs and growls so her voice fills up the whole lodge.

"The people are taken by fear, and they don't know what to do. They run as fast as they can back across the prairie, back into the black hills, and all the way to the cave they came from. But when they get there, the mouth of the cave is covered, and they realize it is another trick played on them by Iktomi: they're trapped forever in the world. At this, they sit down to cry, and then wait to die.

"But this time, though, the Creator spirit hears their voices. He comes to see what's happened, and when he arrives, the people tell him about Iktomi, and about Anog-Ite, and the trick they played. They want the Creator to punish them. But the Creator spirit tells them that there is nothing he can do to those two, because it is their nature to be evil, and they are just being what they are. But they—the people he made—are *not* being as he made them. And so it is them who have to be punished. This is what happened: because they were cold, the Creator gave them long hair all over their bodies to stay warm. Because they were hungry, he showed them where there was grass to eat, even in the snow. But because the taste of meat was what had led them to such trouble, they would never eat it again. And so those people the Creator made ceased to be people, and they became the buffalo herds that lived on the prairie, once upon a time—in the time before *your* time—in numbers so great they couldn't be counted."

Peacekeeper Trimble folded his hands on his lap. "That's how I heard the story," he said. "That's what Maka Oniye is to our people."

Embers from the fire floated high into the night sky. Henry was riveted, and he asked Peacekeeper Trimble (who, he realized, had tricked them himself about being a storyteller), what happened to the people who stayed in the cave.

Trimble smiled in the yellow light. He was still and whole, all his daytime jitters gone in the comfort of his telling. "When the Creator was ready," he said, "he opened the cave again and went in to find them. He led them through the long tunnels and to the surface, stopping to pray as they went, and when they got to the blue sky and their eyes adjusted, he pointed down at the hoofprints of the buffalo-men in the dirt and told them, 'Follow these wherever they go, and from them, you will have everything you need.'"

With that, Trimble was truly finished. Billy was quiet, taking in what he'd heard. Henry Henry was perched in his chair, elbows on his knees, flames flickering in the reflections of his glasses. He did not believe in God. But still, he knew God to be just so: making providence of punishment.

"Tokahe is an Adam," Billy said finally, as if sliding pieces into a puzzle. "From the Bible."

"Or Adam is a Tokahe," Trimble replied.

"No, that's not right," said Henry. "Because Adam breaks the rules. Tokahe is good. Adam is the buffalo men."

"Bison," Billy corrected reflexively.

"Bison, then. But Tokahe listens and the Creator takes care of him."

"Tokahe is Tokahe," said Trimble. "And buffalo are bison." This made him laugh to say, and both Billy and Henry smiled. Then he went on: "The point of the story is that there are places not to go for the simple reason they aren't for you. Maybe 'not yet,' and maybe 'not anymore.' But it's not for you to choose."

"Which is Maka Oniye?" Henry asked.

"Maka Oniye is 'not anymore.' We don't go back to the cave for the same reason we don't climb back into our mothers: it's the place we came from."

Henry thought about that, and about the rock Iktomi placed back over the entrance.

"But have you ever been curious?" Billy asked, sitting up now himself.

"To see Maka Oniye? No."

"You're a storyteller. It would be a story."

Trimble shook his head. "It would be a story running backwards. That's the wrong way."

"I understand what you're saying," said Henry, "but I would like to see it. I wish I could."

"Imagine a hole in the ground. That's what you would see. Our people are what matters from it. We're what came from it." He knew even as he prepared to lash out at them that they did not deserve it. But the flame had already caught: "Your people have refused to see us from the start. You've ignored us and tried to push us away. Your eyes have always been on the land, and what have you done with it when it's stolen? Tokahe is Tokahe and you are buffalo, and worse—because what do you give?"

Knots popped in the fire. Billy and Henry were quiet. What could be said to that? America was a burning thing, and they were three men like embers adrift above it. Whatever it was becoming, none of them would be there to see it. In whatever had set it ablaze, none of them had had a hand. They were late sparks, 'not yets,' 'not anymores,' and that was all.

Trimble allowed his words to sit heavy, but in time, the men found small talk again: plans for the days ahead, stories of the wanderers who had drifted into the Nation before them. The temperatures of the night cooled, and as the fire smoldered down, the three of them drifted one by one to bed. Trimble had opened a second cabin, and as Henry lay down on a real (if also quite musty) mattress, he could see a candle burning in his window. He wondered if he had found it or if he had brought it with him. He watched its glow for a long time.

Who was Trimble? he wondered. Was he Tokahe? The tracker? He'd led them here; but he'd also warned them about where to go. He couldn't settle on an answer, and so his thoughts drifted on. *Who was Billy?* His friend was focused and capable in ways he envied. But he also followed Henry, when he ought to know better. *And who was he?* Wandering from trouble to trouble and catching people in his wake. Brave enough to do something. Afraid to do enough.

Trimble's candle still burned, but Henry's eyes had closed. *Tomorrow,* he thought, *I'll be good,* and the idea was so clear in his mind that he felt sure it would reach his heart and do some new alchemy there. If the way wasn't shut. Henry Henry held all of this close, happy and sad at the same time, and sank deep into sleep.

Buffalo Men

There were animals in the village; even a herd of them. Henry looked through the open cabin door at creatures he'd never seen before. They were the size of deer and similarly built, but their fur was a bright tan, nearly yellow, and the white of their bellies reached far up their flanks and made stripes at their necks. Their faces were thin, with black at the nose and eyes, and on every one was a set of strange and stubby black antlers. Henry watched as they grazed the wet grass where the heat of the fire had finished off the snow cover. He counted no less than twenty of them, and they made him grin like a child.

Billy poured a cup of coffee from the percolator and then came and stood beside him. Steam rose from his mug in a great white plume. "They're the second fastest animal on earth," he said. "Pronghorns."

"How do you know that?" Henry asked, still looking out.

"Read it in the ranger book. I stayed up studying all night."

"That's a lie."

"It is. But I did read it just a minute ago when I saw 'em through the window."

"Is there more of that?" The smell of Billy's coffee had won him over.

"There is."

"Heavens to Betsy," Henry said, and Billy laughed.

"*What?*"

"I don't know. My mom used to say it. I think it means, 'oh my!'"

"That's the whitest thing you've ever said."

"Which part?"

"All of it. Get your damn coffee."

Henry did.

The pronghorns didn't scatter as Henry, Billy, and Peacekeeper Trimble walked back to the parking lot, but they did mosey to the far side of the quad. Russ paid them no mind, and with the sun up again, he was back to his hurrying ways. When he got to his patrol car, he had tossed his things in the back, opened the driver's side door, and sat down behind the wheel before they could think to wish him well.

"You two have fun out here," he said. He started to close the door, and then he paused. "You're good fellas. I didn't mind the time with you."

Billy smiled. "But you'd better not see us again," he said.

Trimble grinned up. "Not in that ice cream truck, no ways."

"Thank you, Russ. Really."

"No problem." Peacekeeper Trimble finished closing his door, started the engine, and then he was gone. They listened to the sound of his car as it disappeared back up the winding road to the plateau. The thrum of it lingered in the still morning air for a long time. And then they were alone.

Henry and Billy spent the entire day with the Junior Ranger book. They drove back up the hill and hiked a nature trail in the cliffs, walking in a short circle around thick and snow-patched dry brush and scrubby pines. The rocky outcroppings of the pale cliffs towered above them. Early spring birds scattered as they passed.

They explored a cluster of paths at the rim which led out from the parking area on boardwalks. One led to a log ladder that climbed to the top of the formations, giving them sweeping views of the prairieland. Another led through a hole in the rock and down into the maze of gray runs and canyons below. They wandered for hours there on no trail, scrambling through the cold and cracked clay. At times, holes in the earth revealed that even the surfaces on which they stood were hollow underneath, gaps in the hardened mud descending in thin pits and cave systems. Everything they touched crumbled in their hands, and they realized that the formations, for all their strange shapes and wonders, were eroding quickly and endlessly, the landscape changing by the year, even by the day, with every heavy rain and snow thaw. The Badlands were never the same. There was not a single cloud in the sky. The two of them were cold and content.

As they walked, Billy said more about his brother, who once held state records in track and now coached high school; about his sister, who raised two children with her husband in Milwaukee and sold monochrome paintings of safari animals at craft fairs there. He told Henry about the mother he'd lost to illness and the father he had never been able to find. He marveled, time and again, about the Lakota nation where they now found themselves and the people who had endured here. People who'd found purpose, he said; people who could see their future. He was desperate for this, Henry realized—simply to know how to matter in the world.

And Henry Henry talked too, if mostly about his past. He told Billy about life as a salesman and a supervisor and then a corporate stiff. He recalled half-friends he'd made and lost; company softball leagues and Christmas parties. He described his home in the suburbs, and the deep resentment he felt towards mowing the grass in the front lawn. He'd never had a green thumb, and when he said it, they'd both looked around and laughed: there were places, they knew now, where green had lost its Eastern stranglehold on beauty. Henry complained about his old HOA, and then remembered a story a neighbor once told him about a woman on his street who had adopted a gaze of wild raccoons. When she'd been found out, she tried to take them to an animal shelter for adoption, but they laughed her out of the building. So she'd poisoned the raccoons herself, lacing the food she left out for them each night with antifreeze and then dumping their dead bodies—more than a dozen, in the end—in the community pool. It stayed closed for the entire summer. "Some revenge," Billy said, and it was the first time Henry had thought of it that way: for the last decade, he'd only imagined her as a crazy person.

As they hiked, they played "Badlands Bingo" in the Ranger book. They crossed off pronghorns and turkey vultures and cottonwoods and prickly pear cactus. They looked for cliff swallows, but couldn't find them. In the center of the game was a picture of an American bison, but there were none to be found.

By mid-afternoon, their legs were tired and they were hungry. They made their way back to the village and set themselves up for the evening. Peacekeeper Trimble had left extra firewood beside the pit in the center of the ring of cabins, and as the sun sank towards the horizon, they lit another bonfire. It wasn't dark enough yet for the light to dominate the clearing, but a stream of gray smoke rose high up into the sky. They ate a dinner of canned peaches and pork and beans. They were quiet.

And then they heard the sound of an engine—a truck—coming up the road from the south. It slowed by the visitor center and then turned in, winding its way to where they were. There was a lightbar on its roof and the familiar red-and-white flag of the Nation stenciled on the doors. Across the leading edge of the hood were the words *PINE RIDGE*.

Neither Henry nor Billy stood as it cruised to a stop not ten feet away from them in the grass. There was a single person inside: a woman in her late-twenties wearing a tan uniform with a silver badge over the breast pocket. She got out, closed the door of the cab, and raised her hand in greeting as she stepped towards them. "Hello there," she said. She told them her name was Evie Not Afraid.

Peacekeeper Not Afraid was short, thin, and smiled broadly. Her hair was a deep auburn and unusually curly; still, she wore it pulled back in a frizzy and loose single braid. She'd been sent to check-in with them by the chief in Porcupine, she told them, and laughed at the confusion on their faces. "New town center down Pine Ridge way," she added; "S'pose it's an odd name for strangers."

"Would you like to sit?" Billy asked her. Trimble had left his chair by the fire and he gestured towards it.

"I would," she said. "Thank you."

"Do you have them?" Henry asked her. "Porcupines, I mean?" They hadn't been in the bingo.

"I don't personally, no," she said, and laughed. "But they're around." She swept her eyes around the Badlands. "A bit more trees where we are. They like those."

Henry had never considered a porcupine in a tree; now it was all he could think about.

"What are you hoping to check?" Billy asked her. She seemed warm and open, and all of his curiosity was back.

"Well, I could say how soon you're leaving. But really just to see if you're where Brule said you'd be and if you've burned anything down yet."

"Not much to burn down here," Billy said.

"No, not much."

Henry offered her the extra cans they'd brought out from the Roving Ranger, and to his surprise, she accepted. She ate the peaches right away, and then set the beans near the edge of the fire to warm. While she waited, she asked them about their day and answered Billy's questions about the former reservation with kindness. She seemed surprised by his interest, and he didn't try very hard to tone it down. They learned she was a rarity in the Nation, as a female peacekeeper: but her father had been a sheriff in the American Way, as she called it, and it was all she'd ever wanted to do. Henry realized he hadn't had a real conversation with a woman since his talks with Cece what felt like years ago. There was no doubt Peacekeeper Not Afraid was easier company.

By the time her beans were ready, she'd decided on an offer. "How long are you going to be here?" she asked.

"A few more days," Henry said. "We were just here in the pass this morning, but I'd like to explore a bit more."

"What about you?" she asked, looking at Billy.

"I'm with him," he said. "So, a few more days."

She took a big bite of beans, swallowed, and then spoke: "Well, about that. Would you want to see Porcupine for a bit? My father knows more about the Transition and the ILA and all that than I do. He's always eager to talk. Might have some questions for you, too: he's curious what's happening out in the wilderness these days. It wouldn't be any trouble."

Billy looked at Henry. "Just me or both of us?" he asked.

"Well," Not Afraid said, "Both. Or, if he's more keen on wandering than you are, you could come back with me and I could bring you back here in another day or so, depending on how long you want to stay. So long as you're here at the cabins, it should be easy enough to find you."

Billy wanted very much to go. He turned again to Henry, hoping it didn't show as much as it felt. "What do you think?" he asked.

Henry smiled. He liked her. "I think it's okay. You should go."

"You'll be alone."

"I've been alone before." It was true, but it suddenly felt strange to Henry to say it.

"Okay." Billy looked back at Not Afraid, who was scraping the bottom of her can now with a spoon. "Okay," he said. "I'll go."

"Good," she said. "It's an hour or so south from here, so not too far. A bit tricky to find if you don't have a map for it, but here's what I think: I'll leave an extra radio here with you, Henry, if you need it. Won't have much charge, but should be fine for a few days; call in if there's trouble."

"Any particular trouble?" Henry asked.

"Can't imagine it," said Not Afraid. "But it's the Badlands, I hear."

"Right."

"Not our name for it, though. It came down from the French, once upon a time." She paused. "Like 'Sioux,' as a matter of fact."

"What's your name for it?" It was Billy who asked.

She looked at him with a spark in her eye. "Don't have one." Then she wiped her mouth with her sleeve. "You okay to leave now? I got another dinner at home waitin' for me."

Billy's eyes widened. This was happening. He was ready. There was another dinner.

He got his things, said his goodbyes to Henry, and then they were gone, too.

The pronghorns were back the next morning, much to Henry's delight. He'd made coffee, but too much of it. Still, he finished the pot and set off with his heart racing. He'd stayed up the night before and scoured the trail maps in the Junior Ranger book and from the visitor center, planning out his day. He'd start with a longer hike at the top of the bluff and then, after lunch, drive the loop road out west. There was a marker for a prairie dog town, and he was desperately curious to discover what that meant. He packed food for the day and filled a water bottle from a spigot in the village. Then he was off again on his own adventure.

Clouds rolled in during the afternoon, but not until the sun had finished its work with most of the lingering snow. The shadows slid over the cuts and ridges of the landscape, drawing out the depth and distances between them that the common bands of colored earth tended to obscure. Henry smiled to himself all day: he'd never been somewhere so beautiful.

The prairie dog town was all he'd hoped for, too. It was two dozen holes in the crusted topsoil with little brown heads taking turns poking up and disappearing into them, just like in the old carnival game. He wasn't prepared for their squeaking: they spoke to each other, taking turns looking around and then sharing what they saw. Their sound was identical to that of a dog toy, and he'd learned they were nearly toys themselves: routine snacks for black-footed ferrets and hawks, but so rapid in their multiplication that the regular losses never held the colonies back.

Although he'd never seen a prairie dog himself, Caleb had once been fascinated by them. He'd downloaded a book from the library and shared facts with Henry on the drive to school. Henry was surprised he could still remember some of them: "they have the most complex decoded language of any animal;" "their mating season is just one hour long." The book told a story Caleb hadn't understood, but one which had amazed Henry. During the Lewis and Clark expedition, explorers had marveled at prairie dogs and Merriweather Lewis, mercurial as ever, had insisted one be captured and sent back to Washington as a gift for President Jefferson. It took the men nearly an entire day to catch one of the rascals. But what amazed Henry was that, once it was caught, one of the members of the expedition had to be dispatched to ferry it east. They were months away from St. Louis by that point, not terribly far from where Henry now stood, and a man who dreamed of the Pacific Ocean was sent home alone with a rodent in a cage. Henry Henry couldn't fathom it, and he tried to kindle the same wonder in his son. But in the age of next-day delivery, it was like trying to start a fire with sticks.

A gentle rain began to fall as he stepped again into the Ranger and began the drive to the cabins. It had been an empty day; a day outside of time. His only jobs were to move and to eat. Everything more *was more*—it was delight. After dinner, he thought, he would radio Billy to check in. He wanted to hear about Porcupine. He wanted to share himself and to be shared with.

The last thing he expected was to see three familiar silhouettes racing down the Pinnacles Road south in the rain on their motorcycles, heading right in his direction.

Porcupine was altogether new. It had been no more than a few mobile homes before the land rights were restored to the tribes, but afterwards, the council at Pine Ridge had chosen it as the place to build something from the ground up. They'd used the monetary allotment which had been held in trust with the Treasury Department for nearly half a century after the United States' violation of the Fort Laramie Treaty was nullified by the Supreme Court in 1980 (gathering interest to the tune of nearly two billion dollars) to finance the construction. There was a high school and a stadium, a courthouse and a county seat. There was a cultural center and a museum. Houses were new, as were the gas stations and grocery stores. The result was a fresh-painted oasis at the edge of the drought-ravaged plains; a marker, to any who cared to see it, of defiance and endurance.

The victory of the Lakota Nation, in the waning days of America, had seemed pyrrhic in the newspapers—but that was because we have always confused freedom with power. The Lakota thrived because they chose to, and there was no longer the will, in Pierre or Washington or anywhere else, to try and stop them. Peacekeeper Not Afraid's father, who had joined the tribal council after his retirement, was proud of the metaphor: "Pȟahíŋ," he told Billy, "never bears the other animals any contempt. But his quills are sharp nonetheless."

"Why do you use the English word, then? Why 'Porcupine?'"

"The warning is for outsiders, not insiders. Who knows what p̌ahíŋ calls himself?"

Billy thought it was a good answer. He said, "Porcupine seems like a home, though. More than a warning."

"There's lots to be happy about for us, that's so. We have a place. But the Invasion changed our people. It changed me, working for it. The language is lost. So is the way we live with the stories. Even still, lots of young folks want to leave. It doesn't matter that your country is falling apart; 'there's always Canada,' people say. Broke things are broke things. You have to learn to live with them as they are."

Billy wasn't sure that was true, but he knew not to say it.

He spent most of the day, though, with Evie. She was, as Henry felt, easy company. He followed her to work and rode with her on calls. Some boys broke a window at a store; a new traffic light kept cutting out on a cross street. He half-expected they would have to rescue a kitten from a tree before the day was done, but in truth, he'd not actually seen any cats.

For her part, Evie seemed happy to have someone around. One consequence of keeping the borders of the Nation closed was a lack of new faces, she said, as well as the stories that might come with them. She wanted to hear about the South and about the other places Billy had traveled. She wanted to know about *him*: a traveler through a country which had once, and did still, mean him harm.

When Henry checked in at the end of the first day, Billy was surprised that he felt bothered by the call. It was, like it or not, an interruption—and Henry was still a poor conversationalist. He talked about finishing up the ranger bingo and finding a storage shed full of more firewood. He did his best to describe the sunset. It was all pleasant enough, but food was waiting, and then drinks with a few of Evie's cousins. Billy said he planned to stay a day or so more. It made sense, when you thought about it: it was still only mid-March, and the highways west would get into the Rocky

Mountains soon enough. If the Lakota would tolerate them, it might mean better chances for clearer roads.

Henry agreed with that. He still had places he wanted to see. His leg was feeling a lot better, he said, but he could use the rest. They'd talk again tomorrow, and for Billy, that was promise enough.

"He's an odd one, yeah?" Evie had been in the room for their call.

"He is."

"What's he up to out here?"

Billy sat back in his chair. They were in the station where she worked. "A quest for his kid," he said. "He died a few years ago. So did his wife. He's finishing a project."

"That's sweet," Evie said. "Maybe strange, too."

"Yeah, it's both. Our country's not cooperating, though."

"Did it ever?"

"It didn't use to be so hard for people like him."

"This is some bitter medicine, then."

"It is."

"You think it will help?"

"I'm waiting to see."

She opened the office door and held it for Billy. He stood up to go. "Be careful you don't get sick, too."

Billy walked out of the station with her.

The bikers drove ahead of Henry on the Loop Road all the way to the cabins. They pulled into the back and parked in a circle around his fire pit. He stayed at a distance; but he followed nonetheless.

The rain had stopped and the sun was blood red on the clouds as he stepped out of the Ranger. He was unarmed, of course. The bikers waited, standing and now holding their helmets in their hands. He walked slowly towards them. He didn't know what to say.

It seemed at first that they didn't either, although they had been the ones to force the meeting. The tallest—a man with a long, black beard and dark, weathered skin—cleared his throat. Then, the road-worn woman with dirty red hair to his left broke the silence.

"What are you doing here?" she asked Henry.

Henry wasn't sure how to respond to that. His mind had been trying to get the very same question out of his own mouth. Eventually, he went with the truth: "I'm just looking around."

The third biker, who was the oldest of the three with a dusty gray goatee and sunglasses still on above it, spoke with gravel in his voice: "Yeah? It's a pretty place."

Now Henry was even more confused. "Yep," he said.

"Yep," said the gravel man.

After a long moment, Henry finally asked them if they wanted something. He still stood more than a dozen feet from the three, and he had no interest in getting any closer.

"No," came the croaked reply from Gravel.

The woman rolled her eyes at that and then hit the bigger man with the black beard in the stomach with her helmet. He finally spoke. "*We been watchin' you since you took up with the reds.*" he said in the deepest voice Henry had ever heard. He wrinkled his nose at the slur, then hoped they hadn't seen him.

"I know that," he lied.

"Now your friend's gone and set in with 'em," the woman said. "Which ain't a surprise. But you was right to stay. You won't see him again."

"That's not true. He's coming right back. He might be back any minute, as a matter of fact, and the officer, too."

All three of them laughed at Henry's bluff. "No chance," said the red-haired woman. "They don't do nothin' fast. Except try to chase folks off."

Henry felt indignant at that. "Seemed like you were the ones chasing us before."

"Not chasing. Warning. You can't be on the main roads here. Look where it got you."

"I'm where I want to be."

"Course you are. Campin' in the Badlands by yourself."

"For now."

"Boy, do you think you're the first man ever thought to drive across South Dakota? All they do is bother white folks. The hate's in their blood."

"Nobody seemed hateful to me."

"Yet."

Henry's heart was still racing and he wanted very much for them to leave. "What do you want?" he asked again.

"Just to share dinner with another traveler," she said.

"And tell him he ain't gotta get pushed around." It was the older man again.

"I don't have food for you," Henry said. *There's just the driver,* he thought.

The man smiled. "We brought our own. And extra."

Henry didn't want to share a meal with them, but he didn't know how not to. The bikers started the fire and got to cooking. To Henry's grief, whatever they had brought smelled incredible. It turned out to be hot dogs.

Henry kept to himself until dinner was ready. He busied himself in the Ranger, organizing and reorganizing his bins, and then pittered around in his cabin. He made his bed. He prepped coffee for the morning in the percolator. He did everything he could not to cross paths with these strangers who had invaded his space. The conversation before, such as it was, had told him next to nothing about what they were doing there. It had also made him sure he didn't really want to find out. But there was only one of him and three of them, and he didn't know how to make them leave. He wished Billy was there; he would know what to do. When he was inside, he saw the radio on a table and thought about calling down to Pine Ridge for help. But was he "in trouble"? Would anyone answer?

"Come eat!" A cigarette-choked voice called from outside. He did.

They actually had ketchup and mustard to go with the dogs, along with buns that were only half stale. Against his better judgment, Henry asked where they'd found them.

That brought more laughter. "Cops got you scared good, huh? Stores around here still take money, even if they pretend not to like who it's from," the redhead told him. Her name, he learned, was Lori with an "i". She said he looked like he was about to shit himself: "What'd they tell you about us?"

"Not very much," Henry confessed. "They said you didn't want any more trouble with them. That you'd already had some, I guess."

"In their dreams," Lori said. "Listen up now: we *lived* here. Before any of their bullshit. All we did was not leave, and it drives 'em crazy that they can't run us off. But how're they gonna do that? We go where we want, and we're faster than any damn cop car."

"*Nomads*," said Blackbeard, grinning in the firelight.

"It's the prettiest place in the world," said Gravel. He put down his hot dog on a paper plate in his lap. "Can't nobody *own* it. These are the best roads there are, and we live on 'em and drive 'em when we want. Don't cause any trouble 'cept what they start with us."

Henry felt his questions slipping away. He fought to keep hold of them: "What's that have to do with me?" he asked.

"Just what you make it," the old man said. "They told you to stay where they want you to stay. We're tellin' you you ain't gotta listen to 'em. You wanna go somewhere, we'll tell you how. You wanna leave when your friend gets back, you leave."

"*White courtesy*," Blackbeard said, and Henry understood both of the things he meant.

"What is it you're out here for, Ranger?" It was Lori again.

"I'm not a Ranger."

"Your truck, dummy. Says 'Ranger' on it. You wanna tell me your actual name?"

"No," Henry said. "I'm going to the parks. Trying to…see the country, I guess. What's left of it, anyway."

"That's what we got in common," Gravel said, the hot dog back in his hand and on its way to his mouth. "The world's endin' and we might as well see it while we can." He took a bite. "You gonna go into the Hills?" he asked with his mouth full.

"I was before. But I'm not now."

"That'd be a damn mistake."

"No need to be scared of 'em," said Lori. "No tribe owns 'em. Almost never anybody *in* 'em. You plannin' to carve a new set of faces in a mountain?"

"No," said Henry.

"Then how they gonna know you was even there?"

"But if they did…"

"*Chicken.*"

"I don't mind moving on. This place…" Henry looked at the jagged silhouettes of the rocks all around him, at the stars coming out overhead "is plenty. And I've got other places to go."

"May be. It's not the Hills, though," said Gravel. "Be a shame to miss 'em."

"Look, if you're scared of 'injuns,' you're scared of 'injuns,'" Lori said. "You ain't the first. But I'll just say this: Buffalo Gap. It's only half a town, and there's an old quarry road west that runs just south of Wind Cave. You can follow the main highway up from there all the way to anywhere you wanna go. You won't see a soul."

"If you did, what're they gonna do? Shoot the tires out of an ice cream truck? They'll just kick you right on out—which is what you're about to do to yourself."

"I need to wait here on my friend," Henry said.

The bikers laughed again, the sound of it loud and ringing through the night. "You won't see him again," the old man repeated. "Or us, neither. Do what you want; that's what we came to tell you. It used to be a free country."

When the food was done, the three of them saddled up and left just as they said they would. They agreed not to come back. The woman, Lori, shook her head at Henry as she put on her helmet. "Keep puttin' the shackles on yourself, Ranger," she said. As they rode, they rode without lights; the moon was enough. When they were gone, Henry sat at the fire without them for a very long time. He watched it burn low, and then burn out. He thought about the radio in the cabin. He wondered, in spite of himself, if Billy was planning to stay gone.

It was five days before Billy returned. Henry had checked in that first night after all; he'd told Billy about the hikes and the prairie dogs, but he didn't mention the bikers.

On the second night, the radio died while they were talking. Henry hadn't thought much of it, as his heart was set on a strange place in another corner of the park map—an old abandoned missile silo he wanted to explore. He'd largely forgotten about his visitors and what they said. He was content. He would go up to the silo the next day, and then head west to camp in the park at Sage Creek. A guidebook he'd found in the visitor center said there might be bison out that way, and he desperately wanted to see one. The route would also take him back past the prairie dog town, and he was eager to drop in on his old friends there. Billy was still in no hurry, it seemed, and he knew he had time.

On the third day, he woke at Sage Creek and headed south. In the morning, he crossed the line without knowing it: he'd followed a road to a ghost town deep in the prairie and wandered among the dried shells of the buildings there. He'd thought the place belonged to the park service, but as he made his way home, he passed a sign telling him he was re-entering the Badlands. He thought about the transgression all evening, as he stayed warm by another fire and then as he pulled the sheets up on his bed. The plains were stubborn and beautiful, he felt; the things that lived on them even moreso. Wanderers, except for the prairie dogs. Orbiters, like he used to be, stretching out their circles until water or pockets of lush grass brought them back. He knew the pronghorns would be there in the morning; they always were.

And then on the fourth day, in tall prairie grass under rolling hills of ponderosa pine, he saw his first buffalo. It was a solitary bull, bigger than a car. A bird sat on its shoulders, digging mites out of its thick, brown fur. Its head was down, rooting slowly and purposefully in the earth. Its horns were cracked and worn and the color of burned coffee. Beneath them, the bison's eyes were enormous and glossy-wet. It watched him, and there was no caution in its stare: it looked with only the recognition one animal has for another.

Henry didn't have the Ranger book with him to cross the animal off. He was far away, miles from his truck and his radio and his cabin. And for a long time, Henry sat beside the bull on the ground and cried. It surprised him, and overwhelmed him. He wept for himself, and for his son, and for his friend, and for this time in which they all found themselves. Providence, God knew, could be made from punishment. But it was punishment, nonetheless. What would it take to bring him home? What was left to discover? How far would be far enough? He saw himself, perhaps for the first time, as he was: a breaker. His reasons for breaking were suspect, as was his hope that he could get far enough away that his clumsiness wouldn't matter. No ghost, no righteousness, no pity. He led people astray. This was the deepest truth he could find.

The wind howled across the plains, ripped at his skin, and spoke nothing to him at all.

When Peacekeeper Not Afraid's patrol car pulled in past the Ben Reifel Visitor Center, Henry was standing by the firepit. It was ten past noon. He had just eaten lunch. He was burning his trash from the last few days.

Billy got out of the car and was all smiles. Evie said her farewells from the window and then backed out the way she came–off, she said, to eat lunch somewhere herself.

As he walked towards the smoke, Billy said, "I brought you a gift. I'm sorry I was gone so long. But truly: you're not going to believe this."

"Yeah?" Henry said. He'd turned to look at his companion, but his feet had not moved. "What'd you find?"

"There was a man in Porcupine," Billy said. "An old friend of Evie's dad's, who had a kind of knick-knack shop."

"Like antiques?"

"Yeah, sort of. It was actually more of a museum: things from the tribes, arrowheads and old cavalry sabers and things like that. But–"

"Like army surplus?"

"Yeah, a bit. But that's not the point!" Billy was radiating with his own excitement. "The point is he had old *park stuff*. Ranger hats and WPA posters and logbooks and…" he paused for dramatic effect "…and *this*." He held out a Junior Ranger badge. It was made of wood rather than plastic, but the shape was the same as the others. The corners were worn and the design was chipped, but Billy was close enough to Henry now that Henry could read the words engraved on the banner. They said *Wind Cave National Park.*

"Can you believe it?" Billy asked.

Sadness crashed over Henry in a wave he could never have held back. His eyes watered. "Oh, God," he said. "Oh, God."

Billy knew Henry would be surprised, but he hadn't expected this. "Incredible, right? I told him what we're doing, and he wouldn't even sell it to me: he gave it to me on the spot." He tried to hand it over to Henry. "Lucky fourteen."

Henry wanted to take it, but he couldn't make his arm move. "Lucky fourteen," he said.

Billy stood there with the badge in his hand, trying to figure Henry out. "You want me to set it in the truck?" he asked.

"Yeah, you can."

"Fortune favors the bold."

"Thank you, Billy. I… I… " Henry's voice drifted off.

Billy shrugged as if it was nothing at all. Things felt strange, but he couldn't place it. He started off towards the Ranger. "Want me to put it in with the others?" he asked.

His back was to Henry now. "Yes," he heard Henry say.

Billy opened the door to the cab, reached under the front seat. The lockbox was where it always was, and he picked it up, undid the latch, and opened the lid. At first, nothing seemed amiss. But as he got ready to set down his prize, his hand hovered over the pile there. Right on top was another badge that looked just like it.

Broke Things Broken

"What did you do?" he asked, panic beginning to rise. "Henry, what did you do?"

"Billy–"

"This is bad, Henry. This is really bad. Evie talked about this, she–"

"Billy–"

"We've got to go. Like, right now. If they find out–"

"Billy–"

"What were you *thinking*? Somebody saw you. Somebody's got to know…" Billy's mind was racing through the options. He realized he'd left some things in the cabin, and he set off for them. They had to leave.

"Billy–"

Billy walked through the open doorway and scanned the room for anything that couldn't be left behind. He realized Henry's things were still laid out, his bed unmade and the radio still on the dresser. "Henry, you've gotta get your stuff. Now. What have you been doing? They have cell phones; all anybody has to do is call this in–" He was busying himself with clothes, books, a comb. Henry had followed him through the doorway.

"Billy–"

"I'm serious, Henry. We've seen what we came to see and got what we came to get. We're leaving."

"Billy, *stop*."

He said it with all the strength he had, and Billy did. He was holding a half-filled bag in his hand. The rabbit's foot key fob was sitting on top of the dresser.

"Stop," Henry said again. "It's okay."

Billy held out the bag. "It's specifically *not* okay."

Henry leaned against the doorpost, already spent. "I mean, it's okay for you."

None of this was making sense to Billy. Henry was an obsessive, but he wasn't an idiot; Billy had seen through that act what felt like ages ago. "What are you talking about?" he asked, without really asking. "Listen to me: they're going to come for us. They keep track of things out there. They know about those dumb bikers and anybody else that wanders around. It's important to them. We've got to go—"

"Then they know you didn't do it, Billy. You weren't there."

"How does that matter?! They'll take the truck—"

It was the thing Henry had needed Billy to say. "No, they won't. *You* will. It's yours now, Billy. You can take it." He pointed at the keys.

Billy put down the bag. "Who cares whose it is! Get your stuff, Hank. I mean it; get it right now so we can go."

"No, Billy."

"What do you mean no?" But he wasn't really asking that question, either. Henry pretended he was.

"I'm not going. I'm not going with you. You take the truck wherever you want. It's yours."

"We don't have time for this."

"Billy—"

"*Stop saying my name!*" His mind was racing now, and he stepped away from the dresser and towards Henry. "Why?" he asked. "*Why?*"

Henry didn't move away. He didn't look away. "You know why."

"I'm asking because I *don't*."

"Yes you do."

This couldn't be right. "Look, you did something stupid," Billy said. "It's not the first time! But right now, just get your things, get in the truck, and we'll figure all of this out. *Together.* This was just a rule. We'll get out like we said we would, and we'll go wherever's next. It doesn't matter."

"I can't do that anymore." Henry said. "It does matter."

"You can't do *what* anymore?"

"I can't let you follow me. You can't come with me anymore. It wasn't something stupid," he said, and with that his eyes began to well. *"It's what I do.* It's what I *always* do. You have to go."

Billy couldn't believe it because he didn't want to. "You can barely walk!" he yelled.

"That's not true anymore. Take the Ranger. Go."

Billy was beside himself, and he was surprised to feel tears in his own eyes now, too. "I don't leave." It's all he could say.

"I know. I know. That's why *I'm* leaving. I'm leaving *you.* I'm leaving the keys, and all the stuff we found, and…" he looked around the room "and whatever all *this* is. I'm the one who's leaving." He'd rehearsed this part of his speech a dozen times, but he still got the words wrong. "You… you just can't come with me anymore. It's not right for you." And then the sentence came back to him unbidden: *There's just the driver.*

Billy was staring. His hands were on his hips now, and he was thinking as hard as he could. "Hank, look: this is dumb. This is *all* dumb. You can't go anywhere." He pointed out the cabin window at the emptiness of the prairie. "This *is* nowhere! They will catch you, and they will lock you up, or they will dump you out somewhere else. That would be *my* fault. You can't be alone. You don't have anything, you don't know anything…"

"You can't protect me from me, Billy," Henry said. And with those words, he finally understood: *buffalo man.* The room was quiet. The two men looked at each other, frozen in their separate places, and neither knew what might come next.

Finally, Billy spoke. "I won't go," he said.

Henry nodded, and it was the movement he needed. He had always been able to count on Billy for that. "I know you won't," he said. And then he walked over to the side of his bed and picked up a backpack that was sitting behind it. *Badlands National Park* was embroidered on the shoulder strap, and it was already packed with clothes and all the food Henry could carry. There was a water bottle attached to a loop on its side by a cheap carabiner he'd found in the gift shop. "I'm sorry," Henry said. "Thank you, Billy. You're good. You're good, and I'm sorry."

And with that, Henry Henry walked out the door of the cabin and set off, limping slightly, into the late-March afternoon.

Billy Faulkner stood still. He'd been with Henry for a month. They'd crossed half the country together. And now he was alone. Or at least he was about to be.

He followed Henry into the empty space between the cabins. Henry was just passing the fire pit, the smoke from the trash he'd burned still rising up into the afternoon sky.

"Hey!" he yelled. Henry stopped. "You're an old fool, Henry! But you don't have to be a lonely one!"

Henry didn't turn around.

"You're wrong," he said, and he hated that these were his last words to his friend, and that he had made them so.

Billy didn't say anything, but he stood there and watched as Henry made his way up the path to the visitor center and turned right towards the rising road into the pass. He thought about the keys and the Ranger and Evie in Porcupine. He knew there were stories there, but he wasn't ready to hear them. He didn't know if he was ready for anything. He was free; he was free.

The wind had picked up, and it was catching between the buttons in his shirt. He was cold. The rabbit's foot would still be on the dresser, he thought, but it would be safer in his hand. He turned to go back inside. The shadow of a cloud passed quickly over the cabin, causing it to flicker in the light.

Inside, dust motes floated in sunbeams and there were no sounds at all beyond the ones Billy made: hard-soled shoes on the floorboards, the clangs of metal as he stacked tin cups and pots and pans. The hinges creaked on the campstove. The paper rustled as he folded up a map. In his own room, he found the badge from the Badlands he'd pinned to his shirt in the visitor center. He picked it up, turned it once in his hand, and looked down at it. Then he tucked it deep in his pocket.

Where could Henry go? He walked north, up the winding road to the edge of the plateau, and then on past the trailheads and overlooks to the edge of the park. He knew the way, having driven it several times in the last week. But it felt farther on foot, and as he hit the straight and empty road through the wide, flat prairie, his leg hurt and he was exhausted. It was late in the afternoon, and the walk was bitter and hard. Still, he moved on over the cracked and faded asphalt as lizards darted across the road and a prairie dog, wandering far from his own home, stood and watched him from the shade of a dead and sun-bleached tree. Henry stared at his own feet, taking one step, and then another.

As the sun began to fall into the horizon, he realized he was getting closer to the interstate, but he wouldn't be able to reach the safe and empty spaces on the far side before dark. For all the time he'd spent imagining being on foot again over the last day or so, he'd thought very little about how to sleep. Up ahead of him, he saw a sign for a place called the Oglala Living History Village; he decided he would turn in.

The site was just as abandoned as he had figured it would be. There were a half dozen outbuildings and wind-shredded trailers, and then beyond them, three traditional tipis set up in a wide circle. The coverings on two had been ruined by snow and rot, but the one in the center from where Henry stood seemed to be intact. He walked to it and opened the door flap so he could peer inside.

He'd never been in a tipi before, and it was more spacious than he expected. The floor was hard-packed earth, dotted with a few half-buried stones and patches of long dead grass. There were two frayed blankets laid out on the ground alongside a straw basket which had been trampled and ruined by someone or something a long time ago. It would keep him out of the wind, though, and so Henry took off his boots and stepped in.

The first truth was that he felt bad about this: it was another act of trespassing and transgression. But another truth was that he felt like he deserved his shame and it would no longer do to hide from it. He settled in for the night, taking care not to touch the things that had been left there, and stared up at the poles crossing in the center above him. He didn't think about them, or about the Oglala, or about the Living History Village. He didn't even think about Billy, or where he was, or what he might be doing now. Instead, he had tunneled deep into himself, and from where he was now, he could think of no place other. He was a cloud, shadowing the ground underneath him. He was rain, eroding every place he touched. He was contaminant, infected and infecting everyone. When sleep found him, late into the night, he hoped only that it would not let him go.

But of course it did. The morning came, and the sun with it. The walls of the tipi glowed with the dawn, and Henry couldn't lay down and die after all because, to his great frustration and humiliation, he had to pee. It seemed an unbearable affront to do it where he was, and so he got to his feet and stepped outside.

And when he did, not twenty feet away was an old police cruiser. Henry recognized it even before he recognized the man fidgeting with something in his hands beside the open driver's side door: it was Peacekeeper Trimble. Henry didn't know what to say.

But that had never been Russ's trouble. "Good morning, Henry Two-Times."

Henry expected him to produce handcuffs, or maybe even a service revolver. But he just stood where he was, absently flipping pages back and forth in his notebook. A hawk flew past in the sky above them, and its shadow flitted across the lightbar on top of the car.

"How did you find me?" Henry asked.

Peacekeeper Trimble pointed at Henry's boots sitting outside the entrance to the tipi. "Your friend called down to Porcupine and they gave me a ring and asked me to come check on you. That was last night; I figured you weren't getting too far, so I drove down early this morning to look."

Henry thought about that. "He told you what I did."

"Yep, he told me."

"And you just want to check on me? Not lock me up?"

"I don't want to lock you up. Hetty might–but just so she'd have somebody to heckle. And chief says no."

"Why?"

"Well, it'd be more expensive than just giving you a ride, he thinks."

"What do you think?"

Trimble put the notebook away. He shifted on his feet and looked Henry over. "I think he's the boss. And I think you seem kinda locked up already, if you don't mind me sayin' it."

Henry squinted against the early sun. "It's okay," he said.

"Where were you trying to get to? I was surprised your friend said you'd gone north."

"It's too far," Henry said.

"Not really an answer to my question."

He paused. He'd seen the word on a map, but it was different to say it out loud. "Medora?"

Trimble laughed in spite of himself. "Medora? That's Standing Rock territory there. Mandan and Hidatsa. And 300 miles from here. You were gonna walk?"

"I am," Henry said. "I know it's a long way."

"No, get your things and get in. We'll go. But you'll owe me some answers to a few questions on the way. We'll have time."

Trimble was already seated and had the door half closed by the end of his last sentence. Henry hadn't moved. A gust of wind rippled the door flap behind him.

He would do his best.

Sink Hole

o you want to ask me why I did it?"

Russ Trimble turned the wheel, backed up the patrol car, and then put it in drive.

"You told me not to. So did Chief and everybody else," Henry said.

Even though there was no traffic, Russ stopped at the end of the dirt track and looked both ways before pulling onto the highway.

"Billy did, too," Henry lied. "He never knew I was going to do it. He wouldn't have gone, ever, if he had. It was just me."

The cruiser picked up speed, heading north. They drove over the interchange with I-90 and were immediately in wide, empty nothing.

"It wasn't the bikers, either. They told me it would be okay, but I knew they were lying."

"You saw them again?"

"Yes, but they didn't make me do it."

"Hmm." Trimble set his speed at 60 and they slid over the surface of the earth.

"I went because I wanted to see. I knew it was bad. I knew it…" Words just kept pouring out, and Henry didn't know how to stop them. "even when I was there, I knew it. And I still kept going. I kept driving, anyways."

"You didn't go for your little badge?"

"No," Henry said. "I mean, yes. But no. I didn't even look for it first. I went… I went…" And then Henry was crying, on top of everything else. He was such a goddamned fool. Russ was quiet. His hands were at ten and two. Endless grasslands swallowed them up, cruiser and all.

"What can I do?" Henry asked. "I can't fix it. What can I do?"

"I'll tell you this, Henry–"

"What? What? Tell me anything."

Russ pursed his lips at the interruption. "I'll tell you this: you ever get locked up one day back in your own country… you get yourself a lawyer."

Henry blinked tears from his eyes. "Huh?"

"I used to watch cop shows when I was a kid. Kinda piqued my interest, now that I look back on it. And Henry," Russ said, "you sing like a bird."

"Oh," Henry said, almost to himself. He thought on it, and something caught. "I did it, though," he said. "And you already know."

"Yeah, you did," said Trimble. "Still, though."

"Yeah."

"Okay."

Their tires rumbled over the gravel track. Henry listened to them, feeling the ridges and pebbles in the soles of his feet. As he did, he tried to climb back up out of himself. After a while, he spoke again: "Russ, what can I do?"

"Hmm?"

"You said you had questions before. What are they?"

Trimble was still looking straight ahead, but the corner of his mouth creeped up just a bit. "You're ready for that, then?"

"I think so."

"Well…first, I was wondering what you saw."

"What?"

"Like I said before, I've never been all the way out there. I'm wonderin' what it was like."

For two days now, Henry's whole chest had felt like it was caught in a vise squeezing harder and harder. He hadn't been able to breathe. Until he'd drifted off the night before, he hadn't even believed he could sleep. From the instant he left Wind Cave until now, he'd wanted to forget every single thing about it, and so he'd put a wall around the place in his mind so that he might never be tempted again. And sitting in that police car, he realized he didn't know how to get back in.

"Russ, I'm sorry," he said. "I know it was wrong. I don't–"

"I know you know that. But it happened, anyway. So, what did you see?"

"I can't–"

But Henry realized that he could. There was a door in the wall after all, its seams hidden but still visible in the surface. He knew where it was, even if it hurt to open it. So, he said in the quietest voice he had, "*It was beautiful, Russ. I'm so sorry. The grass was so tall, and the trees were all shaking–all at the same time–in the wind. There were cliffs and stone canyons between them. Birds in the air, and grasshoppers jumping around in the thousands, Russ. I'm so sorry.*"

"That many grasshoppers, huh?"

Henry coughed softly to clear his throat. "I've never seen so many."

"Sounds like a lot of places in the Hills."

Henry didn't know about that, and he said so.

"I know, though," Trimble said. "What about the cave? Did you find it?"

Henry closed his eyes, remembering. "I saw where it was," he said. "There was a path behind the visitor center. It had a sign. But I didn't go." He looked over at Russ. "I want you to know that I didn't go."

"No?"

"No. I walked around for a long time. And then I went in the center for a badge. But after, I just wandered in the woods. I wanted…" He was struggling to find the thought. Or maybe to finish it.

"You wanted what?"

And then he realized he could say it: "I wanted to see a buffalo," Henry answered. "A bison. I hadn't seen one before. I wanted to find one."

"Did you?"

"No. Not there."

"And you didn't even go in the cave? Even after all that?"

"No."

Russ was quiet for a moment. Then he asked, "Why?"

Henry was all the way back inside now, but the wall he'd built was still there, and it was hard work letting things go back through it. "Because it's not my place," he finally said.

Russ took that answer in, and his eyes were still on the straight road to the horizon. "Yeah," he said. "But what is?"

"I don't know," Henry said.

And then they drove for a long time. The sun poured in through Henry's window, and Peacekeeper Trimble sat cool in his shadow. The sky was the color of muslin cloth. In the distance, Henry saw a cemetery coming up on their left, and then past it a town, maybe five buildings in all. When they got there, there was a stop sign. Russ braked, looked both ways again, and then moved on.

Henry had been holding onto a thought, and as they picked up speed, he let it free. "Where is my place?" he asked.

Russ squinted against the light glinting off the specks of silica in the asphalt. "I don't know, Henry," he said. "Are you sure you're supposed to have one?"

Henry didn't have an answer to that. He thought about Ohio. He let himself think about the Ranger, and about Billy. But those weren't places.

Peacekeeper Trimble rolled his fingers on the steering wheel. "Is it okay with you if I tell you what I think?" he asked.

"Yes," Henry said.

"You're older than me. And you're from a different place, yeah. But you're also–" and he couldn't believe he was saying this "–my elder. So, I might not know anything… "

"Please, Russ."

Trimble frowned. But he went on. "You seem like you're trying to fix something's not made for fixing," he said. "Or trying to find something's not made for finding, maybe. But either way, something *outside*."

"I don't understand," Henry said.

"Yeah. I'm probably not sayin' it right." He decided to go a different way. "Mind if I try a story?"

Henry very much did not mind. "Please."

"Okay. When I was a kid, I grew up on a farm," Trimble began. "My daddy ran it, even if it didn't grow much. We planted wheat mostly, and some alfalfa and soy. I hated it," he said, and grinned. "But it's what we did.

"Anyway, one spring when he was plowing, he lost an axle in a ditch he swore hadn't been there the year before. After he got the tractor out, he had all of us come out to take a look and see, and sure enough, what he'd hit turned out to be a sinkhole, maybe half a dozen feet across. It went down just a foot or so, but it was soft and sandy at the bottom. He shook his head at it, and because I was just eight or nine at the time, he told me to steer clear of it, in case it got bigger. Which I didn't, and which it did.

"So, after my mom had to rescue me and my brother enough times, he set to try and fill it up. We had a little backhoe then, and so he started digging on the other side of the field and bringing over loads to the hole, one at a time. I remember watching him, scooping dirt in one place and bringing it over to the other. Dropping it in…" Russ smiled at the memory and even laughed to himself. "And it just kept taking more and more. At some point, I thought he must have moved enough dirt to fill that sinkhole twice over–not that I probably had much of an eye to tell yet, really. But still, I went over to look… and except for being a different color at the bottom, that hole didn't look a bit different than when he started."

"Where'd the dirt go?" Henry asked.

"That's what he wanted to know. Fact was that the more he put in, the more it pushed into that sinkhole, and it kept sinking. He figured it must have been the dome of a cave that collapsed to start with, and now he was going to have to pack the whole thing to get his field back. I remember him shaking his head at it and telling my mom he must be just about there, just about there. But he stayed at it all day, and the next day, too: moving dirt from one side of the field to the other, and dropping it into that goddamn hole, as he kept calling it. And it never did fill. In the end, my mom finally made him give it up."

Henry thought about what Russ was saying, and he tried to find his place in it. "Am I the sinkhole?" he asked.

"No, Henry, you're not the sinkhole. What I'm saying is, we ended up with two ditches in our yard."

"Oh." Henry scrunched up his nose. "I don't think I understand."

"That's okay. What I mean is that if you keep trying to pull dirt from one place to fill in another, that's not fixing. There is no fixing. You did a wrong thing. Maybe you did a bunch of 'em; that's my guess, anyway. But that hole is already there."

Henry was watching him closely, thinking as hard as he could. Russ stretched his mouth into a long flat line.

"Maybe what I'm gettin' at is this: what do you want to fill it up for?"

Henry thought on that. "I want to fill it because it's my fault."

"But it's not your place," Russ said.

With that, Henry was even more confused. But he was trying.

Russ went on. "People have a right to be mad at you. *I* have a right to be mad at you. You're trying to 'sorry' us out of it because *you* don't want to be mad at you. You think if you dig a big enough ditch in yourself, you're gonna prove it's about us. But you're just gonna end up with two holes."

Henry listened. He looked out the window and wished for interruption in the infinite plains, but there was none. He wondered what was underground out there.

"I'm not mad at you, Henry," Trimble said. "It doesn't matter if I *could* be; the fact is I'm not. It's not because you're sorry. It's because I don't want to be, and it's got nothing to do with you. You want to atone?" He turned and looked at him. "Don't dig another hole."

The car rumbled on and on. "But I always do," Henry said, in a voice so quiet he wasn't sure if Russ heard it.

"Nothing always does anything."

They drove all through the long day. The way led them to places so empty and alone, Henry had no imagination for them. The sun climbed through the vacant white sky, paused at its zenith, and then began its descent in the same way it always did. They spoke here and there, but talked about very little. They ate bologna sandwiches Russ had brought with him. Henry drank his water.

Just past the waystation of White Butte, the road curved and Henry spotted the rusting and faded sign for North Dakota. It had been covered with bumper stickers and peppered with shotgun pellets, and some traveler or other had written upon it in white paint, *if you lived here, you'd be home by now.* They drove through Haynes and Hettinger and Bucyrus. Past a marker for the Last Great Buffalo Hunt. And just before reaching the inexplicably-named town of New England, the road moved west and

Henry saw the first stands of gnarled ponderosa pines he'd seen since leaving the Black Hills.

There was snow on the ground when they rejoined the old Highway 85, and Trimble said they were nearly there. To the north, wisps of clouds were forming high in the sky above them. Henry was getting lost again, but not in himself. He was realizing that he was on the verge of truly being alone, and unimaginably far from any place he knew. There would be more people. There would be more nights huddled in the freezing cold. What seemed like lifetimes ago, he'd walked out of the house he'd lived in for twenty years and left the door unlocked. He'd tricked himself then into thinking it was courage. But he knew now what it really was, and he said a quick prayer to no God he believed in that this time, it might be true.

There was a sign ahead for interstate 94, and just as Henry saw it, Trimble spoke. "I got a good guess why Medora," he said. "But what I'm askin' is this: just talk to somebody first."

"Okay, Russ," Henry said. "I promise I will."

"Good, then. And after here, where?"

"West."

"It'll be cold. Do you have what you need?"

"Yes," Henry lied.

Trimble let him. "Are you going all the way?"

"I think so."

"Well," said Russ, and for the hundredth time that day, he rolled his fingers on the wheel. "Henry, I hope you find it."

"Find what?"

"Your place."

"Me, too."

Russ paused. "Or maybe that you let it go."

The cruiser took a frontage road along the interstate—really, it was just a tractor path—into the outskirts of a small western town like any other. There was no sign. But, looking ahead, Henry could see smoke rising up from chimneys in the mid-afternoon light, and he knew people were there. Peacekeeper Trimble brought the car to a stop. Henry unbuckled his seat belt, grabbed his bag, opened the door, and got out. He thought Trimble might follow, but he had stayed in his seat. Henry bent down and looked back inside.

"Thank you, Russ," he said. "For the ride and for everything."

"Keep the thanks," Trimble said. "It's a day off. It's good to get up here."

Henry tried to put a thought together, and it took him a moment. Then he had it: "Hey, Russ—," he said, turning back to the car.

But the door was closed, the engine was started, and the tires were already rolling across the ground.

Walk Softly

A buck walked down the main street of Medora. He was old, with gray fur around his black and cracked nose. He still had most of his winter coat, but pills were beginning to form around the belly, and as he walked, tufts shook off and floated away on the breeze like dandelion seeds. There was a large scab on his brow from shedding his antlers just two days before—something that happened later and later as the weather warmed, if it happened now at all. He was ten years old.

There was a patch of grass in front of the community center, and as he lingered there eating, he saw Henry out of the corner of his eye. He watched as this stranger crossed the railroad tracks on the far side of Pacific Avenue and then wandered into the parking lot outside the old Dacotah Territories building. The buck kept his head down, pulling grass up with his teeth for as long as he could and waiting to see if the man would move closer.

People were rarely a bother to him; there weren't many left here. He would sometimes watch the ones in town from under the scrub pines clustered at the bottom of the escarpment to the north: they moved in and out of buildings, chopped firewood, played on swings in the park. He would walk and eat and watch. Of greater concern were the coyotes, whose calls, when they started near dusk, were a sign to move back to the higher ground in the badlands beyond.

This human, Henry, didn't seem to know where to go. He stood for a long time on the asphalt, looking first one way, and then the other. The buck kept plucking up the fresh spring shoots. He was ready to move on, but he waited. Finally, the man settled on a course up a far street. He walked down Pacific to the faded and disused crosswalk, looked both ways again, and made his way across. No cars came. No cars were idling anywhere, for fifty miles in any direction. As he approached, the buck raised his head, gave a soft snort, and bounded off towards the distant hills.

Henry Henry meant to be true to his word. As he entered the edge of town, he looked for any sign of the peacekeeper station, but there were none to be found. All he could see were rows of faded marquees lining the main drag to the west and rows of small, well-kept houses running up a half-dozen intersecting streets to the north like tines on a comb. Directly ahead of him were a couple wide and low buildings which might have been city offices, but he couldn't tell for sure. A deer was grazing. He didn't know where else to go.

On the far side, and to his great luck, he saw a small sign with an arrow pointing towards the community center. He figured it would be as good a place to start as any, so he made his way across the green space, over a split rail fence, and to the nearest door.

It was unlocked, and inside Henry found a spacious gathering hall with a tile floor and basketball goals pushed back on swinging racks against the walls. There was a notably unattractive drop ceiling with brown-painted runners and yellow-stained tiles. Fluorescent tube lights shone down from no more than half of the recessed rectangles, and most of those flickered and fluttered in the dimness. The whole place smelled of cigarette smoke. No one seemed to be home, but Henry saw a glass door on the far wall with *Medora Police Department* stenciled on the pane underneath a generic decal of an old sheriff's badge. He knew the words were wrong, but he figured whatever the law called itself around here now, it still more than likely hunkered down in the same office. He walked across the tip-off circle taped down at midcourt.

The bullpen was much like the one in Lower Brule: a long meeting table in the center covered with folders and loose papers, offices to the sides, and a desk facing away from him towards an exterior door on the northeast side. An older woman was stationed there, and she didn't seem to hear him come in. He looked at the wide, gray braid of her hair and then over her shoulder at the game of solitaire she was playing on her computer. All the aces were out.

Henry stayed where he was and apologized for coming in the wrong way. She swiveled to look at him without a hint of surprise. Her name was Louise, she said, and after she listened to his intentions, she called for the chief on the intercom. He was in. He came out of his office and shook Henry's hand. He introduced himself as Chief Ebenezer Poor Fox Johnson, but he insisted Henry call him Ebb. He smiled at Henry's story and told him a wander through the park would be no problem, but he suggested Henry wait at least until morning: things were wilder up there, he said, and the forecast called for snow tonight. He said Henry could likely room for a few days with someone named Ida, so long as he didn't mind doing a few chores for his keep. She kept up an old motel there in town—not that many visitors passed through anymore. Henry asked for the address, and Ebb waved him off, pointing instead at a building on the far side of the lot outside.

"It's a gift to see a new face," Ebb said.

"Thank you" was all Henry could think to say back.

* * *

"Ida" was a woman named Ida Four Bears, and she ran a place called the Amble Inn. It was a half dozen rooms, an office, and a small proprietor's apartment. The place had the look of a log cabin both inside and out, and there was a bearskin rug taking up the entire floor in front of the check-in desk. Ida talked to Henry over the counter, and before he could even think to barter for his keep, she had turned around to pick up a room key from the peg board behind her.

"I don't have any money," he apologized.

"You don't have a roof over your head, either," she said back, and handed him the worn plastic fob. "We'll work something out. The bed's not made, but there are sheets in the dresser." She looked him over. "Come back for dinner." Henry thanked her, too, and he did as he was told.

Ida made a stew, and it was more than enough. She asked Henry where he'd been, and she laughed at his tales of Lower Brule and motorcycle drifters. "I've never been down that way," she said; "Never been outside Standing Rock, except for a doctor once in Bismark." She was old, Henry knew, but he couldn't have guessed her age: her face was leathered by the sun, but the deep crows' feet marching towards her temples and the creases at the corners of her mouth told him that she laughed often. Her eyes were like circles of moonless night, and stars twinkled there. Henry didn't tell her about Wind Cave, but he already believed in his heart that he could.

They drank together after dinner, and by the end, Henry was laughing, too. He asked her about her name, and she told him with a smile about her ancestor, the Mandan chief Mato-tope, who was so profligate, the legends said, his descendents outnumbered the buffalo. He'd ended up starving himself to death during a smallpox epidemic in the 1830s that saw his clan reduced from the thousands to less than a hundred souls. He died swearing revenge on the Whites he'd once befriended, but who had then brought this scourge on his people. "Still," Ida said, "you can't throw a rock in Indian country without hitting a Four Bears." She had a reproduction of a famous painting of him framed on a wall in the lobby of the Amble Inn. The eagle feathers of his headdress draped to the ground. Bison horns were on his head.

When Henry finally said good night, the snow outside was coming down in earnest. A blanket already covered the parking lot, a few inches thick, and Henry huddled against the cold as he turned the key in the lock. But inside it was warm, and he fell quickly into a deep sleep.

He woke early and found Ida reading a book in the office. She told him it was the most comfortable place and had the best light; there would be no guests this day, nor any day soon. What travelers she saw came early in the summer, and they would be mostly Natives from out east with horse trailers looking to ride in the backcountry. Sometimes, hikers came down from Canada. Henry realized the Inn was more of a hobby than a business, and he asked her what he might do to help.

"Not much in the snow," Ida told him. "But there's wood to split out back."

So, Henry spent the day splitting wood. He'd never done it before, and it took him a long while to get the hang of it. His hands were well and blistered by noon, but he kept at it until the logs were quartered and stacked. Twice he checked in with Ida and made easy conversation. Once, in the afternoon, he traipsed through the snow back to the old police station to talk with Ebb.

Together, they put together a plan: Henry could stay with Ida until the snow cleared, and then he could move himself over to the old visitor center and camp for as long as he needed. Chief Johnson looked suspiciously at Henry's backpack and suggested he re-outfit himself when he got to the park: there were old storerooms there which should still have most of the things he would need, and the park service had technically ceded them to the Nation when the ILA took effect. Henry could think of it as a gift.

Henry thanked Ebb again for his help, and as he turned to leave, Chief Johnson told him to wait. He went into his office, rummaged around for a bit, and emerged with another key in his hand. "To the center there," he said, handing it over. "With the weather, we don't want to break the door."

Henry stayed with Ida for two weeks. He didn't know the date anymore, but he guessed it was now the middle of April. The snow had gone again, and prairie grass was pushing its way up through the dark loam. He'd split wood, fixed broken gutters, and repainted the wooden block letters on the side of the Amble Inn a bright white. He and Ida had settled into an easy routine of breakfast coffee, tidying the rooms, afternoon chores, and dinner in her apartment. By the end, she knew him better than he knew himself, and told him so:

"So, you're a runner and not a wanderer," she said, after he'd told her about leaving his friend Billy behind. "But you might learn to wander, yet."

Henry said he hoped so, even if he didn't really know what that meant. "Not supposed to," Ida Four Bears said, laughing with him for the hundredth time.

And then, with gray dawn skies overhead, Henry set off again: west down Pacific Avenue, past the boarded storefronts there, and then north onto the park road. The sign was still there, the words *Theodore Roosevelt National Park* grooved into the wood in those loopy capitals common to the old park service, with the arrowhead to the side. Henry stopped and looked at it for a long moment, remembering Shannon's insistence, many years ago, that their family take a picture by the one in Cuyahoga Valley. He couldn't recall her words, but he did remember squinting against the sun as Caleb made bunny ears over his head and he held out his camera for the selfie. Worlds gone and gone.

The visitor center was close, and he turned in at the employee entrance and used the key Chief Johnson had given him to unlock the door there. He had to kick snow away to give it enough room to swing open. Inside, in the dark, there were the empty racks in the old gift shop nook and the familiar wide acrylic countertop. In the middle of the room was a large glass case with a mannequin of the 26th president of the United States atop a wooden horse. The swings in temperature had loosened the glue holding on his famous mustache, and it had fallen down and stuck to the mane of his steed. There were other displays along the walls: a mold of the skeleton of a prehistoric crocodile; a plaster tree stump displaying artificial rings; an enormous rack of elk antlers on a touch desk for children. Henry did as he always did and made his way behind the ranger counter. He bent down to look for the box of junior ranger supplies and found them. He extracted his token and put it deep in his coat pocket without so much as a look.

On top of the desk was a stack of park maps, and he picked one out and unfolded it. A little light streamed in through the front windows and a skylight overhead, but it wasn't enough to read by. Still, he could see the line of the park loop road winding up from the visitor center, over the nearby interstate, and then in an enormous, curvy loop through the badlands beyond. There were icons for turnouts and trailheads. Inset photos of bison and wild horses. A picture of ancient Native pottery shards. The room was cozy, despite the cold outside, and Henry felt safe. He felt, strangely, home.

As his eyes adjusted, he saw a laminated piece of paper beside the register:

MALTESE CROSS CABIN TOUR SCHEDULE:

10:15 am

11:40 am

1:00 pm

2:25 pm

4:00 pm (*last tour!*)

ranger reports 10 min. prior

He wondered about the cabin, but he decided to leave it for another day. He was planning to spend at least one night in the wilds of the park, and he knew he would need more than the old sleeping bag stuffed in the bottom of his backpack to stay warm. He looked under the counter for keys and found them on a small hook; his third set since he arrived in town. Then, he headed back into the offices to search for the supply closet he'd learned about from Ebb.

It was just where Chief Johnson had said it would be and perhaps even more well-stocked. He found parkas, boots, slip-on snow tracks, emergency blankets, and even an old bivvy sack in service-issue green. There were racks of walkie talkies still on their chargers, and for a moment, he thought about taking one down and trying–in open defiance of science and logic– to radio Billy in the Ranger. He wanted to imagine their conversation, but he could get no further than exchanging "hellos." He sensed the words that lurked just under that easy surface, but he knew he could not yet dredge them up.

He left the radios where they were and stepped back into the atrium. He didn't have a watch, but he guessed it was around ten in the morning. The walk to Wind Canyon, where he planned to stay the first night, was just under ten miles, and he trusted he could make it there by late afternoon. Ida had given him food for three days, which he thought was more than he would need. He threw his pack over his shoulders, hitched up the straps, and tipped his cap to Teddy on his way out.

Snow slowed his progress; as did the surprisingly steep incline of the road up into the hills. In less than a mile, he reached a vantage point that afforded him a view of the whole of Medora in the flats down below, maybe eight blocks in all. He saw the odd, sweeping roof of the Amble Inn, and the community center housing the peacekeeper station. He saw the railroad running behind the long row of the Dacotah Territories building. Smoke rose from chimneys, and deer grazed in a small herd, maybe five or six animals in size, between patches of snow in the town park. Henry's breath steamed in the early spring air. He knew he would be back.

Henry turned away and set out again. He could see the ridges and gulleys and cliffs of the badlands, and he was struck by their difference from the ones he'd visited to the south: whereas the landscape in Pine Ridge territory was towering, stark, and compact, a labyrinth of stone castles and canyons in the washed-out break of some plate of the world's crust, things here were wide and wonderful, the eroded earth spreading out in water- and wind-carved spirals of buttes and prairie. Scrub trees and sagebrush dotted the red- and gray- and yellow-lined faces of the cliffs, and the naked tops of cottonwood trees rose up from the banks of the Little Missouri as it snaked through the basins. There was no hiding the life here, even in its harshness.

Henry saw all of this as he hiked, winding from one viewpoint to the next, until he officially began his journey on the loop road just past a small campground at the edge of the river's floodplain. To his delight, there were pronghorn there: at least a dozen, maybe a hundred feet away from him and foraging for shoots of fresh grass in the melting snow. He smiled and spoke to them, or perhaps to himself, and decided to sit on a fallen tree along the road shoulder. It was early afternoon now, and he made himself a sandwich and ate it without ever taking his eyes off his hosts. When he was done, he cleaned his bread knife with a handful of snow, put it back in his pack, and walked on.

There was no wind and no sound at all beyond his own footsteps on the cracked pavement of the road. The sun the day before had finished off the ice on the tarmac, and it ran now like a narrow black ribbon through the white wilderness. He smelled earth. He was content.

Once, when Caleb was 13 years old, he confessed a crush to Henry that he held for a girl in his class. She was tall and athletic and already very beautiful. Her name was Breonna, and Caleb said she could have her pick of the guys. Caleb was short for his age, and his caramel-colored skin was dotted with acne. He didn't yet know what to do with the hair on his head, or the fuzz beginning to shadow his chin and upper lip. There was some event or other coming up at school, and he was working up the nerve to ask her to go get ice cream with him after. He was afraid she was too pretty for him, and he told his father so. Henry smiled at his son and asked if there were other girls he thought were cute. *Not like her*, Caleb said.

There are other ways of being pretty than just being pretty, Henry told him. *One day, you might like them more.*

Yeah, he remembered Caleb saying to him. *But for now, I think I like pretty in the regular way.*

Henry wondered what happened to Breonna. She hadn't gone out for ice cream with Caleb, or with any other boy: it turned out she had a crush herself, on a girl Caleb knew from their English class. Caleb had gotten over it and gone on to new crushes and new experiences with the same old fears. He'd never dated; Henry hadn't thought about that before. As he did, some new sharp thing poked him in a soft place deep inside, and his eyes watered as he walked.

Caleb nervous. Caleb happy. Caleb scared. Caleb whole. Caleb detached and wandering further and further into himself, to a place where he would one day get lost and see no way out. Caleb wearing down. Caleb eroding. Canyons and rills and runoffs and depositions. Henry and Shannon like travelers over that landscape, squinting and taking pictures as they went.

He'd not known his son. He'd not cared to. He'd thought noticing would be enough: warm thoughts as he watched him go through his days; half-thought advice shared from the corner of the bed. Love as a kind of gentle admiration, making his own heart more full.

A hawk flew over the badlands, its shadow racing to keep up on the thinning blanket of snow below. All of this, so beautiful and fleeting. Mysterious and wonderful.

Pretty in the regular way.

He tried sleeping the first night in a patch of grass near the parking lot for the Wind Canyon trailhead, but the wetness of the earth chilled him even through the flooring of his tent and the lining of his sleeping bag. He would doze for a half hour or so, wake up and roll over, and then repeat the cycle again. Around midnight, he gave up and decided to pull his tent, with his things still inside, over onto the black top. The ground would be harder, but he hoped the asphalt might still be holding some of the heat from the day's sun. He would be wrong.

But after his things were in their new place, and before he ducked back through the flap of the tent to try and sleep, he paused and looked around. There was no moon, but he realized he could see what seemed like miles in every direction. He could count the spines on a cactus. He could see the shadows of bats on the ground as their small furry bodies zoomed by above him. And when he turned his eyes up, he saw more stars than he could ever hope to count. The wispy green of the Milky Way wrapped around the earth, and beyond it were other galaxies impossible and innumerable. His breath caught in his lungs and he held it there in awe.

He slept little the rest of the night. He was up before the sun, but the sky was already glowing pink in the east. He ate dried cereal, packed his meager things, and began to walk. The Wind Canyon trail was a short loop, just to the edge of a cliff and back. From the viewpoint, he could see down to the Little Missouri, which was still shadowed in the pre-dawn darkness and running there smooth and slow. He made his way back to the park road and carried on.

When the sun finally broke over the horizon, he was in a wide valley between eroded buttes. Their grass-topped summits were no more than a hundred feet above him, and he decided to scramble up the side of the one nearest to him for a better view. When he did, he realized a small herd of bison were just then waking on the far side, and he looked down at them as they rose from their beds in the short grass and shook their enormous heads to clear them for the day. He heard the sounds of their grunts and snorts, still impossibly deep even as they bounced off of the rocks in the hills and echoed back to him. There were two calves in the herd, cinnamon-red in color and no more than a month or so old, and Henry watched as they stretched out their wobbly legs and began to nurse at their mothers. The largest bull in the herd, almost twice the size of the average cow, walked to the edge of the group nearest to the park road and stood sentry. Henry watched them there for a long time, until every beast was roused and the herd began to move slowly towards the far side of the plain. When they were nearly out of sight, he scrambled back down the same side of the cliff he had climbed and set out again.

By noon he was deep in wild country. The road rose and fell through hills and small groves of ash and juniper. From time to time, he would see spur trails and follow them a few hundred yards into this clearing or that one. He ate when he was hungry and rested when he was tired. By the time the sun was half way back down, he had already crossed the bridge over Paddock Creek and was coming up on a parking area for a path to the old eastern entrance station. There was a black and white picture on the signpost by the trailhead of an old stone gatehouse in its heyday, cars lined up behind its lowered wooden crossbar, and then a color photo of the overgrown ruins as they now were—or at least as they were in the last days of the park when it was a park. He thought: ruined or no, they would make a warmer place to sleep than the open ground. And so he went.

Along the way, he saw his old friends again, the prairie dogs. The trail led over a narrow wash and then straight across the floor of a wide basin where hundreds of burrow mounds dotted both sides of the path. There were dozens of heads poking up from the holes, and he smiled at the sound of their chittering as he walked between them. The braver souls scurried into the dirt in front of him and stood on their hind legs there, sniffing the air and waiting until the last moment before darting off to find cover.

On the far side of the flat, he saw a cluster of trees and the horizontal line of an old rockwall. There was maybe an hour of daylight left when he dropped his backpack through an empty window opening of the gatehouse and then climbed in after it. The space was dusty but whole, and it was still covered by a sturdy wooden roof. There was no snow or pooling water on the ground, and Henry knew he had found shelter. He left the tent in his backpack, laid out a sleeping pad and bag, and sat down atop them to make his dinner.

His legs were tired and his sleep was heavy. He dreamed, for the first time in many years, of his mother. She was impossibly young in his dream; a person he could not have recognized aside from photographs, but who he knew nonetheless. He realized he must be a child himself in this memory, no more than two or three. She smiled down at him, and her teeth were so white, her lips painted bright red. She was holding a hose, and she was watering the roses in their garden. He realized he had been calling out to her, because he was hurt in some inconsequential way; a scraped knee or bee sting perhaps. But she would not come any closer. *Oh, Henry, Henry*, she said, still smiling, still watering. *Oh, Henry, Henry, Henry. Oh, Henry*. He kept trying to speak to her, but his voice wouldn't come out. He was trying to cry, to will tears for her attention, but his eyes were dry and staring straight ahead. *Oh, Henry*, she kept saying to him. *Oh, Henry, Henry, Henry. Oh, Henry.* Her perfect teeth. Her eyes enormous and kind. The row of rosebushes, he realized, was getting longer, pushing her further and further away. *Oh, Henry*, she said. *Oh, Henry, Henry.*

It was early in the afternoon of the third day when he saw the low roof of the visitor center appearing again from the far side of a gentle hill. The snow from the week before was entirely gone now, and a carpet of green spring grass had taken its place. The sky was blue and clear, and the world around him had the tangy scent of new life. Henry hadn't spoken a word aloud in days. His feet were sore, but they felt strong. *He* felt strong, like he could walk forever.

But instead, he made his way back to the employee entrance to the visitor center and went inside. There was more light this time, and he had his heart set on the Maltese Cross Cabin out back. He rummaged through the ranger office for a key and found it in a lockbox in the back of a closet: his fourth, now, in Medora. He went out the back door of the visitor center and made his way down the short path to the structure. From the outside, it looked like any other frontier home: two windows on the front framing a simple wooden door; a steeply-pitched and bark-shingled roof. There was no Maltese cross, as best Henry could tell, but there was a rack of deer antlers on the western gable and a thin chimney pipe poking up from the center ridge. The door was padlocked, but the key fit and turned easily. He had to give the planks a shove with his shoulder to get it to swing open, but it was otherwise no trouble.

Inside there were two small rooms: a combined kitchen/study and a bedroom. The kitchen was outfitted with period antiques, including an iron stove, flour mill, and coffee pot. The study consisted of a bookshelf, writing desk, and rocking chair. And the bedroom held a table, a mirror and chiffarobe, a single narrow bed, and a large duck-skin trunk with the letters *T.R.* painted on the lid. Henry knew right away whose it was; he was realizing, too, where he was standing. He sat down in the rocking chair and put his pack on the floor. The wind had picked up over the course of the long day, and the glass panes rattled in their fittings. The ancient wood creaked under the floorboards. He thought about lying down in the bed and finally did so. He looked up at the exposed beams of the roof and tried to think about something important, but all he could muster was a memory about a settling crack in the drywall in the ceiling above the bed in his own home. Shannon had always hated it; he'd always pretended not to care.

A snort from somewhere close and outside brought him back to the present. He tried for a moment to identify it without getting up, but no luck: there wasn't room, back in the little grove where the cabin sat, for a buffalo, and he hadn't seen any deer for days. So, he sat up and looked out the bedroom window, and he was suddenly eye-to-eye with a large white horse. The gray hair of its mane was fluttering in the wind, and it's speckled nose was pressed against the glass. He could see into its nostrils; they widened as it snorted a second time, and steam fogged the pane. Henry stared, and the horse flicked its ears.

"Hello," he heard himself say, his voice raspy after days of disuse. "Hello, there."

The horse said nothing back, but it kept on watching him. He'd read in the brochure that wild horses roamed the park, but he hadn't seen any in his wanderings. "What's your name?" he asked, stupidly. The deep black eyes of the animal looked at him.

Henry moved to get up from the bed, and when he did, the horse started. It stumbled back a few steps, and Henry could see more of it now: its white coat was still thick from winter growth and speckled gray at the flanks. The horse flicked its long tail in agitation, watching him now warily.

"I'm sorry," Henry said. "I'm sorry about that. You don't have to go."

The horse stared for a moment more, and then it turned away and lowered its head to the grass. Henry looked after it, and he realized he couldn't leave the cabin now for fear of scaring it away.

Once upon a time, the cabin in which Henry stayed that night traveled the country. After Theodore Roosevelt was elected president, this small refuge from his time ranching in the Dakotas after the deaths of his mother and wife on the same day in 1884 became a public attraction. Circus men bought it off his former partners and loaded it on train cars, first to towns further west, and then all the way to St. Louis for a World's Fair Exposition. It sat on the state capitol grounds in Bismark for fifty years, where tourists came from far and wide to carve their own initials into the wood of the door frame and window sills. They are there still.

For Henry, though, it was a shelter from the cold and a way to avoid spooking a wild horse. Eventually, he settled in under the stiff museum blankets on the tiny bed and slept soundly through the night. He did not dream again. In the morning, he thought about trying to fire up the wood stove to make coffee, but he didn't know how to work it, and he had no grounds besides. Instead, he made his bed, brushed his teeth, re-packed his things, and locked the door behind him before setting off back into town.

He'd left the place much as he'd found it, with one single exception: a small gray lockbox, its lid open and contents emptied, sitting in a thin layer of dust on what may have once been Teddy Roosevelt's writing desk.

PART THREE

Abandon

Invisible Man

illy Faulkner knew he would never go back to Porcupine, but that didn't mean he had any idea where he was off to next. He spent much of that first night alone sitting at the pit in the middle of the village in the Badlands, keeping the fire there stoked and watching embers float up into the clear night sky. It was cold, but not excessively so, and anyways, he believed the chill helped him think.

Henry had left him the keys to the Ranger, a drum and a half of old vegetable oil, and enough food to last him a few weeks. He could make it back to Chicago, he knew. He could also get most of the way to the coast, if he set out that way. There were people he'd met in the Nation who cared for him, like Evie and her father. But it still seemed to Billy he was an outsider in any direction he went, and an alien where he was if he stayed. Once upon a time, he'd left home thinking he could make his mark on the world. But he hadn't even been able to make a mark on one sad widower from Ohio. Goddamn Henry.

Billy remembered playing with his sister once, during the summer before she started high school and he started sixth grade. They had built a fort in a culvert running under the railroad tracks a few blocks north of their home, making a door from a wood pallet they'd found behind the corner store and lining the curved, concrete bottom of the space with broken-down cardboard boxes. They lived in Chicago then, in a neighborhood of old row houses built during the heyday of the meatpacking industry called Back of the Yards. They were the only Black family they knew, and the neighbors were mostly Latinos who had moved in during the early 2000s and a handful of poor Whites holding on by their fingernails to generational housing. Billy had learned Spanish in school. He spoke it still.

One afternoon, a storm rolled in, and Busola came to the fort with a map and a flashlight. Billy and his sister huddled in their little cave while the rain fell outside. A minor stream had formed in the bottom of the culvert and ruined the cardboard, forcing them to crouch on opposite sides of the tube in the dark. His sister was showing him the line of the railroad that ran right over their heads. *Look here*, she said, *it goes all the way to the airport.*

That's gotta be at least a mile, Billy said back, knowing already what was on his sister's mind. She was a born explorer.

It's four, she said. *I measured. We could walk it on Saturday, just to see. We'd be back before dad got home.*

Even now, Billy remembered how serious she'd been when she said this, as well as how afraid it had made him feel. Four miles was too far, and the airport—Chicago Midway—was all loud sounds and barbed wire. *There's trains*, he said.

Not here, said Busola. *And we could just stay on the side if one was coming.*

Billy thought about the steep gravel of the right-of-way, then about feet slipping as boxcars screamed by. He found his way out: *There are bridges*, he said. *We might get stuck on one.*

He was right, of course. And with that, Busola's vision of her own adulthood—her capacity to do a grown up thing—came crashing down around them both. *You're such a dumb baby*, she said angrily.

I'm not a baby.

Yes, you are. You're a dumb baby and a chicken. I was going to bring you with me, but I don't want to babysit anyway. I'll go by myself.

I'm not a baby!

Busola rolled her eyes and let out the loudest *Ugghh!* Billy had ever heard in his life. Then she kicked down the door of their fort and stomped off in the rain.

He'd picked up the pallet after she left and tried to make things right again. It had been covered in mud, and his hands got filthy as he handled it. He remembered the smell of earth and refuse under his fingernails. He remembered going home to wash them.

Even without his sister, Billy kept going back to the culvert for the rest of that summer, and the summer after that. He made it a clean and quiet place where he would read comic books and then, later, waste time on his phone. He kept it tidy. But Busola never came back, and when school started, she made new friends and left him behind. Growing up, he'd always thought this was just as well; they'd never had much in common. Except that neither of them ever walked the train tracks to the airport.

At the campfire, Billy thought about his sister, who was not so far away now in Wisconsin. She had a family there, and a full life. They didn't talk often, but they were friendly and kind towards one another when they did. Still, her home wasn't his, and there was more out there to see. More to find. It felt strange to admit he'd had fun in the middle of the Apocalypse, but it was true: the world had fallen apart, but it was beautiful nonetheless.

He wouldn't chase Henry Henry, at least not tomorrow. Before he'd lit the fire, he'd used the radio to call Evie and tell her which way he'd gone, and he knew she would make sure he was safe. But he also knew where Henry was headed in the end. And he had time to decide if he really wanted to see the end of the line.

*　　*　　*

In the morning, Billy packed his things, cleaned the cabins he, Henry, and Trimble had used, re-locked the doors, scattered the ashes in the firepit, and got into the Roving Ranger. He squeezed the lucky rabbit's foot on the key fob and turned the key in the ignition. It started just as he knew it would. Before putting the truck in drive, he looked over at the diner seat bolted into the floor beside him where he had often slept. The vinyl was cracking now in the sun, and there were spots and splatters of mud on the door side. He reached into his pocket, pulled out his Junior Ranger badge from the Badlands, and tossed it into the wide beam of sunshine pouring in through the open window. It was a warm day for the first of April–April Fool's Day. Billy thought to himself, *That's just as well.* Then he adjusted the mirror, buckled his seatbelt, and set off.

He traveled north first, back up the winding pass through the naked crags and spires of the park, then to the rim of the plateau above. He turned left onto the park road and cruised along the edge of the cliff break with the mid-morning light now behind him. Looking out over the floor of the prairie, he could see clouds forming over the grasslands below, and he wondered if it would rain before the day was over. He wondered, for that matter, how far he would go, and what ways he would take to get there. When he had been drinking his breakfast coffee earlier, he'd flipped through the old Rand McNally atlas Henry kept under the driver's seat looking for directions, but Henry had torn out the pages of his cross country itinerary. Billy assumed he'd burned them the day before so he would not follow. But the pages for South Dakota were still there, and although the roads were vague in the southwest corner, he knew if he could hunt signs to a place called Maverick Junction, he'd be able to work his way around the southern end of the Black Hills and into Wyoming. He didn't expect to run into real trouble there: the Great War everyone had feared didn't seem to have come here; at least, not with the same energy he'd seen in the South. Still, he suspected this country would always know its violence. He would be careful nonetheless.

Today, though, Billy would only know rain–if not for a while yet. The clouds swelled behind him, and he cruised along. About an hour into his drive, he saw an old, bullet-riddled sign for Roberts Prairie Dog Town, and he pulled over to the side of the road and put the Ranger in park. When he stepped out, he didn't see anything at first: just pan-flat and dusty ground. But when he looked closer, he spotted burrow holes there by the dozens, and more than a few of them hid little yellow faces. He watched wet noses sniffing the sharp air and heads turning first one way, then the other. Then, to his surprise, one dog climbed out from its hole and began creeping towards some bit of food not very far away from where he stood. He noticed the bristling golden fur on its back and the tiny brown-black claws at the ends of its paws. But the shadow of a bird somewhere above passed over the ground between them, and the prairie dog squeaked a warning to its kin before running back to its home.

Billy laughed as it disappeared again. "Don't go, little buddy," he said, mostly to himself. And then he did something that would have made his sister furious: he reached into the breast pocket on his button-down shirt and pulled out a soft pack of Lucky Strike cigarettes. They'd been a parting gift from Evie, who flew straight as an arrow when she was on duty but smoked like a chimney when she was off-shift. Billy had hated the smell of cigarettes growing up because his father burned through two packs a day. But he'd picked up the guilty pleasure when he'd worked as a substitute teacher, and he would smoke them whenever they were around. It was another way to talk to people, he had always thought. Another part of living to learn.

The cigarette was nice, but he didn't finish it. Half way through, he rolled the filter in between his fingers until the remaining tobacco and paper fell down to the dirt, then he scattered them with the toe of his brown dress shoe. He kept the filter and carried it back to the truck, dropping it in the open mouth of an empty soda can in the cup holder. He took out his handkerchief and cleaned his hands. The can was a Coca-Cola, from a deli in Missouri now a thousand miles away.

By midmorning, Billy had found Maverick Junction, and once there, highway 18 through Edgemont to the border. He crossed out of the Nation into Wyoming without so much as slowing down. The checkpoint was marked only by an empty wooden booth and a sign declaring Wyoming to be the home of "Sovereignty and Equality," whatever that meant. When the road ended at an intersection between two towering weather-monitor antennas, he turned right towards some place called Newcastle on little more than a hunch. He could tell it was north, which seemed like something. It also took him away from those still-darkening storm clouds.

He drove, and it was another two hours to the town of Sundance. On his approach, he'd started counting down the miles on the highway signs, his curiosity building as the numbers got smaller. He wondered what he would find there; his thoughts were of the Sundance Kid, and then of Butch Cassidy. He'd never seen the old movie, but he knew the names and the basic gist that they were bandits in the wild West. He had continued to talk out loud to himself since the stop with the prairie dogs, and he said "*out*-laws" now, in a little sing-song whisper. "*Out*-laws from *Sun*-dance."

But Billy was wrong about the *nom de guerre* of Harry Longabaugh, who was actually from Pennsylvania, and he was also wrong about the town. Despite appearing on signs for 100 miles, Sundance had barely half the population of the high school Billy'd once attended. The main drag was complemented by no more than a dozen or so side streets, each running out from it and lined with short rows of small, clean homes. A bluff rose on the north side of town, and there was a gas station, grocery store, and liquor emporium. As he turned west onto Cleveland Street, he passed an old-timey barber shop, complete with a spinning candy cane poll, and a car wash.

Then, at the intersection under the only stoplight in town, he saw those ubiquitous sawhorses. *Who was still making these things?* Two men stood on either side of this particular set, and they looked more bored than anything else. Neither seemed to be armed. Both wore button-up farm shirts, jeans, and dusty cowboy hats. As Billy coasted the Ranger to a stop and rolled down his window for the one closest to him, he saw a lanyard around the man's neck with a piece of paper slid into a plastic sleeve. The word *DEPUTY* was printed on it in black capitals.

"Afternoon to ya," the man said, walking over in what could only be described as a mosey.

"Good afternoon," Billy said back.

"You're'n the first one through today," he said, "It's good to see ya. Yer not an outlaw, ain't'cha?"

There was no logical answer to that question. "I don't think so," he said. "I'm just out wandering. I saw the signs for Sundance and thought it might be the famous one."

"Nah, ain't the famous one," the man said, laughing. "That's the right dog, wrong tree. You're'n welcome to visit anyway, though. We got a museum down just a piece, and a rodeo come summer. But it's still too cold out now."

"I'm sorry I missed it."

"Sorry's fine; maybe you'll come back." The man hitched at his belt. "Gotta ask, though: where ya headin' to?"

Billy didn't know how to answer that question, either. "I don't know," he said. "Down the road, I guess. I've never been to Wyoming."

The man sniffed. "Well, it's a place. Lots to see. Not many folks travel these days though, which's a shame."

"It is."

"Yeah. I gotta ask ya, too: where'n you come from to get here?"

Billy wondered about this, and he had the sudden sense that he was walking into a minefield. "South," he said, trying to remember the map in the atlas. What was down there? Cheyenne? But capitals were usually in the middle of states, weren't they? "Up from Denver," he finally said.

"Well, that's a good-god-damn way! You do it all today?"

"I did. I've got family in Boulder." Billy was bluffing like crazy, and he pushed his luck. He looked up, expecting to see those storm clouds, but the sky was clear blue. "Left early this morning," he said.

"Musta drove like hell. Surprised they let you out. Meanin' no offense, now. S'just that we hear things're rougher south."

"They can be."

"Yeah, well. Like I said, that's't folks say. Ain't that kinda trouble here though," the man said, his hand now resting on the window slot of Billy's door. "Sheriff's just got us checkin' who comes through. Stoppin' cars 'n' all. Makin' sure we't least lay eyes on 'em..."

"Make sense."

"It does, it does. Got time for't, of course; s'just barely gettin' on spring yet. Not sure what his summer plan'll be. Maybe get older folks'ta stand here. Older'n me, anyhow!"

Billy was getting the sense that this man might talk to him forever. He kept his hands at ten and two on the wheel, and then he tried something else: "You said there's a museum. Anything else around I might be able to see?"

"Well, there's the museum, like I said. Ain't much, but some nice cowboy things in there. It's for all Crook County, the sign says. And we got a statue of the Sundance Kid right that way..." The man pointed off behind him "...even though he weren't really our'n. Still fun to look at, though. All bronze." He picked up his hand and hitched his thumb back through that belt loop. "Main thing 'round here's the Tower, though, s'far as close goes."

Billy craned his neck to look at the low mountain on the north side of the town; he'd pretty much had his fill of towers. "Yeah?"

"Devil's Tower, yeah; 'bout a half hour up on 14 here. Then you can't miss it. It's somethin' to see. You watch that movie *Close Encounters*? Prob'ly before your time…"

Billy hadn't, but he knew what the man was talking about: it wasn't a tower at all, but a mountain like the stump of an enormous stone tree. He realized he would like to see it. "Is it safe to visit up there?"

"It's safe enough people do it," the man said. "No rangers up there n'more, but the road's clear unless'n there's some trees down from winter."

Trees, Billy thought. It had been so long since he'd seen more than an isolated stand of them.

"Mind if I go that way?"

The man took a step back from the Ranger. "Not at all, s'long as you take care of the place. Indians get sensitive about it when they come through, and seein' as we got 'em on all sides here, we try'ta keep the peace much's we can. Don't miss that museum, though."

"Okay. Good," Billy said. "I won't. It's just up here?" He lifted a hand to point past the barricade and up the road.

"Yessir," the man said. "And the statue, too: the Kid."

"Right. I'll see 'em both."

"Alright, then." The man walked over and took hold of the leg of the nearest sawhorse in the barricade. He pulled it off to one side. "Head on through, outlaw," he said, and gave Billy a sly wink. "Enjoy Sundance."

"I will," Billy said, and shifted the Ranger back into drive. "Thanks for the hospitality, sir."

"Sir's my pappy," the man said, "Thanks'll do."

The man gave a little wave as Billy drove by. Billy looked in the side mirror as he passed, and he saw the man pull the sawhorse back into the street and step over to his partner to recap their conversation. The scene made him smile again, and he hummed a little to himself as he idled down the roadway. There were more than a few people out, walking in and out of stores in what passed for the downtown. Up ahead was a cop cruiser, parked outside the small police station. Just past that was a sign for the Crook County Museum, and he decided to turn in. *Out-law*, he thought to himself as he spun the wheel of the Ranger.

Out-law.

When he got there, the sun was setting and the rain was close. Still, Devil's Tower took his breath away. He stayed two days, parked underneath a canopy of budding trees beside the old Park Service visitor center. It was a Monument, Billy saw, and according to the faded and crumbling brochure he picked up from a little wooden box hanging from the side of an area map kiosk, it was the very first: set aside by Theodore Roosevelt himself in 1906.

The formation itself was a wonder. It was 500 feet high and looked at first like a perfect column of solid rock. But as Billy walked the loop trail around its base the next morning, he saw it was made up of hexagonal stone columns bundled together like the strands in a fiber optic cable. The storm had passed in the night, and the channels between the columns had turned briefly into dozens of narrow waterfalls in the dark. Billy hadn't seen them, but he could see the near-black streaks left on the rock from their passing like a tiger's stripes, or like the ink lines of some giant artist. He walked the loop five more times, staring up through the grooves in the tower's side on each lap and imagining what strangeness might be there at the top.

He read that no one quite knew what the tower was. Some thought it was the fossilized core of an old volcano, the sides eroded away over millennia by the harshness of the prairie. Others thought it was some great worm of stone pushing up from the mantle of the earth. The Kiowa believed it had been a refuge for a group of young girls once running from an enormous bear, who jumped on a rock and prayed to the Great Spirit for rescue; the rock grew up into the air, and the bear dug its monster claws into the sides as it rose. Billy liked that story the best.

The air on both days after the rain was crisp and clear, and animals were everywhere: birds sang in the trees, chipmunks darted across the cracked pavement of the walking path, and Billy could hear mule deer bounding away from him through the underbrush as he approached. It didn't occur to him to look for a badge in the old visitor center until his second morning there, and when he did, he found the doors unlocked and things mostly in the same places they always were. It was a paradise, Billy thought, and he was happy. As he slept the final night, he thought of nothing and nowhere else.

There was frost on the prairie grass as he drove west, and the sun rose slowly behind a shroud of clouds that had no end in the sky. He wandered through Gilette and Spotted Horse and another sleepy barricade in Clearmont. He skirted to the north of Sheridan, which seemed almost a city from a distance, and thus a place he'd rather avoid.

And then suddenly there were mountains in his way. They were the first true mountains he'd seen, and they rose up in sharp, snow-covered, and altogether fearsome peaks. He realized not just *where* but *when* he was: it was still barely April, and the roads through the Rockies wouldn't be clear for another month yet. He pulled over on the side of an empty road and got out the atlas. It was open country, and his food wouldn't hold out. Things were different than they were in the South, and there were no white-stripe diners to hole up in or abandoned convenience stores to raid. Empty here meant empty, and he needed an actual plan.

He saw a town ahead on the map called Crow Agency, and he pegged it for the center of the former reservation just over the border in Montana. His best guess was that it would operate in a way that was similar to the Lakota, and he thought he might seek refuge there for a while, if they let him in. He could find food and barter for more vegetable oil. At worst, he could backtrack to Sheridan and take his chances there, where at least the few hundred dollars he still had folded up in a side pocket of his duffel bag might spend. And so, he decided to go north again. As he drove, his thoughts were of Trimble, and Hetty, and of Evie and her father. He was eager to meet the Crow.

But this Nation, as things turned out, did not seem to exist. Billy crossed the border into what was once Montana without knowing it, and the first place he came to—a place his atlas said was Wyola—was a ghost town. Further on, in Lodge Grass, he found only the skeletons of a few houses which had burned down long ago. And after that, it was miles to a cluster of old tribal offices at the edge of what signs told him was the site of the famous Battle of the Little Bighorn. But although the buildings there were still intact, Billy could see they had long been abandoned, too.

"Where is everybody?" Billy said out loud to himself. "Where'd you go, Crow?"

He parked the Ranger in the empty lot of the Department of Enrollment and PerCapita, under the shadow of a darkened sign for an old casino. The steeple of a novelty wedding chapel at the edge of the property jutted up into the white sky. A cold wind had picked up as the morning wore on, and the only sound Billy could hear was the fan of the heater in the Ranger. He sat and looked around.

The casino was out of his view and down a paved road on the other side of a wide patch of spring grass. In front of him was a derelict, graffiti-covered motel, the windows intact but empty, and a broken gutter dangling all the way from the roof to the asphalt below. The main building was a bit to his right, and as Billy watched, an actual tumbleweed passed in front of the Ranger and bounded that way.

The tumbleweed was enormous and still covered in morning frost. Billy had never seen one before, and he was surprised by just how right all the old cartoons were: it skittered and bounced on the worn concrete, lifting all the way into the air with each bigger gust of the wind. He was fascinated, and he kept his eyes on it as it crossed through his field of view. He saw it catch for a moment on a parking block, and then roll off to the side and jump away again. It caught the curved side of a light post and changed direction, moving now towards the covered entryway to the old office center. "Where're you off to?" Billy said to no one else. Then it was entering the shadows of the PerCapita building, where the white of the frost on its outer branches kept it traceable. But it stopped on something again. Billy saw it pause for a moment, and then roll away. And as it did, whatever it had hit under there began to sway in the darkness. It was just a shadow, but it seemed to be hanging down from the crossbars of the awning. At first, Billy thought it might be a broken panel from the roof or a strip of dangling insulation, swaying in the tumbleweed's wake. But he could see color, see white, and something was genuinely off about the shape. He kept looking at it.

And then Billy realized he was much too late. His mind had caught up to his eyes, and he understood: he was staring at the naked feet of a hanged man's body.

White Sheets

Henry walked for four days straight, and for the first two of them, he felt like a new man. But by the third day, his feet were blistered and his back hurt from sleeping on the ground. His clothes were filthy, and the beard he'd been ignoring for months was tangled and itching down at the skin. Before he left Medora, he took the Junior Ranger badges from the tin and pinned them to the front of the hoodie he'd kept since exploring the Everglades forever ago. They jangled as he walked, catching the spring sunshine and making a constellation of reflected stars on the pavement in front of him. He'd stuck to rural roads heading west, but the berm of I-94 was never very far away, and he kept it to his north as a marker that he was on the right track.

Not that he quite knew how to get where he was going. His next stop was Yellowstone National Park, and he'd done his best to memorize the way before he burned the itinerary pages in the atlas. He knew it was in the far corner of Wyoming, which meant he needed to head southwest from where he was. He knew the interstate led to Billings, which seemed to be the biggest town along the way, and if he could get there, his next target would be a place called Red Lodge. From Red Lodge, there was an extraordinarily curvy road south that should take him to the park boundary. It was all a very long way—hundreds of miles—and to tell the truth, his body was starting to tell him it was a pipe dream. Rode-hard and hung-up-wet, he reached the outskirts of a place called Beach just on the near side of the border to Montana.

Beach was about the same size Medora had been, and it seemed just as sleepy. There was no beach there—nor any features at all, really. A woman hanging laundry on a clothesline waved to him as he scuffled by on a gravel road running arrow-straight from horizon to horizon, and he was grateful she didn't shriek and run away. Or get a gun: he must have looked like a perfect goblin.

Further into town, he found an empty baseball field in a park, and he rested on a bench there in the shade of a covered dugout. He took his backpack off his shoulders and rummaged inside it for the things he needed to make himself a sandwich. After he ate, he laid back on the bench and napped. No one seemed to notice him, and he slept for an hour there in peace. But while he slept, something unexpected happened: the temperature had been warm all day, sunny and maybe in the mid-fifties; but he woke to the sight of his breath in the air and an inch-deep dusting of snow on the ground. He sat up and looked at the baseball diamond. It looked like a perfect white sheet with a slight rise in the center where the pitcher's mound must have been. No snow was falling, and the gray sky seemed content with what it had left behind. It was cool, but not cold; Henry wouldn't have thought it was even near freezing. But the flurries covered everything in sight.

He dusted off his backpack, lifted it onto his shoulders, and started to head out. Leaning against the chain link fence was an old wooden baseball bat he hadn't seen when he came in. It was splintered at the end, and he understood it had been abandoned there. He picked it up, tested it with his weight, and walked on, using it like a cane. He never looked back. But if he had, he would have seen a trail of perfect footprints, an occasional round hole at their side.

* * *

The border was quiet, but after he crossed, he noticed the ridge of the interstate had drifted to the north out of his sight. He kept walking that straight road west, and he trusted 94 would make its way back to him eventually. He figured it had to. It was getting on in the afternoon, and he was starting to think about what sleep would be like that night.

But there was nothing anywhere that he could see. Although Henry thought he'd gotten used to the utter emptiness of the country here, the place he was now was more barren than he thought possible. Under that thin layer of snow, he was walking across a single fold in the center of an infinite sheet of white paper. There were no rocks and no shelter. There was only the road itself and a straight line of crosses made by the powerlines running alongside it. The sky had not regained its color since his midday nap, and Henry couldn't have felt more alone if he was walking across the surface of another planet.

Except that, as he scanned the fields around him, he realized he wasn't alone at all. There, to his south, was a wobbly dark speck on the horizon. It must have been more than a mile away, but Henry was sure he was seeing *something*, and he stared for a long time. He held up his hand over his eyes to block the nonexistent sunshine and squinted. And his confidence grew: it was another person.

There was nothing for Henry to do but walk on, so that's what he did. As he walked, he kept his eye on the only thing there was in ten miles to keep an eye on. He couldn't be sure, but it seemed like the figure was moving closer to him. It was little more than a smudge in the distance, but it seemed larger than it had been, and after another five minutes, it was larger still. Henry could see the shape of it now, too: it had a hat on its head the color of spring grass, and it looked like a little beacon of color gliding across the blank and naked horizon. Five minutes more, and Henry could see that whoever was underneath that hat was wearing a blue shirt and darker blue pants. It was definitely a man, he thought, but there was something strange about him: his clothes were odd, old–maybe Amish. Although he was still a few hundred yards away, Henry thought he could make out actual suspenders, the metal of their clasps winking at him across the ocean of snow.

It dawned on Henry that the reason the man was getting larger was because the roads they were each traveling on were going to intersect. Horrified, he tried to do the geometry in his head. He considered slowing down or speeding up to avoid the confrontation, but he wasn't sure which choice would make things better. And he knew the man must see him by now, too; he must be working the same numbers. Despite all the empty space in the world, Henry realized he was trapped, and he felt his body flood with worry.

Still, he walked on, and so did the stranger. They drew closer and closer to each other. Then Henry could see their crossroads up ahead: it was just a hundred yards more, and there were thin slivers of what must be stop signs on the other man's path. When the man arrived at the intersection, he stopped. When Henry got there, he stopped, too.

They looked at each other, and it was the stranger in homespun clothes who spoke first. "You out here for the last days?" he asked. Henry realized he had a single stalk of wheat dangling from the corner of his mouth, and it bounced as he talked. Henry couldn't imagine where he'd found it.

"I don't think so," Henry said.

The man was young, and for all his strangeness, there was something familiar about him. He looked Henry up and down and then spoke again: "I figured you must be out here for the church convention. But I guess those're odd clothes for it."

"Church convention?"

"Starts tonight," he said. "S'pose I'm a bit early."

Henry was afraid to look away from him, but he couldn't help himself. He glanced down the road in the direction the man was heading, and then he scanned the entire horizon. There was absolutely nothing to see: not a farmhouse, a barn, or even a tent in a field.

"Can't be too much longer, though," the man said. "No, I'd say we're just about here to the end of things. Don't you think?"

Henry's mind was all blinking lights, and the brightest of them was a neon sign reading *Ghost!* But he'd never imagined ghosts to be particularly apocalyptic, and this odd fellow—just more than a boy, really—seemed tangible enough. Henry could see the blond hair sticking out from under his hat and a day's stubble on his neck over his Adam's apple. He realized he was waiting for Henry to speak. "I guess it's got to happen sometime," he said.

"Truer words," the stranger said, smiling. "Preacher says it's 'once coming, twice deserved.'" There was light this time when his eyes met Henry's again. "You're more'n welcome to tag along, friend," he said. "Be nice to have a fellow traveler."

"I'm heading that way there," Henry said, pointing down his own path. "Gotta get somewhere to sleep for the night." *Stupid,* he thought immediately, chastising himself for the admission of plans.

"Oh, won't be much sleep tonight, I don't think. You'd miss the show."

"Yeah," Henry said. "Well."

The kid shrugged his shoulders like he didn't have a care in the world. Or like this wasn't a world worth having a care in. "Suit yourself," he said. "Til the hereafter."

"Til the hereafter," Henry heard himself say back.

The kid moved first, crossing the intersection and rambling on. Henry watched him go, and when he'd gotten a decent ways off, he looked both ways and crossed himself.

The sun neared the horizon behind its veil of clouds, and the entire sky turned a radiant pink. Another few miles on and Henry finally found a place to hole up for the night. There was an old homestead just off the road without a single intact window in the place. He nudged the door open with his foot and called out anyway, but there was no answer. Inside, he tried to find a clear spot for his sleeping bag, but the floors were all a mess: boards missing, broken glass, springs leftover from old mattresses and ruined furniture. The air smelled, despite its dryness, of mold. In the end, he settled on the horse stable, where at least the ground was clean and dry after the snow.

Despite his exhaustion, it took a while for him to fall asleep. He'd given up trying to figure out where the kid he'd met was going, but the sky had cleared, and as the stars came out overhead, he couldn't help but wonder if it was his last night on earth. He'd grown up in a nominally Christian family, and he'd heard his fair share of prophetic ruminations about Jesus and his coming army of angels. He understood God's anger at the mess of the world, and at times, he'd felt that anger himself. But out here, in the empty middle of it, he was beginning to suspect that whatever bones God had to pick with his people, the land had nothing to do with it.

He closed his eyes, but his thoughts fought back. He did his best to resist them, to rest. But old habits won out, and he looked up again to stare at the sky. When he did, he was shocked by what he saw: curtains of green were swaying in the air, rippling with eerie light. Patterns on top of a sea of stars. Movements with no beginning and no end.

Henry had never seen the aurora before, and it was entirely beautiful.

On the morning of the next day, Henry gave up the ghost: he turned right at an intersection and set off in search of the interstate. It was five miles until he found it, and he walked down an eastbound exit ramp and got back to walking on honest pavement. It was easier on his feet, and even if it only came in the form of an occasional passing car, he was eager for company. By midmorning, he had made his peace with hitchhiking, and he decided he'd stick out his thumb for the next motorist to come along. He'd seen only one so far, and it was going in the wrong direction. He thought about setting down his things and resting while he waited, but it seemed a bit too much like putting all his eggs in a single basket.

The sun was out, and it had made quick work of the strange snow from the day before. There was a real wind blowing across the prairie, and Henry would have found it pleasant, if not for the grit it kicked up and peppered across his face. Eventually—around noon—a truck did pass by, but the driver either didn't see Henry's thumb, or he didn't want to have anything to do with the man holding it out. So Henry kept walking.

The landscape was beginning to change. The sky still stretched to the edge of the earth on all sides of him, but if the feeling he had was like being on the sea, the Great Plains were at least beginning to have a few waves. Hills rolled out from the sides of the road, and Henry could see rows of shrubs and dwarf trees in the creases between them which held water. There were clouds now, too—blown in with the wind—and he could see their shadows gliding across the stubbly spring grasses. It was a pleasant day, but by the end, he'd done twenty more miles, and his feet weren't going to let him push them much farther. He'd been seeing signs for a place called Glendive up ahead, and he had to lean hard on his baseball bat to get properly into town.

Glendive was auto shops, a few seedy motels, and a Seventh Day Adventist church. Its main claim to fame seemed to be that it spanned a two-hundred foot wide stretch of the Yellowstone River, and although Henry was glad to see the word in print, he wasn't eager to cross the bridge: for the first time in forever, he saw an honest-to-God police barricade in the middle of it, flashing lights and all. Without Billy around to help explain his oddness to strangers, he thought it would be best to find another way.

He stayed on the near side and wandered through town. There were people, but they seemed to be going out of their way to pretend he wasn't there. Eventually, he realized it was because they took him for a vagrant—which, he was surprised to admit to himself, is precisely what he was. There was something both horrifying and liberating about this discovery for Henry: he was rightly and finally invisible. But he also felt ashamed, and not for anything he had done. He decided he didn't much like it.

But as with most bad things, there were upsides. The sun was already setting when Henry caught sight of a place he wouldn't have noticed in his previous life: a trainyard. The grounds were quiet, and they contained the near ends of three long rows of boxcars. The place was dark, and there were no fences or guard posts blocking it off. The trains were right there, Henry thought, for anyone to explore. And so that's exactly what he did.

The rows of cars seemed impossibly long. The engines were well out of sight somewhere to the south, and he had no idea if they were even operational. He had no memories of whistles, or of the trails of smoke in the sky that he assumed all trains still made. When he climbed over the hitch between two cars in the closest row, he found himself in a sort of open-roofed hallway formed by the lines. It was claustrophobic after weeks on the prairie, but it also felt strangely safe. He walked the row, and in short order, he was standing by an open and empty boxcar. It was late, and Henry remembered that he *was* a vagabond, after all, so *what the hell?* He shrugged, for no one but himself, before he lifted a knee and started to climb in.

The inside of the car was perhaps fifty feet long and floored with worn timber held down by thick rusted rivets. He walked to the far corner, took off his backpack, and sat down. It was quiet and dark, and the sky outside the doorway was a fading purple. He unrolled his sleeping bag, made another simple dinner, and smiled as he came up with a new nickname for himself: *Hobo Henry,* he thought; *Henry the Hobo. Hobo Hank?* He settled on Hobo Hank.

At some point in the night he realized he was moving, but he did not allow this to wake him. He was in his worst day again, and though his dreams often took him to that place, this time he lingered there like a man holding his palm over a lit candle.

Caleb was dead, and the paramedics who had placed him onto a board and tied him to it, as if he might get away, had covered him with a white cloth. He remembered his first thought when he saw it was that it was like a scene in a movie; that the sheet was like a prop. It had creases in it where it had been folded before and stowed away. He had wondered if it was new, or if there were boxes of white sheets, folded and individually wrapped in plastic, in the corners of every ambulance and firetruck in the world. He had hoped so: the alternative was that his son was wearing the same shroud someone else's son had worn before him.

The strangers in his home carried Caleb down the stairs as if they'd done it a hundred times. They kept his body level on the stretcher. The sheet was tucked in around his sides. He was a mummy in white, floating down the steps he'd walked up on his own only hours ago.

Henry remembered the procession going by over the shoulder of an officer asking him questions. Shannon wasn't there yet, and he had needed her, and he had feared her coming. He had been afraid every single day of his life since. His thoughts drifted to corpses in their spacesuits on Mars, to a hand holding his umbrella, to a sense of moving along while lying still. But he made himself come back.

Who are you? an officer's voice asked. *What's your name?*

It's Henry. Henry Henry. He's my son…

Is this your address?

What? Yes. 1422 Laurel… this is our home—

Are you the boy's father?

What?

Are you his father?

What? Yes, I am. Is he?

Was he alone in the house?

I'm here.

Was he alone?

They were always questions with no right answers, information leading nowhere. Years and years of digging fresh holes while the most important things drifted by.

And then the scene changed, and he was with Shannon. It was dark. They were at the kitchen table. *You don't get to know,* she was saying. *You don't get to know what it means for me to have lost my boy.*

Caleb—

Don't you say his name. Don't you say his name to me.

Cheeks streaked and eyes closed. A hand palm up on the table, despite the anger behind it. His own hands pressed flat around the bridge of his nose, as if in prayer.

The boxcar thumped beneath him, but Henry would not wake. He stayed in these dreams, and then the next:

He was at the table again, but this time Caleb was with him. It was the day after Halloween, he knew. Caleb had eaten leftover candy for breakfast. He had gone out trick or treating the night before dressed as a werewolf.

Where do ghosts go during the day? he was asking.

There are no such things as ghosts, Henry said.

I know, but even in stories and things. Why do they only come out at night? Shouldn't they always be around?

Henry thought about Caleb's costume from the night before and remembered they were hunting logic: without a full moon, a werewolf is a man again.

They're still there in the day. It's just too light to see them.

Really?

Yes. They're pale, and it has to be really dark for them to show up.

That's sad.

Sad? No way.

Yes, it is! He was up and getting his lunchbox out of the refrigerator now. *Why is it sad?*

He put it in his backpack and looked at Henry. Oh, God. *Because then they're invisible when people are awake and not invisible when people are asleep.*

So?

Caleb rolled his eyes. *Even ghosts need friends.*

And Henry flinched.

He woke to the sound of brakes squealing beneath him. He realized the train was stopping, and alarm bells went off in his waking mind. Where was he? He sat up in his sleeping bag and looked out the door of the boxcar. It was dark outside, but he could see stars in the sky and the shapes of mountains forming a horizon. Their movement slowed. As he watched, a long, low platform slid past, and there were lights on it at intervals. The intervals grew, and just as the car came to rest, he could see a sign on a fence railing at the far side of the platform. It said *Red Lodge*: Henry had traveled, by accident, more than a hundred miles in the right direction.

He got out of the boxcar, patted the sliding door once in gratitude, and set out. As the sun began to rise, he found a sign for Yellowstone and started down the road. He'd made nearly a dozen miles by noon, and the going was easy. The weather was cool but pleasant, and he walked for hours in the shadows of lodgepole pines. The smell of the needles was rich and sweet. He ate an early lunch at a campground just off the shoulder, and all seemed well.

But by mid-afternoon, he wished he'd stayed the night there, or taken a different route entirely. He was on a road called the Beartooth Highway, and with no warning, it began climbing in steep switchbacks up into the mountains. It had not been plowed this season, or seemingly in any season: banks of winter snowpack ten feet deep made the path almost impossible to follow, and all Henry could do was try to stay in the lane of white between the stands of trees. His legs ached and he labored for every step. His boots punched holes through the icy surface of the snow, and if not for that baseball bat, he would have broken his ankles a dozen times.

There was a small pullout for a place called Vista Point, and as soon as he turned in, he collapsed on a rock wall poking up from the snow like an island. The sun still had hours left in the sky, but he was entirely beat. He scrambled into his sleeping bag, huddled against the cold that began creeping in the instant he was still, and longed for rest.

The next three days were no better. His food ran out, and he had to teach himself to make drinking water from the snow by shoveling it into his water bottle and tucking the bottle in under his coat against his bare skin until it melted. His lungs hurt with the altitude, and after he climbed above the treeline, he lost all sense of direction. He stumbled and scrambled over summits and through valleys, wanting it all to be over. He thought he would die there, lost in the mountains. He was so weak and hungry.

And then, on the third day, he realized for the first time in years that in his deepest heart he wanted to live. It wasn't a survival instinct; it had nothing to do with what he felt he deserved, or didn't deserve. It was purely this: Henry Henry wanted to see what was on the other side of these mountains. He wanted wonder. And, in his delirium, his thoughts caught on something that surprised him: if he died here, Billy Faulkner would never know what happened to him. He would never know that Henry didn't get to all his parks. He thought about Billy, and he even began to speak to him.

Really wish I had that ice cream truck right now, Henry said in his mind.

Lotta good it would do you.

It would be warm.

It wouldn't get down this road.

You would have found a better way.

I would have told you this was a dumb one.

I'd have listened to you.

Yeah?

Yeah. I should never have left.

Don't start with that.

It's true, though. I hope I get to tell you sometime. I mean, really tell you.

Because this is a figment of your imagination.

Because this is a figment of my imagination.

Apologies don't count here. That's cheating.

That's cheating. Yeah.

You gonna live?

I'm gonna try.

Think anyone will see you?

I hope they do.

That's a first.

Even ghosts need friends.

* * *

By nightfall on the third day, Henry found trees again. By noon on the fifth, he was in the abandoned town of Cooke City. He hadn't eaten in two days. He raided the storeroom of an old market and gorged himself on canned beans and individually-wrapped Twinkies. He slept for twenty-four hours.

On day seven, he kept walking. And then he found it: America's first national park. He had made it to Yellowstone.

No Hemingways

When Billy closed his laptop after the last virtual course of his college career, he wanted to be Ernest Hemingway. He wasn't the first man in America to feel that way, and he wouldn't be the last in whatever this country was going to be next. It wasn't the books or the bravado that seduced him: it was the sentences.

During his junior year, there was a brief semester where students were permitted to attend classes in person. Everyone wore a mask, and more often than not, they still worked on computers sitting at their desks. Waves of sickness always kept a quarter of the students in quarantine, and several of the professors refused to be in the classrooms, anyway. Life was staring at rectangles and clicking a button to raise your hand.

His journalism professor never intended to come back. And on one Friday afternoon, he instructed his TA to clean out his office, pack up the books he wanted delivered to his house, and give away the rest. The TA brought the ones in the last category to class, and Billy and a few of the other students browsed through them after dismissal. He found one called *By-Line* by Hemingway, and he didn't recognize the title. It was thick and heavy. When he got home he realized it wasn't a novel, as he'd first supposed. Instead, it was a compendium of the articles Hemingway had written during his time as a journalist. They covered European affairs, mostly; dispatches from his time with the *Star* papers in Kansas City and

Toronto. But towards the end, Billy found a run of articles written for the North American Newspaper Alliance covering the Spanish Civil War from 1937 to 1939. He fell in love, and he knew just what he wanted to do.

Billy was a child of American wars: he was born the year the Iraq War began, and Afghanistan was white noise during his childhood. Then Trump, then Ukraine, then Russia. But none of that touched him, or touched most anyone in Chicago. So at 22, reading Hemingway's crisp, run-on sentences, Billy felt like he could see the last real magic trick: taking chaos and folding it into the tiny box of the right words to contain it.

When Billy floored the accelerator of the Roving Ranger and made for Hardin, Montana, he did his best to wield that same spell.

Dead man in Crow Agency, hanging from a rafter. A sign reading 'So All White Men' dangling from his neck.

No, that won't work– 'dead man… hanging' is three words to say one thing; 'dangling' is limp and imprecise.

'So All White Men' read the sign draped on the corpse's neck.

'Draped?' Like a tablecloth?

A murdered man hangs as a warning to others like him in Crow Agency.

'So All White Men,' the sign on the dead man's neck warned.

He couldn't get it. And as he raced to tell someone what he had seen, he thought so hard about how he would say it that the thought of who he might find down the road could find no purchase.

*　*　*

There were no peacekeepers in Hard Town. But there were the Crow, and the corpse Billy had found was no surprise to them. It was also not the only one. Just past the sign marking the city limit, a makeshift gibbet had been built over the roadway, and there were three more white bodies hanged there, swaying in the morning wind as the Ranger passed beneath them. They were young and male; two still wore biker jackets, and Billy could read the words *Billings Boys* on their shoulders in heavy gothic script. The third was stripped naked, his skin torn and streaked with dried blood.

A Native woman stopped him outside Cricket Pawn. She was unarmed, but she stood in the middle of the roadway and held up her hand. She left it up until Billy had taken the keys out of the ignition and rolled down his window to show them to her. She did not speak. Instead, she came to Billy's door, opened it, and pointed at a place for him to get out and stand. Once he did, she took the rabbit's foot from his hand, got into the Ranger, closed the door, and drove away.

Billy watched until the Ranger was entirely out of sight. He stood there, alone and afraid. He began walking in the direction the woman had gone, and there was no sound. The smell of smoke in the air stung Billy's nostrils. He followed after her.

He'd made it perhaps the length of a football field when he reached a railroad crossing. The instant he touched it, two boys carrying rifles came out from a small stand of trees and held out their own hands, stopping him again. Neither could have been older than fourteen. After he complied, one gestured up the road with the barrel of his gun, and Billy walked in the direction it pointed. They fell in behind him, marching him towards he knew not where.

*　*　*

He spent the next five days locked in a horse stall at the county fairgrounds. The woman from the pawn shop brought him food. There was a bucket with a seat bolted to it which she emptied for him each day at sunrise and sunset. She still did not speak to him. It was cold at night and hot during the day. It rained more than once. Outside, Billy could hear engines and voices from time to time, and he understood the fairgrounds were a staging area for something he could not see or entirely understand, but something that was busy and frightening. There were louder noises sometimes, which seemed perhaps a mile or so away, and he knew they were gunshots. He'd found violence, and the sounds erupted in back-and-forth bursts like firecrackers. He was blind, and he waited.

On the third day, someone else was brought into a stall on the other end of the barn where he had been kept. They didn't come quietly: he heard them yelling, and he heard the wet and heavy sounds of another person's fists on their naked flesh. *Fuck you!* the damaged man would scream. *Fuck you! Fuck you!* But no one argued with him, and his voice was muffled at times with phlegm or with blood. When he was eventually left alone, Billy heard him whimpering and cursing under his breath.

Hours later, and well after dark, Billy called out to this stranger. He had been quiet, and Billy wondered if he was still alive. The man didn't answer him at first. When he finally did, he wouldn't share a name, and he took Billy for a spy. But at a point deep in the night, the man began to rant—maybe to Billy, or maybe to himself—and Billy understood he was at war.

The beaten man cursed the "red bastards" who had seized his home and his land and swore vengeance and promised death to each man, woman, and Indian child.

"Thieves and murderers," the white man called them. It was their nature, and he would be "damned to hell" before he let them live one more day in "his country."

"White Montana" was God's destiny, the prisoner swore. The time of the "reds" was over. He would die for this, God knew.

Billy tried his best. He listened to all he could. He wanted to understand, and to trap his understanding in words so all the things he did not yet know might cease to terrify him and he might control what is uncontrollable and master his own fear.

But they were no Hemingways.

If you ever have to shoot a horse stand so close to him that you cannot miss and shoot him in the forehead at the exact point where a line drawn from his left ear to his right eye and another line drawn from his right ear to his left eye would intersect. A bullet there from a .22 caliber pistol will kill him instantly and without pain and all of him will race all the rest of him to the ground and he will never move except to stiffen his legs out so he falls like a tree.

\-   "On Being Shot Again," for *Esquire,* June 1935

The man in the other stall was killed on the morning of the fifth day. Guards Billy could not see came for him and took him out screaming and kicking at the wood boards of the pens. Billy heard the shot seconds later. It was somewhere outside, and the sound hit the sheet metal walls at the far end of the barn and bounced back to him in an echo. Afterwards, a man came to Billy's cell. He was old, and he wore a stained yellow t-shirt and cargo shorts. His feet were bare.

"What do you want here?" he asked looking down at Billy, who was sitting cross-legged in the straw.

"I came to warn you," Billy said. "I saw a man a few miles south. In Crow Agency, by the Department building. It was a corpse, hanging. It was a dead man." He knew was using too many words. "I don't know what's happening here."

The man nodded, but at which part Billy couldn't say. "What's happening here is war."

"Between who?" Billy asked.

"Between everyone," the man said. "It's war."

"Are you Crow?"

"Every man is Crow."

Billy pointed in the direction of the dead man's stall. "Was he Crow?"

"He wasn't a man."

"Why did you kill him?"

"He shouldn't have been here. He meant us harm."

"He said he'd been harmed."

"Nothing was taken from him. That was his…" The old man's nose wrinkled. "confusion. He sees things more clearly now."

"What did he do?"

"What was in his heart to do. He had a sickness." The man looked at Billy, and Billy knew what he was seeing because he was a Black man and he'd felt that look all his life. "Their kind all have it. They take and can't give. It's foreign to them. They only understand…" Billy watched as he searched for another word. He gestured with his hand, as if Billy should help him out. He wouldn't; but he knew what the word was. *Violence.*

The man gave up the hunt and shrugged. He changed topics. "We can't keep you," he said, and pointed towards the empty plate sitting on the straw beside him. "You cost too much. We can't keep you, but we can't let you go."

It took ten words for Billy to realize, for the first time since he had been marched to this stall, that he could die here. Even the other man's murder hadn't seemed like a real threat to him. *We can't keep you, but we can't let you go.* What he had thought was an unspeakable thing swept into him with a cold rush and took him over. "What are you going to do?" he asked.

The man's face was weathered and stiff at its seams. He gave nothing away. "What are you going to do?" he asked back.

Billy didn't know what answer might save his life, or if any answer could. The man waited for a long moment.

"They hate you, too," the old man said finally. He stepped back out of the horse stall and closed the door, but he did not lock it. Now, Billy could only hear his voice. "And they are not men."

The smaller rooms in the back, on the side away from the shelling, were considerably more expensive. After the shell that lit on the sidewalk in front of the hotel you got a beautiful double corner room on that side, twice the size of the one you had had, for less than a dollar. It wasn't me they killed. See? No. Not me. It wasn't me anymore.

   -   "A New Kind of War," for *NANA Dispatch*, April
      14, 1937

That afternoon, Billy decided to try and save himself. He left his stall, which the old man had left unlatched, and emerged from the far end of the barn into the blinding light of the fairgrounds. There was a rodeo arena and grandstands and white tents set up in a grid across the dirt there. People were everywhere. Vehicles of all sorts were parked haphazardly in every empty space. Everyone he saw carried rifles over their shoulders. One of the trucks had a .50-caliber Browning machine gun mounted on a tripod bolted into its bed. It was war, but not the war from the movies. No one was shouting. No helicopters were churning up tornadoes of dust while a commandant tried to convince his square-jawed general to move two platoons to cover the eastern flank. There were not even uniforms: everyone Billy saw—old men, old women, teenage boys—wore just the sorts of tired farm clothes Billy had seen in Lakota. But it was war. Smoke drifted out from a long tent where a man was cooking food.

Billy wandered the space without purpose or direction. His feet felt heavy. He looked for the Ranger, but he did not see it. He looked for the woman who had taken it from him, or for the man who had threatened his life and also set him free, but he did not see them, either. Card tables had been set up under the largest and nearest of the tents, and he saw both men and women huddled around them. He walked that way.

No one paid him any attention. They were caught up in their own conversations, pointing at spots on a large map spread out across the tables. Billy didn't understand the geography, but he could see salt shakers and coins set in particular places which he understood to represent people. A woman reached across to move a bottle of ketchup, and another man put his hand on her arm and stopped her. She muttered something under her breath, angry with him.

And then suddenly a car was honking. The sound wasn't coming from the fairgrounds, but it was getting closer and growing more insistent. Billy looked around, and he could see a cloud of dust moving down the highway in their direction. A pickup truck raced through the open gate at the far end of the parking lot, and the people at the table stopped what they were doing and moved as one towards it, already shouting questions at the men preparing to jump down from the bed. Billy watched all of this, and then there was a new sound: a muffled thunder, from somewhere that was not far enough away. He saw a plume of black smoke rise above the treeline to the west. The voices were barking orders now, and everyone else in the fairground was running towards one vehicle or another. Billy stood still, trying to catch it all, and in less than a minute, he had been left completely alone. There were the sounds of a dozen or so engines receding down the highway away from him, and the dust trailing up after them. And as his eyes followed it, he was finally distracted by the emptiness of the wide blue sky.

> *If you want to know something, get someone who was there to tell you. If you wish, and I can still remember, I will be glad to tell you sometime what it was like in those woods for the next ten days; about all the counterattacks and about the German artillery. It is a very, very interesting story if you can remember it. Probably it has even epic elements. Doubtless sometime you will even see it on the screen.*
>
> - "War in the Siegfried Line," for *Collier's,* November 8, 1944

In another world, Billy was a wolf, like his brother. In yet another, he was a hawk, like his sister. A bear, like his mother. Even a beaver, like his father. But in this one, Billy was a prairie dog, and in the new silence of the town he wandered the streets looking for a burrow to duck back into. He wanted his ice cream truck.

He hadn't seen it in the westbound caravan. It wasn't parked along the main street of town. But he felt sure it was somewhere, and in his eagerness to find it, it never occurred to him that he didn't have the keys. Dazed and tired and hungry, he walked and searched. He didn't know how long he had. He didn't know if anyone cared to find him at all.

A few blocks from the fairground, he discovered a bowling alley with its door propped open and went in. The lanes were dark and stacked with boxes. Red and blue and green balls were still lined up in rows beside the returns. The main island where the rental shoes were kept had been turned into a kind of ammo stockpile, and green metal tins were stacked there three feet high and organized by caliber. No one was around to watch them, and Billy assumed they had gone out with everyone else.

He hunted in the dimness looking now for food, and he found an old cafe in an alcove along the south wall. Inside were boxes of old potato chips and a spoiled pack of hotdogs in a plastic cooler. There were individually-wrapped snack cakes in a drawer, and taking all he could hold, he sat down in a small booth in the dark to eat this relative feast.

Afterwards, he explored the rest of the space. It was cooler here, and he hoped to enjoy the shade for a bit longer. He opened doors to broom closets and wandered the narrow walkway behind the abandoned pinsetters. Aside from the depot in the front, there weren't any signs of activity or use, and no one had bowled for a very long time. A door behind the pin machines led to an alley and a dumpster, and Billy found himself almost in another house's backyard: a chain link fence had been built to separate the properties, but the diamond mesh had been removed and only the posts, spaced at ten feet intervals, remained. Billy looked down the odd row and then went back into the bowling center. He would grab the extra bags of chips and head north towards the high school. He'd seen a sign before, and it could be the Ranger had been stashed there in the lot. It was as good as any other guess. Hardin was home of the Mustangs.

But as he walked past the end of the lanes, he heard a noise towards the front and Billy realized he was no longer alone. The sounds were coming from the shoe stand, and he knew it was someone rummaging through the tins of ammunition there. He could see the person now, even in the dark: his hair was blonde, and his neck and shoulders were thin. From this distance, he seemed like little more than a kid. But he was rooting purposefully through the stockpile, and Billy could see a four-wheeler parked out front through the open door of the alley with mud splattered on its piping and rifle sitting in the seat, its barrel pointed up at the sky.

Billy stood perfectly still and watched. As he did, the kid's bare hands came up over the side of the kiosk and he began stacking the ammo boxes on the countertop in sets. They were lined up there like shoes: two, four, six. On his next lift, he finally looked up, and the instant he did, his eyes locked onto Billy's. He was only the length of a bowling lane away. It was too dark to read the expression on his face, but Billy could feel the boy's fear in the air. His head ducked down again, and Billy thought he was trying to hide. Billy found his own voice:

"I can see you there," he said. "Hey! It's okay. I don't want any trouble. I'm not a fighter."

There was no response.

"Hey!" Billy said again.

But this time, when the boy's head came up, he was holding something in his outstretched hand. Billy couldn't make it out, but as he stared, he saw a flash of light and heard a sound like a popping balloon. It reverberated around the hollow room, or maybe just in Billy's ears. Strangely, he felt suddenly quite certain that the sound was a bowler: some phantom in the alley, nailing a vicious strike. Billy needed that to be what it was.

But the kid was already grabbing the tins and hauling ass out the door, and Billy could feel something wet and warm—too much of it—underneath his soiled and wrinkled dress shirt. He didn't want to look because it would be real. So he sat down on the cold, tile floor and stared at the doorway until the kid had loaded his things and the four wheeler had sped away and the fading afternoon sun had changed the color of the parking lot yellow and then orange and then red and then Billy closed his eyes, still sitting there on the floor, to let himself sleep.

Geyser Gazers

What happens when you let something die? Who are you, to think it can be stopped? Henry knew and didn't know. But he would not die at the mouth of the Hayden Valley, under the towering peaks running out from the Absaroka Range and walking along the cracked pavement beside Soda Creek. There were too many words for it, and Henry had learned that real death tracks after silence and does not precede it. Death is cold punctuation, with only rumors of sentences to follow.

The dawn was still breaking, though the sun had been up for an hour or more. The shadows of the mountains drew back to them, uncovering spring grass in patches amidst the melt of high-altitude snow. Already, wildflowers were blooming. Ancient whitebark pines rose in their multitudes from the hills. Mist still shrouded the creek, but it had only moments left before the light of the day would touch it and send it away until the next morning. Or so Henry thought. Henry was as tired as he had ever been in his life, but he didn't feel like a phantom of himself: he could sense every muscle and sinew of his body, and he put his waking mind into using them to lift first one foot and then the other. He walked in amazement.

Something was moving down the road towards him. It was low and dark, and it approached in a trot that hugged the northbound shoulder of the road. His mind fixed on the shape of a dog, but it seemed too large, and as it neared, Henry realized it was a wolf. Its pelt was jet black, and its tongue lolled out of its mouth. It did not break its stride, even as it met Henry on the path. It was only feet away, but the wolf merely looked at Henry out of the corner of its eye and ambled on. He could hear the pant of its breath and see the trembling of its sides. He stopped as it passed and turned to watch it continue back towards the pass through the mountains.

When he began walking again, it wasn't long before he saw a truck up ahead crossing the valley. It was on him quickly, but he did not feel afraid. It was an old pickup, dirty white except for a green stripe down the side. As it pulled to a stop, he could see the old park service arrowhead on the door. *Ranger* was printed on the fender.

But the driver wasn't a ranger, at least as far as Henry could tell. She seemed ancient, her pale skin turned to leather and her gray hair cropped short at her shoulders. She wore a yellow rain jacket over a pale blue t-shirt. Her eyes were even more blue, and somehow even more pale, though they sparked when she smiled in greeting at Henry.

"You saw a wolf!" she said with a level of excitement he struggled to square with his presumptions about her age. He didn't quite know what to say back.

He pointed up the road. "It went that way," he said.

"She always does," came the reply. "Killed a calf a few miles west this morning and headed home." The woman was still smiling, and Henry was confused.

"Are you trying to catch her?"

"No!" the woman said. "Not hardly!" Something registered in her face, and she held a hand out the window of the truck. "She's God's own. I'm Lydia."

"Henry," Henry said back.

"Where ya headed?"

"I don't know yet. In, I guess."

"In is right," she said. "I'll getcha there."

Her name was Lydia Fairleigh-Hayes, but her friends called her Lee. Henry was instantly her friend, and he sensed that was typically the way of things. They drove west through the valley and into the heart of the park. Henry realized maps betrayed the sheer size of the place: Yellowstone was larger than several of the old United States, and it held places like none he had ever seen. As they went, Henry split his attention between his host and the landscape. They passed through a wide and spare bottomland between enormous, snow-capped ridges. The earth tumbled around them in rolling hills, and twice they passed through herds of grazing bison numbering in the dozens, if not the hundreds. Lydia would slow the truck to a crawl and sit up at the steering wheel, watching for sudden movements among the bulls or cows.

"They don't spook," she said to Henry. "You seen many bison in your wanderings?"

"Not too many," Henry said.

"Well, they'll just stare atcha. If they get in your way, there's nothing to do but wait for them to move on; a honk'll just get you a snort back. They couldn't care less about you."

"Do they charge?"

"Oh no! Not at a car. But if you get too close, they'll put a hoof through your door."

"Through it?"

"Just about."

Henry wondered where he was going and who it was that was taking him there. "Are you alone in the park?" he asked Lydia.

"Alone? Not a chance!" she said. "Got all these guys, for starters."

"I mean people?"

"I know! I got a herd of those, too."

It was another three hours before Henry knew just what she meant. Soon, they crossed the Yellowstone River on a narrow bridge near Tower-Roosevelt. More steam rose up from it, and the water bubbled on beneath them towards valleys and canyons below. It was fearsome and momentous. Once they had crossed, Henry's ferrywoman turned onto the main loop road of the park at a junction across a parking lot from what looked to be the burned shells of a dozen small visitors' cabins. In fact, everything there seemed burned: the trees were still standing, but they were naked and black at the stump. "Fire in '28," Lydia said as he leaned forward in his seat to stare. "Ran right down the west side of the river. Burned a thousand acres."

"Was anyone hurt?" Henry asked.

"Hurt? No, no. Hardly anybody here in '28! But the party was getting started."

"How long have you been here?"

"Oh, just a year or so. I'm not a Gazer like most of the rest; just somebody travelin' through. Probably the same as you. But it's felt like forever."

They pushed on together. The Grand Loop Road wound through the wilderness, past forests of pine and spruce and trailhead after trailhead. They saw more bison. Eventually, the road turned south and rose in switchbacks past the steaming terraces of an enormous hot spring. Henry wanted to stop to see it, but he didn't know how to ask. He'd already noted a dozen places he thought he should return to.

They drove and drove, eventually reaching more flatlands, this time surrounded on all sides and even to the horizon by plumes of white smoke rising hundreds of feet into the air and drifting in unison in the direction of the wind. The ground was white and bleached, and the smell of sulfur filled the cab of the truck. But if it was hell Henry had entered–if he had, in fact, died there in the Beartooth Pass–Lydia was proving a strangely talkative Charon. And as they went along, Henry believed he could make a second life of it. The sun shone down, and Henry listened and nodded, smiling both to his host and himself.

Their destination turned out to be the old Old Faithful Inn. It was nearly noon when they arrived, and the first stop of Lydia's tour was the cafeteria. It was located in a wide wing of the enormous building, and Henry couldn't help but marvel at the place. The lobby was positively cavernous. There were balconies for each of the three levels and nothing else between the slat floor and the tree-trunk beams of the exposed ceiling some eighty feet above him. Everything was made of rough, unfinished wood, from the staircase railings to the light sconces along the walls–which were lit, Henry noticed. Actual electricity hummed through the space. The only exceptions to the lumber seemed to be the glass in the windows, the moose antler chandeliers, and the biggest stone fireplace Henry had ever seen: it was 500 tons of rhyolite wider at its base than a car, and it reached all the way up to the steep slant of the roof.

People seemed to be everywhere. Henry saw them leaning over the railings and crossing this way and that across the atrium. Most seemed old to him–perhaps retirees–but they moved with purpose in their feet. A surprising number had matching t-shirts on. But Lydia's focus was food.

She hustled Henry through the Inn and paid no attention to his mumbled questions about the place. Instead, she led him through a set of doors and into a place called the Bear Pit Lounge. The ceiling here was lower, and there was another impressive fireplace. Tables were everywhere, though all but a few were empty. The ones that were occupied sat more eager-eyed geriatrics, all deep in excited conversations with each other.

Henry and Lydia weaved through the room until they made it to a buffet line on the far side. She handed him a tray as if what came next should be entirely obvious to him. Henry's mind raced backwards in time to the last time he'd been inside a Shoney's. He went with roast beef and mashed potatoes with a side of macaroni and cheese, and holy shit, was it a feast. They sat together in wicker chairs beside a window. Henry ate in a near-frenzy, hunched over his tray and shoveling in food with both hands. There were dinner rolls. He drank an actual fountain soda, and Lydia watched him. When he was nearly finished, she spoke.

"When was the last time you ate?"

"Real food?" Henry asked with his mouth full.

"If that's what you think this is!"

"No idea," he said. "I have no fucking idea."

Lydia laughed. "I guess not! Typically I'd offer to say a blessing first. But if He knows anything, the good Lord knows how to wait."

"Mmhmm," Henry grunted, his stomach already beginning to ache. He swallowed, took another sip of soda, and felt his whole body fizz as it went down. When it settled, he went searching for his manners.

"Lydia, thank you," he said. "Lee, I mean. Thank you for bringing me here."

"You're most welcome, Henry. But you might want to wait until you find out where 'here' is before you get too grateful." The words were ominous, but Henry wouldn't believe them. The Old Faithful Inn was full of food, lights, and grandparents. Whatever else it might be, it was at least heaven.

"Where am I?" he asked, still floating somewhere above his body.

"Well, Yellowstone, for starters. But you already knew that," Lydia said. "Beyond that, you're in the Valley of the Geyser Gazers. The Last Watchers in the First Park. You've fallen in with clock keepers and note takers, I'm afraid. The accountants of the apocalypse." Lydia was smiling, but Henry had no idea what in the hell she was talking about.

"Watchers of what?" he asked.

"Everything out there," Lydia said, gesturing at the window with an upturned palm. "They track the water levels and temperatures, the little earthquakes, the eruptions. They're obsessed."

"Earthquakes?"

"They're hard to notice unless you're paying attention. They're not the knock-the- pictures-off-the-wall kinds. It's more subtle than that. You feel them in your feet." She raised one of her legs so Henry could see her dirty white Keds. He wondered if some factory somewhere still made shoes like those; they didn't seem particularly old.

"So, they gaze at the geysers? I get it, I think."

"That's what they do."

"I didn't know you could predict things like that."

"You're in the 'Old Faithful Inn.'"

Henry had never thought about the nickname before, and he felt like someone had just explained to him that bluebirds are blue. "How many geysers are out there? Are all of them..." he went looking for the word "...schedule-able?"

"Lots! That's the best I can tell you. Hundreds at least. And no, not all of them are 'schedule-able.' But the Gazers have a pretty good sense of things."

Henry realized she kept talking about them as a *them*. "You're not a Gazer?" he asked.

She laughed again. "No, not hardly. Too nerdy for me. And too boring! They'll sit out there on the benches for hours and hours. But I like to see them when they go, and somebody or other is always getting excited and saying, 'This way! This way! It's Steamboat! It's Excelsior!' Makes it easy to tag along."

"What do you do here, then?"

"Oh, not much, really. Talk with people. Walk. Chase the wolves."

"Why the wolves?"

"I've always liked dogs! The regular kind aren't really welcome around here; they're too easy pickin's for their cousins. So I make do with the ones I can."

"Where are you from?"

"That was about to be *my* question!"

"My answer's not very interesting: Ohio. But you?"

"Spokane, once upon a time." She said it like pe*can*, which was the way Henry's mother had pronounced the word when he was a boy; she had always thought pe*con* sounded pretentious, and she would say so.

"Did you come here in '26?" That was the year so much of the trouble started, although Henry had noticed so little.

"No, my husband and I didn't wander off until a bit later. No kids, and we'd already retired. Left Spokane in '28, and husband left me in '29."

"I'm sorry to hear that," Henry said. "I was going to ask if he was here."

"Not likely. He's dead and gone. If he ever got his act together, he's on past the Pearly Gates."

Henry's plate was clean and he was thinking about more. But Lydia sensed she might have him where she wanted him, and she wasn't going to let him go. "Quite the collection of flair you got there," she said, pointing at his chest. He'd taken his winter coat off when they sat down, and he realized now that the old Everglades hoodie he had on underneath was still covered in gold plastic badges. He didn't know what to say.

"There's a story to those. You're not my average drifter."

"Do you have an average drifter?"

"You'd be surprised. Not much left to do in this country but fight, hide, and wander. Folks pass through, and I like giving rides. But tell me about your badges."

"I collect them," Henry said, and it was the simplest answer. Although it felt more hollow than it used to.

"Was that a Before hobby or an After one?"

"'After.'"

"And was hiking the Beartooth in a thirty foot snowpack part of a plan to get another one, or to stop altogether? Because it was an act of commitment either way." Her eyes stared hard into his, and Henry knew she was searching for something in him. Or she was investigating its absence. He couldn't remember the last time he'd held someone else's attention like this, but the truth was that he didn't know, and he said so.

Something changed in her face and it was suddenly soft and kind as well as curious. "I'm sure there's one of those around here somewhere. We'll find it. But you'll have to earn it before you get to add it to the collection. Does that sound fair?"

Henry could have asked what she meant. He could have asked what he would need to do. But those were Before questions.

"Sounds fair," Henry said, and he felt ready for After.

"Waves on Grand!"

The call came from the doorway of the Inn, and suddenly everyone was moving. Henry could hear the pounding of feet racing down the stairways and the lobby filled with white hair and purple t-shirts. The only word for this was commotion. He and Lydia fell in with the crowd and made their way into the midday sunshine. When Henry had entered the Inn, he'd done so from the "road side," where the sheer size of the building had blocked his view of the geyser basin beyond. But now, he was walking along a path in a bubbling and smoking wilderness. Everything smelled of rotten eggs and the air made his eyes water. The ground was bone white, and rivulets of steaming water ran at intervals below the boardwalk. In some places, the water took on strange colors—yellows, browns, reds, and greens—that signaled, according to Lydia, the kinds of bacteria thriving there. These colors tracked with the temperature; pink was the hottest.

As the Gazers crossed a footbridge over the Firehole River, the path wound around the stump of Tardy Geyser, which rose in a bleached and popcorn-mottled mound, then past a bright yellow and green pool. After that, it broadened into a bench-lined arc that formed a semicircle around the main attraction.

There was no sinter cone for Grand: just a wide pool of water with odd rings of water pushing out from a bubbling plume in the center. There were other geysers on the odd plateau there, which leftover signs from the park days labeled "Vent" and "Turban," and the latter was already erupting, shooting spurts of scalding water a few feet in the air. But the real show was set to begin.

The steam rising from the center of the scene seemed to speed up, rising in a tumbling and roiling cloud. Henry expected to hear something: a rumble perhaps; or the crack of rocks somewhere below. But the crowd had gone strangely silent, and the only sound was the splashing of water around Turban.

"When does it happen?" Henry asked Lydia, and she shushed him.

"*Just wait*," she whispered.

And then it did: with a roar and a hiss, a fountain of boiling water shot straight up into the blue sky. The vapor plume was enormous, but it could not keep up with the geyser, which spouted nearly two hundred feet into the air. Henry expected it to quiet after that initial burst, but it did not: the water kept coming, in spout after spout, as the Gazers erupted in loud cheers. Some patted each other on the back, others high-fived, and a few even wept tears of joy. A voice not far from Henry kept repeating, "Oh my goodness, oh my goodness!"

The show lasted nearly ten minutes, with the column of water falling and rising in fresh bursts, each of which brought more "oohs" and "ahhs" from the watchers. Henry couldn't fathom how many hundreds of gallons he was seeing spit out from the earth. He wondered at the scale of the oceans beneath his feet and the heat so immense and near to them. The piping of the rocks through which it funneled and then erupted. It was like nothing he had ever seen.

When it was over, Lydia did something unexpected: she rested her small chin on his shoulder and gave him a hug with one arm. "That was Grand," she said. "Some sight, no matter how many times I've seen it."

"How rare is this?" Henry asked her, still swept up in his awe.

"Few times a day," she said. And Henry sat stunned.

"How do I earn it?" Henry asked. He and Lydia had walked back to the Inn, and she seemed like she was trying to find someone to pawn him off on. He wanted to ask her while he still had the chance. "A badge, I mean."

"In a hurry?"

"Not at all," Henry said, and it surprised him how much he meant it.

"Well," Lydia said, still moving quickly around the lobby, peering towards this hallway and that one. "I'm betting Bob would love to give you a few shifts, so you can start with those."

"Shifts?"

"Gazers have to gaze! He'll have one in mind for you to keep an eye on. He's their schedule guy. He used to be their walkie talkie guy, but he swiped Kenny's job when Kenny wasn't looking and now he's got to stay on top of things or they'll give it back. Which would just be a commotion."

"They don't all get along?"

"They fight like cats and dogs! Everybody's an amateur, but everybody's got an opinion. If there was another place in the world like this one, they would have split up a long time ago. But Bob's a good guy, if a bit full of himself. And Kenny is, too, bless his heart. Just not as good with the schedules."

They found Bob after all: he was in a makeshift office behind the old registration desk. He was a heavy man not terribly older than Henry, and he was sitting in a chair apparently meditating over a dozen clipboards spread out in front of him. His eyes were closed, and he seemed to be whispering to himself. Or praying. Henry had picked up on Lydia's presumably Christian devotion, but whatever faith Bob was practicing, she seemed to have little patience for it. "Bob!" she yelled through the doorway, startling him. "I've got somebody!"

He swiveled in the chair and looked Henry over. "Where'd you find him, the bottom of a ravine?"

"He hasn't had a chance to take a bath yet." *There were baths?*

"Well, the water out there'll kill ya, so don't get any ideas. 198 degrees *on average*. Somebody falls in, you don't get 'em out, you just point down at their bones and say, 'There goes…'" Bob made a face and looked at Lydia.

"Henry."

"'There goes Henry; he was dumber'n shit.'"

"Language, Bob."

Bob rolled his eyes at her. "Don't jump in's all I'm saying. You're lookin' for work?"

It was a Before question, and it took Henry a moment to wrap it around himself. "I think so," he said.

"Well, good. The pay is zero, but everybody who helps out gets a room and food, so long as they take a turn cleaning up after the cooks. That work for you?"

"That works for me."

"Not like there're better deals out there." He swiveled back and started picking up clipboards. "You think you can handle a golf cart?"

Bob and Lydia set Henry up at a smaller geyser basin on the shore of a positively enormous lake some twenty miles from the Inn. He was given a watch, a clipboard, a pen, and a paper bag with two roast beef sandwiches, an apple, and a bag of potato chips. His instructions were to watch the basin, record any eruptions, and come back at midnight. For the commute, Bob gave him a tiny key for a golf cart he helped Henry roll off the trailer he kept hitched to his pickup truck. The key was on a rabbit's foot fob.

"What if I don't see anything?" Henry asked as Bob turned to walk away. Lydia had stayed behind at Old Faithful, and it was just the two of them. Bob hadn't spoken on the drive, except to ask if Henry had a drinking problem or had ever killed a man. Those seemed to be the only disqualifiers for the job.

"You will."

"Or if I miss one?"

"You won't."

"I just don't want to mess this up," Henry said.

"Don't see how you could, Hank. You got eyes; you got a hand. Just write it down and bring your notes back."

That last part made Henry nervous. It suddenly occurred to him that twenty miles was a lot farther in a golf cart, and he would be driving it in the middle of the night.

"How do I find my way?"

"You take the road," Bob said. And with that, he hoisted himself into the seat of his truck, pulled down on the gear shift, and drove away.

Henry was alone, and looked out over the steaming and bleached basin hissing at him from the edge of Lake Yellowstone. He was at a minor elevation above it, and he could see the boardwalks below, meandering between the sinter cones and deep blue and green pools there. The white bones of dead trees rose up from the poisoned ground. There didn't seem to be life anywhere: no deer, no chipmunks, no birds in the air. *But it isn't hell*, Henry thought to himself. And he took his things and started down the path to his stations.

It was midafternoon, and his wards included Lakeshore geyser, the Cones (Big and Fishing), and the Twins, "Maggie" and "Jiggs," who had not erupted in more than a decade. Henry had no trouble finding each of them, as the old park service signs had been kept up by the Gazers. Lydia told him before he left that West Thumb Basin—where he would be—was typically quiet, and thus infrequently monitored. But an extra person around meant an extra set of eyes, and there was no sating the gang's hunger for data. So, Henry would keep watch, and he would check times, and he would take notes, and in the end, it would all count for something.

As far as he could tell, all was as it should be. He took his time making rounds on the boardwalk loop. He gazed down as deep as he could into the biggest hot spring pools—Abyss and Black—and was struck by their sheer clarity. Aside from the heat shimmers in the water and the clouds of steam, looking into them was like looking into blue crystal. At the nearest point to the parking lot where he had been dropped off (and where his personal golf cart now sat) there were mud pots that bubbled in thick gray globs which made perfect popping sounds when they ruptured.

But by far the most grand sight was the lake itself: he was at the western end of a large bay, and at its mouth, the tree-lined shores to his north and south pushed nearly together to form a kind of sea gate through which he could see the larger waters beyond running nearly to the horizon. Above everything—above the waters and the trees and even the hills through which he'd traveled—were distant purple mountains, all still topped with winter snow. The sun loved them, and their peaks shone like banks of flood lights rimming the park entire and illuminating the great basin below.

What Henry did not yet know was that this sense of being encircled was entirely accurate: Yellowstone sat within the caldera of one of the largest volcanoes on Earth, and those mountains formed the rim of a crater almost fifty miles across. A week from now, he would find a sign explaining that its next eruption was already more than 200,000 years overdue. All of human history had been lived in stoppage time, and as best as anyone could predict, the next time Yellowstone blew would be its final whistle. Oh, what a time to be alive.

And for this afternoon and evening and night, living is what Henry would do. He kept his watch, and when Big Cone hissed and sputtered—at 9:44 p.m.—he took note. There were gurgles at Lakeshore, but nothing else. A little geyser that wasn't on his list, named Thumb, spent more than three minutes launching buckets-worth of water perhaps four feet in air just before midnight, and Henry added a column for it on his paper and jotted down the time and duration. Then, at midnight exactly, he walked back to the parking lot under the banner of a billion stars, put his key in the ignition of his golf cart, and started the journey home.

*   *   *

"You're a man reborn," Lydia said to him as he found her in the Bear Pit at lunchtime. Henry had showered, shaved, and put on his cleaner set of clothes. He still wore his hoodie, but that morning he had done a thing that surprised him: he'd taken a clean rag to each one of his fifteen badges.

"I hope it sticks this time," Henry said, entirely for her benefit; he had given up on resurrections. There was little for him to do until the middle of the afternoon, when he was due back in West Thumb, and he was hoping Lydia might be willing to show him around.

"I heard you were 'sufficient to the task.'"

"Bob's words?"

"Absolutely. I told him I knew it."

"I'm glad to hear that."

"You should be! He's usually skeptical of my finds. But they're rarely so 'sufficient.'"

Henry smiled for himself. "I wanted to thank you. Again. You didn't have to pick me up."

Lydia reached over the table and gave his arm a good push. "Don't even think of it. It's a trick I play to make myself feel important."

"You seem important."

"To you, maybe. But around here, I'm just Crazy Old Lee."

"You are important."

At that, Lydia blushed.

She did end up showing him around. She was worried with all the fuss over the geysers, he might miss her favorite place.

The drive took them more than an hour, and as they rode, Henry struggled not to think about the time. If what she had planned was going to take awhile, he might be late for his shift. It was strange for him to care so much, and to care so suddenly, about punctuality; but in a land of watchkeepers, it was hard to remain unaffected for very long.

The consequence of his worry was a lack of attention to the land: although Lydia's truck wound steadily uphill, Henry paid this no mind, and when they turned south at a junction near an overgrown and abandoned campground, he was dumbstruck when the forests of narrow pines parted and what seemed like the entire park spread out in the valley before them. He could see the blue waters of the lake and bright green meadows and steaming white basins. He could see a thousand cumulus clouds, all holding common altitude and extending to the horizon like words printed on the cobalt page of the sky. He felt sure this was what he had been brought here to see, until Lydia turned away from the vista and onto a cracked and potholed side road surrounded again by trees. He was on the verge of asking her where she was going when the truck coasted to a stop and she put the gearshift in park.

"This won't take long," she said. She had read the worry in his face forever ago. "But you'll remember it the rest of your life."

They got out and walked over to a trailhead. It led to Lookout Point, and Lydia was quiet—even reverential—as she led the way. The path took a quick right hand turn, and as it did, Henry realized where he was:

There, in a crease of the ridge they had skirted, a river had carved an enormous canyon into the ocher earth more than a thousand feet deep. The walls of the canyon were not cliffs, but steep rocky slopes the very color of a field of summer wheat. It bent towards them from someplace further to the north and then snaked, just so, towards the edge of the caldera. And right there, where the flow of the waters running from Lake Yellowstone (*yellow stone!*) met the upthrust of soft rock on which they stood, a waterfall twice the height of Niagara poured in a perfect white rush down to meet the thin line of deep blue below. A rainbow refracted in the cascade. The tiny shapes of osprey hovered over the tumult, and Henry had to crane his neck downwards to see them. It could not have been more beautiful, and it could not be forgotten.

"Now you see it, don't you?" Lydia asked him.

"I do," Henry said, and meant it. But he couldn't stand the thought of missing her meaning, too. "See what?" he asked.

"What God can do."

On the drive back to Old Faithful, Lydia finally evangelized, and Henry let her. She told him she had been lost, but then she had been found. She told him about stained glass and old hymns, and then about wishing for children until that wish became ashes in her mouth. She talked about her husband, Ruther, and the anchor he had been until the sands washed away and he'd lost his hold on both her and himself. But mostly she talked about a God who remained with her—who was at her side no matter how foolish the paths were that she had chosen. In the end, Henry did not find her passion either conniving or convincing. Instead, it seemed to be an explanation, holy or otherwise, for why it was worthwhile to befriend half-starved and nearly-frozen vagabonds who crossed her path. For this at least, Henry would always be grateful.

He stayed in Yellowstone for a month. He kept up his rounds. He spent time with Lydia, and with other Gazers he got to know. He ate at the cafeteria and showered every morning with hot water. He wondered about that, and one day he asked a man who seemed like he might know. When he heard the answer, he realized it should have been obvious: they drew heat from the ground.

After he learned about the volcano, he finally put his thoughts together enough to ask Lydia: *if everything in this park would end—if one day the vents of the geysers and pools and hot springs would cease to be enough, and the pressure would build until the most powerful force on this planet brought utter desolation to this magnificent landscape he'd found here and final punctuation to the people he'd met who cared so much about watching it—why did everyone bother?*

She smiled at him, in the very same way she always smiled at him, and answered with one word: *love*, she said.

"Love?" asked Henry.

"It's always doomed, isn't it?" she asked him. They were drinking fresh coffee and sharing a scone. Henry's badge count was now officially at sixteen.

"It doesn't seem like it should be," Henry said.

"If it wasn't, we could never be worthy of it."

"This is a God thing," he said, and she laughed.

"No," she said, "It's a 'me' thing. God doesn't get the love he deserves. Not from me, and not from anybody. Some of us do our best to pay attention to him, but it's pennies down a well. What I mean is that because I know I'm not going to be here forever, there's a bottom to me. I can be filled up. If I wasn't doomed, how could anything count?"

Henry thought about the time sheets and predictions. He thought about the living roots of understanding digging into this place, and the grief and loss when the world decided the time was up. And then old thoughts and lost chances crept into Henry, and his face told on him.

Lydia saw. "Do you want to go somewhere?" she asked.

Henry thought of places he'd seen on a map and still hoped to explore: Mammoth, Fishing Bridge, Tower-Roosevelt.

And she saw this, too. "It's not in the park," she said.

"Oh," Henry said, suddenly doubtful.

"But it's in another one."

No Quarter

Get up, Billy heard Busola say. *Get up, you dumb baby. Get up.* Her voice was clear, but her face was hazy. His mind tried to focus on where he was. On when he was. He could feel the ground with his hands and his back; Busola was standing over him. *Get up.* Had she pushed him? No, he'd fallen. From a bicycle? Had he tripped on a lip in the sidewalk? He didn't know. He didn't remember. *Get up!*

Billy opened his eyes because he was not dead, and because there was a fire somewhere in the bowling alley. He could hear it crackling, and he could smell what was not woodsmoke, but the acrid and sour odor of burning plastic. His shirt was sticky and wet. Aside from the orange glow of the flames, the room was dark. He understood that he had bled quite a lot, but that he was not bleeding so heavily now, and that if he did not move, he would not live.

He did not know if he could stand. Slowly, he shifted his weight to his legs and tried to lift himself up. When he moved his left arm, he felt something tear and lightning bolts of pain flashed through him and made his fingertips go numb. He was filthy and covered in his own blood and he knew what had happened to him. Still, he stood.

When he did, his head swam and the room darkened, but he knew that darkness was coming from him and was not the room; the room was getting brighter. He turned his head and saw that the far wall was burning and brown smoke was billowing out from it and towards the open door, and he did not think he could go that way. But he remembered the other door behind him, behind the walkway with the pinsetters, and he staggered on his legs and moved there.

The door was closed and he did not think he could use his hand to turn the knob, so he fell into it with all his weight, and the pain exploded through him again. He felt the electricity in the soles of his feet and tips of his toes. But the door gave way, and he was in the alley. He kept his feet. Outside, it was deepest night. *The house*, he thought. There was a house there, behind the bowling center, on the other side of a fence with no chain. He had seen it before, and it was still there now. He fixed his eyes on it, and he saw there was light in one window. No; the glass was reflecting the orange of the building on fire. No; it was something inside the house: a lamp, or a candle. And he stumbled towards it.

It was no more than ten steps, but each one was agony. As Billy moved, he realized there were other sounds besides the hissing and popping of the fire in the bowling alley: there were gunshots, and they were not far from him. His memories of an old world convinced him he heard sirens, too. But he did not. When he got to the back door, he collapsed against this frame, too. He did not want to fall asleep again. Perhaps because he had found a certain courage, or perhaps because he knew that if someone found him he would need to be able to contain his condition in words, he reached his right hand to the left side of his chest and felt what was there.

His shirt was stiff and sticky and cold, but he could not find the hole. His fingers retreated a bit to the line of buttons where they fumbled with one until it was undone, and then he pushed his hand through the hole and underneath to touch his skin. It was warm and wet, and his mind revolted against what he was doing, but he did it anyway. Just below his left nipple, a sudden flash of pain at his touch caused the darkness to return. He lightened the pressure of his search, but he searched on: there was a soft line of warm gore there that ran perhaps a few inches towards his arm pit, and then it disappeared and he felt his own skin again. Then, further back towards his shoulder blade, he felt something more that was ragged and wet and still seeping. He pulled his hand back through his shirt and looked at his shiny fingers in the dark. He understood he had been shot, and that his rib had deflected the bullet enough to not kill him. But also that it was broken, and what had happened inside his body was still happening.

He tested his lungs. He could breathe, though not fully. He took his wet hand and balled it into a fist and banged it against the door as hard as he could. "*Help!*" he yelled. "*Help! Somebody please help me!*" He did this again and again. For a long time, it was quiet inside the house, and he began to wonder about the light in the window. He did not want to die; God, he did not want to die. He knocked again, and this time, he heard something coming from inside: there were footsteps, and the sound of moving furniture. He heard voices talking. He kept hitting the door.

"*Help me! Somebody please help me! I've been shot! I need help!*"

Now the voices were closer. They were just on the other side of the wall, and it took Billy a moment to realize they were speaking to him, and no longer to each other.

"Go away!" He heard one say. "Get away from the door!"

He thought perhaps the door opened outwards, and he was blocking it with his own weight. So with effort and pain, he pushed himself off the frame and stumbled back a step to give them room. "Thank you!" he yelled. "Thank you! I need your help."

But the door did not open and the voice kept repeating itself: "Go away!" it said. "You have to go!"

There was plenty of space now, and Billy didn't understand. "I need help!" he said again. "Please, let me in!"

"We can't help you! Go away!"

"*I need help! I'm shot!*"

"*Go!*"

Billy closed his eyes against the pain, the everything pain, and he did all he could to keep standing up. "I need help!" he said again. "Please!" But the door did not open, and when he looked again, he saw the light in the window was out.

"*You have to go away!*" the voice said again. "*Please! Go!*"

He didn't know what to do. He swayed on his feet, and again, he heard the rattle of gunshots somewhere close. The entire bowling alley was now in flames behind him. "*Where?*" he asked, hoping this voice, which would offer him no comfort, might still answer.

But no words came.

In time Billy found he could walk, so long as he kept most of his weight on his right leg and held his left arm tight against his chest. He did not know why the pressure on his ribs helped him—his own touch was intensely painful—but so long as it was steady, he could endure it. It was only the sudden shocks that tempted him to fall to his knees.

He stumbled on in the flickering light of the burning building. He ignored the gunshots now—how many they were; how close—because they were outside of his body. Except for the one, of course. He went to another house, and again there was no answer. It seemed empty. When he went to a third, he heard the sounds of the people inside shushing one another so he might not believe they were there.

No one was going to help him. He saw other fires and knew that what had been coming for this place was truly here, and that was why. There were voices besides his own crying out in the darkness. There were truck engines rumbling in the distance. He didn't know what to do but walk on and for as long as he could. He was still struggling to accept this coldness: he was not a fighter; he was not in any way a threat. Surely someone must at least have light, and water, and a needle and thread. He felt weaker and weaker with each minute that passed, and he began to curse his sister in his delirium for the role her phantom had played in waking him up. To asphyxiate in a bowling alley would have been better than dying a leper in the street.

He wandered north because it was away from the bowling alley and away from the fairgrounds where he had been a prisoner. He'd gone perhaps two blocks, and whenever he could summon the air to do it, he screamed for help. But still, no one answered. So he went as far as he could. And then, as he neared the school complex at the edge of the small town, he saw the angry simplicity and smallness of all this violence in its very nakedness. Moving down the road towards him were a half dozen pickup trucks and another half dozen four wheelers, their engines deafeningly loud. They were in some sort of a formation, driving slowly in the opposite direction and using both lanes, as if in a parade. As the caravan neared, he saw pale men standing in the beds of the trucks holding guns and shooting at nothing in the sky. Old American flags, as well as flags of the failed Southern Confederacy, rippled in the night breeze beside them. They were yelling and chanting as they rode, some drinking from big, dark bottles, and others lighting rags dangling from the ends of less dark ones until they filled with fire and were thrown haphazardly at the houses on either side. *"White! Montana! White! Montana!"* their voices roared, and with each explosion of a bottle, there was fresh laughter. *"White! Montana!"*

And Billy, who was not white, who was soaked in his own blood, stood in the middle of the street and found himself suddenly furious that this would be how he met his end. There was nowhere for him to go. There was no way for him to get there. They were coming, and he hated them, and he hated this country, and he prayed for fire from the sky to consume them all and leave not a single false prophet alive.

But when it arrived, this petty army paid him no mind at all. They jeered and cursed the burning houses, but when the first truck neared him, it gently turned its wheels to give him wide berth. The ones that followed it did the same, parting for him like the waters once parted in the Red Sea, and Billy was left standing there between them, clutching his hand to his side. To him, no one spoke a word: their malice was directed elsewhere. In less than a minute, he was alone again under the darkened street lamps of the Hardin Junior High parking lot.

He gasped for ragged breaths and did not turn to see where they went. He listened until the shots of their guns were more distant and their cheers couldn't be heard, and then he walked on, rounding a turn towards the back of the building. Where else could he go? There were dumpsters and old school desks there in an enormous pile. There were big black bags full of trash. But there was something else, too, and when Billy saw it, he wondered for the first time if he had in fact died in that bowling alley; it seemed like the only explanation for what he was seeing.

Because there was only one vehicle left in the lot. It was dusty and battered and hard to make out in the dark. But he was sure he saw a raccoon on the front fender, and a wood duck paddling between cypress knees on its tall, flat side. He blinked, and blinked again. He could hear his own heart beating in his ears.

Of all things, he had found the Ranger.

*   *   *

The door was unlocked, and the lucky rabbit's foot was sitting in the middle of the driver's seat. The engine roared to life the instant the key turned in the ignition. And somehow, Billy drove.

He couldn't travel fast, and he struggled to keep the Ranger on the road. The world behind him was on fire. But the streets were empty, and he kept going until his headlights reflected off of a sign for Interstate 90. He took the ramp and followed it west. As he drove, he expected barricades, or additional caravans of racist boy-soldiers who might see and seek to amend the mistake the last band had made by ignoring him. But none came, and he drove on and on. He knew he wasn't far from Billings, and Billings would be large enough to have a hospital; he thought if he could make it there, he might figure out what was wrong with him and what else he was facing.

But although he found Billings in less than an hour, and found the hospital shortly after that, it was no immediate help. The sun was rising, and he could see ambulances and more pickup trucks backed up in the Emergency loop there. Several of the trucks in the loop displayed the same flags he'd seen in Hardin, along with a new one reading *Billings Boys* in the font he had seen before on the jackets of the hanged men. There was smoke in the sky, but it wasn't from here. It drifted in from somewhere farther away, and everything was gauzy and white. It could be from Hardin, he thought. It could be from anywhere. The line of vehicles didn't seem to be moving, but there were people running everywhere. He saw gurneys and men and women with stethoscopes around their necks. He realized that these, too, must be casualties from this odd local war. It came as a relief: he would have to wait, he was sure, but at least another bullet wound would come as no surprise. He sat back heavily in his seat and closed his eyes, eager for rest.

But the very instant he let out his first long, ragged breath, someone banged their hand against the Ranger's hood. He had been seen. He opened his eyes, and there was a man wearing the clothes of a sheriff's deputy pointing in his face and then pointing away. Everything about him was angry, and he was insisting that Billy could not be there.

"I'm hurt!" Billy shouted back through the windshield. He held up his blood-stained hands for the man to see, and he waited for him to offer directions to wherever else it was he expected Billy to go. *"I've been shot!"*

But the man kept pointing furiously, first at Billy, and then back towards the main road.

"I need help!" Billy yelled again, still holding up his hands. *"I need the hospital."*

This time, he knew the man heard him. But he yelled back, "I don't fucking care! Get this fucking truck out of here!"

Perhaps because he was dying, or perhaps because he did not want to die believing it, Billy convinced himself the man simply did not understand. He thought he could explain himself. And so, with excruciating effort, he rolled down his window and tried to get his attention again.

"I'm hurt!" he said. "I've been shot. I need a doctor. Please, I need a doctor. I drove all the way here–"

"I don't give a fucking shit, you black bastard!" the man screamed. "Now go!" He kept waving his arms like this was nothing at all. Like Billy was some rube blocking a fire lane. Like he was a stupid child, or a dog in the street.

Billy rolled up the window and struggled to breathe. The man walked back to wherever he had come from, confident in his firmness and clarity, and Billy realized that he would move the Ranger. He was watching himself from above now, like a character in a movie. An astronaut could have seen his helplessness from space. But bleeding and cold and impossibly thirsty, he turned the truck around and went back to the highway. He had no choice but to move further on, first through the town, and then west against the dawn.

Hours passed. He finally risked a nap near Bozeman. It was midday, and he realized could not keep the Ranger on the road any longer. He also knew the bleeding along his ribs had stopped, but he did not know what lasting damage had been done there. He shivered, even though the cabin of the truck was warm with sunshine. He was unsure where to go. In the back of the Ranger, he still had food.

He had been confounded by the day: the luck of finding his home again, and the terror of everything else. The fear he knew he still felt, but towards which he was becoming numb. The anger that was rising and rising, becoming a kind of life ring to keep him afloat in the sea of it. He did not want to cling to it, or to give it lasting purchase inside him. But he did not want to drown, either. He did not care about Montana. He did not care about the Crow, or the Whites in Billings. He did not need to understand this violence or its reasons. He needed to live, and to escape, and fuck their problems forever. But as he looked at the sign for Bozeman just in front of where the Ranger was parked on the shoulder, he did not trust that his troubles were behind him. He felt wholly on his own.

Billy slept, and he did not dream. He realized at some point that he was far away, and he was waiting for his sister's voice to call to him: *Get up! Get up, you dummy!* But if she was crying out, he was too far gone now to hear, and there was only this space through which he drifted, through which he fell, and all the while tumbling on. He didn't hurt here, he realized, and somewhere in him he began to wonder if he should ever come back.

* * *

But Billy woke at dawn the following day nonetheless. He checked his wound and knew he would not die. He knew he could breathe. And so he did what came first to his mind: he found water, a rag, and clean clothes from the duffel he kept under the seat. He washed himself and got dressed. He knew he would bleed again, and in the old first aid kit he found wide flat pads of gauze and some tape. He made a bandage and emptied the small tube of antibiotic ointment on one side, then pressed it to his ribs. He wrapped himself with the tape and buttoned his shirt. He could tell something was still wrong with his breathing. The air rasped and wheezed in his lungs. But he did not know what there was to be done about it, or if anyone was left in the world who might show him. So he crawled gingerly into the driver's seat and got moving again.

He went south, away from the end-of-winter mountains that were in his way and towards the signs he saw for Yellowstone National Park. He knew he was traveling to the west of it, and if he could avoid it, he would not stop there. The places where people were had become war zones, and he held out very little hope for the places people weren't: the last thing he needed was to stumble on some commune of crazed cannibals.

But he was also wary of how far he could go on his own. He was genuinely surprised that he made it through the first day. He stopped frequently to rest, and he did his best to find back roads around the occasional towns in his path. When cars passed, he slouched low in his seat so their drivers would not see him. If he had enough warning, he would pull the Ranger far off the road and wait until the coast was clear. Twice, he passed people walking along the side of the highway—both times children, both times Native—and he felt his pulse quicken with fear. He steered the truck far into the oncoming lane and floored the accelerator until they were specks in the rearview mirror.

In the afternoon, he began to suspect the insanity of all this. He was a shot man, his ribs were broken, and he could not fix himself. But there wasn't a person left in Montana to whom he would speak, and he wished for some sort of code or marker he might trust as he had once trusted the green balloons and firewood signs littered throughout the East. And then he remembered he had once believed he could create just such a thing, for just such a purpose, and he was swallowed up by his sorrow, because he knew he would die for lack of himself.

When darkness came, he was nowhere at all, and he stopped. When the sun rose, he realized it must be at least Idaho, and he went on again.

By the middle of the day, Billy knew he had a fever and his vision was blurry. He was infected. He convinced himself that he could smell something in his wound, and then he convinced himself he couldn't. But he could not bring himself to stop. He drove slower and slower, the Ranger weaving slightly at first, and then in a way that was genuinely out of his control. He closed his eyes to rest them for an instant, and then for more than a minute at a time. He was utterly alone on a two-lane blacktop weaving gently through barren hills.

And then he was not moving at all. He had stopped, suddenly and loudly. His face was pressed hard into the steering wheel and he felt the urgency of his confusion fighting to overcome the heavier weight of his resignation to whatever ending this was. For a moment he was outside of his body again, watching these two forces battle for his will: to wonder? Or to quit? He felt genuinely interested in the contest, and at first he had no idea about the outcome. But even this level of curiosity turned out to be its own answer to the question, and with some effort, he returned to himself and sat back in his seat.

He had hit something. He was no longer on the road. With significantly more effort, he climbed down from the truck to see what it was. He limped to the front of the truck, and when he did, he saw that the front bumper of the Ranger had become more-or-less wrapped around a perfectly brown and unremarkable boulder. The boulder was perhaps three feet high and slightly less than that wide. It was fixed to the ground, and even with the impact, it had not moved.

Billy scratched his head. He turned first one direction, and then the other. He scanned all the way to the horizon, looking to see if there were other rocks like this one. But there were none of any size or sort anywhere, and he saw only patchy hills around him baking in the afternoon sun. He realized he had drifted from the shoulder, down a slight embankment, and hit the only obstacle in sight.

And as he took all of this in, along with the pain he felt in his body, along with the poison he could feel spreading in his chest, he finally understood that no matter where he went under heaven, there would be no quarter. He would die, unlucky and unseen, and it would not hold the interest of another soul on earth. *You dumb baby!* He wanted to hear. *Get up, you chicken!* But it was just the wind and his wish for it. It wasn't her.

The sun beat down upon Billy in all this misery, and the first thin wisps of black smoke began to drift up from under the Ranger's hood.

The Mirror of God

Henry Henry's legs were not used to a bicycle, although he had been riding one for a week. Every muscle in them hurt, along with most of the ones in his back. The skin on his thighs was chafed and sore, and he was frighteningly sunburned and genuinely filthy. However, his lungs felt strong when he breathed, and his face as he pedaled had become stuck in a kind of haggard smile. In short, Henry was alive.

He was also somewhere west of Thompson Falls, Montana. When he'd cycled through it, he'd known right away it was a ghost town. The houses were overgrown and the parking lots along the main street were sprouting trees from the cracks in the pavement. His nostrils—which had begun to feel like jet intake manifolds—filled with the rich scent of dark earth. There was no smell of trash, or diesel, or any other trace of people. He'd given some thought to stopping at the local grocery, or even the liquor store, on his way through. But instead, he had settled for an empty bakery called the Huckleberry Patch. He'd never tried huckleberries before, and even if there wasn't going to be a fresh basket of them sitting in the dark on the counter, he thought there might at least be a few pictures he could use to learn what they looked like.

He had already been amazed by the number of wildflowers and berry bushes on the roadsides. Traveling by bicycle was shockingly exhausting, he felt, but it was also almost perfect: fast enough to cover 40 or 50 miles a day, but also slow enough to really see the places he passed. If his body could learn to handle it, he thought he would do it forever. When the sun was too hot, he found shade. When it rained, he took shelter under either the towering hemlock and spruce trees or the plastic tarp Lydia had given him when she sent him away. If he was in an empty town, he simply sought cover beneath the awnings of whatever buildings were near.

On his first day, when he had still been more afraid than anything else, he had waited out a thunderstorm in the darkness of Hungry Horse Antiques. He hadn't needed to break in: if there had ever been a front door to the building, someone had requisitioned it for some odd purpose long ago, and he'd been able to bring his bike right over the threshold inside. While the rain was coming down, he had wandered the dim and musty aisles. There had been a surprising amount of used cookware there, though most of it was not very old. He'd found pewter spoons and a souvenir stein from someone's trip to Dresden. On one shelf, there was a sizable collection of drinking glasses decorated with paintings of old Looney Tunes characters.

At a point late in his search, he'd thought about his park badges and decided to check the glass case beside the register where open pocket knives and pieces of costume jewelry twinkled in the soft blue light. He hadn't found one, of course, but he'd caught sight of his own reflection in the dusty counter of the display. He'd seen himself there and smiled.

As he mounted up again now outside Thompson Falls, Henry realized he had no idea what day it was, but it must have been at least the first or second week of June. The 31st of May would have been his birthday. He was 51 years old.

*   *   *

"*Where are we going?*" *Henry had waited nearly six hours to ask this question, and in his mind, he felt he had been very patient.*

"*It's a surprise,*" *Lydia said, and then took an actual, full-mouth bite off the top of her ice cream cone.*

"*Oh my God,*" *Henry said, watching her. It made his own teeth hurt to look at it.* "*How did you do that?*"

Lydia laughed with her mouth full and raised a napkin to hide the mess she was making. She forced a swallow. "*My teeth're fake,*" *she said.* "*I can't feel a thing.*"

"*Still!*" *Henry said, shaking his head.* "*There's the brain freeze; that has to be awful. No!*"

Her shoulders were shaking and her eyes were squeezed shut as she kept chuckling to herself. "*I'm an old woman, Henry! Leave me alone!*"

"*Jesus, Lydia.*"

"*Leave the Lord out of it,*" *she said.* "*And I told you: Lee.*" *She opened her eyes and they were wet with tears.* "*You're making me laugh. My time is short and I want to eat as much ice cream as I can. Don't trifle me.*"

"*I'm not trifling. I don't want you to have a heart attack. Or a stroke. That much in one bite can cause a stroke.*"

"*Wait'll you see the next one,*" *she said, and it was Henry's turn to lose it.*

They were sitting at a picnic table in what looked like a tiny abandoned Old West park. There was a saloon and a sheriff's and a jail. An old Conestoga wagon with the fabric long since disintegrated sat by the roadside. Oakwood barrels were stationed at intervals along the pine board arcade as trash cans, and altogether inexplicably, there were life-sized, chicken wire-and-plaster dinosaurs roaming the parking lot. This tourist trap was named Choteau, but it didn't seem to hold a soul. The ice cream came from an old shoppe *at the end of the row. By some strange miracle, the buildings here still had power, and they found forgotten tubs of it in a walk-in freezer. God knew how old it was, but they ate it anyway; you only live once.*

"*Seriously, Lee: where is this? Where are we going?*"

"You're thinking about Bob."

Henry was. Lydia had told him to call out for his next few shifts at West Thumb watching the geysers, and he was already feeling guilty about it. Bob was ornery, but the little grunt and nod he gave Henry each morning when Henry handed over his filled-in watch chart had started to feel like purpose. It had started to feel like the old days.

"Don't worry about him. We're getting you another badge," Lydia said. "To add to the collection."

"Glacier, then," Henry said. He knew they had been heading north, and he knew that was the only park up there.

"That's the one."

"Why do you want to go there?"

"Because I've never been!"

"And I'm a good excuse."

"As good as any I've met yet."

Henry thought about that. "What do you think is up there?"

"I don't really know. My husband went once, a long time ago. He said it made him feel as close to God as he'd ever felt. I thought that sounded nice." Lydia talked often about Ruther, but always descriptively: he had been tall, he had been stubborn, he had been lonely in his heart. But she didn't talk about their relationship, or about what had happened to him.

"Was he religious? Like you?"

The corners of Lydia's smile flinched, but only for an instant. Still, Henry saw them. "No, never like me. The God-in-the-Clouds was always good enough for him. The God of Nature. He thought I was at least a little bit crazy to go in for the son."

"Did you ever think about changing your mind?"

Lydia surprised Henry again. "All the time! I think about it most every day. It's not always easy to square what I believe with the world the way it is. I used to tell myself, 'God has His ways, and they aren't mine to judge.' But I do wish it was easier to see the kindness in them sometimes."

Something seemed to be bubbling up in her, and Henry had spent enough time with the geysers to recognize the signs. Waves on Grand! Waves on Grand! *But Lydia's smile came back, and she took a regular lick of her ice cream cone while she changed the subject. "Enough about me. What's really got you out here, Henry? Why are you taking orders from a little old woman?"*

Henry was warm in the sun, and he was tired of not knowing, and there was a Triceratops with naked chicken wire where one of its horns should be that seemed to be watching him. He trusted this person. And he thought, if just this once he started talking, a real answer might come out. "I had a son," he said, because that was supposed to be how the story started. "I had a son, and he died. And I had a wife, and she died, too. And back when the world was ending, I thought: 'but my world is okay; so long as things are normal for us, we can keep going.'"

Lydia watched him and listened. Her face had grown more serious, but it was still kind. A laugh wasn't too far away, and Henry went on: "But then things weren't normal anymore. And then they were... really bad. After they were both gone—when I was alone—I started to think about all of it, and I realized that everything broke while I wasn't paying attention. When I was just...working and doing dishes and watching TV. And the broken things weren't just in the world, they were in them, too. And I didn't do anything. I didn't lift a finger to stop any of it."

"There was a lot of that going around."

"I know," Henry said. "I know there was. I'm not trying to beat myself up. But when I left home, after they were gone, I thought at first I was doing it because they would have wanted me to. They wouldn't have wanted me to just die. So I thought I could... maybe honor them somehow? I don't know. But I went to all these places that they talked about, or that they wanted to go. My wife always wanted to travel. My son collected these..." And as he said this, Lydia saw that Henry's wide hand shook as he reached to touch the badges on his chest. "So I was getting more of them. I know it was stupid, but I thought I could get all of them. I had this box..."

He thought she might interrupt, or even make a joke. But when he looked, she was fully there. "It doesn't matter. But then I felt like he didn't want me *to have them, you know?" He knew his eyes were welling up. "Because he wanted to have them. He wanted them for him. And I can't do that. I can't make that happen. I could have, but I didn't. And so… so…"*

"Henry, it's okay—"

"It's not though. I mean it. I know you want to be kind, but it was wrong," he said. "I started going to all these places and seeing all these things that he didn't get to see, and then you know what's even worse? Those places started talking to me. Do you understand what I mean? They started showing me me. Over and over again, that happened. And now, when I go to them, I keep seeing my reflection and not his anymore. And I'm terrible, Lee, and he was not. But these places are beautiful, and I know I don't deserve any of it."

"Who's to say what you deserve?" Her ice cream was melting, and she let it. It was an incredible day, in spite of everything.

"I think I am," he said. And then Henry was finally out with it: "Because I'm the one who shouldn't be here."

And that was all the pressure Henry had in him. He cried, and his new friend held him in this ridiculous place, and the clouds rolled over them on and on and on.

It was Lydia who gave him the bicycle; it had been in the back of her truck the whole time. She had never intended to give Henry a ride back to Yellowstone, and she did not plan to go back there herself. He'd been bamboozled, he realized, but as Henry biked northwest through the Clark Fork Valley and towards the old Idaho state line, he was grateful nonetheless.

The weather was holding out, and signs told him he was on state road 200. This seemed hard to imagine in all this wildness; he couldn't fathom how there could be 199 more. Aside from clusters of empty houses every few dozen miles and the cracked and worn pavement beneath his wheels, there weren't any signs of other people anywhere.

He'd learned to scavenge berries from the bushes along the shoulders after all. He'd mastered the art of weaving downhill on foot through the underbrush to fill his water bottles in the Fork. Even squatting on the ground to go to the bathroom was starting to feel mostly normal. And as much as a person could be at home on a bicycle, Henry was.

Crossing into Idaho was entirely unremarkable: the sign had actually been knocked down, and Henry didn't even realize he'd made it over until he saw the route numbers change. However, as he made his way across a low bridge over an old railroad line, the valley he'd been traveling finally opened up, the rocky palisade he'd been pedaling underneath for days disappeared, and he was suddenly in the wide, wide world again. The river poured into an enormous basin–Lake Pend Orielle–that was as perfect as water could possibly be. The mountains on the far side rose in ridgelines layered in lighter and lighter shades of blue, all the way to the horizon. The sky was clear. Crisp air filled his lungs with each deep breath. Everything–every drop of water, every pebble in the pavement, and every leaf on every tree–received the sunshine and reflected it back.

Henry saw it all and he didn't stop pedaling for an instant. There would be more around the next bend, and more around the one after that. And so he crossed Idaho in just one day, biking the entire 70 miles before dusk fell and he settled in at a campground just over the next border in Washington state. He'd had an easier time finding the line this time, and he slept under dark and towering trees, warm in his sleeping bag on a bed of soft pine needles.

When daybreak came, Henry packed his things into the saddlebags on the bicycle, stretched his legs, popped his back, and then set off again.

When they first arrived in Glacier National Park, Henry had been terrified. The last two hours–which was all that had remained after their ice cream stop–had taken them back into the barren wastes of the Plains. The line of the Rockies remained visible to their left, but it seemed to diminish with every mile, and Henry couldn't shake the feeling he was traveling backwards. They passed through the remains of the old Blackfeet Reservation, but it, too, seemed to have been abandoned. Lydia told him that wildfires, failing crops, and dried-up ranches forced the Native people there east not so long ago. But Henry didn't believe it: the places they passed through seemed as if they'd been lost for centuries.

In the remains of Browning, they turned west again, and the sharp peaks of the mountains rose ahead of them once more. They entered the park through a broken gate and, before long, the road began to climb along the shores of a long and oddly turquoise-tinted lake. When Henry asked Lydia about the color, she simply shrugged: "some mountain thing" was the only explanation she could give him.

The scale of the place did not register to him until after they had ascended past the lake and began weaving through the real crags of the park. Suddenly, snow-capped and sediment-lined cliffs were everywhere, all of them curving upwards a thousand feet in steep parabolas which rose from the river-threaded valleys somewhere impossibly far below. Henry and Lydia were driving on a road carved directly into the sides of those bowls, and they were protected from imminent death sometimes by low rock walls on the downslope side of the two-lane highway, and other times by nothing at all.

When their path wound into the creases between the mountains and switched from one southern face to the next, Henry saw truly magnificent threads of waterfalls cascading down from the cols above and either disappearing between stone arches somewhere below the roadway or crashing into the asphalt itself, making bright rainbows of refracted light as a new and brief river formed across the pavement and then continued its descent on the far side.

The wheels of Lydia's truck splashed through water and every place he looked sparked wonder. His heart seemed to climb into his throat as he faced the wildness of things. It was impossible and impassable; he was traveling across the crown of the earth.

We shouldn't be here, *he thought—though he had intended to say it out loud.* No one should be here. *But when he dared to look over at Lydia, her hands were at ten and two on the wheel and she was grinning from ear to ear.*

Once, this was called the Going-to-the-Sun Road, *she told him. But now it seemed to answer to no name at all.*

Henry stayed along the river until he got to Tiger, Washington, and then he headed west into the Colville National Forest. It was rich and dark there, and he wondered for the first time in all his travels what was really gained and lost by abandoning these wild places. He understood the logic of preservation, especially in the East where the appetites of people and industry were rapacious and there seemed to be no forest or hill or river which could not be directed to some human use. There, setting aside a place so it might stay as it was felt generous and good.

But out here, things were different. Colville was filled with woods, as the mountains alongside the Pend Oreille River had been filled with woods, and as the mountains in Montana had been filled with woods before that. The roads and homes and farms had fallen into disuse, and now Nature was the voracious one, swallowing them back up into itself. The national ordering of things into what is permissible to destroy and what isn't suddenly seemed impotent, Henry thought, and more than that, a bit arrogant. It was perhaps hateful, above all else: that the world was a thing to be pushed back or dominated—or even allowed to live—by a people who couldn't keep their shit together for 400 years. Who all the while were lashing out and dooming themselves. There was something both audacious and sad about saying, "we will save this place from ourselves."

It was true that when the Park Service disappeared, good work disappeared with it. But the Service only ever existed to broker some temporary peace between the world it came from and the world it was in.

If the ones who made it, hoping it was the better angel of their own nature, were now gone, then there was not much point any longer in such a truce. There was also no real question of who would win in the end.

Henry wondered what watched him from the trees, but he was not afraid anymore. Where limbs were piled in the road, he would go around. Where the pavement was washed out, he would lower himself from his bike, lead it down into the softness of the exposed earth there, and carry it out again on the other side. Then he would get back on, put his feet up on the pedals, and ride whatever miles he could.

On their last evening together, Henry and Lydia sat on the rainbow-pebbled western shore of Lake MacDonald. They were in a place that used to be called Apgar Village, but falling trees had done away with most of the buildings there and the weight of winter snows had finished off the rest. Where they sat, there were still a half dozen canoes pulled up from the water and resting upside down on the rocks, mostly still intact. A little yellow buoy, faded from the sun, floated a little ways out from the shore. Past that buoy, the lake stretched on and on back towards the U-shaped valleys and the mountains beyond.

"They were carved by glaciers," Lydia said, staring out.

"That's why they look like that?"

"So I read. Years and years ago."

"Is that why it's called what it is?"

"Maybe so. I think there used to be a lot of glaciers here, too, though. Before."

"Yeah."

There was a long pause. "You told me your son died," Lydia said. "But you didn't say how. I just want you to know that I think I know."

Henry didn't look at her. Instead, he stared out at the lake, too. "He shot himself," he finally said. "When he was sixteen. He had gotten himself into some trouble, at school and with his mom and me. And I think he thought that was the only way out."

"What was his name?"

"It was Caleb."

"That's a good Bible name," she said. "Surprising, coming from a 'Henry.'"

Henry had no idea about this. "His mom picked it out. Her name was Shannon. Is that in the Bible, too?"

"Not that I know of."

"Hmm." They watched the little waves on the shore, and Henry wondered if there were tides; if the place they sat might shrink away if they stayed there long enough. "Who was he?" he asked. "Caleb in the Bible, I mean."

"He was a spy," Lydia said, and Henry immediately began to regret his question. But she went on: "He was one of the Hebrews God rescued from Egypt. He was a boy then, during the Exodus. But as the people wandered in the desert, he grew up. He knew Moses, and his best friend was Joshua. They became a little trio."

Henry listened as Lydia went on. "When the people finally neared the Promised Land," she said, "Moses sent Caleb and Joshua ahead to see what was out there. The people had wandered for a generation, and even though they wanted a new home, they were very afraid to fight. In fact, they were afraid of most things. So, they hoped the spies would return with good news."

"What did they find?"

"Bad news. The land was wonderful, but it was home to a city of giants. Joshua and Caleb came back, and when they told the rest of the Hebrews, the people cried and tore their clothes. Which was a thing they did quite often." Henry tried to imagine it, but it only seemed like a scene from a movie. He couldn't make it look real, and he gave up.

"What about Caleb?" he asked. "Why does anyone remember him?"

"Because even when the people doubted, he and Joshua weren't afraid. They told Moses that God would hand the giants over if they all went in. Even though the rest of the people didn't listen, the two of them had courage."

"Then what happened?"

Lydia paused. "I don't remember, actually. God was mad for a bit, and then things worked out. For the Hebrews, anyway."

"*That doesn't seem particularly fair; that everyone ignored them, and God didn't care.*"

"*No. And He did care: 'But because My servant Caleb has a different spirit and follows Me wholeheartedly, I will bring him into the land he went to.' That's what God said about it. He saw who they really were.*"

"*So, Caleb did make it? In the end?*"

"*He and Joshua did. They were the only two; not even Moses crossed over. I remember that.*"

Henry had warmed to the story after all. "*Because he was brave.*"

"*Because he was wholehearted.*"

"*Because he was wholehearted.*"

A haze drifted over the lake, and it caught the sun as it was beginning to go down behind the distant mountains. It fired orange, and the place where they sat began to gray and fade with the dusk. The shore smelled clean and cold, like snow. The whole world was quiet.

"*Henry,*" *Lydia said,* "*I care about you. I really do. And I say this with kindness. But your Caleb gave up.*"

Henry felt a rolling weight in his chest, as if some heavy stone was being dislodged there. But he did not get up, and he did not run. Instead, he said, "*I didn't do enough for him.*"

"*Oh, absolutely!*" *Lydia's voice was oddly bright, and Henry felt that weight suddenly flash and transform into anger, and then into fear. But Lydia went on regardless:* "*You should have done a lot more, Henry! You should have loved him more, and held on a lot tighter.*"

Henry was so stunned, he realized he couldn't speak.

"*Do you want to hear what I think?*"

"*No!*" *he finally said, and he meant it in every way it could be said.*

"*Well, I'm going to tell you anyway; I'm old, and you can't stop me. I think you taught him that. You taught him how to give up.*"

This time, her words didn't sting, they burned like fire in a wound. He felt the anger again, and then the fear, and then something even more different and awful. It wasn't shame, which was something he always knew. It was guilt. Because what she said was true.

"What the fuck, Lee?" was all Henry could muster.

"Language, Hank. No. I'm sorry that hurt, I really am. But it's true, and you should hear it. You're a runner. You're selfish. And you seem like you were a crap dad."

Henry now felt entirely nailed to himself, like a bug pinned down and writhing. He wanted to be free, but when he spoke, the words that came out of his mouth were, "I know." He looked at Lydia for pity, or at least some sign of regret for what she had said. But she was still staring out at the water. He realized she hadn't turned to look at him for this entire conversation, and Henry focused on this and let it bring him back to this beach. She was speaking because she felt she needed to, and she was also afraid. Still, her next words were:

"But you don't have to be a crap ex-dad."

"Fuck!" Henry said again, and this time, she let the swear slide.

"I know that's mean. I don't want it to be. But the thing is: I was a crap wife, once upon a time. To Ruther. I was so in love with being loved, I didn't work very hard at staying lovable. Truth was, I always thought he was a character in my story. An important one! But not like me. And then I wasn't lovable anymore. I wasn't any of it. When I look back, I know some of that was his fault, too. He wasn't always kind. But that doesn't make it feel any different."

With that, she finally turned to face him, and Henry saw her eyes were red, too. "But I'm not going to be a crap ex-wife, Hank. It's not for him; I can't fix that. It's for me. I need to see. Do you understand?"

Henry's own wounds were still open, and had even been salted. But now there was something he needed to know, and he asked her. "Lee, what happened to your husband?"

He didn't know what he expected for an answer, but it wasn't a smile. "You wouldn't believe me if I told you," she said. The smile was strong and old, and water bubbled beneath it.

"I would," he said, using as sincere a voice as he could muster. "Try me."

And then she started to lose herself. Her shoulders began shaking, and Henry saw that it wasn't sadness that was taking her but laughter. Waves on Grand! he thought in spite of himself, and he marveled at the heat and pressure of her heart. Lee's shoulders were shaking, and Henry was still torn to pieces inside. But at the sight of her, he couldn't keep his grip on that pain, and it began to mix in with everything else: the air, the laughter she was trying to hold back, the breeze coming in now off the water.

"I'm serious, Henry," she said. "I'm serious. I don't think I can say it out loud. It's too much."

"I'm serious, too. Tell me. You just tore me apart; you have to now."

She took a deep breath to still herself, and it took her a few good seconds. She looked like she was practicing a mantra, and she closed her eyes to focus. "He gave up, too," she said. "In his own way. Like Caleb did. He gave up on me, and he disappeared into the woods. And he didn't come back."

Henry felt his eyebrows pinch together. "Like, the actual woods?"

And with that, she broke. When her laughter came, it was all body and no sound: Lee squeezed her eyes shut, opened her mouth, and looked for all the world like someone in a silent film. Henry watched her in complete amazement. When her voice finally came—one big HA!—she sucked in a fresh breath and just shook her head. Her shoulders were bouncing.

"The actual woods," she said, "Yes, the actual woods. It's so dumb!"

"What did he go there for?" Henry asked.

"This is the crazy part!" she said, gasping again. "He walked out on me… and went looking for a Bigfoot."

A part of Henry was sure, absolutely sure, she was yanking his chain. But the rest of him knew perfectly well that she was not.

Lydia put her hand on his shoulder, looked him in the eyes, and pressed on: "He swore to me that he'd seen one," she said, "Years ago, and I never believed him. He hated that. And then one day, he looked at me, and he said, 'You're gonna eat your damn words.' And then he left. He did it just to prove me wrong! But he never came back. He *was gone for months and then a year, and then one day, I woke up, and I knew in my heart that he had died out there. I can't explain it. But nobody ever found him, and I knew: 'my Ruther is dead. He's gone crazy as a caterpillar.'"*

Now Henry was laughing. He didn't mean to—or even think he wanted to—but he was laughing all the same. Lydia watched him, smiling. "Are caterpillars crazy?" he finally asked between his own deep breaths. "I don't think caterpillars are crazy."

"I don't know!" she said. "I don't know if they are or not. But it rhymes."

"It doesn't rhyme!"

"Yes it does!"

"It definitely doesn't! And... and I really don't mean to make fun. That's awful, what he did."

"It's okay. It is," she said, and then she puzzled for a moment before she went on. "I guess caterpillars are crazy enough to think that dying is the best way to become something different. Which is what he must have thought. And God... well, he's crazy enough to let them do it, even if it sends a pretty unhelpful message to the rest of us. Like Ruther."

Henry's belly hurt, and so did just about everything else inside him. But he was thinking about what Lee had said, and he realized that beneath the wreckage, some new space was opening up. "I would have liked to have met him," Henry said. "Caterpillar or not."

Lee wiped the tears from her cheeks with the pad of one thumb, and then the other. "He wouldn't have known what to do with you," she said. "My Ruther was a selfish man. In the end, that's what got him. And I was a selfish woman, which is why I let him go. The fact of the matter is that I'm still a selfish woman! But I think I can still make a little room for new fools. It's not gonna do much to save the world... but it keeps me from being lonely, and that's all selfishness ever gets you."

Henry smiled and looked back at the lake where the darkness was finally settling in. He was dizzy from all of this, but a thought still stuck: "Unless there really is a Bigfoot," he said.

Lydia had found herself again, too. "Unless there really is a Bigfoot," she said. "Poor Ruther."

"Poor Ruther."

"And poor Caleb."

Henry's breath caught in his chest. "And poor Caleb," he said.

They were watching for the stars now, and he realized they were not far away.

"You said you see yourself in places like this," Lydia said. "You learn things."

"I think I do."

"Can I tell you one more thing?"

Henry thought about it, and he said she could.

"Be careful with that."

"Why?"

Lydia slid close to him. She reached over and took his hand in hers, interlocking their fingers. Then she rested her head again on Henry's shoulder. "Because it's not the world's job to tell you anything. You're not the main character, either."

Henry thought about this, and he thought about her. "Do you mean God?"

"Maybe," Lee said. "I don't know. Could be there isn't one. But if there is, I wonder sometimes what he sees when he looks around down here at all of us. What we tell him about himself by being the way we are. What we tell him about his world."

"Do you think he needs us? If he's really there."

"I think he's there, and we're here. So we say something."

"Maybe we're spies," Henry said, and he thought to himself, looking for giants.

"That's a notion. Go on, Henry." Lee's voice was quieter, and he felt her attention beginning to fade. She found comfort in his voice.

"We can report back. And say whether the land is good."

"It is," Lee said. "It is."

"And be wholehearted."

"Mmhmm." Henry knew she would be gone soon.

The first stars were out now, along with Venus and Mars and Jupiter. For millennia, people just like the two of them had sat in places just like this one and sewn them together in their minds, stitching a hundred patterns and pictures. Telling stories. Tying themselves to the world and to one another. Henry thought for a long time, there with his friend's head on his shoulder. And as he did, he spoke a kind of prayer:

God, *he thought,* make yourself better. Make yourself better, so I can be better.

It was a sacrilege he knew. He dared not share it with Lydia. And he didn't know if it was really true, or if it just felt that way. But that weight that had been rolling in him felt like it had moved on somewhere, had gone on to join the million other pebbles on this wide and quiet beach, where glaciers a thousand feet deep had once slid past and left beauty in their wake.

On the far side of the national forest, Henry came across a highway sign pointing south to Spokane, just some 80 miles away. When Lydia had lifted the surprise bicycle from her trunk the morning after their night at the lake, he had asked her if that was where she might go. She'd said, "God forgive me, but *hell no*," and aside from that, she would not say. When she asked him a version of the same question–"Are you going back to Ohio?"–he had just smiled and shook his head. It seemed their final destinations would remain a mystery to each other.

He took the other road and cycled on. Henry didn't have a map, but he knew what way west was. He knew there would be more deserts ahead, and then more mountains beyond those. If he remembered correctly, they were the Cascades, and there was another park there–if he could find it. He knew he wanted to see. And after that, there were rainforests, of all things, on the edge of the biggest ocean in the world. What a wonder that would be. After that, he wasn't sure where would be next. But he knew he could go there.

Craters of the Moon

The world was black and it was not night. The bird was black, too, and it floated above the landscape of soot and cinder looking for some new carrion there. Ancient lava flows had hardened and baked into cracked hills of younger earth below her, and being old herself, she watched this place more and more often now because it was easier on her eyes. Patches of sagebrush, seeded by the wind and resilient in the thin soil, held all sorts of future prey. But killing was not her nature: Death was. What she needed was starvation and sickness; the snakebit hare left under the rock until its breathing stopped and eyes closed. She would eat then, leaving her molting and lice-filled feathers behind for some other creature—a field mouse, a Brewer's sparrow—to carry off and use in their bed.

She had seen the man the instant he stepped out of the metal box that had brought him there, and he smelled like soon. Her circle began two hundred feet above him, and she watched him patiently. But before long, a second smell caught her attention: it was fire. Fire had shaped her home, but it was rarely found in it. She looked, and the scent came from the box, where it was growing quickly. Plumes of black smoke bellowed up and rose up to her. She paid them no mind: it wouldn't be long now. She could wait.

* * *

Billy sat on the volcanic ground and lit a cigarette. The Ranger was belching flames from under the hood, and he didn't care anymore. His body hurt, and he was tired. He wanted to sleep, but he could not. It was too hot, and his nose stung with the smells of burning rubber and plastic. He had imagined that when a person was where he was, they would have deep thoughts. They would reflect on the world and stare unblinking at the horizon as it drew closer and closer. They would face the end with clarity and courage; perhaps curse their enemies, or pray to God. But Billy found that he didn't want to do any of those things. All he wanted was not to die; that was it. So he smoked, and he closed his eyes. And then he heard her voice.

The fuck is that? she said.

He looked up for Busola, but whether he did this in the world or just in his mind, he didn't know.

What? he said.

The cigarette, dummy. You're smoking?

Seems that way.

That shit'll kill you.

Billy just laughed. It sounded like someone rattling a can of spray paint in his chest. The voice went on:

You're just like Dad.

What do you care?

One of him was enough! You look fucking stupid.

Yeah?

Yeah. Like you got a damn lollipop in your mouth.

Like a baby.

Like a grown man acting like a baby.

Billy didn't have anything to say to that. Or to think to it. He felt annoyed that the only ghost who deigned to visit him in the end was Busola.

You seem like you're in a little trouble.

It's turned out that way.

What happened?

You should know.

Why's that?

Because you're me, talking to myself. Doesn't seem like I should have to rehash it.

So you *say. Do you have something better to do? Too busy being cool, with your stupid cigarette? You got any sunglasses on you to go with it?*

I might. That's a good idea.

Tell the fucking story, Will.

She never used his real name and it sounded strange in her voice.
Well, Busy, I ran into some trouble.

Give it some detail.

I left Dad and went South. I ran into a guy and got it in my mind to try and be helpful. It didn't work out.

Riveting work. Really.

Are you just here to bust my balls, Busy?

You need my help with that all of a sudden? Humor me: who was the guy?

Ulysses. But with no home to get back to.

Huck Finn, then?

367

What do you know about Huck Finn?

> *As much as you do.*

Yeah. But he wasn't a good one. Not enough charisma. A pretty poor protagonist, actually.

> *So why are you making him one?*

Billy's cigarette was burned up. He flicked it away and got out another one, but he didn't light it yet. *I don't know. Not a lot of options out here these days.*

> *Jesus Christ, you're going to kill me before you kill yourself. This sad-sack, mopey-ass shit. Just like Dad.*

I'm not the Artist.

> *The hell are you talking about?*

The Artist was always you, B. Remember?

> *Because I paint shit, I got a monopoly on 'Artist'?*

You were the explorer. Creator. Going places, making stuff.

> *Wow! You ever tell me that? Woulda solved my entire life. 'I'm the Artist'! If she knew that, it woulda paid her bills and raised her kids right away. You been sittin' on that gold for how long?*

Don't act like it's nothing. Mom always said that: 'Robbie's the Athlete, Busy's the Artist...'

> *And poor Billy?*

'...Billy's the Achiever. Billy's the Academic one.'

> *B-fucking-student Billy?*

Why am I imagining you so mean?

> *Ask yourself.*

You were something, Busy! You and Robbie both. You did it, and people saw it.

Not you, though?

Not me. I couldn't figure it out. I had one idea, in my whole life. And it got me killed.

Couldn't even get a 'B'?

You're lookin' at what I got.

That's it, then?

In about an hour or so.

'Here lies Billy the Achiever.'

Yep. That's the size of it. Billy finally lit the cigarette.

You're so stupid, Will. Really, you are.

Because of this? He let smoke drift out of his nostrils.

Because Author, dummy.

What?

Your stupid A's. Athlete. Artist. It's not 'Achiever,' it's 'Author'.

Billy tried to laugh again, and it went about as well as it did the first time.

You never thought about your own name? Mom's the one who gave it to you.

That was Grandma.

No, it was for Grandma. When you were born, Grandma wanted you to be Jerome.

Jerome?

That was her daddy's name.

No shit?

Mom picked William. And it's good she did, too, because 'Jerry' would have just made me feel sorry for you.

'Billy' didn't make you nice.

It made me creative. Let me ask you: you think you're out here to find a story?

I did.

And did you?

A lot of things happened. I don't know if they're a story.

How you gonna put them together if you don't bring them back?

I would if I could.

And how you gonna tell it if you hate everybody that's in it?

Billy thought on that. *That's who they were.*

And you?

Maybe me, too.

And that's all?

Can't make 'em any different.

Dummy, that's the one thing you can do.

Not from here. The second cigarette was half out, and Billy chanced a look at the Roving Ranger, which was now entirely in flames. He wondered when the tires would pop.

I'm gonna lay some real ghostly shit on you, Will. Stuff I'm not supposed to know, because it's stuff you don't know. You ready?

I guess I am.

Do you know where you are?

Craters of the Goddamn Moon. National Monument. *It's not a Park.*

You read the sign.

I read the sign.

Do you know what this place is?

I do not.

10 million years ago, a volcano erupted not too far from here. And the whole earth slid over it, and then it erupted again. And the earth slid, and it erupted again. And a whole valley formed from where the world kept blowing up and then moving on, and you can see it from space. Right now, that volcano is sitting underneath—

Yellowstone. I read that sign, too.

Yellowstone. The prettiest place in the world. And it's going to erupt, too. When that's over, it's going to look just like this. And then it'll look like something new. This shit is just a garden waiting to be a garden, Will.

More story yet.

More story yet.

I don't know how you know that.

Ah, you musta picked it up somewhere. When you were Achieving. Academically.

Billy dropped the next butt on the ground and toed it with his shoe. It disappeared into the earth. *I like it though.*

You should. You came up with it.

I wish it happened faster. I'm afraid I'm still going to die out here.

You're the blindest person in the world.

What are you talking about?

There's a Ranger Station right over there.

Billy put his hand over his eyes and scanned the horizon. Sure enough, Busola was right: he could see a long, dark roof just over a ridge of cinder not a hundred yards away. He had passed the driveway for it when his eyes had been closed, just before he had crashed his ice cream truck.

That dummy you were following around: he teach you anything about those places?

Just where to find badges.

What about bandages?

I guess I know where to find those, too.

Probably some antibiotics in there.

Probably so.

Billy?

Yeah, B?

Don't quit out here. she said. *Walk the line. I know you're afraid.*

Thanks, Busy.

Now get up, dummy.

And Billy did.

*　　*　　*

The vulture watched all of this, her circle narrowing and descending, pass by pass, in a funnel. The smell of the cigarette smoke was in her nostril, alongside the other, sweeter scent. But she was still not very close, and she was waiting. Her ears did not hear well anymore, but she caught sight of the man's movement and adjusted her path so her wide wings might catch the next updraft and take her higher again.

He wasn't ready. She watched, and the man found his feet again and walked on. She saw him stumble over the lava field and towards the building there not far away. He disappeared into its shade, and even through her deafness, she heard the sound of breaking glass and knew he was gone from her forever. It was no real matter.

As she pulled the tired muscles in her shoulders to make a new way for herself, she saw a new shape drawing closer along the gray line of the road. She looked, and she had seen it before. It was a truck, deep blue in color, churning up a fresh cloud of dust in its wake.

Many Apocalypses

When Henry Henry was nine years old, his father went away on a business trip. His older brother, Michael, was away at Scout camp, and it was the middle of the summer. He remembered his mother outside watering her roses when his father squatted down to look him straight in the eyes. A duffel bag sat on the floor by his feet. "You're the man of the house this week, Henry," his father said. "You take care of your mom and be good. Okay?"

It was the first moment in Henry's entire life when it occurred to him he might be the main character of a story. He'd always been happy to tag along before: with his mom in the garden, or his dad at the grocery store, or his brother playing in the fort they'd built in the woods. He was an accessory to his friends: when someone told a joke, he laughed; when two people got in a fight, he formed part of the circle. In tee ball, he played catcher, because nobody trusted him in right field. But that day, at just under fifty pounds, Henry tried to imagine what it would be like to be a grown up.

After dinner, he did his best to follow his father's routine. Without saying a word, he put the family dog on her leash and took her outside to pee. But the instant they walked out the door, Callie–who was the same age as Henry–yanked hard on his arm… and his tiny fingers gave way. She ran into the street in a straight line, the leash trailing all the while behind her. He could still remember the skittering sound it made as it dragged along the pavement. And he remembered the sound kept going, well after she was gone in the dark.

Two days later, a neighbor brought Callie home limp in his arms. Her fur was matted and stained red. She'd been hit by a car. Everyone cried, and no one blamed him. But the truth was that she was dead because Henry had let her go.

Henry watched his mother dig a hole in the backyard from the window in the attic. She had to work at it, because it was summer, and because she used her garden trowel. As she dug, Henry cried and wondered what his father—who was a man, and who was good—might say when he came home.

The first signs of wildfire didn't appear until Washington Pass. Henry had picked up highway 20 in Okanogan on the western edge of the dry flatlands between Colville and the fearsome peaks of the Cascades, and he had followed it through the sleepy town of Twisp and the long-burned shells of Winthrop into the lower reaches of the mountains. But his first real trial in more than a week came on the ascent: the road rose in a steady and endless incline between a steep ridge of lodgepole pines on one side of him and the thin white sliver of Early Winters Creek on the other. The snow-covered summit of Silver Star Mountain towered high above, but each time he looked for it in the gaps between the trees, it got no closer. His legs burned and his lungs gasped for air.

When he finally reached the gap in the opposite ridge which would lead him west, he looked down at the road that had just whipped him, and he realized he could no longer see where it began. The asphalt ribbon disappeared far below into a thick haze before it reached the valley beyond. The air was dim, and although he knew the sun was shining and there were no clouds, he could not feel its heat on his skin. The smell in his nostrils was woodsmoke, and he understood that somewhere up ahead of him, the mountains were on fire. But as he scanned the sky above Silver Star Mountain for clues as to its whereabouts, he came up empty: the world was a faint and uniform brown, and the sun was just a disc of light overhead. Henry didn't know what to do or where else to go, and he knew highway 20 was the only way across. So he got back on his bike and cycled on.

In another hour he arrived at Easy Pass, but he did not want to get off his bike there. *Bull shit,* Henry thought to himself, reading the sign and feeling the aching in his legs. His breathing was becoming more and more difficult.

An hour after that, he reached a vista overlooking what was supposed to be Diablo Lake—but he could barely see it now through the haze. The waters spread in strange arms around the hill on which he stood hundreds of feet above it, and he knew them to be the same turquoise as the lake he had marveled at with Lydia in Glacier. But all he could see now were flat bits of blue-gray in what had become an increasingly sepia-toned landscape. It was no postcard, and Henry was sad to miss it. And he was beginning to be worried.

He went on again, and the smell of fire grew stronger. When he passed into the steep valley around the Skagit River, the air thickened, and he realized he could no longer see more than a hundred or so yards ahead of him. There was ash now along with the smoke, and it swirled in the air as if shaken in some dark snowglobe.

Henry was officially concerned. It was mid-afternoon, and his body was already spent from the day's effort. He was hot, and he couldn't tell if it was his exhaustion or heat from the world around him. The road had been tilting downhill since the lake, and he did not think he had the strength to get back up it if he turned around. Which meant he would soon be trapped here, stuck again, and his mind began to race in search of some memory of shelter along the way. He could think of none. But he knew Newhalem was not far.

To call Newhalem a town would have been generous: it was little more than a disused power station built over the river and surrounded by a dozen or so cookie-cutter homes once constructed for the workers there. Everything looked to be at least 80 years old. But it also looked like, until very recently, it had been inhabited: front doors were left open and clothes still dangled from lines in the side yards. The brown haze obscured everything in sight now above the rooflines, hovering in a thickening cloud some thirty feet above him. He knew there was no longer any way out.

So Henry pedaled faster and faster, hoping only to escape the mountains. But as he went, something not far ahead on the road shoulder caught his eye: it was a set of blinking orange lights, piercing through the smoke. As he got closer, he saw that they were attached to a dusty Subaru station wagon with a mattress strapped to the roof rack. The back hatch was open, and Henry could see stacked boxes, piles of blankets, and a lamp crammed in sideways above them. And then he saw something else, too: it was a woman, pacing in the haze with her elbows out and her hands on top of her head, like a ghost in the middle of the road. She wasn't alone: there was a smaller shape sitting on the ground against the car beside her.

Henry was on them in an instant, and the woman waved him down.

"Oh my God," she said, "what are you doing here?" There was fear in her voice and it tried to spread to Henry, but he dodged it—in a very un-possum-like way—and then stopped his bike.

"What's wrong?" he asked back.

"What's—it's our car," she said. "It won't start; I don't know if there's gas… it's… oh my God, we have to go! It's—I don't know what to do…"

"It's okay. Everything is okay," Henry lied, both to her and to himself. "Please slow down. Where are you trying to get to?"

"There!" she said, pointing down the mountain and towards deepening smoke.

"Isn't there a fire?"

"Yes, but not that way. It's a mountain over, I thought–Dorado. I don't know if it's spreading. We were at home–the neighbors left–they didn't even knock. They didn't even knock, oh God–"

"What's down that way?"

"Marble–Marblemount! There's a shelter. It's upwind... they said that's where to go... they have a fire department... Jesus Christ, the car won't start..." She had not stopped pacing, and her shoulders heaved with each panicked breath. "My daughter!" she said, and then held both of her arms out towards the child like this explained everything in the world. Which, even to Henry, it did. "Oh, God..."

"Okay," he said. "Okay. What can we do?" Henry had a bicycle, a backpack, and a sleeping bag to his name.

"Take her!" the woman said. "Please, take her. Oh my God, please..." She didn't know what else to say. Henry was still standing over the only seat.

But what he said was: "Okay. Can she hold onto my back?"

"Yes! Yes!" The woman was moving quickly. "Sweetie, come here. Come here..."

The girl stood, and Henry sat back down on the bike and let the woman lift up the child to situate her behind him. But his pack was in the way. "Hold on," Henry said, and he pulled his arms through the straps to take it off. "You hold this. I'll come back for it. How far?"

"Oh, God!" the woman said. She was crying.

Henry looked at her and repeated: "I'll come back."

The little girl—who must have been only six or seven—was in shock. She did not cry. She did not ask her mother or Henry anything. Her eyes were glazed, and she was suppressing the sounds of her own coughs from the smoke. Her mother lifted her up again.

"Wait," Henry said. "One more thing." He fumbled his way out of his hoodie then, and as he did, the plastic badges rattled against each other. He took it and wrapped it backwards around the girl's shoulders, tying the arms together loosely behind her head to make a sort of bib from it. He spoke to her: "This can cover your mouth, okay?" he said, and then showed her how to pull the hood up over her nose. "See?"

The girl nodded, and then her mother lifted her up a third time and got her as settled as she could be on Henry's back. She wrapped her arms around his waist and held on. He scooted as far forward on the seat as he could so she might have at least a little room. Henry looked at her mother.

"I'll take her to town," he said. "I'll get help, and then I'll come back. As fast as I can. I promise. There's time."

The mother's eyes were red, and her face strained every muscle into an agonizing shape. "Please," she said, and it was the only word she could make. "Please," she said again. "Please."

Henry pedaled away, heavier now with the girl's weight, and trying to hold himself up on the handlebars.

He did his best to go slowly, for fear of the child. But the grade of the road was steady, and he picked up speed anyways. As they went, the girl was quiet and Henry spoke kind things to her. He worried that, in her state, she might think she was being kidnapped, and he did his best to explain that once she was safe, he would go back to her mother and bring her along. Before long, he realized he was mostly talking to himself: "You're going to be okay," he said. "You're going to be okay."

The smoke thickened as they descended, but he did not see fire. It was ten miles to Marblemount, and it took them an hour to get there. But he didn't have to go far into town to find help: a cluster of residents, disheveled and with fear all over their faces, stood smoking cigarettes outside of the Community Hall. They were looking across the street, where the remains of an old iron truss bridge had collapsed into the river below. The damage was recent, and Henry could see the stark white of freshly broken concrete by the roadside. Rebar poked up from it like strange candles in a ruined birthday cake.

He began talking to the people the instant the bike crossed from the roadway into the gravel parking lot where they stood. "Hey!" he yelled. "Hey! We need help! Help!"

A middle-aged man who looked quite a lot like him tossed away his cigarette and jogged over. "What's going on?" he asked.

Henry was already trying to unhook the girl's hands from around his waist and lower her to the ground. "I need someone to take care of her," he said. "Her mom is still back there in the mountains. She needs help."

"What? Who?"

"I don't know her name! She was stuck back there; we need to get her—"

"Who is this?"

"I don't know! She's her daughter—their car broke down—"

"How far up?"

"Maybe eight miles? Please, someone needs to go back—"

The man had helped the girl down from the bike and was squatting in front of her. "Sweetie, you need to be brave," he said. "What's your mom's name?"

But the girl just stared at him. Henry spoke: "We need to go get her mom. Somebody needs to drive back up the road. I can't make it back up, but I can show you—"

The man looked up at him. "There's no cars," he said.

"What?"

"Everyone went over for the fire, but the bridge went out behind 'em."

"There's not a single car? Not one car?"

"Buddy, I said 'everybody,'" the man said. "No one can go." He turned back to the girl. "We need your help, honey. Who's your momma?"

Henry had been confused at first, but now he was becoming angry. "Her mom's *back there*! Go get her and ask her yourself!"

The man ignored him. "Honey, where were you coming from? Were you up by the plant? Newhalem, sweetie? Did you see fire there?"

Panic was getting closer, and Henry was doing his best to push it away. "Can you watch her?" he asked. "Is there someone here who can take care of her?"

The man finally looked up at him. "We've got her. We need to know who she is."

"But you've got her?"

"What'd I say?"

"*Fuck!*" Henry said, mostly to himself. And then he turned the bike around and set off again back up the hill.

The ride back was terrible, but he made it quickly. Everything in him burned, and the things around him were beginning to burn, too. The smoke was even thicker now as he ascended towards the pass, and he could see the first licks of yellow flames high along the mountain ridge to the east. At least, he thought it was east; the sun was long gone from the sky, and the world had entered some red nightmare twilight.

He found the woman a half mile downhill from her car. She had pulled what things she could from the trunk and put them in a hamper that she was dragging behind her. Her face and clothes were sooty. The air itself was now hellish and black. She was still a phantom in the smoke, and Henry didn't know what to do. He had never known what to do; not once in his entire life. He'd gone and gone, attention always elsewhere. If it even was attention. But the world was on fire, and he needed to be here, now.

When he got close, he braked the bike and found the words the woman had to hear: "She's safe," he said. "She's safe—with people—in town. No fire—there. She's safe." Henry was gasping for each breath and spending it all on every sentence. The woman dropped the handle of her basket and ran to him, throwing her arms around his neck. They were so thin, and she squeezed him so tightly.

"*Thank you,*" she whispered in his ear. "Thank you, thank you, thank you."

"You've got—to get to her," Henry labored. "We've got—to get you down."

She was sobbing into his shoulder. Henry was searching frantically in his mind for any sort of plan. The only pieces he had to work with were a laundry hamper, two adults, and a bicycle. All of that only added up to one thing. And then he knew.

"Take—the bike," he said to her, and he took her wrists from around his neck and held them so he could look her in the eyes. "You take—the bike. Go back—down. Go back—down to her. She's at—the Hall."

They didn't have time. The woman stared back into his face, terrified and unbelieving.

"Take the bike," he said again, his whole chest aching. "Go."

As this last word came out, he realized he was still sitting on the seat, and he lifted his leg and stood to the side, still holding the handlebars. "See?" he said. "You—take it." He took her hands and put them where they needed to be. Then, when he was sure she had a grip, he backed away.

"You?" she asked, her whole self trembling.

"I'll walk. I'll figure—it out. You've got to go."

She began nodding, both to him and to herself. "I can't," she said. But she got on anyway.

"Can you make it?" Henry asked her. "Can you ride–a bike?"

She nodded again, emphatically this time. And then something lit in her face: she turned to him one more time. "What's your name?" she asked.

"It's–Henry," Henry said. "Henry Henry."

"Okay," she said "Don't get fucked, Henry."

"I won't–I won't–"

"Promise me." It was a silly thing to ask, and an impossible thing to do. But Henry promised anyway.

When he was sure she was gone, his mind turned to the trouble he was in. The entire ridge was on fire now, and he could feel it sucking the oxygen from the air. He didn't have much time, and he felt like the world had closed in so there was only a narrow and straight line of actions left for him to take. There were no more branches, and there were no more choices: he could keep moving down this one path–or he could die.

The first action was to go back to the car. He chose it, and he ran as fast as he could.

The second was to put the gear shift into neutral–which was something he realized much too late would only be possible if the keys were still in the ignition. It was a gamble, Henry knew; but when he looked behind the steering wheel, they were right where they needed to be, and this was the first gift. He turned them, and then he shifted.

The third action was to get out again and take hold of the doorframe. He would push with every bit of strength he still had left in his tired self, and he had to hope against hope that the car would begin to roll–or he would die there. He closed his eyes, grunted, and pushed with all his might. The car rolled, and it kept rolling. This was gift number two.

The next step was to jump back into the moving car and buckle the fuck up. Henry was fifty-one years old and as beat as he had ever been in his life. But he knew this was what he needed to do, and he would do it. He did, the latch on the seatbelt clicked, and he closed the door.

The fifth thing was speed: he needed the grade to be steep enough to keep him moving through the level spots, but not so steep he would overshoot the turns. He didn't have any power steering in the wheel, and he could only turn it so hard. He knew the road from the lap on the bicycle, and he wasn't sure this would work. But still, the odometer crept up… enough, but not too much. And this was a gift, too.

Avoiding the hamper the woman had left in the middle of the road was optional. This was good news, because he hit it going maybe eight miles per hour. It dumped over to the side, and he needed it to miss the tires. It did, and spilled who-knows-what into the roadway. This was a loss, and not a gift. But it was not fatal.

And then there was just one last need: a road that didn't catch on fire. But the wind—that goddamned *wind!*—was picking up, and the line of yellow and orange from the ridge moved closer, and then closer still. He couldn't believe the speed of it: a half mile away, and then a quarter, and then less. He was still barely moving, not even going ten miles per hour, and everything began to unfold in impossibly slow motion: the car crept on, and the flames spread down. He tried to time out the impending moment of their intersection, but again he could not—or he would not allow himself to. He crawled ahead, and there was not one thing in all the world for Henry to do.

He sat. He watched. He waited. His eyes darted between the road, the fire, and the gauges.

The car picked up speed: ten miles per hour, then eleven, then twelve.

The fire moved closer: fifty yards away, then twenty, then five.

The road stretched on: eight more miles to Marblemount. Then seven and three quarters. Then seven and a half.

And Henry moved through a tunnel of flame.

One car and one passenger.

One road and one prayer for it.

One single line of actions.

And gift after gift after gift.

He turned into the parking lot on two wheels, steady at twenty-five miles per hour and afraid to touch the brakes. The mother was waiting on him, her daughter on her hip. When the car finally stopped and Henry stepped out, she put the girl down and ran to hug him. "I didn't get the hamper," Henry said, nearly in a state of shock himself. "I mean, I hit it. But I didn't get it."

"That's okay, Henry, that's okay," she said, crying into his chest. "Thank you. Thank you. Thank you." She was wearing Henry's backpack on her shoulders and he could see the frayed stitching of the upside words over her shoulder: *Badlands National Park*. He knew he wouldn't ask about it. He knew that whatever he had was hers.

Later, after they had sat and eaten and laughed together, Henry spoke to the girl. She asked him who he really was.

"Just Henry," he said. "Somebody out wandering around. Who are you?"

"I'm Clare," she said.

"That's a nice name."

"My dad gave it to me." She was drinking from a juice box.

"My dad gave me my name, too," Henry said. "Do you like yours?"

"Yeah. Do you like your name?"

Henry smiled. "I do. It suits me. You had a scary day today."

"*Too* scary," Clare said. Henry realized, for the first time, that she was still wearing his hoodie: she or her mother had turned it around and put it on properly, and it swallowed her up so only her fingertips poked out of the sleeves. *I Survived the Everglades*, it said. The Junior Ranger badges were still lined up like medals on her chest.

"You were pretty brave," he said.

"No I wasn't! I was really scared."

"It's okay to be scared."

She frowned at that. "I'm supposed to be *big*."

Henry thought about heroes and fathers. He thought about the smell of salt along the rocky coasts of Maine and the rot of swamps in nowhere, South Carolina. He thought, of all things, of a goddamned crocodile.

And he said "Fuck that" to Clare, whose eyes went wide at the word. "People will tell you to be big," Henry went on, "but you don't listen to them. You can be small."

She giggled. "I *am* small," she said, holding up the oversized sleeves as proof.

You take care of your mom, and be good. The sound of a leash skittering down a street in the dark.

"Be kind," he said. "That's what you can be."

"Okay."

"Okay."

When Henry left the Cascades, he did it on that same old bicycle. He kept going west, out of the mountains and all the way to the coast. It took him two days, and he couldn't believe the Pacific when he saw it: it was gray and white-capped, shrouded in infinite mist. The waves pounded the shoreline in rhythm with the beating of his heart. He had expected to feel small when he got there, but he did not. Instead, he felt… well, he felt *interesting*.

It wasn't because he couldn't name things, but rather because he finally could. He was Henry Henry: a scared son and a poor father and a selfish husband. An inept adventurer and an opportunistic truck thief and an ongoing fugitive from Southern justice. An obsessive. A reluctant friend. And then a good friend. And then a bad friend. A ghost, hiding from everyone. A geyser gazer. A guy in the right place at the right time, only because he was foolish enough to be in the wrong place at the wrong time before that.

And for the first time in his life, it occurred to him that he didn't have to add them together, or to subtract the bad from the good, hoping not to end up ashamed. This wasn't because who he was didn't matter to him. It was because who he was did now: he was Henry Henry, and though he was ever a fearful man, he had still crossed a country so afraid of its own becoming it would rather die than ever see it. Before, he could have related to that—a river of grass, a buffalo man, a mirror of God. But the Pacific Ocean didn't really care who Henry was. It just came to him, in wave after wave, and it was finally joy to see and know that neither he, nor this country, nor this continent was at the center of the earth.

He stood on the shore for a long time, until well after dark. The little birds on the shore watched him and gave him wide berth. Sea lions barked to one another, their voices carrying to him from far away on the wind. Whales spouted a mile off shore, kelp forests twisted and billowed in the heavy green current, and mollusks and sea stars by the tens of thousands tumbled in the surf until their feet could find purchase on the ancient and stubborn stones still buried there. When the moon rose, Henry laid down on the sand and slept.

In the morning, he regretted at least the last of his choices, and he dusted himself off, got on his bike again, and tried to learn something from the itching in his socks and the chafing under his armpits. He rode south, all the way to Seattle, and he found something new: the city was quiet and full. There was no power. People lived in buildings with open windows or in tents lined up in the parks—so many of them. On the pier behind Pike's Market, he met a man who was grizzled and dirty and ancient. He told Henry it was no big thing for a country to fall apart. He had been homeless twenty years before the missed elections and secessions and militias got started: "Somebody's world ends everyday," he said. "But then they don't end with it."

"Why not?" Henry had asked him.

The man only shrugged. "We missed the first bus. Gotta wait around and catch the next."

From the end of the ferry dock that had once kept service for Bainbridge Island, and with the disused and slowly eroding concrete of the Space Needle still towering above him, Henry could see mountains across the Sound to the southwest. He knew they were another park. He knew the tallest was Mount Olympus, and it gave the place—and the whole strange peninsula—its name. And he knew he wanted to go there. Henry didn't need a badge anymore, of course, because he'd given the rest of them away. But it was somewhere to be next. And so Henry went.

To Let Go

Billy Faulkner sat in a diner in Forks, Washington and ordered steak and eggs. It was the Fourth of July, but there were no old flags out front or fireworks for sale. The era of American patriotism had passed—particularly in Forks, Washington—and what had swept in to take its place was darker and more bitter.

The diner was called the Twilight Kitchen, and there were pictures everywhere from a series of movies that had been released more than two decades ago. They were faded with the sun and dusty on their frames— sharp-jawed vampires and brooding werewolves. Aside from this decor, the place looked like any other diner in any other town in what used to be the United States: a chrome-lined counter with a half dozen stools bolted to the floor in front of it. Booths against the glass windows with red vinyl seats. A checkered tile floor. A cash register.

Billy sat at the counter because he was hungry, and because he had twelve dollars left in his pocket to spend. He wore a white linen shirt for the heat and pleated brown slacks. His shoes shined. There was a hat perched on the stool beside him. Two months ago he had very nearly died, but now hours passed—maybe an entire morning—and he would not think about that. A bullet fired by a child, and a White child, had broken two of his ribs and torn a long line in his side on its way through his body. He knew the child had not seen his skin in the dark, but just his otherness: he was not like him, and that made him afraid. But Billy did not forgive him for his fear. Billy's capacity for forgiveness had dried up.

It was morning, and his steak sizzled on the grill. His eggs were already plated and beginning to cool, but the waitress was waiting. Billy sat quietly and waited, too. Then the electric bell over the door rang behind him, and he heard the sounds of boots on the tile: one pair, two steps, and then a long pause. He knew the person wearing them was staring a hole in his back. And then the boots moved again, off to a booth at the far end of the diner. There was the sticky sound of a body sliding into a seat, and Billy looked at the waitress. Her eyes darted between the booth and his own. She picked up her order pad from the pad and walked over.

"What can I getcha today, Sammy?" They talked more, but Billy only half-listened. His steak was up.

The man who found him on the floor of the ranger station at Craters of the Moon was named Ellison. He was old—in his late seventies—but that was not what Billy noticed first about him when his eyes fluttered open in the cab of his truck. What he noticed first was that he, too, was Black.

He remembered he had been talking with his sister, Busola, and she had led him to a box of medical supplies in the office of the station. He had taken a handful of long-expired antibiotics there and emptied a tube of ointment into his palm and smothered it on his side. But the pain of his touch had been explosive and blinding, and he realized that he had passed out, and he did not know for how long. He tried to speak to the man to ask him who he was, or how long he had been unconscious, or anything at all. But when he did, no sound must have come from his mouth because the man did not look over at him but just drove on.

They went to a house not too far away. It was old and weathered and did not have power. The man was wiry and strong, and Billy could feel the muscles in his arms and his shoulders tense as he lifted Billy from his seat and helped him inside. There was a bed there, and the instant he laid down on it, he fell asleep.

He was two bites into the steak when he risked another glance at the booth. As he did, he saw the other man's eyes dart away to find something to stare at outside the window. This gave Billy a chance to look him over: he was in his late twenties. Thin. Black hair and a short black beard. He wore a stained red trucker cap with *Take America Back* written on it, along with a blue-gray flannel despite the heat. He was in jeans, and the boots Billy had heard before were splattered with mud. The sleeves of the shirt were rolled up, and his arms were hairy and tanned. He had a tattoo on his neck, but Billy couldn't make it out. He'd seen him before, he thought— or he'd seen many like him. He watched the man's Adam's apple bob up and down nervously. He was holding a menu, but he didn't seem to need it.

Billy went back to his lunch, and he felt the man's eyes come back to him when he looked away. He cut another bite of the steak and put it in his mouth, chewing slowly. And he felt an old heat rising up in him. There was a single key in his pants pocket, and it fit the ignition of a deep blue truck in the parking lot that was the same age he was. He could finish his meal, pay the waitress, and go.

He could.

Later, he learned the reason Ellison hadn't heard him in the truck—or when he called out from the bed the next morning to see if his host was still there—was because Ellison was deaf. Billy learned this when he spent the energy he'd found in his sleep to get up from the bed and walk through the bedroom door into the only other room in the house. It was small and the ceiling was low overhead. There was a worn and patchy couch against the far wall to his right and a kitchen to his left. In the center was a simple table and two chairs. Ellison sat in the one closest to Billy, but his back was turned. He was playing solitaire with a deck of Bicycle-brand cards, Billy knew they were Bicycles because they were the same as the ones his father had used.

"Hello?" Billy asked. "Hello?" But nothing happened.

When he limped into the periphery of the man's view, the man flinched and put the cards in his hand down on the table. He turned, and the look on his face was worried and sympathetic. He reached for a pad of paper on the table next to him and wrote, in all capitals,

U SHOULD REST

Billy spoke without thinking, and the man watched his lips. "Where am I?" he asked. The man wrote again:

U R SAFE

Billy took that in and tried to focus. "Who are you?"

ELLISON — FRIEND

Billy nodded. "How did you find me?"

SMOKE

From the Ranger. Billy nodded again. A wave of sadness crashed into him, and he wobbled on his feet. When it receded, it left fear behind. "Am I going to die?" he asked. Ellison wrote.

NOT TODAY

* * *

Instead of finishing his meal, instead of paying the waitress, instead of walking calmly back to the truck in the parking lot, Billy put both hands on his plate and looked back at the booth. This time, Sammy didn't turn away. The two men stared at each other, and Billy saw deep into him. Then the newcomer broke the silence:

"You need somethin'?" he said. He wanted his voice to sound like acid, but it was unconvincing.

Billy picked up his plate and stood. "I think I do," he said. "You care if I sit?"

"Not over there."

Billy smiled. But it wasn't convincing, either. "See, I don't believe you about that."

"I don't care what you believe."

"You got a problem with me being here?"

"I got a problem with this."

"Yeah, I know. You're Sammy, right?"

"I didn't tell you that."

The waitress was watching them from behind the counter. "Okay, boys," she said.

"It's alright, Shelly," Sammy said. "He's got somethin' on his mind." Acid hadn't worked, and he was trying to be smug now. It came easier. Billy crossed the tile floor and put his plate down on the opposite side of the man's table. He slid into the booth. His heart was racing and his blood was on fire, and he decided right then and there to let it burn.

He got used to writing things down with Ellison. The old man could often read his lips, but at times—and with larger words—he would need help. Billy did his best to learn to sign, but in the end, Ellison settled on something simpler: when occasion arose, he would take a card from his deck and write a word they used often on one side and its opposite on the other. This began with YES and NO, which went on a joker he never used. Then NOW and LATER, on the other joker. MINE and YOURS on the two of hearts. GO and STAY on the two of spades.

Billy learned they were in what was left of Ketchum, Idaho. He learned Ellison had lived there all his life, and this was the home in which he was born. He had never had power—even before the After. He kept food in an ice box. His father hadn't put in running water until the mid-1980s.

Ellison had never married and he had no siblings. He'd worked when he was younger in a market at the meat counter in town. He had been born deaf, and only his mother ever learned how to listen to him without reading. She had lived the longest, and died not that long ago, at the age of 99. Billy slept in what had been her room. Ellison slept on the sofa, where he had slept all his life.

When Billy was well enough to explore, he took to walking through the empty and abandoned town and up the Sun Valley Road to the golf course there. It was wild and overgrown, except for the greens: the grass there had stopped at just above the heights of his ankles, and when the winds caught it, it rippled like water on the surface of a pond. He liked to look at it. He could feel himself getting stronger, and he would strain against the hurt in his side to fill his lungs as full as they could go.

One day, he went further on the road than he had gone before, past the lightning struck ruins of the old clubhouse and on towards the mountains. A creek drew near to the road, and then he saw something strange: on the far side of a little gravel lot, there was a short obelisk of stone rising up from the weeds with a bust at the top. He walked over and recognized the face. Then he realized why the word—why Ketchum—had looked so familiar to him on the pad of white paper where Ellison had written it down. The bust was of Ernest Hemingway, and this was where, in 1961, he woke early on a July morning and put a shotgun under his chin.

Billy brushed the tall ricegrass away from the plaque at the base of the small monument and read what was written there:

Best of all he loved the fall
the leaves yellow on the cottonwoods
leaves floating on the trout streams
and above the hills
the high blue windless skies
…now he will be a part of them forever.

Later, he asked Ellison about what he had seen. The old man smiled and went over to a small bookshelf there beside the sofa. He picked one up and brought it back to the table where Billy sat, exhausted now from his walk. He opened it to the title page—For Whom the Bell Tolls—and pointed to a scrawled signature. He nudged it over to Billy and reached for his paper.

I MET HIM – WHEN A BOY –
FATHER WORKED ON HOUSE

"What was he like?" It was the only question.

LIKE HIS BOOKS

But then Billy found another: "Kind of 'macho,' then?"
Ellison shook his head and picked up the joker:

NO.

And then he wrote:

SCARED

"Scared of what?"

Ellison picked up the two of spades, and Billy knew what was on it by now: "Scared to 'stay'?" he asked. He knew the story: an aging writer, whose skill was leaving him, deciding to make a dramatic exit rather than stick around.

Ellison shook his head and turned the card over.

Scared to go.

"What did you see?" Billy asked. He was sitting with his back to the door.

The man's eyes were pale blue, and they would not settle on his own. They looked at Billy's edges: the stubble of his black hair—the line of his jaw—the handkerchief in the pocket of his shirt. "I don't know what you're talkin' about," he said.

"Yeah, you do. The minute you came in. You looked at me and you saw something. What was it?"

"I didn't look at you." Sitting there, with Billy so close, he didn't have the starch he'd had before. They both felt the power shifting.

"Yeah, you did. I was right there. I watched her watchin' you watch me. Then you came aalll the way down here. So what did you see?"

Finally, the man's pupils stopped moving and they bored into his own. Billy didn't blink but gave the stare right back. "You know what I saw?" he said, "Somebody who doesn't belong here. That's what I saw."

"And why's that?"

The man grinned. "It ain't yours, that's why."

"But it's yours?"

"It is."

Billy picked up his knife and his fork. "I'm gonna eat, Sammy," he said. Sammy didn't say anything, but he watched as Billy cut a piece from the steak and put it in his mouth. When he was done chewing, he swallowed and asked, "What did you order?"

"Not your business."

"No," Billy said, "It's not. I was just curious." He took another bite. When he was finished, he asked, "How long you been here?"

Sammy had tried meanness and he'd tried disdain, but Billy was still there. He thought disinterest might be worth a shot. "I'm not tellin' you anything. You wanna sit here, sit here. But eat your damn food and get on."

"I'm doing that. When I'm finished, where should I go?"

"You talk a lot."

"I wanna know, Sammy. Where should I go?" Billy asked. "Anything around here worth seeing? Where should I 'get on' to?"

"Look–"

And then Sammy called him the word Billy knew was in his heart.

"–I don't care."

The air froze. The waitress's mouth hung open and her eyes went wide. Billy stopped chewing. Sammy's eyes locked onto something outside the window and the Adam's apple bobbed. Everyone and everything was still and waiting.

And then Billy's closed fist came down hard on the table. The plate jumped. Eggs flew up in the air. The silverware clattered.

"Yeah, you do," Billy said. "Yeah, you do."

On his last day with Ellison, he told the old man where he would go: he'd set out to see the ocean, and he would find it. There was a point he remembered from the map– Cape Flattery–that was as far west as west could get. Ellison wrote something down for him:

CAN'T WALK

"You can always walk," Billy said.

TOO FAR – TOO HURT

"You know I'm up for it. I've been walking for weeks now. I'll be alright."

NOT SAFE TO GO

Ellison flipped over a joker on the table: LATER.
Billy took this in slowly and then turned it over. "It's summer," he said. "You can't keep me forever."
Ellison pointed at the joker again. LATER.
Billy smiled at Ellison and loved him. "You took good care of me. But I'm not afraid."
Ellison let out a long breath and shook his head, if only slightly. He wrote.

OK

"Okay," said Billy.

LEAVE TOMORROW

"Okay."
Ellison pointed towards the door and the driveway beyond. Then, he wrote again:

TAKE TRUCK

Billy looked at the words on the paper. "I can't do that," he said. "I can't do that; you need it."
Ellison pulled out the two of hearts: YOURS

*   *   *

The anger in Sammy had flashed and evaporated. What was left was naked fear.

"He didn't mean it," the waitress sputtered. She was still standing by the counter holding her notepad. "Don't worry about the tab—you just need to leave. Get on to where you're gettin' to. The steak's on the house."

Billy didn't look at her. He was still talking to Sammy. "Why's it yours? Somebody give it to you? Did you take it?"

"I didn't say that," Sammy said, and he seemed to be talking as much to himself as he was to Billy.

"Yeah, you did."

"I didn't."

"You did. You said you owned the whole town. Wasn't a place for someone like me in it. 'Sam's Forks,' you said."

"I didn't say 'Sam's Forks.'"

"I'm just passing through, Sammy. I'm just eating breakfast here. I don't want your damn town."

Sammy was quiet.

"You know why you said it? Because I do."

"Why, then?" Billy could see in his eyes that he was searching for his nerve again.

"You said it because you're already losing it. You never even had it. And I made you remember that, just by sitting on that stool."

"Fuck you," Sammy said now, but he should have waited: the words were still an empty shell.

Billy lunged over the table and the waitress gasped. He grabbed the bill of Sammy's hat and flipped it off his head, sending it flying through the air and onto the floor. "*You and this dumb hat!*" he said. "You don't need it! You don't need to take anything!" Sammy had flinched and now he had

401

his hands up to defend himself. "Just let it go!" Billy said, and with that he knew he was spent. "Let it go, you *asshole*. You'll live longer."

Billy stood up, and he knew he was breathing too quickly. His side hurt in the way he had nearly gotten used to. He ran his hands down the front of his shirt to smooth it and then reached for his wallet. He turned his back on Sammy and went to the counter. He took the twelve dollars he had and put them on the counter. "Thank you for breakfast," he said to the waitress, whose back was against the wall. "I've got somewhere to be."

He took Ellison's truck and was grateful for it. He drove west through Fairfield and Mountain Home. He skirted around Boise to the south and drove through the arid wastes of eastern Oregon to Burns, then 395 to Wagontire, then 140 to Bly. The roads were scarce and empty. The sun was hot in the sky.

He didn't have vegetable oil to rely on anymore, so he found gas whenever and wherever he could. Sometimes, he would barter with an attendant. Sometimes he found abandoned pumps that still worked if you kicked them hard enough. He burned through most of the American money he had, and the people he gave it to seemed happy enough to have it.

In Klamath Falls, he saw an old sign for Crater Lake National Park and he followed it. At sunset one evening, he stood on the rim of the deepest water on the continent and looked at the perfect blue of it until night fell and he could see the starshine reflected in the surface. He went to the Visitor Center. He got a badge.

He went north then, crossing the Columbia River Gorge at a place called The Dalles where the road wound down to an old bridge that was maybe twenty feet above the water. Seagulls nested on rocks there, a hundred miles from the ocean.

In mid-June, he spent a week sleeping in his truck on the shoulders of Mount Rainier. The mountain was bigger than he could have ever imagined. The summit was hidden in a halo of clouds.

Billy didn't know what drew him to these places anymore. It wasn't Henry. It wasn't something he had come to understand about himself. He only recognized that they were wild places people had pretended for a time were not wild. But they had never cared. They were endless, and still busy becoming.

After Rainier, Billy realized he could not put off any longer what he had set out to do. He understood he needed to see if there was really a place where things stopped. He knew the Olympic Peninsula was more than fifty miles across, another fifty miles long, and almost entirely pinched off from the rest of Washington state by the creeping inlets of Puget Sound to the east and the Chehalis River to the west. All that saved it from becoming an island were the foothills of the Olympic mountains, which rose in a narrow spine between the waterways and then climbed to fantastic peaks in the heart of this strange, enormous diamond of earth.

Billy made his way to it north of Aberdeen, and then he wandered the narrow lanes of the old national highway through wild forests of fir, spruce, and pine. The road wound west towards the coast, and as he drew closer to the water, he noticed the underbrush transitioning from scrub trees and tall grasses to massive clusters of ferns. Green moss grew on the hemlock branches that stretched out across the pavement. The air grew more humid and thick.

When the water finally appeared, he saw it as a gray line between the trunks of prehistoric trees shrouded in mist along the coast. Sea stacks of towering rock jutted up from the beaches and seabirds turned in wide circles above them. It took Billy's breath away. But he did not stop.

On the second day of July, he followed an old park service sign inland to the Hoh Rainforest. The word itself seduced him: he thought of Amazon jungles and waterfalls in Hawai'i. But the Hoh was something different. It was a new denseness of wood and leaf and color. Shaggy vines draped over every tree. He rolled down the window in the truck and breathed air that was cool and rich with the smell of the earth. The road narrowed and was nearly washed out in places by the river. He slowed his speed to a crawl and wondered, as the truck tumbled in and out of each enormous pothole, if he would be able to drive back. But he had set his heart on going as far as he could go, and he drove on.

Miles later, he knew he was nearing a visitor center there: he had seen signs, and the numbers on them had been counting down. But he couldn't find it. The road simply vanished ahead of him into the forest. He parked and set out on foot, but he could only find the pavement for another hundred yards or so before it was lost, too, in soil and growth.

Billy stood there, at the road's end, for a long time. He listened to the bubbling sounds of the river as it raced past the pebbles on its shore. Somewhere in this wildness was whatever was left of a building. Inside that building was a silly plastic badge. People had built this place once so they could get closer to this country. Though it was everywhere around them. They had stationed rangers there to watch over it, and to keep it safe from themselves. But the rangers were no more. They had let it go. And it had become something else without them.

When Billy went back to his truck, he turned the key in the ignition and did not give a single flying fuck if anyone was watching him go. He sped north through town and didn't breathe deep until he had crossed over the trestle bridge spanning the Sol Duc River and was lost again in the thick pines. He wanted to stay gone forever.

Six months ago, someone had poured sugar into the gas tank of his dead mother's car so he would leave town. Someone wanted him gone so badly they kept him there. He couldn't make sense of it; hadn't known that he *needed* to make sense of it. But the sense was this: whoever had done it wanted control. They wanted to be the reason. They wanted to matter. Billy had wanted that, too. But he would no longer accept such gravity.

*   *   *

The road to Cape Flattery began in Sappho and went on to Clallam Bay. Clallam Bay was nestled into a scoop carved out of the Strait of Juan de Fuca, and Billy was surprised to find it alive: fishing boats puttered in the small harbor and there were people riding bicycles along the streets. He drove through slowly, marveling at what looked like the country's last intact place. Across the water, he could see the mountains of Vancouver Island, snow still blanketing the highest peaks there. He traveled west along the coastline, meandering there between forests and sea, until he reached a place he did not expect: a sign told him he was exiting the "Sovereign State of Washington" and entering Makah Nation. He had never heard of the Makah.

There was no gatehouse or fence. There were no peacekeepers or police out on patrol. But before the next mile was out, he found himself in another town called Neah Bay, and there was a simple wooden sign staked alongside the highway reading *Visitors Check-In @ Museum*. He didn't see any signs for a museum, but he did see a grocery store ahead, and he thought that was as good a place to stop as any.

He parked Ellison's truck in the lot and walked up to the old-style sliding doors. There were no handles, and he expected that he would have to knock. But as he approached, the sensor saw him and the doors parted and opened. He was in a grocery store, the lights on and the shelves stocked, and he saw a woman there in a simple green vest.

"I wanted to check in," he said. Her name tag said she was Niko. "I'm a visitor, but I couldn't find the museum."

"We never built it," Niko said. "So you're in the right place."

"Is it okay that I'm here?"

"It's five dollars," Niko said. She was close to Billy's age and friendly. Her hair was black and worn loose over her shoulders, but it still framed the simple and lovely oval of her face. "It's five dollars for a pass, I mean."

Billy scrunched his face up in a way that showed more frustration and sadness than that price should ever warrant: he realized he'd given the last money he had to the waitress from before. He had insisted on paying. "I don't have it," he said. "I'm so sorry. I didn't mean to waste your time."

Niko pursed her lips and then clucked her tongue. "What are you here for?" she asked.

"That's a big question," Billy said. "I think I wanted to see how far the road goes."

"I guess that depends on if you turn around or not," Niko said. "But it goes out to the Cape."

"I wish I had the five dollars then."

Niko paused. "Don't worry about it," she said. "It's just five bucks."

Billy looked at her to really see if she meant the offer. She was smiling, if only slightly. "Are you sure?" he asked.

"It's somewhere to go," she said. "No reason to keep it from you."

"No, no reason." He felt stupid when the words came out of his mouth. "Thank you," he said, and this time, he felt better.

"No worries. Turn left at the crab house. Have fun."

Billy left the grocery in Makah and moved on. The road to the cape took him deep into the forests and around bend after bend. He expected the destination to be close, to be just a bit further up the coast, but the drive took him nearly an hour, and by the end, he had no idea where he was. He couldn't see water anywhere—just trees and fields.

Finally, the path began to ascend towards some hidden promontory. The forests grew closer, and then he entered a disused and narrow parking lot and drove to the far end. He saw an old shed where there had once been restrooms, but a falling tree had caved it in. Where the pavement of the lot stopped, his eyes paused on an old wooden sawhorse with the words

CAPE TRAIL painted on it in white. An old bicycle was chained to the post beneath it, and he laughed at the thought of someone trying to steal something this far from anywhere and anywhen else. Why would they want it? Where would they go?

And then Billy turned off the ignition, stepped down from the cab, and took a deep breath of the salty air. It was late afternoon, and he didn't know how much farther it was to the Cape. He also didn't know what he would see when he got there. But he set out for it just the same.

The path was broad and sandy at first, but it quickly narrowed. It went further into the woods than he thought was possible–further than made any sense to him–and he felt sweat beginning to form on his forehead and underneath his linen shirt. He had been foolish to wear his dress shoes, he knew, and he had to watch his feet as he walked.

A quarter mile in, the way changed from a dirt trail to an uneven boardwalk. Its wooden planks were wide and rough-hewn. They were nailed down to the support trusses with what looked like railroad spikes. He hiked on, moving up and down little sets of steps \ in the pathway and weaving between tall and ancient trees. The smell of saltwater grew stronger, and he could hear the ocean. But all he could see were walls of deep, mossy green.

The path forked, and Billy stayed right; the left branch seemed to go down into a ravine, and he trusted that wherever he was headed, it must still be uphill. When the way turned to the right again, he caught his first sight of water: there was a break in the trees, and he could see out to a fifty-foot high finger of rock jutting out into the sea. It formed a tiny cove with the peninsula he was walking, and there were sea caves where they came together. He watched the waves swirling and crashing at the base. The sound of them was deep and dangerous. He knew he was getting close.

The forests on both sides of him began to drop away, and Billy realized he was on his own little ridge now. The trees thinned, and the path straightened, and for the first time, he could imagine the end. There was one dip of the boardwalk left, and then a rise, and now just visible through the trees, he could see the horizontal lines of what must be a viewing platform. The blue of the ocean was peeking through the screens of limbs and leaves. The air was rich with the scent of pine. The light in the sky was already shifting from violet to orange.

And as Billy climbed the last steps on this corner of the continent, he saw someone he thought he would never see again. He knew him: he was the most lost man he had ever met, God bless him. But he hadn't stopped moving after all, and now he was here.

"Henry?" Billy said softly.

The man at the end of the boardwalk was holding onto the railing and looking out at what he had imagined would be the empty ocean. But it hadn't turned out to be empty at all: the land he had driven and walked and ridden and fled ended, to be sure. But just there, only a few hundred more yards away, was the loveliest little island he had ever seen. The ocean sputtered and foamed against its steep cliffs, and nestled among the hedges and grasses that lived upon it was a perfect lighthouse. Its beacon was still lit and circling, shining out into the dusk. There was more. There was more, and he couldn't believe it.

And so lost was the man among his thoughts, so amazed by his own endless foolishness, that it took hearing his name a second time for it to register:

"Henry Henry?" the voice repeated.

Instantly, this time, he knew it. The man's heart bloomed inside his chest. His shoulders lifted up and his hands let go of what they were holding–but only for a moment. Because he knew he would turn, his eyes wide and his face beaming out, and run to wrap them around his friend.

EPILOGUE

Eruption

On the morning after Henry and Shannon buried their son, the police report arrived in the mail. They left it sitting on the island in the middle of their kitchen until lunchtime. Neither of them wanted to open it. But eventually Henry gave in. He slid a bread knife under the fold, broke the seal of the envelope, and pulled out what was inside. It was just three pages of copy paper.

The first had the reporting officer's name at the top and listed the minutiae of things: the time, the address, the type of incident, the name of their son. Henry couldn't read it, and he slid it across the marble to his wife.

The second had Henry's name on it underneath the words *Witness Statement*. He saw everything he had to say about his only child listed in four hand-written bullet points:

- *No prior knowledge of victim's intent*
- *Present in home but absent from scene*
- *Found unresponsive*
- *Called 911 (check about time)*
-

He read them over and over, and they sank deep inside of him: *No knowledge. Present but absent. Check about time.* He kept the second page for himself.

Then he read the third. On it was a silhouette of Caleb's body. There were marks on the drawing, and words describing his injuries. There was an estimate of the time when his heart stopped beating. And then, in a thin box below, a list of his personal effects. The officer had noted the color of his shirt, the sizes of his pants and shoes, the presence of his cheap, plastic wristwatch. But beneath this, and in all capitals, he had written:

NO NOTE FOUND

Henry passed the paper over to Shannon and she read it, too. When she got to the end, she looked up at him. "I didn't look," she said.

"I didn't think—"

But Shannon was already running up the stairs. Henry followed, and by the time he reached the landing, he could already hear her turning Caleb's room inside out. When he got to the doorway, she was holding the foot of his bed in the air and moving it to the side so she could look beneath.

"It could have fallen…" she said. "Did they look in his desk drawer?"

"I don't know—" Henry did not want to cross the threshold. He did not want to be there, sharing his wife's panic and feeling the force of her grief. She dropped the bed and was on her hands and knees then, running splayed fingers through the filthy carpet and tossing aside dropped Cheerios, forgotten Lego bricks, broken stubs of colored pencils. Henry saw a single sock, stained and dirty. A lunchbox from years ago he'd thought they had thrown out.

"Look in his desk!" Shannon yelled at him, not looking up from her work. "Come look!"

But Henry was paralyzed, his hands gripping the doorframe.

"Henry!"

And then he went in. He searched the desk, the drawers in the dresser, the pockets of clothes in the laundry hamper. But they couldn't find it. They couldn't even know if it ever existed.

For four years, Henry had held tightly to this last memory. He needed it, he knew, because it filled the same space as another memory hidden underneath it, one from that same room, and he kept them together like two pictures stacked on top of one another in a single frame. He did this because this was the memory that was more bearable–the one that could be permitted to be visible–and he thought of that lost note often. He imagined what it might have said. He imagined who it might have blamed. And all this time, he had believed that what he and Shannon were searching for on that final sheet of paper was an explanation: that their question was "why?"

But there at Cape Flattery, as Henry hugged the friend he had lost and then who had found him again, he understood an answer was never what they had wanted. What they had wanted was *more*. One more note of their child's voice. Just another living word–confused or angry or kind–to hear and to know. *I hate you, Dad. I forgive you, Dad.* It wouldn't have mattered, so long as it was him. It wouldn't have mattered, so long as it didn't end.

Henry realized this, and he held it close. He missed his son. He missed his wife. His heart broke open from all the things in it he had failed to let out, and for so long. *But let him decay.* Henry wouldn't defend himself from them anymore. *Let him erode.* He would feel this, and he would be made different by it. *Let him abandon.*

Because Henry Henry had dug his claws into the earth for long enough.

Billy and Henry walked back to the trailhead and fireflies glowed in the dark of the woods around them. When they reached the parking lot, Henry went to the old bike by the sign and unlocked the chain. As he did, Billy laughed and shook his head. "Did you ride that all the way here?"

"A lot of the way," Henry said, looping the cord around the frame and closing the latch again. "But I had help at a few spots. What about you?"

Billy pointed at the only other vehicle in the lot. "I got that from a friend. It's just the second truck I've ever owned."

Henry thought for a moment. "The Ranger didn't make it, huh?"

"She gave it her best. But I ran into too much trouble."

Henry heard that and knew he could ask questions later. "That's a shame," he said. "I wonder what'll become of her."

Billy thought about the old ice cream truck, burned and rusting in the wild spaces of this great country. "Something yet," he said.

"Something yet," Henry repeated. "But what about us? It's the end of the road; where are we going to go?"

"It's only the end of the road if you don't turn around," Billy said.

Henry gave him a look. "You didn't come up with that."

"I didn't," Billy said, smiling. "I didn't."

"Still, though: where to?"

They didn't have the old atlas. They didn't have a lucky rabbit's foot. There were no answers, and there was every answer. So Billy paused, his hand resting on the hood of Ellison's blue truck, and asked: "Have you ever been to Alaska?"

Henry's eyes went wide and he grinned. "Can we even get there?"

"I don't see why not."

Something occurred to both of them at the exact same time, and they spoke in accidental unison:

"Passports?"

"Passports."

"We'll have to sneak across," Henry said, and when he did, Billy loved him, too.

"Let's go," he said. And then he opened the door.

The two of them drove back from the Cape, through Neah Bay, and late into the night. The moon was bright and they kept the running lights on. As they rounded the southern edge of Puget Sound near Tacoma, they could see campfires in the city streets from the overpasses of the highway.

It was no longer the fourth of July when they cleared the last suburbs of Seattle, but it wasn't quite the fifth. The clock in the dash read four in the morning, which meant that far off to the east, the sun was already shining down on the places where this nation briefly was. But through Smokey Point, and Skagit City, and Mount Vernon, that light was still hours away. They drove on in the dark, and if the fog from the sea had not drifted in over the rain-drenched flatlands west of the mountains, if the smoke from wildfires there hadn't blotted out the stars, Henry and Billy could have seen something wild and magnificent happen not so far away from them. Something that had not happened in almost 200 years.

Mount Baker, the third highest volcano in the old state, blew its top. The eruption moved faster than the speed of sound, and a shockwave ran out for more than twenty miles. Rocks larger and heavier than a house shot up into the night, and even though they could not see it for the sky, Henry and Billy felt the ground rumble beneath their feet.

"What was that?" Henry asked.

"I have no idea," Billy said.

And as the earth rained back down upon itself, a pillar of ash began to rise through the darkness from the hole where the top of the mountain had been. It was four thousand feet across and roiled in great tumbling plumes, higher and higher. In time, a deep red glow began to refract through the cloud at its base, and then beneath it, as if birthed from the smoke, an eager mouth of lava crested around a fork in the lip of this brand new crater, slowly beginning its long descent to the sea. And as it moved, it looked for all the world like a crocodile of fire.

Billy and Henry couldn't see it from where they were, and they did not know to search. But the flow of molten stone slithered down those slopes, snapping up everything in its path, every tree and rock and earthworm, eating them all with a hiss and then licking spittle from its lips. It crawled on and on, devouring the world like some ancient and elemental beast; like some primal god, too bright in its glory to look at without burning the eyes out of your skull.

And if Henry had been there, if he had found the wonder he had once gone searching for, he surely would have stared until he was blind, stared until it snapped him up with the rest and deposited him as virgin earth in the cooling of the sea. And he would have known, fully and truly, that this entire world is living, living, living.

1 July 2022 - 9 July 2023

ABOUT THE AUTHOR

Kenneth Camacho is the pastor of a small church in Annapolis, Maryland. Raised in the South, he is a former English teacher and holds a doctoral degree in American Literature from the University of South Carolina. He loves baseball, hiking, road-tripping, and stories about people who go looking for Bigfoot. His favorite national park is—of course—the Badlands.

This is his first novel.